"Bittersweet Summer"

William Batt

Bittersweet Summer

ISBN: 9798389818019

DEDICATION

To all my friends and family that both believed in me and gave me the encouragement to keep going! Most of all to my grandfather, for being the most special man in my life.

CONTENTS

Bittersweet Summer

ACKNOWLEDGMENTS

"Thanks to Steph. I couldn't have written it without your inspiration".

1 "MIKE"

All I want is someone who cares. The same thought kept coming into her mind as she got into her Mercedes and looked up at the cheap and sad looking hotel.

She put the key in the ignition, looked down at her high heels, slowly took them off and dropped them into the passenger side. Being naked in bed was one thing but for her, driving with naked feet was an amazing feeling!

As she started the engine, she lowered the roof, and looked up again. One last glance. And as she left the car park, the "come down" was already beginning to bite.

The drive home was around 40 minutes, 30 if she really tried, but she didn't feel like trying today. So the sun beamed down, the music was loud, "*C'est la vie*" should have been her motto for life. But despite the Mercedes, the house, the shoes, and all the trappings of a beautiful life, she knew what was missing. She pressed the accelerator a little harder, she could hear the exhaust snarl, and the come down was already complete. She pushed replay and turned the volume up a little louder, the Stereophonics were right..."*C'est la vie*."

She pulled into the drive. Thank God Tommy wasn't home. She stopped the car and put the roof up. Only when she went to the boot to get her bag, did she see the dent. She had totally forgotten about the bloody dent. MERDE! She got back into the car and carefully parked the front end in the hedge. Just so he wouldn't see it, at least not today.

The key slotted easily into the lock. She needed to shower; she needed to get him off her, to cleanse herself.

What had started as a drunken fumble a few years ago, had become an all-consuming drug that was both awesome and awful in equal measure. She looked around. A quick drink, and shower. She didn't need to go to the drink's cabinet, there was always a bottle in the kitchen. The rum was spiced, and she didn't need ice, or anything to mix it with. Just a hit. It burnt her throat, but she needed it. Now feeling composed, it was time for a shower.

She stripped naked, watching the dress fall to the floor just as it had a few hours earlier. She caught her reflection in the glass of the oven door: lace bra, lace thong, hold ups. She still looked bloody good, despite her 48th birthday having just passed. She removed her bra. Her breasts hung, only a little, and the advantage of having 36B breasts and not those enormous 38DD things was, you could still look at them and think they belonged to a woman 10 years younger! She smiled and began to remove her hold ups. No matter how many times she had done it, she always managed to feel provocative as she peeled them down, even if there was no one else around to enjoy the spectacle. He had demanded she kept them on earlier, he definitely liked the look. Her hands went to the waistband of her thong, and she stopped, just for a second, and went back. The memory made her frisson, and unlike the few hours earlier, not in a good way. She had enjoyed "performing" for him. Allowing him to be the dominant male, be in control. Roughly he had pulled at her thong. Desperate to expose what he wanted, and she had let him. But now, alone, the memory made her uncomfortable. she slid them down, could barely allow herself to look at the pile of clothes on the floor before scooping them up, and putting them into the machine. She needed that shower more than ever. As she bent over to load the machine, she checked herself and slowly lowered her body into a more elegant posture. Her mind was still too fresh as he had taken her bent over. Another shudder, as she threw the tablet into the machine, selected the programme, and heard the water start to fill the new Bosch.

She padded softly out of the kitchen, the cold tiles feeling good on the soles of her feet, and she climbed the stairs. Thank God for a sunny day, and golf. She checked the clock that read 18:30. She had at least an hour before Tommy came back, maybe more if he spent any time at the 19th hole. She heard herself let out a sigh and as she reached the bathroom door, she felt sick. She wobbled a little then had to run, shit, she was going to throw up! As she spat the last remnants of the prawn mayo sandwich into the toilet, she heard Tommy pull into the drive. Why is he back earlier than she wanted, than she needed? The bloody Aston Martin was so loud, most of the neighbours knew he was home too. She flushed and watched the loo empty, as she rose to her feet, stabling herself with the toilet basin. Feeling her empty stomach too at least made her begin to feel better about herself.

She turned the shower on, as the key entered the door, and a slightly slurred "hello!" boomed out from downstairs; she said nothing, but stepped into the shower, and stood in its direct path, feeling the hot water pound her head. She ignored the setting and turned it up hotter, the water was almost too hot for her skin. But she wished it could be hotter, to burn the memory away. Why couldn't she just find the perfect affair, she thought to herself as she reached for her favourite L'Occitane shower gel. She knew it would cleanse the smell of him away, but the memory would take a little longer.

She muttered, "hello" as the almost scalding water turned her skin red, pointless, as she knew he couldn't possibly hear her, but at least she could say she had responded. She began to wash and scrub her face. She could feel "his" stubble touching her as she rubbed harder. She could smell his stale sweat, why couldn't

3

he have bothered with some kind of deodorant or aftershave? And a bloody shower! Even though she quite liked the stubble, the smell was overpowering and unpleasant. Although she had heard some women liked that, she definitely didn't.

She moved her hands to her breasts. She remembered he had pulled hard and pinched her nipples and she didn't want to admit it but she liked it. But because of his overpowering, unpleasant stale sweat smell, she started to massage her body hard, wanting that disgusting stench gone, wanting *him* gone. She was rubbing between her legs now and she couldn't escape the fact that he had felt good, hard, really hard. She started feeling lightheaded as the shower was too hot. She needed to get out of there, back to reality and to normality.

Finally cleansed, she turned off the shower as Tommy staggered into the bathroom. "I FUCKING WON!" he shouted, and opened his fly.

Holding on to the wall as he urinated, she said quietly, "good for you baby."

He turned and smiled. Looked longingly at her as she stepped out of the shower and dried herself, and continued to pee as she left the room.

She knew the drill by now.

She put on her silk robe and went back to the kitchen. Pinot was needed before he came down, so she opened the fridge door. Excellent, three and a half bottles. She wouldn't need to risk him hearing the "snap" of the seal, so poured a large glass, and downed half in one go. She refilled it, as she heard the bathroom door close, and rolled her eyes. Tonight would go one of two ways; he would either pass out drunk or stoned, or she would have to give herself to him. A thought that she genuinely despised.

She went to the living room and waited. Flicking the TV on, she didn't particularly care what she was watching, she just needed some company that would be anything but him. At least her

4

mind was nowhere, aimless drivel on the television taking away the memories. Allowing herself to be empty, she waited for him to come down the stairs. As she flicked through dozens of channels, Mamma Mia, the first one, and definitely the best one, appeared on the screen. It was only five minutes in, so she decided to stick with a chick flick and wine. What the hell else did she need tonight? Her mind was fucked. She had been fucked, and now, at that moment, she felt her life was fucked too. A feel good movie, get pissed, and fall asleep was perfect.

She kept waiting, poised, listening, craning her ear to check if the stairs would creak as he came down. It was now starting to get dark, the wine was going down well, and most importantly, he hadn't appeared. .

She said to herself, "he had more than I thought." Perhaps he only played 9 holes, then went to the club. Then, "shit he shouldn't have driven."

She remembered when she had said that before to him, when he had come home and could barely stand.

He had looked at her, almost with a look of disdain, and simply said "don't you fucking *dare* tell me what to do." He had pushed her onto the sofa, and leaned over her, "know your fucking place." Not shouted, but in a deep menacing, almost whispering quiet tone that had scared the life out of her. The man she had loved so deeply had become a monster. She had never mentioned drinking and driving again.

After the threat, he had stood up, quietly left the room, his point made, and he had gone to the dining room. As she had heard the decanter clink, and the gentle pouring sound, she had known that her night was done then, and she would be going to bed alone. He would pass out in the dining room, wake at 2am, and go into the living room to find solace on the sofa.

At least this evening she had not let her thoughts come out. And as she sat with the TV on, the wine went down easy, she welcomed the cold crisp feeling in her mouth, and she let her mind roll back to earlier in the day.

2 "CHARLIE"

The shopping trip with the girls had been planned for a while. All along, however, Michelle had also planned her "meet". She had told the girls, Tatiana and Grace, that she had a hair appointment, made her excuses and left. She knew Tommy was at golf and would be for some time yet. All the girls used their phones all the time. They sat having coffee and bitching about Valerie. Tatiana and Grace could be quite cutting when they had the chance. She just nodded, smiled and laughed in the right places. All the while, her own phone was open, chatting - to Mike. She had only discovered the website by chance, pissed one afternoon. Michelle Googled, "adult relationships," and there they all were. From match.com, to fuck a slut," and everything in between. She scanned down quickly and was shocked. At the time, she had closed the page, but the seed had been sown and it could only go one way. It had not taken her much "Dutch Courage," (less than one bottle of wine) it was easy to join one of them: create a fake email, make up a username, nothing sexual like others were, and display a photo, nothing too sexual. Just a shot of her legs in stockings and high heels, would be enough to provoke their interest, and within what had seemed like seconds there were men practically begging her for sex. That had all been so innocent and so long ago. Now, as the girls bitched, she was planning Mike, and smiling at the girls, sometimes in all the wrong places! But the girls didn't notice, they were too busy taking Valerie apart.

"I'm off now girls," Michelle said. It was no surprise, they had already agreed that 1pm was pretty much time (unless booze was involved), they couldn't do more than two or three hours together before they wanted to go anyway. Pissed, dancing, loud music ... That was different. But today, three hours of "your hair looks great," or "did you hear what Valerie did?" was more than enough. Two coffees, five times as many cigarettes, and not enough genuine laughter and friendship meant she *needed* that hotel now. They kissed on both cheeks, the other girls insisted. "It's the French way darling!" And bid each other farewell. It wasn't that she didn't like them, but, after her upbringing,

She sometimes struggled with fitting into the new social circle she had been thrust into when she first met her now husband. They all waved, as they always did, and she watched the other two leave. She hung back, checking her phone once more. The two girls both drove convertible BMW's. She had to be different of course, so told him she wanted the Mercedes two-seater. Michelle didn't have kids, and was not planning them, so why the hell would she want a bloody great 3 series? Besides, a silver Mercedes was the perfect car to disappear in. They waved again as she approached her car, and she smiled and waved, that pathetic wave like the Queen does.

She looked around. The Louis Vuitton bag in the boot contained all she needed for the next part of her day, but she was already slightly late. The hotel was around 30 mins away. Mike had told her 2 pm in the bar. It was now 13:15, shit! she needed to get changed. She looked around, scanning the roof for cameras. Sod it; she couldn't be late, she hated being late. After all, it was a dress, and some hold ups. The Agent Provocateur underwear was already on, she unzipped her jeans, and the thin cream jumper she slipped over her head fell to the floor almost as quickly as she slipped the beautiful black Chanel dress back on in its place. Admittedly it didn't look so good with the jeans, but they slipped down easily enough, and she had kept most of her modesty intact. She placed the bag back into the boot, and grabbed the hold ups as she got into the car. Christian Louboutin heels would complete the look. She deftly pulled the hold ups on, proud of her legs despite the fact she was nearly 50.

She normally wore very little makeup, but she lowered her mirror, applied some lip gloss and smiled at herself. She liked what she saw. A new record, dressed like an elegant slut in less than fifteen minutes. Perfect!

She started the engine; the roof would have to stay up for now as she didn't want to turn up windswept. With a final look into the rear-view mirror just to make sure she was presentable, she pushed the throttle, and the Mercedes began its journey onto her next man.

Oh no! It's now 13:45, I need to stay calm. The hotel is only another five minutes away. She is back in control and checks her phone. The lights are red. *Shit!* More time wasted. As the Mercedes slows to a halt, she sees the BMW Z4 in front. It's old, but she kind of likes them. Maybe she can ask *him* for a newer one. It feels like she has been waiting forever. She stares up to her left at the lights, waiting, *urging* them to change. As they hit amber, she hits the accelerator. And as she looks ahead, she sees the brake lights, and *screams*! *"Fuck!"* It's too late. She pulls the wheel to the right and hits the brakes as hard as her naked feet will let her. And she can see the Z4 getting closer. Fuck! He was turning right. Shit!
The dull thud seemed deafening. And as the car stops, her mobile flies out of her lap, across the car and hits the dashboard. Panic sets in; not for the car, but for her phone. She looks around. Her first thought was, I *need* my phone. Only then does she see a face at the window, she screams again.

 He is clearly pissed off. "What the fuck?" she hears through the window. Thank God it's up. She locks the doors. And she can begin to hear herself sob, suddenly tears are falling. Shit! this is going from bad to worse. The guy outside, his expression changes. He sees the tears, and now his persona changes. No longer pissed off. He wants to make sure she isn't hurt. He knows the accident was nothing, but she seems totally shaken. He calls, "are you OK?"

softly, not wanting to make her upset any more than she clearly is. She looks at him. Thank God for waterproof mascara. He looks nice, warm and friendly. He speaks a little louder now. "*Are you OK?*"

Of course I am OK. Except she panics again. I just hit his bloody car, and he is asking *me* if I am ok? He taps the window. Come on Michelle, pull yourself together. She winds down the window. He is dressed scruffily, a builder perhaps? She looks up at him.

A crooked smile appears, "are you OK?"

She warms a little. "Yes, I'm fine, I'm *so* sorry. Just as she says the words, she hears her mobile ring. Fuck! Panic again. It's *him*.

"Do you want to get the cars out of the middle of the road?" Her mind comes back to 'crooked smile man'. Warm eyes, nice biceps.

"Yes, I suppose we should."

He walks back to the Z4, nice arse too, and he shouts, "follow me," and slowly moves the BMW to turn right. The road is quiet, and she follows. Her phone still lit up from the missed call. The lay-by isn't far, and she parks behind him. She leans over, grabs the mobile. A missed call from him. *And* from Mike. FUCK, MIKE! it's 2pm, *oh shit!* Her mind is racing. As 'crooked smile' approaches the car. She blurts out, "I'm so sorry" again. It's pathetic, but she is lost. Her mind can't think straight.

"It's ok, there isn't much damage." The relief is visible. "Do you want to see?" he asks.

"I'm kind of late," she blurts out. Her French accent was there for him to hear.

"OK," he says, puzzled. "Well, let's swap numbers for insurance, and give me your name and address, and I will get you on your way."

Inside, she is already asking herself, how the *hell* can he be so calm? She looks down. She is dressed like a high class slut, she smiles inside, he *wants* her phone number!

She watches him walk back to the BMW. Very nice arse indeed. Bit of a beer belly, but nice arse. He comes back with a tissue, and a pen. "Sorry, best I could do."

"That's just fine." She smiles for the first time since the day had seemed to go so horribly wrong. She scribbles her name, address, and mobile number.

He is using her car to lean on and leans close to the window as he gives her his details. She can't help thinking that he smells nice. "I have a mate who has a car repair business if you don't want to use insurance."

She still hasn't got out of the car. "OK, thank you," is all she can manage.

He smiles, that crooked smile, "you best get on your way if you are late already."

She smiles, wishing right now she wasn't late for Mike, and as she does, the dial chat message appears. "Where are you?"

She looks again at the crooked smile man. He says, "Hi, I'm Charlie."

She looks up. "I'm Michelle."

As she puts the Mercedes into drive, she picks up her mobile and dictates a message to Mike, "give me five minutes."

She pulls into the hotel car park, sweating slightly and stressed. She opens dial chat.

"I am just pulling up, get me a glass of wine please," and she presses send. Hoping Mike won't read immediately. Shit, he does! OK, get your game face on; you have done this dozens of times, focus Michelle. It's sex. As she steps out
of the car, putting the heels on, her mind wanders back to 'crooked smile', nice arse man. And she walks to the front of the car, surveys a dent, fist sized probably, and some blue paint. She mutters shit! under her breath. With a glance
into the window, she makes her way to reception, it's now almost 14.30. As she enters the hotel, and looks around, she sees Mike, and her heart sinks. Yes, it's definitely the guy on the profile, but probably 10 years older, definitely 10kg heavier, and with a complexion that suggests he enjoys more than the odd bottle of wine. She smiles. And walks towards him.
He smiles, "I got you a Sauvignon."

She smiles back, "thank you." And as she leans in to kiss him, the smell is overpowering. Unpleasant and stale sweat.

3 "DAVID"

It's 6.30am, and just briefly as she wakes, she isn't quite sure where she is. Shit, her head hurts! She looks around the room, the two empty bottles of wine are laying on the table, and so is the glass, the rest of the house looks like a show home. White leather sofa, elegant stone-coloured cushions and carpet. It's classy, tasteful. She designed most of it of course. He wouldn't have a clue, but he was the one who paid for it all. Slowly, she lifts her head from one of the cushions. Good God, her head hurts! She glances down at the empty wine bottles. Secretly, she is just a little proud that she drank both bottles and wasn't sick. And just at that moment, she realises she needs to rush to the downstairs bathroom. The wine came back. Hard. Ugly. She made it, just! But she regretted both the emotional low, and also good God, the physical act of throwing up. Finally, she stopped retching and stood up. Looked in the mirror and muttered, "Michelle, you look like shit."

She walked to the kitchen slowly staggering, she needed water. She opened the fridge and saw the can of full fat Coke, perfect! Sugar, now! She poured a glass, and drank it, not too fast, or she knew it would be coming back again. But yes, the sweetness definitely was both needed, and being absorbed greedily by her dehydrated body. She poured more, and only then did she begin to piece together the day before. Why hadn't *he* come downstairs after she had got out of the shower? The usual pattern was, if he had won, he would be semi pissed, but in a great mood. So she would have to succumb to his advances, to keep his mood buoyant. Yet last night he had not followed her downstairs. She decided to creep upstairs, curious as to why he had changed his usual routine.

As she got to the top, she could hear the snores. The master bedroom was magnificent. Clean, white again, with deep wine-coloured accents. Even *he* admired the bedroom and en-suite. But the only thing he was admiring this morning was the top of the duvet. He hadn't even bothered to get undressed. She found it unusual, out of character. Sure, he had come home drunk before, and occasionally he had also fallen straight to sleep. But she couldn't put her finger on why, this just felt different. She grabbed a pair of comfy cream joggers, and a top, and made her way out of the bedroom. He was oblivious to it all. She needed a shower again, and to brush her teeth, but she could do that all in the guest bathroom. Less elegant, and not quite so lavishly furnished, but still clean and immaculately presented. It served the other two bedrooms, and together with the downstairs loo and shower room, meant there were more than enough places to go to the toilet or wash when parties or guests were at the house. It seemed a long time since anything like that, except for *his* friends. No, not even friends, his mates had come around, direct from the club. Pissed, and gradually got more pissed. She usually shuts herself away on those nights.

She decided to go back downstairs and empty the washing machine, (the Chanel dress was dry clean only, but she really didn't care, she had machine washed it before and no one noticed) but she carefully made sure the clothes were hidden amongst the others hanging in the warm utility room. He wouldn't notice anyway, but you could never be sure.

Returning back through the kitchen, she decided that the downstairs shower room was safest. He wouldn't hear the water, and she could hopefully escape before he woke. She hated Sundays! If he wasn't playing, it made for some very quiet and awkward days.

She stepped out of the silk robe, and into the large shower enclosure. Turning the valve, she felt the water and immediately it made her more alert. She opened the valve fully, the shower room had a powerful pump fitted and, on the right setting, the water almost hurt if it hit in the right place at the right angle. It could make you orgasm too she thought, and she smiled to herself. The water felt good, hot and powerful, she wasn't dirty, and just needed the shower to wake her and drag her out of the hangover. She didn't need long in there to feel awake. Rejuvenated and alive, she stepped out. Dried herself, and then decided she would just put her hair up. Sod it, she wasn't going anywhere. She pulled on the joggers, and the top. It was a little risky, no bra, but her still reasonably firm breasts meant she was ok with it. At least her tits were not on her knees yet! She was feeling pretty chilled, and glanced at the clock, 8am, not so bad. She had no idea what time she had fallen asleep, much less what time he had. But one thing was for sure, he had definitely had more than her to drink. The glass decanter was still beside him upstairs. She had no idea when he had come down to get it. And thank God he hadn't spilled anything this time.

Slowly, she began to come back to normal. And it was then she remembered the car. Shit! The dent! How the hell was she going to explain it? Maybe she would just see how he was before she mentioned anything. In fact, that's definitely what she would do. He may just sleep all day, she could only hope!

As her mind wandered back, she thought about a crooked smile man. What was his name again? Charles? something like that. He had been so calm. She would have gone ape shit. She decided she was going to go and check out the car. She went to the fridge: wine, cheese, and a few tomatoes. Great, she really needed to shop too! She would go to the car., check the damage, and go to the garage. Bread: eggs, and bacon. At least she could start the day with something for her. And perhaps *he* would be awake when she got back, and a bacon and egg sarnie might put him in a good mood too.

She closed the front door quietly and slipped into

the Mercedes. She looked into the passenger foot well. Shit, her shoes! Oh well, he clearly hadn't seen them, so she would put them in the boot later, before he could comment. At £800, she knew he didn't mind her having them, but chucked in the footwell of the car wasn't his idea of taking care of things, and she had to agree.

As she pulled out of the drive, she was amazed at how, no matter how drunk he was, he always parked the Aston perfectly. It was his pride and joy. Second hand, but only 2 years old, and had cost well over 100k. She secretly loved it. The noise, the looks, the speed. But she wasn't allowed near it and wouldn't dare ask.

The garage was not far, she needed petrol too, so she could do it all. And then maybe she would check out the dent and decide what story she needed to come up with. David in the garage had known her ever since she lived there. And they always had a little laugh and a smile for each other. This morning, a cheery greeting from David, and a friendly face was just what she needed.

As she pulled in, she was relieved to see that no one else was in the garage. She pulled onto the pump, and smiled as he looked out of the window. He gave her a small wave and she felt warm inside. She smiled back, and instantly she just felt a little better about her day. She filled the car, and stepped inside the small shop.

"Good Morning Michelle!" came the bright greeting from behind the counter. She blushed, feeling herself go red. And had no idea why, but she just felt a glow inside. That she needed right now.

"Morning David!" she beamed back.
She collected all she needed, and placed it all on the counter.

"You must have been unlucky Michelle, your beautiful car."
She looked at him. Then the dent. "Oh yes, bloody car parks," she said.

15

David looked at her. "I hope you get it fixed."

"Me too," she said, and paid for her shopping. "See you!" she smiled as she left the shop. He smiled back. He liked Michelle.

She looked at the car. Shit, It was a dent! Not massive, but fist sized, *his* fist size. She walked around and got in. She took a deep breath as she sat down in the driver's seat. Threw the bacon and the other stuff on the passenger seat, and opened the glove box. She saw the tissue. Charles wasn't crooked smile's name, it was Charlie, and there was his number. It was 8.45, on a Sunday. She took out her Samsung.

4 "THE HANGOVER"

She slowly pulled out of the garage, smiling again at David, as he waved to her. He was a nice man.

The phone was ringing, shit, she felt the panic rising as it rang much longer than she expected! She was just about to put it down, when a bleary voice muttered, "hello?"

She felt the panic again, though she couldn't really explain why. "Hi, it's Michelle, we, er, met yesterday?"

"Michelle?" came the reply, and instantly she felt rejected. "Oh, Michelle! the good looking woman who drove into my car!" A muffled laugh. She relaxed and felt herself go red with embarrassment.

"Er yes, that's the one. I'm so sorry to call so early, I was just out picking some things up, and wondered if you were awake."

"I am now," came the laughed reply.

"So sorry," she said, again, feeling a little rejected. She didn't take rejection particularly well, and especially when she actually *wanted* him to be interested!

"It's fine, I had a bit of a late one that's all. Are you ok after yesterday? Did you make your appointment OK?"

She felt herself go red again. "Er, yes, I was a little late but it was OK." She could almost hear the smile at the other end of the phone.

"That's good then," he said, and she worried if he wondered what she had been up to. "So, how can I help?"

She smiled, and thought, God, you have no idea how you could help. "I wonder if your friend could take a look at the car fairly quickly? My husband doesn't know I have hit it, and I would like to keep it that way!" She could hear the smile again.

"No problem. Let me give him a call and see how he is fixed, how soon are we talking?"

"I don't suppose today is an option is it?"

"Let me make a call. He won't be up yet, he was out with me last night! Can I ring you back?"

She panicked. "Er, no, best not to. I will give you a ring after lunch."   She swore he was grinning at her at the other end of the phone.

"OK, no problem, speak after lunch."

"Thanks." She ended the call. And couldn't help but allow herself a smile.

She drove home a little quicker than she planned and carefully put the car next to the hedge. She collected the shopping and went indoors. Phew! She could hear the shower running and rushed to the kitchen, where she took out the frying pan, and began to prepare breakfast.

Shouting "DO YOU WANT BACON AND EGG?" Knowing full well he would, and also that she would not be heard with him in the shower. Another smile to herself, perhaps today would be a good day after all. She heard the shower stop running and smiled to herself again. The bacon began to sizzle.

She shouted up again, "do you want bacon and eggs?"

"That would be nice," came the reply in a decent voice. She felt good. As she flipped the bacon she tried to make it as crispy as possible just the way he liked it.

He came downstairs holding his head slightly, "do we have any paracetamol?" he asked.

She smiled, he clearly had more than she thought, and definitely more than she had!

"I will get you some," she said, turning the bacon again. She bent over to retrieve the pills from the "medical" cupboard, and he couldn't resist smacking her on the rear. She smiled, and let out a squeal. She only wished the mood would last. As she turned to give him the medication, she opened the fridge and passed him a bottle of water.

"Thanks love," he said.

Sounding genuinely grateful. His head was not in the best place, mentally or physically. He took the pills, and asked how long it would be for the bacon.

"Only a couple of minutes," was her reply. He sat at the breakfast bar. Looking slightly dazed, empty. Despite all the things she disliked him for, after the best part of 20 years together, she couldn't hate him totally.
"Are you OK?" she asked. "Do you want coffee?" As she looked up, she could see he was much worse than hung over. She had no idea what was wrong, but she had never seen him like this.

"Yes, please."
She turned away again. Went to the coffee machine, and began to make his brew. She still drew breath at almost £1000 for a *coffee* maker! But it did make bloody good coffee. She poured, and watched as his eyes kind of glazed over.

"How many sugars do you need this morning?"

"Two please"

"Had too much yesterday did we?" she smiled as she said it, wanting to avoid confrontation, wanting to show she was just making conversation.

He looked at her, and just for a moment she panicked, then she saw his face soften, "yes, I suppose I did." His expression wasn't entirely convincing, but she said nothing more.

She ate her sandwich, and asked, "what plans do you have for today?"

He looked at her again, and she was uneasy, he just wasn't himself. "I said I would go back to the club today, there is a charity match on. Come down if you want?"

She was taken by surprise at the generosity. "I might just do that," she found herself saying. She could see the disappointment on his face, "but I have a couple of things to do first." "What time does it start?"

He looked at her again, "around 12 I think. I feel a bit rough. I think I will have to go and sort myself out."

She smiled. "OK baby, well, if you have finished, why don't you go and have a lie down?" She could see he still wasn't quite with it.

"I might just do that," he said, and finished up his sandwich. He still looked slightly worse for wear, but was enjoying the food and the sugary coffee.

She said nothing more, but left the kitchen, and padded upstairs to organise his clothes. He couldn't say or do anything. His body was still in "come down" mode, from the excess of yesterday's drugs and booze, despite the length of sleep. But he wasn't about to show weakness, or tell Michelle what he had been doing. He placed the plates and cup neatly next to the sink, and followed her upstairs.

She watched him go to the bathroom, and called out, "do you want your full tiger woods?"

He shouted back, "why the hell not!"

She smiled. She would be able to get the car looked at this afternoon at least, and perhaps she might even make it to the club to please him too. She began to go through his wardrobe, and found him a bright yellow polo, his check plus fours and matching jumper if he wanted it.

She walked to the bathroom and said, "clothes are on the bed. I am just going to pop out and will come down to the club a bit later."

He gave a simple thumbs up as he brushed his teeth for the 2nd time that morning, and she was again puzzled. No resistance. No protest. "See you later and good luck with the golf!"

She practically ran downstairs, grabbed her keys and purse, and went out to the car. Shit, I need my phone! In her haste she had left it charging. She desperately needed her phone, but didn't really want to go back inside the house. Oh well, she would have to go in, she couldn't call crooked smile without it. Softly, she opened the door and listened, silence, perfect! She grabbed the Samsung and rushed back out of the house, closing the door with her key to make it as quiet as possible. She jumped into the car and reversed out of the drive as the car connected to her mobile. She pulled out, and slipped quietly down the road. A grin, a sigh of relief, now, where was that bloody phone number.

5 "CALLUM"

It was ringing. She felt her stomach become a little tight. Pick up please!

"Hello?" The voice was a little puzzled and confused.

She replied, "Hi, it's Michelle, I crashed into your car," she wasn't sure if the laughter was a good thing or not. But it made her giggle too when she heard herself and what she had just said. She said, "God that sounds so bad!" And laughed timidly.

The reply came with a giggle too, "well, it's a hell of a way to introduce yourself, but, hi."

"I wonder if your friend might be able to look at the car for me? I know it's Sunday, but my husband is out and hasn't seen it yet and I just wondered."

"He is about today, yes. I told him you might call. Why don't I meet you there? It's Lornden Lodge farm. Want the postcode?"

"No thanks, I know it," she had been there for a few riding lessons at different times.

"OK, Shall we say 30 mins?"

"That would be perfect," she said. "Thanks again, see you there." She ended the call, and slipped the gear lever into drive. He was right, it was a hell of a way to introduce yourself.

She cruised along now. Feeling a little more relaxed. She decided to pull over and lower the roof, whilst it wasn't as hot today, it was dry and with watery sunshine that made the day feel warmer than it was. As she did so she looked down at what she was wearing, she couldn't believe she went out in joggers and a top, hair barely done. What was she thinking! Oh well, it was too late now, and she was only getting her car looked at. She didn't need to rush as the farm was barely 20 minutes for her, and she was comfortable it was both out of the way of the golf club, (totally opposite directions thankfully!) and also, the last place *he* would ever look for her. He really had never been interested in horses, and certainly wouldn't be wanting to be anywhere near a stables. So she could afford to relax, even if she was more than a little disappointed in the way she looked. She had absolutely no idea what there was about Charlie, but that "movie moment" had definitely happened. It had been brief, but the look as their eyes locked told her there had been some tiny spark. She shivered, and had no idea what was actually going on in her mind, but she knew there was just a tiny *something*, a niggle, a thought, a glint. She couldn't even explain it, but she *knew* he had felt it too.

As she pulled into the farm, she could feel her cheeks redden slightly, and she had absolutely no idea why. It probably was the fact that the blue BMW was already there, top down despite the chill in the air, and there he was, leaning against it, laughing. Jeans, white trainers, white shirt, and shades resting on his head. She liked what she saw, and couldn't help thinking he was a bloody show off! Only then did she notice the guy standing a couple of feet away from him. Shorter, stockier, big arms, and a big beard! That must be Callum. She could see they were really relaxed, like true "mates". A look she had seen from her husband when he had been at the club many times. A camaraderie and friendship that was quite deep, and something she had never really experienced. Callum was dressed, well, like a mechanic really. Covered in a little grease and oil, and with overalls and his cap on backwards. Both men turned as she drove in, and then looked back at each other. Were they talking about me she thought? There was that bloody glint again, as Charlie looked at her. What the *hell* was it about him? She noticed then that Callum was much younger than Charlie. And her mind began to wonder. Why? Charlie was (she guessed) in his 40's, late probably, the hair more grey than brown now, the stubble had flecks of grey too. But the smile and eyes were bright and felt and looked much younger. Callum she guessed was mid to late 20's, shorter, and bigger built. Definitely not a bodybuilder, there was a belly there, but also a warm smile and *shit*, she looked at his eyes. Then quickly back to Charlie. They were more than just mates, weren't they? She parked the car and opened the door.

The men looked at her again, and smiled.
"Good Morning," Charlie said.

And Callum chipped in, "mornin!"

She smiled back nervously, and whispered, "hi."

"This is the lady that very kindly drove into the Z4!" he said, and she felt herself redden again.

"I'm so sorry," she apologised, and shuffled uncomfortably.

He laughed. And pointed to the dent on her Mercedes. "You came off worse," he said. She looked at the BMW, it had barely a scratch.

"How did you manage to have *nothing* happen to your car!"

"I guess I was just lucky," he replied, and winked at Callum. She wasn't quite sure of the dynamic between them, but the body language said they were definitely comfortable with each other.

Charlie turned and smiled that crooked smile. He could see she was pondering what on earth was going on. "Callum is my son," he said.

She stepped back, more than a little surprised, but also it was great to see how they were with each other. "Oh, I see! I had no idea!"

"Why would you?" came the reply, and she blushed.

"Why don't I put the kettle on, and you can show Callum the damage? Do you want tea or coffee, and I hope a mug is ok?" "Coffee please, black, and a mug is fine!"

Callum smiled at her, "let's go take a look at the car."

It was hardly far, and certainly you didn't need to be a rocket scientist to see the dent. Callum bent down and began to survey the damage. He made some strange noises and tapped at the metal in a few places. She watched him closely, puzzled. Did he really know what he was doing? He began to almost caress the metal, and she thought she had seen it all. A man giving a car a massage!

Then things got more bizarre. As Charlie returned with the coffee, Callum disappeared into the workshop, and came back smiling and carrying what looked to her like a slightly odd looking hair dryer. He smiled as he took a big gulp of his hot tea, and grinned at Charlie.

Looking back at her he smiled and said, "blow dry madam?"

She smiled nervously, and was just a little worried she had done the wrong thing coming here, before Charlie said "don't worry, it's a heat gun, he needs to warm up the metal," he looked back at Callum and said "behave!"

Callum grinned, and said, "yes father," and muttered to himself, "nothing like a blow job, er, I mean dry, on a Sunday!" He laughed to himself as he flicked the switch, and she heard the gun begin to blow out hot air.

Charlie turned to her, there was a slightly awkward silence before he said, "coffee OK?"

She smiled back, "it's perfect, just what I needed."

"Had one too many last night did we?" he asked.

She laughed nervously, "Yes, I think so, I find a can of fat coke, or an ice lolly is the best cure."

Callum stood up, and said, "when did you last have a hangover!" and almost as quickly knelt back down and carried on with the heat gun.

She thought she saw Charlie grimace just a little, before he smiled and said, "yes, perhaps it's been a while." There was that bloody crooked smile again. She liked it.

Suddenly, without warning, Callum stood up and swung his fist at the car. She screamed, and dropped her coffee. The thud was almost as loud as when she hit Charlie's car.

"I'm sorry," Charlie said, as Callum beamed with pride.

"You dozy git, poor woman shit herself."

"I am sorry, Callum beamed, "but look!"

She approached the front of the car. The dent had almost gone, she was amazed.

Callum beamed again, and his dad was also clearly impressed.

"Bloody hell mate, that came out alright!"

She smiled, "that's amazing," she said, a little bewildered. "How did you do that?"

Callum looked at her, and said, "years of practice, and the old man helping to teach me to know where to hit them!"

Charlie smiled. A little shyly. And she saw him look humble. "Well, I have been doing this a long time," he said with a crooked grin. She smiled back. "It's perfect," she exclaimed.

"Not quite, Callum replied, "but it's pretty good. If you get really close you will see it still has a little indent here and there, but overall, you would have to look hard to see it."

"How much do I owe you?" She questioned.

"Talk to the old man," was the reply, "he is the brains of the outfit!" and he laughed out loud as he began to go back inside with the heat gun.

Charlie looked at her. "Well brains?" she smiled.

"Let's say this one is on the house," he said, and winked at her.

"You can't be serious?" she replied.

"Of course," he said, "it's nothing." "One condition though"

She looked at him, puzzled. "OK, what condition?"

"You let me buy you a drink."

She blushed. a deep scarlet she couldn't hide. "I'm married,'" she said.

"I'm not," he replied, and grinned again.

She said, "Are you sure I can't give him anything for what he has done?"

"Oh, there is one thing," Charlie laughed, "you owe me for a bloody coffee mug!"

She felt herself go red again. "He made me jump!" she shuffled her feet awkwardly.

Charlie laughed again. "I'm sorry," he offered his reply.

"I guess I better be off, my husband wants me to go to the golf club."

"That's nice,'" he said patronisingly, and swung his arms like a golfer might before he took his tee shot.

"I hate golf" she said, "but it's all for charity today."

"Lucky charity!" Charlie smiled. "I best let you go get ready then." Only then did she remember her sweat pants and top. "Er, yes, OK, thank you so much."

She looked at Callum, who was now back in the sunlight after putting the tools away "anytime," he said, and gave her a business card. "Tell your friends," She looked down. SUMMER Autos. She looked up again as she slid into the car. "Drive carefully," Charlie said as she slipped the car into reverse, and looked over her shoulder. As she drove out of the yard, she saw father and son standing together. And she watched Charlie make a "figure" shape with his hands and point at the Mercedes. She smiled, I've still got it she thought to

herself, and she pulled out of the yard.

She couldn't take the smile off her face as she drove, and she felt rather pleased with herself. Jogging bottoms and a top, no makeup and her hair untouched, yet she had still managed to get Charlie's attention. And she certainly wasn't about to complain about that. She found him very attractive. Not in a pretty boy way, but kind of rugged and down to earth and there *was* something, she knew it, and he knew it too.

6 "SINGING"

As she swept into the driveway, she felt a sense of relief, the Aston was not there. It was such good news. She at least could take her time, and make sure that, even if she hated the golf club, no one would see it, and most of all, that *he* would be proud of her.

He must have not long left; she could smell his aftershave, he always smelt good. She remembered that from the first time they ever met all those years ago. It was time to get her game face on and put on a show for him. Even if it just was to keep the peace, she knew he would be expecting her to turn up, perhaps not for long, but enough to save face at the club. She was still a good looking, slim petite woman, and despite the fact age had made her reconsider the length of skirt she wore, she was quite proud of herself, and she knew he was too.

First things first, she needed to wash her hair. She was feeling good, and had a spring in her step as she almost ran up the stairs and turned the shower on. As the water ran, she stepped into the bedroom and out of her clothes. It was seconds, and she was naked. She grinned, she had gone out this morning with no knickers, no bra, and Charlie had no idea - or *did* he? She threw the clothes into the corner, and went back to the bathroom. Just as she was about to step into the shower, she stopped, and decided she needed a musical fix. "Alexa, play Stereophonics C'est la vie." The Sonos speakers that were dotted around the house then began to bang out the guitar riff, and she smiled and stepped under the powerful jet of water. As the heat penetrated her head, she began to think about what had brought her here all those years ago. She looked around, and still couldn't quite believe that the girl who had almost literally come from nothing, could now be enjoying all of this luxury. It had been the smell of his aftershave that had begun the drift back to the past, and she now allowed her mind to begin to wind back the clock.

Michelle was born 23rd March 1972 in a small village in France. During her early years, she hadn't really noticed her mother was not there and she was often left with her mother's friends. But as she grew older, she saw more and more what her mother was. The injections in her arms, the empty expressions on her face. Her mother had met a man who had taken them to England when Michelle was around eight years old. She couldn't remember too much of him, other than a beard, a loud voice, and beating her mother. He had not stayed around long after they arrived, he had left them both at the disgusting hostel to fend for themselves. The UK had been kind. And even though there was no way of her mother paying her way, with a young child in tow, initially, her mother had been given a house, and benefits. It wasn't much money, but it made it much easier for her mother to get the drugs her sad and ravaged body and mind so desperately needed now. As she approached ten, her mother's drug use became total. She told herself she had no idea of a home, she had tried to shut out her early life. But every now and again, the emotions took over her, and she allowed herself to dive back into the past. Ever since she could remember, her mother had "slept" a lot. She was always in bed, and most times not alone. Or she was totally out of it, arms by her sides and looking completely vacant. Eventually the people came; she had no idea who they were, but her mother was angry. She heard and saw her mother screaming at the man and woman in the suits. But there was no turning back, they were adamant. Michelle would no longer be living with her mother. She felt herself scream too, and she remembered the tears. Then fighting the man in the suit, but he was too strong. She couldn't fight anymore. She gave in and went with the suits. Her mother stayed quiet, she was shaking. And Michelle knew then she would never see her again.

The children's home wasn't too bad really; it was clean, he remembered that. She remembered the smell of bleach and everything being beige. Ordinary, calm and normal. Except it was *nothing* like normal. She could feel herself beginning to cry. As the shower pounded her head, the tears released themselves, and she began to sob uncontrollably. The hurt. The anguish. Her mother gone. And in truth, little prospect of another human being to fill the gap. She was determined from a very young age that she would not become her mother. She would know who she was. And be proud she had a direction and had made something of her life. She had kept her head down. Gone to school. Never been very academic, but she tried. She was Michelle Bogarde and she was proud of it. It didn't stop the girls at school taking the piss because she was French. Bogeys they called her. She laughed, but inside she was bitter. At her useless drug addict mother, and also at her weakness for accepting what they said without a fight. But she was determined. She would get to 16 and leave school. And make sure she and *only* she was in control of her life. There was *no way* she would be told what to do and what to say. Things hadn't quite turned out that way. She had never quite stood up to the bullying. It had gotten better, and she had shown fight and spirit. They had begun to leave her alone. And there was a degree of respect after her fight back.

"DONT YOU FUCKING DARE DISRESPECT MY FAMILY NAME," she screamed, she had finally had enough of the "bogeys" taunts, and the explosion was inevitable.

It worked and the older girls now at least knew she would not take any crap. It had made her feel better at least. By the time she was 13 she was able to look after herself but she was still intimidated by the older girls. She was determined never to show it and it would carry her through for the rest of her life. She also knew by the age of 13 that her body was changing, and she had experimented sexually with fingers and objects and enjoyed the feeling.

She had also realised that she was never going to be super clever. When she got her grades at school, she was constantly being told they were below average and she must do more to improve. At 13, that wasn't what you wanted to hear and the only solace she found was in something that she didn't actually know she had until around 11-years-old. She had a voice! And she could really sing. Initially it was singing along to 80s pop stuff that she heard on radios. The girls had initially taken the piss out of her but slowly they realised that she could actually sing and that she was good at it. From that moment on her life in the children's home had become easier. If nothing else they respected her voice, and had actually begun to ask her to sing stuff on request. She had no idea where it had come from, she certainly had no idea if her mother could sing, but she knew she could, and if the teenage bitches in the home liked her voice, then she would make damn sure that one way or another, she would use it to her advantage somehow. So she stayed quiet. She ambled through school, almost completely disinterested in anything except music. Her music teacher had become someone so important in her life, she sometimes wished she just lived with him. He was in his 50s, she guessed. Married and boring. Always dressed in beige with patches on the sleeves of his jacket. Your typical boring teacher. Until he began to talk about music. And then you could see the passion he had for what he did. He loved the way she sang, and rarely criticised, which she either took as a compliment, or that he flattered her and wanted something in return. In truth she knew he was as straight as an arrow. Mr Brock was a little boring, a little ordinary, but he too was possessed with a voice that could really sing. He could also play a mean guitar, and the piano, and his boundless enthusiasm made school bearable, and if she was truthful, she loved his lessons, and always gave her best attention. It was that way from the age of 13 when she really discovered how to use her talent, and would continue as she carried on through her school life. As the shower pounded down, she heard herself shout. "Alexa play Trouble by Pink," and as the song began, she allowed her mind to wander again, but this time, with her voice as the accompaniment. She let herself get lost in her memories again, and her singing the pink song wasn't difficult, but it made her smile as she belted out the lyrics, and remembered being 16, and taking her exams, oh what a waste of time they were. All except music. Mr Brock had definitely driven her to succeed, but she put all the work in, and she felt rightly proud of her "A" even if the other subjects put together wouldn't have added up to a C minus. She left school with nothing more than her love of music, and an exam which told the world just that.

7 "THE GOLF CLUB"

She smiled as the song came to an end, so did her thoughts, and she snapped back into reality. The bathroom was full of steam, she always had the shower too hot! Shouts "Alexa, play Craig David," and wraps the towel around her as she pads to the bedroom. "7 Days" begins its melodic chant, and she smiles, as she drops the towel, and peeks at her body in the mirror. She looks at the time, it's now close to 2pm. 20 mins or so should be just about perfect. She towelled her hair but had no intention of drying it; she was proud of her curls, all her own, no perm here! She spread the moisturiser over her body slowly, and, had anyone been watching, they would have thought it incredibly erotic. She did too, and allowed her mind loose, as she massaged her skin with the cream, she found herself closing her eyes, and letting Charlie slip his hand inside her underwear. She touched herself, and felt that warm sensation as she reached her clit, and felt her whole body shudder. She sat on the bed, laid back, spread her legs and allowed Charlie to fuck her in her mind, it felt good, and she knew she wouldn't take long to orgasm. She rubbed her pussy, and could feel the orgasm build. Crazy, hot, intense, but she couldn't stop now, her mind was telling him to fuck her hard. She could feel him on top of her; and as the orgasm built, she closed her eyes, and felt her legs grip him as she came hard, the orgasm was hard, intense, and she enjoyed it immensely as it swept over her. She lay there, spent, and with her breath coming in short bursts. She hadn't experienced a climax like that in a very long time, and it took her a little while to "come back" and gather herself. She lay on the bed, legs spread, her clitoris swollen. She looked at the clock, shit, almost a record when she had played with herself. She reckoned it had taken her less than 5 minutes to come!

Time now to get her game face on, and make him proud of her at the club. As she took a wipe out of the pack her phone rang, it was him. She answered, "hello baby."

He growled "where are you?"

"I'm sorry," she said, "I wanted to look my best for you, so I spent too long in the shower."

His voice softened perhaps a little too quickly, "ok, how long do you think you will be?"

"Give me 20 minutes would you?"

He said simply, "ok," and the phone went dead. She smiled and opened the wardrobe. A see through blouse, a lace bra, and a reasonably short skirt should be perfect for all those old perverts at the golf club. She grabbed a pair of heels, slid her burgundy thong on, and clipped the matching bra. With a cream skirt, well above her knee, (but not too tarty she thought) and burgundy chiffon blouse, she slipped the cream heels on, dusted her face with foundation, threw her head to settle the curls, applied a little serum, just to keep them in check, and applied her lipstick. She would make sure she made an entrance, and make *damn* sure *he* was impressed. He would be too pissed to notice how rushed the minimal makeup was, and the clothes were all designer, so she would have no problem looking the part. With a final glance in the mirror, she picked up the car keys, her phone, and almost skipped down the stairs. As she went, a throbbing in her underwear told her she wanted a little more of Charlie than just a thought of him inside her. She smiled, set the alarm, and closed the front door.

She swept in through the gates at the club just after 2.40. As she did so, she pressed the button to lower the hood on the Mercedes, (well she wasn't going to ruin her hair on the journey!) As the roof clicked into place, she parked neatly beside the Aston Martin, and looked down. Thighs on display, a check in the mirror revealed the curls looked good, and she smiled as she hid behind the Ray Bans. She would make her entrance.

She didn't bother to lock it, and looked back, just to make sure the dent really didn't show, before walking carefully across the car park. Whilst she knew she could carry off the red bottom heels, she didn't always feel totally comfortable wearing them. But today was a heels kind of day. She looked around the car park, spotting both Tatiana and Grace's car next to their respective husbands' vehicles. Her heart sank a little, oh joy, more gossip! At least this time she didn't have anywhere to be, and could at least chat to others too, which meant she didn't have to constantly smile and agree with those two.

She swung the door open, and almost bumped into Geoff, on his way out to his car. He was already fairly drunk, and smiled and looked her up and down as she moved aside and he then stumbled slightly down the stairs. That was all she needed to know. She looked good and my God didn't she feel it!

As she walked along the corridor, she couldn't help but glance in the mirror. For some reason, she still felt nervous, despite the fact she knew she was looking good. She pushed against the heavy inner door, and as she stepped into the large hall, she immediately saw him at the bar. He was definitely well overweight now, too much good food, good wine, and excess of most things, but he still commanded a presence, and as he turned to look at who had come in, he smiled, and exclaimed, "here she is, my little singing star!" She could feel herself blush as the voice boomed out across the room. If she had wanted to make an entrance, she had certainly succeeded in doing that! With her cheeks glowing, she walked up to him, and kissed his cheek, and as she did so, she saw Tatiana and Grace give each other "that" look, and she knew they were ready to chat. He asked, "Do you want a wine, my lovely?" She smiled, and he shouted "large Sauvignon over here!" the barmaid looked up, and immediately went to the fridge.

"Large?" she exclaimed! "Are you trying to get me drunk?"

He grinned, and probably for the first time she noticed how much his gums had deteriorated. An odd observation, but she just thought, he never smiles much anymore. He had paid for her to have immaculate teeth, one thing he had loved right from the start was her smile, and he wanted it to be the best.

"I would LOVE to see you drunk princess," he grinned. The one thing he knew was that she rarely got drunk with him. Usually, it was him barely able to stand, and her watching him as he slurred his words, and she watched him fall against the wall or onto the bed.

"You never know," she smiled up at him.

He handed her the wine, and she turned, to be greeted by Grace and Tatiana. They both smiled, one of those "we need to talk" type of smiles.

He saw it, and said, "Would you ladies like a drink?" knowing full well both of their glasses were full.

"That's very kind Tommy, but we are fine thanks," came the reply.

He smiled, and replied, "I will leave you lovely ladies to it then," and with a kiss on her forehead, he wandered off to see more of his mates.

"OK," Grace said with a grin, "what have you done, and isn't he rather charming."

She looked baffled. What are you talking about?"

Grace grinned. "Angie's daughter has riding lessons, she said she was certain you were in the garage at the stables earlier."

Shit! Initially Michelle panicked. But she knew the two girls had enough secrets of their own, so she acted cool, and laughed! "For Christ's sake don't tell him I hit the car. The bloke I hit said he had a mate who could repair it, so I went there this morning!"

Grace and Tatiana looked at each other and laughed, "you jammy cow," said Tatiana laughing, "I would love to have that rather delicious man hit me!"

"Who?" Michelle mumbled, slightly embarrassed, acting naively knowing full well who she meant.

"Charlie Summer, of course!" Tatiana blurted out. "He is rather nice don't you think!" And she peeled into laughter, joined by Grace. Michelle didn't quite know what to say. The girls saw the look on her face.

"Don't panic," Grace giggled, "it's ok to fancy him. Bit fat, but nice arse."

Michelle went red. "How do you know him?"

Tatiana smiled, "Summer Autos, service with sonshine," and they both fell into laughter again. "We have all had our cars repaired there from one time to another Michelle." Tatiana exclaimed. "And not always because they needed it!" And she erupted into laughter again.

Grace had calmed a little. She saw Michelle was uncomfortable. "We are just kidding Michelle, but he is rather nice. And he does do a good job with his hands!" And off she went, laughing again.

Clearly both girls were well ahead of her in the wine tasting, and she could see that this was becoming a little awkward if he overheard. "Yeah, he is alright," she said, as coolly as she could, "but his son is the mechanic. He did a good job, Tommy hasn't noticed it." The girls had calmed down now, they both knew Tommy had an awful temper at times, and suddenly realised that their friend was right, if he found out, she could have hell to pay. Michelle had regained her composure. "I'm just glad he was nice enough to help me, because God knows what shit I would have faced otherwise." Both girls knew she was right. The only problem was, she knew they were right, he was kinda hot, and she knew they knew!

"Besides, I bet no one stands a chance after you two have had your claws in him!" Michelle spat out. They both laughed again.

"No one has had their claws into him sadly darling," said Tatiana, "rumour has it, he had a girl, about ten years ago, and it was close to marriage, what was she called Grace? Martina? Marie?"

"No you silly cow," Grace slurred, "Marina."

"That's it, fucking Marina! I ask you, who calls their kid after a boat yard?"

Michelle smiled, so he was single.

"Exactly," Grace chirped, "and he has not had another woman since!"

"Don't be so ridiculous," Tatiana snapped, "of course he has, but no one *significant*," she ended the sentence very dramatically, and all of a sudden, Michelle had heard, and seen enough, they were both pissed, and she definitely needed an "out" before the dent in the Mercedes slipped out unintentionally.

She spotted Valerie in the corner. She knew the other two didn't really like her. Valerie's husband was the Chairman of the club, and whilst Grace and Tatiana would never admit it, they were both jealous. He had power and money, lots of money! He may have been fat and ugly, but he was very powerful. And, like Tommy, had an enormous amount of respect and presence, both at the club and outside. Whilst their husbands were nice guys with good jobs, they envied the Aston Martin, and the Bentley, and all the trappings that both Michelle and Valerie enjoyed. It was funny, but the men didn't really see it the same way she thought, they just saw golf, a nice car, and a pint and a lewd joke or three. She wished Grace and Tatiana could do the same.

Michelle and Valerie had never been close friends, but she respected the fact that Valerie was a strong woman, and she also had a good idea of everything that went on, including the shallow nature of the other two women. They had been to lunch on the odd occasions, and certainly as the men in their lives had grown closer as friends, they saw more of each other. Even if most of it was at the golf club, or the odd dinner. Valerie's husband Giles wouldn't be seen dead in Tommy's nightclub, it was full of nothing but youngsters and "modern" music according to her husband. Giles was in his early 60s and could not think of anything worse. Michelle always felt a little uneasy about their friendship, but she and Valerie had certainly blossomed a little lately. Perhaps because Valerie could sense that there was something wrong with Michelle and her behaviour. Michelle didn't especially care. She was too deep into what she was doing to notice, and, as long as Tommy didn't find out, that was ok. Valerie on the other hand was more discreet, and, if there was anything untoward going on, Michelle didn't especially know it. She had always thought Valerie was a little aloof, and liked to just keep things at arm's length. She was about to find out why in no uncertain manner.

8 "VALERIE"

"I have to pee," she said, and made her way to the ladies. As she stood, she saw out of the corner of her eye that Valerie was on her way too. She thought nothing of it, and left the bar. She swung the door open, looked back, and there was no sign of Valerie. She made for the furthest vacant cubicle, and locked the door. She heard the door to the bathroom open, and sat quietly. When she heard the cubicle door lock she knew that Valerie was inside, Michelle thought this would be the time to make her escape. She finished peeing and wiped herself dry. As she stood up to smooth down her skirt, she was sure she could hear noise, but had no idea what it was. Only then did she make out, it was a phone playing a voice note. She could hear a man's voice, and definitely heard the word love at least twice. What was Valerie listening to? As she flushed, she heard the volume go down, and she knew that, whatever it was, Valerie certainly didn't want her, (or anyone else) to hear. She opened the door, and made her way to the basin to wash her hands. As she did, and turned the tap on, the volume went up a little. She let the water run, but crept over to the door straining to hear. She heard, "I don't have much more time, and I need to tell you I love you, and how wonderful it feels to have you here for me at the end." Michelle smiled and felt a pang of sadness. Valerie had been seeing another man by the sound of it. Michelle coughed, and the phone went silent. As she washed her hands, the cubicle door opened, and a red faced Valerie stepped out.

Michelle turned. "Are you OK Valerie, you look a little peaky?" Internally Michelle smiled, and wondered how Valerie would cover it up.

And then the strangest thing happened. Valerie burst into tears and looked Michelle in the eye and said, "can I trust you?"

As the tears ran from her eyes. Michelle was completely taken aback, but could see and almost *feel* this poor woman had something inside her that she needed to let out. And she was certain that it wasn't good, and even more certain that the last people who needed to find out were Grace and Tatiana. "Of course you can," she said, "what goes on in the ladies, stays in the ladies," and gave her a comforting smile to make Valerie feel better.

Valerie mouthed, "thank you," and sobbed. She pulled Michelle into the disabled loo, and sat down on the toilet and tried to gather her thoughts.

"What is it Valerie?" (She knew she hated being called Val, having slipped up more than once and had that acid tongue give her a dressing down for it) "are you OK?"

Valerie looked up. The tears were drying now as she is dabbing at her face with a tissue. "I'm not sure," she said, "but I don't have anyone else to talk to, and I think you might at least be able to listen and not judge."

Michelle was worried now. Both for her "friend" (though they were far from close, but the two men in their lives certainly were) and also for herself. "Well I certainly won't do that," Michelle replied. "What's on your mind?"

Valerie had by now composed herself, and looked at Michelle, a hard deep stare with her eyes red from crying, which were both intense and alarming all in one. "I know you have been having an affair," Valerie said bluntly.

Michelle almost fell against the door. "I am *not* having an affair!" she blurted a reply.

Valerie smiled. "I *know* you are up to no good, Michelle, please don't think I am stupid." Michelle blushed. Valerie continued, "and the reason I know is because I have been having an affair on and off for the last 13 years." If Michelle had managed to pull herself together after the first comment, she lost it again now, and found herself falling against the door again. Valerie smiled again. "So let's cut the bullshit and start fresh, I need someone to talk to, and those stupid bitches out there wouldn't know respect or discretion if it came along and slapped them around the face, but you, I think at least will be able to listen and not judge if I have your character right."

Michelle was taken by surprise, but also felt a little glow inside. It was the first time this woman had become truly human in her eyes, and clearly she had a side to her that no one knew! And she respected the fact that Valerie had at least had the "balls'' to confide in her, never mind trust her with this information. Valerie continued. "Now isn't the time or place, and I have no idea what you heard or you thought you heard, but yes, that was me, and my lover. And I would appreciate it if this stays between us. Now, why don't we go have a drink with the boys, and let's make a date to have a girly catch up?"

Michelle smiled weakly. "Yes, I think I would like that," she replied.

"Good," said Valerie, "and I can assure you, you can trust me too." "Now, let's go get that drink, and enjoy what might be a long evening judging by how all the boys are talking." She wiped her eyes, and took out her powder. With a deft flick she applied just enough to cover her reddened eyes, smiled once more at Michelle and said, "Sauvignon right? or shall we hit the rum?

She clicked the lock, and with a flourish opened the door just as the outer door opened, she looked at Michelle with a smile, and said, "my round."

Michelle followed her, and walked back into the hall slightly bemused. She now knew more than she had ever dreamed possible about a woman she hardly knew, yet felt an empathy with her that no matter how much her mind tried, she could never feel with Tatiana and Grace.

She looked around the room. It was now close to 5pm, and the general look was slightly/extremely pissed. And they would all say it was "for charity" but in reality, it was the same most weekends. Never ridiculously late, but always pretty drunk. She avoided the club as much as possible.

She saw the kids outside. Grace had had her kids late. So, whilst Tatiana had just the one child, late teens, who it seemed was everything you have ever heard in a teenager all rolled into one, and avoided the club and her parents like the plague, Grace's kids were 5 and 8 and loved to wreak havoc at the club, running around and playing tag as only two brothers could. Some of the older members frowned, and certainly there had been the odd altercation at times, but Giles, Valerie's husband, had always put his foot down. He loved kids, though he and Valerie had never had children of their own, and it was something he deeply regretted. So he made sure he would always have time for Grace's kids, Oscar and Leo, as they brought a spark to him that Valerie saw, but wanted nothing to do with. She didn't mind the children, but nothing would make her regret her decision not to have them.

She surveyed the scene further. Feeling almost detached, a little surreal, she gazed around. Tommy was deep in conversation with Giles; Grace and Tatiana were laughing in that stupid drunken manner that all people get into when they have had too many, and whatever the subject, it isn't that funny but you just laugh anyway. Although the room was full, she felt empty and alone, her mind in turmoil. "Michelle!" Valerie shouted again and she poked her gently in the ribs.

Michelle snapped back into the room. "Oh, thank you," she smiled at Valerie as she passed her the large Sauvignon Blanc. She took a big gulp.

Valerie smiled, "I have just done the same," she said, and probably for the same reasons. Michelle smiled, nervous, yet perhaps warming to this woman. "I see the boys can't get enough of each other it seems!" observed Valerie, seeing Giles and Tommy together, and she suggested that they chat outside.

As they both stepped outside, Michelle was glad of the fresh air. Valerie looked around. No one could overhear. "I would appreciate you being discreet about what you know, as I will. And please don't try to deny it Michelle, one *knows*."

Michelle blushed again, she knew there was little point in fighting. "Don't worry, your secret's safe with me."

"Good!" came the reply, "so, do you fancy an afternoon shopping soon and perhaps we can have a proper chat?"

Michelle blushed again. "That would be great," she replied, slightly embarrassed.

"Good, see you tomorrow then, about 11:00 am, don't worry about the boys, I will make sure I take Giles's credit card, and we can have a catch up."

And with that, she went back inside. Michelle felt for the second time in a very short space of time, bewildered.

As she walked back inside, she heard Tommy's voice. "She sings like an angel." She glanced at the clock, it was approaching 6pm. The crowd was thinning out a little, but the sunshine meant there were still plenty of people in the club. She knew what was coming next, and, almost on cue, his voice said "Why don't you give us a song?" It was then she noticed the two men behind him, smartly dressed, and with "trouble" written all over them. He must be wanting to impress, she thought. She had no idea who they were, but she could feel the eyes on her, and she knew there

would be no way of getting out of it. Tommy must either be totally pissed,
(which he certainly didn't seem) or he wanted to show off,
to let them see he wasn't just some flash git, he could back up his stories.

For all her self-doubt, once she sang, she could lose herself in her. She smiled and replied, "but we don't have a band."

He grinned. "We don't, but we have a piano, and we have a Jason," he looked across the room. A short, slightly fat balding guy smiled back and gave a pathetic wave.

She sighed. This was why she never came to the golf club, he thought he owned it. Giles did own it. And between them, they ruled the roost. She smiled up at him. "What do you want me to sing?"

"Son of a preacher man," he said.

She beamed. It was easy to sing, always sounded cool, and she knew it well. Not to mention he *loved* hearing it. "OK," she said, "but just this number."

He grinned like a Cheshire cat, "can't we have at least an encore? Take it away, my little singing star!" Jason sat at the piano. He began slowly playing the intro.

She took a deep breath, "Billy ray was a preacher's son," the room stopped and admired. No matter how often she sang, she was still able to command the room. As she sang, she felt strong, and lost herself in the song, not noticing anyone, or anything. She only really sang in the shower now, but when she did go for it, she really went for it. As the song came to a close Tommy began the applause. But it didn't take long for the whole place to erupt. She felt flushed with success, and her beaming smile couldn't hide the fact.

"MORE!" came the cry.

She blushed. She wanted to do another, but felt embarrassed. She looked up. And caught Valerie's eye. She mouthed, "MORE!" and Michelle walked over to the piano. She whispered to Jason, "do you know wild horses?" He looked up at her, "yes, I think so."

She walked back over to the stage, and decided, if he wanted her to sing, she would perform! As she stepped up, Tommy clapped loudly. She thought, "this could be a long evening," but she was determined to enjoy it. She began to get back to her old self; moving around the tiny stage, performing to the best of her ability. The old adage, "the crowd went wild" was certainly not far from the truth, and the men in particular were definitely enjoying the show.

Tommy stood silent. He hadn't seen her like this in a long time, and as he stood Giles leant over, "she has still got it dear boy," he said.

Tommy smiled, turned, "she certainly has," and turned back to clap at his wife as she ended the second song of the night.

Michelle's chest was beating, she was buzzing, and Valerie sat and took it all in. While Grace and Tatiana viewed her with envious eyes.

She smiled. "Do you want another?" she shouted; and the crowd erupted, all except the three women. Valerie smiled, and the other two glared even harder. Michelle laughed to herself. Fuck them, tonight she was going to show off and enjoy it. "Etta James!' she yelled, "I don't want you to be no slave." She paused and the piano player Jason smiled and banged the keys a little harder. It was going to be a good night, whatever happened! After indulging in a couple of "guilty pleasures," and noticing that the clock was gradually getting close to 8pm, she assumed not a soul had eaten yet, (including her) she thought it might be best to begin to wind the evening down. She looked for Tommy, and could see him outside with Giles, deep in conversation. About what she didn't know, but the body language, and the shifty looks around and almost comical whispering told her it probably wasn't good, and certainly was not something she wanted to either know or get involved in. "This will be the last one of the night," she announced, and she then walked back over to the piano, leaning forward, she whispered to Jason, "do you know Empire state of Mind by Alicia Keys?" He grinned, and touched the keys as she opened her mouth. The room was captivated, and fell silent as she let herself be completely wrapped in the music and her singing.

She went back to her earliest days, to when she first met Tommy. She had gone into the slightly run down club, having left the children's home, and school, with pretty much nothing. She had done nothing to help herself admittedly,
and the only thing she knew how to do was sing. So, as she walked along the main street, she saw the sign. "Singer wanted," and basically thought, bollocks, I will give it a go! She had marched in through the back door and shouted, "who is in charge?"

It had rather taken aback the guy in his maybe mid-twenties. "Who wants to know?" he had replied, and smiled, if nothing else this woman had some balls!

"My name is Michelle, I'm a singer and I need a job."

He couldn't help but smile at this young kid bursting into his club with her fake attitude and her ballsy mouth. She had a nice arse, and legs too. "Sure you are love," he said, patronisingly. Michelle took off her jacket. He thought to himself, "nice tits too."

She smiled, and began to sing. Kylie Minogue was all that would come into her head, and she felt herself go red, but "The locomotion" acapella would have to do. He smiled, and after only a few bars shouted "stop!" She panicked. Shit, I have blown it! "I can't STAND that shit song," he said, "but OK Michelle, you can definitely sing girl." She felt elated, only 17 and she had a job. She had no bloody idea where she was going to sleep tonight, but she had a job.

"Come and see me at 8pm tonight, and we can discuss your wages and what I expect of you," he smiled.

She blushed and put her jacket back on. "OK," she muttered, "erm, I don't even know your name."

He smiled back. "I'm Tommy, and I own this place," he looked suitably pleased with himself. She tried not to show it, but she was impressed, he didn't look old enough!

"See you at 7!" she said.

"I told you 8!" he retorted.

"I want to make sure I get everything right, so I will be here at 7." She smiled, turned on her heel, and walked out the same way she had come in. Tommy sat in silence, just a little stunned. But she DID have a nice arse.

As Michelle finished performing the song, with even Tatiana and Grace singing "New York," Tommy and Giles came back inside and began the applause. Tommy smiled, but it was an uncomfortable, almost uneasy smile. Giles looked at her, then whispered something to Tommy, before clapping loudly himself and shouting "BRAVO!" at the top of his voice. She had no idea what they were up to, but it didn't feel good.

Valerie looked at her and beckoned her over. As Michelle stepped off the stage, Valerie handed her a large glass of wine. "Wonderful," she said. "See you at around 11am tomorrow?" and with that she walked up to her husband, touched her head in a manner that suggested, "I have a headache" and she was gone.

Michelle drank the wine as Tommy approached. He was fairly drunk now. "You were amazing," he said. "I had forgotten just how good you are."

She smiled and said, "thank you."

He turned to the room. "Who is up for a curry?"

She certainly wasn't, it was well after 8 now, and the last thing she wanted was a load of spicy food. "Are you OK if I make a move?" she said.

"Don't you want to eat?" he replied.

"I had something before I came out," she lied. He clearly had forgotten her earlier excuse about the shower.

"Oh, OK then." She could hear the disappointment in his voice. His "trophy" wanted to go home.

"I'm just a bit tired Tommy, it's been a long time since I did that." She had only performed for maybe an hour or two, but it was true, she did feel it had taken it out of her.

"OK baby," he said, "go home and get some rest, you were great!"

"Thank you," she said meekly, and made for the door. She turned as she put her hand on the handle, and saw Tommy roar with laughter as Giles said something. She slipped quietly out. She knew she shouldn't really drive, but she just wanted to get her PJ's on, and put the TV on with a glass of wine and some cheese on toast. The night was clear now, cooler. She threw off her shoes, started the Mercedes, and pushed the button for the roof. It was only 15 mins to get home. As she pulled out of the golf club, she was pretty sure she wouldn't see Tommy tonight.

9 "COFFEE"

She woke up with a start. And just a little bit of a headache.

She turned over in the bed, and quickly realised he wasn't in it. She sighed in her mind, and cast it back to the evening previous, and figured he was downstairs. Her head was telling her she should have eaten more yesterday, and perhaps she should have stayed for the curry, but a coffee and some toast would fix that. Perhaps an extra sugar in the coffee too. She slipped out of bed, and into her dressing gown, as she walked back to the bed, she opened the curtains to be greeted by a pale-yellow sun, a bright blue sky, and the sound of birdsong. It felt like a good day. She looked down into the drive and saw no sign of the Aston. Slightly surprised, she figured he must have put it into the garage, it was his baby after all, and she knew how much he treasured the bloody car. She needed a shower, but she needed a coffee more. She opened the bedroom door, and slowly descended the stairs. As she entered the living room, she was surprised once again, he wasn't there. Now a little concerned, she decided to turn on the coffee maker, and then would start her "search." A ridiculous thought, but he rarely stayed out without letting her know. And then her mind finally started working properly. Where was her mobile? She had definitely had one too many last night, of course he would have let her know, she just had to find the bloody phone and read the message!

She now needed to start a different search. The one for her handbag containing the dreaded mobile monster! As the coffee maker began to utter those absurd noises, she decided coffee was most definitely the proper way to start the day, and as she watched the machine dispense the black steaming liquid, her mind began to focus a little better. Shit! Her bag was either in the car, or it was still at the club! She gulped, and then began to calm. Of course it was in the car you stupid woman, calm down! She slipped on her UGG slippers and opened the front door. It was warm, and the bright sun made her smile more than it probably should have as she walked across to the car, she hadn't even locked it! There was her bag, on the passenger seat. She could feel the relief sweep over her. She grabbed the bag, and just saw the light reveal that bloody dent. You had to be looking for it, but it was definitely still there. Shit, she muttered under her breath, I will have to go back to see that mechanic. And as she said the words to herself, she grinned, and remembered his crooked smile, and his nice arse. Perhaps that wasn't such a bad thing!

As she walked back to the house, she felt her bag vibrate.

She hunted for the phone, and, once she had taken it out, her head spun slightly, the text read "coffee first, or shall we shop and then lunch?"

Oh Christ, Valerie! she looked at the time.

Phew! It was just after 9. Even in her drunken state, she knew it was scheduled for 11am.

She texted back, "I think coffee would be great, my head could certainly do with it! Shall we meet in Costa at 11?"

The reply was almost instant. "Let's make it closer to 10." Michelle said to herself, *really?* But replied, "OK see you then."

Somehow, Michelle could almost *feel* the desperation in Valerie's text, and she wondered what was actually behind the shopping trip, but she was pretty sure it had nothing at all to do with shopping. Michelle rushed back into the house. With the drive to Costa being at least 20 mins, she had only around 30 to make herself look fabulous. (She was pretty sure Valerie would be immaculate, as always, and certainly did not want to play second fiddle to her!) She ran upstairs and rushed into the bedroom, and across to the en-suite. She turned on the shower, and slipped out of the robe she was wearing. She hated rushing, but today, rushing it would have to be! She opened the wardrobe, trousers were the order of the day this time. Something light, black trousers, and perhaps a lighter coloured top. Thong of course, heels, yes, the designer labels made it all work. Now get in that bloody shower woman. It was still puzzling her exactly what Valerie wanted, or needed, but she knew that it felt like a "cry for help." And she definitely wanted to know what Valerie thought she knew about her! It was amongst the fastest showers she could ever remember having. She definitely didn't have time to wash her hair, but she also knew it looked awful after last night's restless sleep. *Oh my God.* She had to do it. Just a soaking, she could let it dry naturally, the curls always masked if it was wet. She was wide awake now, the pressures of time, and the curiosity at what Valerie had to say had made sure the booze was well and truly forgotten! The shower lasted less than ten minutes, her head clearing as the water ran, and her mind still spinning with all the thoughts, and if she thought back, a smile at her "performance." Something she had enjoyed, and suddenly felt very passionate about. Her mind drifted back to last night. God, it had felt good to let go, drink in the music, and the atmosphere, and just go back to a simpler, happier time. As she smiled at the thought, her eyes looked at the phone on the cabinet, oh God, it's 9.30! Ok, *focus* woman, you have a "friend" (she had never *really* thought of Valerie as a friend) who definitely needed a chat. Time to forget herself for a moment and get ready! She turned off the shower, and stepped into the thick bath robe. That would dry her whilst she sorted her hair and clothes. She tousled her hair and looked in the mirror. She actually liked her slightly crazy curls, and as she squeezed a large handful of mousse into her hands and scrunched it into her head, she knew guys *always* looked at her curls. It made her smile, and she decided a skirt was going to be the order of the day. She made her way into the bedroom, and as she opened the wardrobe, the beige knee length was perfect. Cream blouse. Yes, beige was the colour of the day and she would look as elegant as Valerie. She grabbed her makeup, this would not be her most spectacular make up day! A quick slap of YSL foundation, a little blusher, and a hint of pink lip gloss would be OK, along with a little mascara and eyeliner. Should only take ten minutes. She grabbed the phone, she *hated* being late, but needed to let Valerie know it was going to be closer to 10.30am.

The reply came back quickly, "no stress, we have all day." Michelle was surprised all over again. This woman had barely acknowledged her at times, why on *earth* did she want to spend the day with her?

The curiosity only made her hurry more. She was now *desperate* to understand what Valerie wanted. Makeup and underwear sorted, Michelle began to dress. She found her cream Steve Madden heels, and a small brown All Saints leather jacket. Even though she said it herself, she looked very respectable this morning!

OK, she was good to go. Had her Louis Vuitton bag, keys, purse, phone. Let's go! Just as the thought entered her mind, she heard the Aston. No! Even though she knew he wouldn't stop her, her mind just didn't want him around, and now her mind was full of Aston Martin and her husband.

She opened the door just as he struggled for his keys. He looked pretty rough, and she asked, "are you OK?"

The grunt came back, "feel rough," "where are you going woman?"

Michelle smiled, "I'm going to see Valerie, don't you remember?"

The truth was, he didn't have a clue. The drink and drugs last night had been enough to stop a horse, let alone his meagre memory, but he smiled weakly and said "oh, of course."

She knew he was lying, but it didn't matter, he had been pacified. She was out with Giles's wife, and that made everything ok. "Don't wait up!" she laughed.

He smiled again, "enjoy," and shut the door with not so much as a backward glance.

As she walked to the Mercedes, she wondered what today had in store. But one thing was for sure, after today, she was fairly sure she would never look at Valerie in the same way again. She put the key into the ignition, dropped the roof, and slipped the ray bans on. She glanced in the rear-view mirror, thought "you look good girl," and slid the car into reverse. She still needed coffee. And as she left the drive, sent a simple text, "on my way."

The reply was even more simple. "GOOD" in capitals.

10 "VALERIES CONFESSION"

"MICHELLE!" came the voice she couldn't fail to recognise. She looked up to see Valerie waving totally uncharacteristically, and felt even more convinced that this meeting was something Valerie was almost *desperate* for. She raised her hand, but didn't respond with her voice. As she got closer, she pointed to the counter, and once again Valerie almost shouted, "I got you a latte!" It was only then she looked around, and saw the place was completely deserted. She glanced at the board outside. Her mind said, "it doesn't open till 11," and as she did so, she glanced at her watch. It was 10:22am, what the hell was going on?

She looked back at Valerie as she approached the table. She was (as always) immaculate. Hair perfect. Nails are perfectly polished. The clothes, all designer, the shoes, not Louboutin, she thought them vulgar, but Geiger perhaps. Valerie always had a class and style that she never let slip. Except, Michelle saw a sadness in her that she had probably never registered there before, but, if her mind tried hard enough, she could remember seeing.

"So sorry I am late," Michelle blurted out. "I thought this place didn't open till 11?"

Valerie smiled, "it doesn't, unless your husband is chairman and owner of the golf club, and the owner of the coffee shop plays the same course."

Michelle's mind did a double take. Perhaps she underestimated Giles and the amount of influence he actually had on everyone. Michelle smiled, as Valerie continued, "no point having some influence if I can't use it sometimes." Michelle smiled again, a little nervously this time. "Don't worry," said Valerie, "it's just two friends having a coffee, if anyone asks," and it was her turn to smile. "But on this occasion, I will be doing most of the talking."

Michelle sipped her coffee, and swallowed hard. "Why me?'" she asked.

"It's simple," said Valerie, "you are the only one I could trust, because you have some sense, some sensibility, and because you are cheating on your husband and he doesn't know."

Michelle spat her coffee out. "What?"

"Don't try to deny it. You have either been having an affair, or are screwing around and have been for a while."

Michelle felt herself go red. "OK, I'm listening," Michelle replied sheepishly.

Valerie grinned. "Good, so I won't say a word, and you can tell me all when you feel ready, right now I need to talk to someone. And, as I said, I can only trust you, and if I don't talk to someone, I will explode, so here it is, I have been having an affair for 13 years. Same man."

Michelle spat her coffee out again. "Shit!" she exclaimed.

"Yes, it is to be honest, he is dying, and I am hurting like hell, so I needed to let it all out and at least get it out of me. I'm sorry it's a bit of a bombshell, but to be honest, I have never felt so relieved as I do right now."

Michelle sat, a little dumbfounded. And looked at Valerie, who had wet eyes, and was clearly feeling extremely emotional.

"How, when, why, where?" thoughts that smashed into her brain like a freight train. Michelle muttered, "I'm so sorry!"

"I don't need sympathy, just a friendly ear."

Michelle smiled, "well, I can certainly do the listening part, and I have a tissue too."

Valerie looked into Michelle's eyes, and Michelle could see the tears. Valerie took a deep breath, grabbed a tissue, and said, "I don't know where to start, so I will start at the beginning."

"It started almost 15 years ago. Giles was always working late, or had meetings, or was probably screwing his secretary, and I was simply fed up with it. Lonely, as I didn't have many real friends, and certainly not any who I liked spending much time with. Yes, I know I am a stand offish old cow, and I don't suffer fools gladly, and I suppose that's why people see me as cold, but I don't really give a shit, I had a tough upbringing, and I guess I got made that way." Michelle was dumb founded. This woman who she had never really got close to was seemingly pouring out her life. She didn't say much, just sat and listened and let Valerie carry on. "So I decided I would go swimming, it was always something I liked as a kid. I really enjoyed it even if I wasn't exactly a channel swimmer, I thought it would get me out of the house and perhaps meet new people." Valerie sighed. "And boy, did I meet someone!" Michelle looked at Valerie's face light up. She could see there was joy behind the sadness.

"It all started when I lost my locker key. It came off the stupid elastic thing they give you, and I was getting all flustered coz I could see it at the bottom of the pool, but wasn't brave enough to go down and get it. I knew I could swim, but underwater wasn't especially comfortable for me. Anyway, this guy could see I was stressed, so came over and asked me if I was ok. I told him what had happened, and he just dived down and got it. Simple as that. He handed me my locker key, and smiled as he got out of the pool."

"Don't lose it again," he said, "because I'm off now!" and he disappeared into the changing room.

"I watched him walk out and smiled. He was kind of cute! Anyway, I thought I had probably best get out soon too. Didn't want to run the risk of losing my key again, so did a couple more lengths, and then got out of the pool."

"The changing rooms were separate, but the lockers were communal so off I went to get my towel and stuff.
I get to my locker, and there is a business card poked in the side of it. J Henderson financial advisor. I turn it over, and a smiley face has been drawn on it with "don't lose it!""

Michelle grinned. She managed to say, "Oh my God, how cheesy!"

Before Valerie said pretty much the same thing!

"I know, so cheesy!" "But," said Valerie, "it did make me smile, and I wondered, was there more behind the man who had rescued my locker key, or was he just a nice guy?" "So I decided to call him for some financial advice!" Valerie laughed, a nervous, shy laugh, and Michelle saw her face change, and she drifted off to a distant place just briefly.

Michelle took another sip of coffee. She was totally dumbfounded by the outpouring, but realised that Valerie clearly *needed* to do this. She replaced her coffee cup, and said, "So what happened?"

"What happened is I decided I need some financial advice," Valerie laughed out loud. "So I called him, I went to his office, we sat opposite each other, chatted about money, he told me what I needed to do for the future, and how best I could use Giles's money to look after me if anything was to happen to him. He was very professional. But I knew pretty quickly he was looking at my legs, and every now and again I would catch him out. So I decided to "play the game", and crossed my legs just a little more slowly. He definitely knew I had hold ups on and black panties,"

Valerie laughed, a more relaxed, slightly embarrassed, but altogether relieved sound.

Michelle smiled, and thought of the "meets" she had been having, and how she dressed most of the time, and could picture herself in holdups and playing for the guys. She reddened slightly, and turned away a little from Valerie.

Valerie continued. "And that is where it all started. I was not too far off 40 years old, a bit lonely, and a bit left out. Had all the trappings of a luxury life that a woman could want. Nice cars, ice clothes, nice food, and nice wine. And a total emptiness of what I really desired, to be loved! Giles was wonderful in terms of what he provided materially, but that was where it ended. He was too busy enjoying the power and prestige of being him. The adoration of the grovelling little so and so's who thought he could help them get somewhere. And no, that doesn't mean Tommy, he at least can piss with the big boys! The truth is Michelle, Giles has never been very good in bed. But once he got fatter, and drank more and more, he couldn't even get it up. We never talked about it, he felt inferior, bought Viagra, but it never really happened. So I guess from about 38 I was almost celibate."

Michelle was totally bemused. What could she do, or say? "Is that why you never had children?" she blurted out.

Valerie laughed, "sorry," she said, it didn't mean to sound patronising, "no darling, I can't stand the things! I Never wanted kids, and Giles certainly never hinted he did, though he adores Leo and Oscar. In fact, it's another thing we never really talked about!" Her eyes saddened, and she looked to the floor. "Giles sure as hell can get his cock up for his secretary though!" As her eyes rolled to the back of her head.

Michelle almost choked on her coffee. Valerie continued, "I had been passing the office, it was fairly late, I guess around 8pm. I just walked onto the lobby, and couldn't see anyone, but Giles's car was outside, so I went to his office. Obviously, as I got closer, I didn't need to be a genius to hear "suck it harder" so I

just turned and left. I parked across the road, and I guess around 15 mins later, they both came out. Stupid bitch, she can't have been more than age
20-25. Legs up to her armpits, short skirt. No wonder he can get his cock up her, or the next one, or the next one."

Michelle looked sad for her new found "friend". Valerie was in full flow now, and Michelle neither could, nor wanted, to shut her up.

"That's when I decided I might need more than financial advice," Valerie grinned and leaned back in her chair. "The first time I met Jamie, despite the fact I knew he was eyeing me up, and I had teased a little, there was nothing else. I simply thanked him for the chat, and left."

Michelle butted in, "why didn't you say anything to Giles when you "caught" him?"

Valerie laughed again. "What was the point my dear Michelle? The fact is, I wasn't 20. didn't have legs up to the sky, and clearly, that's what rings my fat arrogant husband's cock bell."

Michelle looked sad again. "So you just accepted it?"

"Of course I did, for one thing, it meant I didn't have to screw him, which wasn't especially pleasant, and for another, look at my life Michelle. Bentleys, Mercedes, a pool, a 5 bed house, an apartment in Spain, diamonds, jewels, why on earth would I want to change it?"

Michelle shuddered. And all too clearly, her own life came into view.

"Sounds familiar?" said Valerie.

Michelle looked her in the eye, her face hard, cold, and said simply, "yes."

Valerie smiled. "Now do you understand why I felt I could tell you?"

A small glance, and Michelle nodded. "Yes."

Valerie took a swig of coffee, "shall we have something a little stronger?"

Michelle felt like a parrot who had just learned one word, "yes."

Valerie laughed again. "Get your coat girl, this is going to be a hell of a day!"

As Valerie downed the last of her coffee, she stood and grabbed her coat. Michelle did the same, and Valerie shouted, "charge my husband would you, Ricardo!" she waved as she swung her cashmere coat over her shoulders, and swept out of Ricardo's, with Michelle following like a puppy dog.

Michelle smiled. This woman who had always been slightly aloof, slightly too big for her own boots, certainly had another side to her, and she began to realise that her overweight, loud, cigar smoking husband had much more of an influence and it was far more reaching than she had ever realised.

"Where now?" Michelle asked.

"I think we deserve a little pampering don't you?" Valerie replied.

Michelle smiled. "Certainly sounds good, but what did you have in mind?"

"Leave it to me," Valerie smiled as she said it. She took out her phone, and flicked through the directory. Within a few seconds, she was speaking in low tones to a male voice. Michelle couldn't hear everything that was said, but heard the word "private" more than once, and she smiled. Valerie may have been a cold bitch, but she knew exactly what she wanted, and exactly how to get it!

Valerie finished her call. "I think I shall call my driver," she smiled. "Just need to let my darling husband know I'm having a proper girly day, he gets emotional unless he knows. He couldn't actually give a shit to be honest, but when he gets the credit card bill, it makes him feel better if he knows before I spend his money!"

Her fingers flashed across the screen of her Samsung, and she shrilled "hello darling! Just want to tell you I'm having such a lovely time with Michelle, would it be OK if we do a bit of pampering? I know I have spent a lot lately, but I wanted to take Michelle for a spa?" She smiled, a sickly "I've got him just where I want him" smile.

The booming voice on the other end came back, "only if she can sing "Preacher man" again at the club, it was wonderful!"

"I will make sure she gives another performance," Valerie winked at Michelle. "Love you," and she ended the call.

"Well," Valerie said, "let me call Barry, it's going to be a great day!"

Michelle replied, "what about my car? If we get a cab, I will need dropping back here to pick it up?"

Valerie looked slightly perturbed. "I will get Barry to drop it at your home," she smiled. "Give me your keys, nothing is going to spoil this!" Michelle looked puzzled. Valerie smiled in return. "My dear driver Barry, he is simply wonderful and does all I ask. Barry will get your car home. Let's have a drink." Before Michelle could argue, the black Mercedes arrived. The two ladies slipped into the back.

"Hello Mrs Valerie," Barry spoke brightly.

"Hello Barry darling, this is Michelle," Barry smiled. His greying hair couldn't hide a youthful glint in his eye.

"Hello Miss Michelle!" Michelle smiled in return.

Valerie turned to Michelle. "This is between us OK, it's *our* day, and I know I can trust you not to breathe a word."

Michelle was still slightly bewildered. "Of course," she blurted out.

Valerie smiled. "Don't worry Michelle, your secret is safe too, now, just enjoy the day, and comfort yourself in the fact that Giles is paying, and all you have to do is sing one bloody song at the club again!" Valerie burst into fits of giggles. Michelle smiled, and began to laugh. It was a little more nervous than Valerie's laugh, but she began to let go, to relax, and her mind began to wonder what else lay in store.

They chatted, small talk. Giles and how vast his empire was. How much he liked Tommy. How Giles was even thinking about getting an Aston, (secretly he knew his belly wouldn't get behind the wheel, but he liked to think he still had the ability to have one). How much Tommy enjoyed
Giles's company, and the golf, what their handicaps were. Michelle couldn't help but wonder at the "other side" of this cold, almost aloof woman. A side she had never seen. But Michelle was beginning to understand it was purely because of trust.

11 "RITA"

Within 30 minutes, the Mercedes pulled into what could only be described as a beautiful manor house, with a wonderful open gravel drive approach, and an imposing yet stunning building at the end of it. Michelle looked suitably impressed. "Wow!" she exclaimed. "What is this place?"

Valerie once again took control. "This my dear Michelle, is Oakleaf Grange."

Michelle smiled. She had heard of it. And had always thought it was a little like the priory, somewhere you go to "dry out" or get off drugs. "I thought this place was for rehab!" She exclaimed.

Valerie grinned. "Who said it isn't," she smiled. "But it caters for those who are not old soaks or junkies too, sometimes, depending on your influence, you can come here, have some "private" time, and no one asks or questions a thing."
The look Valerie cast Michelle was one of, stop there Michelle. Don't say anymore, just enjoy your experience.

Michelle understood, nodded to say as much, and as the car drew to a halt, Valerie said simply, "follow me."

Michelle did as she was told. The day was already completely surreal, so she figured it was time to just run with it, and let the day take its course.
"Should I let Tommy know?" she asked.

Valerie laughed out loud, "you can, but I'm fairly certain he will already be fully up to speed." Michelle nonetheless took out her mobile and sent a simple text, "out for the day with Val."

Tommy replied almost immediately. "Enjoy baby, Giles and I might have a round."

Michelle smiled and looked at Valerie. "I told you" she said, and threw her head back as she laughed again.

Michelle suddenly felt a little uncomfortable, like she wasn't in control.

Valerie noticed the change in her face. "Don't worry Michelle, I just had every idea that Giles would tell Tommy straight away. Probably going to the club I should imagine." Michelle couldn't do much except nod. Valerie continued "I don't know what they are up to, nor do I want to, but I just know that Giles likes Tommy, likes his company, and his golf too." "So, now both the men know where we are, relax, embrace and enjoy your day."

Michelle smiled. A slightly more relaxed smile. "OK, I will." She noticed that they hadn't gone into the main entrance, but round to the side through a large oak door. She followed Valerie, who certainly seemed to know where she was going. It was beautiful! Very tastefully decorated, lots of white, marble floors, chaise longue in the corridor, and a general feeling of opulence and relaxation.

They walked along the corridor. The click clack of their heels breaking the otherwise almost silence.

As they approached a small desk, a woman looked up from it. She smiled at Valerie, and greeted her with, "good morning, Mrs Williams, how can we help you today?"

Valerie replied, "my friend and I would like a little relaxation, and a little private time too." The woman smiled back, stood up, and Michelle noticed she was tall, a little more plump than perhaps a woman in a spa should be, but also clearly massively experienced at discretion and certainly knew better than to question anything.

"Certainly madam," she returned, "can I take your coats?" As Michelle handed her coat over and her bag, she reached to grab her phone.

Valerie laughed. "He won't be calling today I'm sure," and she winked at the blonde holding their coats.

Michelle felt herself go red. "No, perhaps you are right," she said.

Valerie said sternly "you don't need your phone today, it's our time."

Michelle got the message and waved away the blonde.

"I will be right back," she said. And she was. When she returned, she had two robes with her. "If you would like to follow me ladies" she said. And she started down the corridor.

Valerie swept her arm out in front of her. "After you," she said, and grinned, a mischievous, naughty smile that surprised Michelle yet again. This woman was a total surprise so far.

Within a short time they had arrived at two oak doors next to each other. The blonde pointed and said, "if you would like to get changed, we can start the experience," and as she did so, she expertly opened both doors and Michelle looked inside to see a glamorous, slightly dimly lit yet very plush dressing room. The blonde handed her a gown, and said simply, "leave your clothes on the dresser."

Michelle looked at Valerie, slightly bemused. That wink again, and then Valerie said, "I will see you out there!" and she disappeared into the changing room.

Michelle shut the door and looked around her. She was in a kind of a daze. There was definitely something strange she couldn't quite put her finger on. But, for now, she was happy to "run with it". The one thing she was sure of was that Valerie was in total control, and this wasn't the first time she had come here.

She suddenly felt a little self-conscious as she began to remove her clothes. She looked into the long mirror, and sucked her little paunch in. She knew that cakes and wine were being less than kind to her, and she wished she had better self-control sometimes, and that went much deeper than just a cake and a glass of wine!

Naked now, she picked up the robe. It was deep and thick and welcoming. Very expensive she imagined, and it felt remarkably good against her skin.

She opened the far door, and stepped out into a fairly dim, but soft mood lighting illuminated room, decorated sparsely but elegantly. The lack of light was actually really refreshing. She adjusted and felt warm and comforted.

"Michelle!" she jumped inside a little, as Valerie emerged from her changing room. Valerie looked at her, "sorry, I didn't mean to make you jump," she explained. "I thought we would start with a massage if that's OK?"

Michelle smiled. This sounded perfect. But she looked around the room. And couldn't really see how or where?

"Oh, not here" replied Valerie, "this is for the Pilates and exercise classes, we will have our own private rooms."

"Oh, OK" Michelle replied.

And as she did so, two doors leading off the room opened. Michelle wasn't sure quite how to react yet. There were two good looking, slim, relatively tall women, dressed in black trousers, and with white blouses. "Good morning ladies, if you would like to follow us, we will make you comfortable and start the experience."

They beckoned the women forward, and Michelle stepped inside and allowed the door to close. The room was small, warm, and lit a little brighter than the hall outside. "If you would like to remove your robe?" the woman asked. "I'm Rita, and I will be looking after you for this experience."

Michelle wasn't quite sure how to take it, but she slipped out of her robe, and said, "thank you Rita'' and laid the robe on the chair.

Rita directed her to the table, and said, "if you would like to lay face down first, we can see about making you relax,"

Michelle did as she was told. The table was vinyl covered, but warm and comfortable. She placed her face in the cut out, and let her shoulders relax as Rita's hands reached for the oil.

Michelle felt the pressure on her shoulders. The warmth of Rita's hands pressing hard at her skin, and she let herself embrace the feeling. She hadn't felt this good in a long time. No pressure. Just a relaxation, and a feeling that she was with another woman who was going through something that she believed Michelle could understand. As her mind began to empty, she noticed Rita had moved to her lower back now, pressing harder, and also she had lowered the table slightly. Michelle assumed this was just to allow her to get more pressure and drive the tension out of her. It was only when Rita got to her buttocks that she began to think otherwise.

The oil was now poured onto her buttocks. She felt it run between her cheeks, and was both shocked and also so ready for a sensual touch that her mind became a little confused. She had played around a little with girls when she was in the children's home. But she had never had a real experience with a woman. She kind of felt she was about to get one. Rita opened her cheeks, and parted Michelle's thighs a little. She didn't resist. Willingly she let Rita's expert fingers work their magic, and she felt almost powerless to stop her. As her fingers found her soft lips Michelle heard herself moan gently, and spread her thighs a little more. And at the same time, Rita's fingers entered her. Michelle gasped, but wasn't shocked. This was erotic, sensual, beautiful, and she wanted it. Rita fingered her softly, caressing her clit and making Michelle wet. She was feeling amazing. Her body receptive to the touch of a woman. It was both unusual and wonderful.

"If you could turn over Michelle," Rita stopped what she was doing. Michelle felt slightly disappointed. But did as she was told. As she did so, Rita smiled and said "relaxed?"

Michelle smiled back, "oh gosh yes"

Rita patted the table, and Michelle laid back down. She was definitely not apprehensive now, and wanted the touch of Rita again. As she poured the oil, it was perhaps a little too warm, but she enjoyed the sensation, and gasped as Rita massaged her breasts, a little roughly. Perhaps more harshly than she had expected, but it felt good, she wanted her nipples pulled. The tingling between her legs became stronger, and Rita obliged. Michelle began to lose herself in the feelings and eroticism that she was experiencing. Rita's fingers massaged her breasts expertly. But Michelle needed her clit touched, as if she could read her mind, Rita began to move lower. Her hands running across Michelle's belly, and Michelle wanting them lower. Rita must have sensed it. As she moved her hand lower, Michelle willingly spread her legs and allowed Rita access to her thighs. Michelle moaned softly, as the slippery hands of her masseuse ventured ever closer to her pussy. Michelle opened her eyes, Rita put a finger to her lips, to indicate the need for quiet, and at the same time she slipped one finger inside her.

Michelle's eyes widened, and she felt herself grab the sides of the bed tightly as she edged herself closer. Rita responded, and slipped another finger in. Pushing harder and deeper now, enjoying the response of Michelle's body to the pleasure she was giving. It may have been a job, but she loved it when the response from her client was a little unexpected. The sensations Michelle was feeling had not been experienced in a very long time, and now she had felt similar sensations twice in a very short space of time. Fingering herself to orgasm while thinking of Charlie had felt great, but what Rita was doing was just sublime. She knew she wanted to come, Rita could feel her getting wetter. She was now rubbing Michelle's clit and using her fingers harder. She could feel the tightness and knew Michelle needed to orgasm. Michelle's head began to spin, and she was losing herself in the orgasm, trying desperately to be quiet, but unable to contain the pleasure, she sighed deeply as the orgasm swept over her.

Breathing heavily, and feeling a little drained but also satisfied, she slowly let herself "come down". As she did so, she opened her eyes. Rita was smiling. "I hope your massage was satisfactory," she said.

Michelle beamed. "Oh, it was perfect!" she replied.

Rita smiled. "Perhaps when you feel rested and have freshened yourself up, you might like to put your robe on, and follow me to the sauna, I believe Mrs Williams may be waiting for you."

Michelle had totally forgotten about Valerie! It then dawned on her, perhaps she had planned this all along? She was beginning to get an idea of the fact that, no matter what she thought she knew of Valerie, she wasn't even close to understanding her!

"Thank you Rita," Michelle said. "That was both unexpected, and also, whilst I didn't know it, totally needed!"

Rita replied. "My pleasure madame, now, when you are ready, the sauna is back out through the changing room, and then into the corridor, turn left, and it's the 2nd door on the left."

Michelle needed to take just one more minute. She swung her legs off the table, and stood. Just a little unsteady and with her clit still throbbing, she quickly regained her composure. Rita held out the robe, and Michelle slipped her arm in. She wrapped the robe around her, and fastened the belt. She smiled once again and whispered, "thank you," as she slipped out of the door quietly and walked towards the sauna. Michelle was still slightly in shock from what had just happened.

12 "JAMIE"

Michelle composed herself but she didn't quite know what to do as she got to the door.

She knocked, and was greeted by Valerie, beaming. "Did you enjoy your massage?" she grinned. She knew now, it was both planned, and she was pretty sure Valerie had had the same experience more than once.

"I most certainly did," Michelle replied and returned the smile. "I feel incredibly relaxed!" She winked.

"Good," said Valerie, "because you are going to need it!" and her face fell slightly.

Michelle saw the change in expression, and wondered what was in store. Whatever it was, it didn't sound quite as good as the massage had been.

Valerie knew her way around this place. Michelle couldn't hold back anymore. "How on earth do you know about all of this?"

Valerie smiled. "Because I designed it that way." Michelle looked gobsmacked. "Giles has a building company, a few years ago, the government decided to throw money at projects to help addictions and stuff. Giles has enough contacts and knows enough people to be first in the queue. So this place was built, and I told Giles I wanted something for me. Somewhere to relax. Somewhere to bring my friends. He of course agreed, because it means he can get a blow job or a hand job every now and again. But make no mistake, I employed all the girls. And I know just about everything that goes on in my little side wing!"

Michelle looked suitably blown away. "So does no one else know about this place?"

"One or two," Valerie replied, "but they are not daft enough to say anything, and the girls here are paid very well! So it suits me, it suits them, and it suits Giles. Not to mention, the government paid for my spa," and she smiled.

Michelle grinned, "you are a dark horse Valerie."

"You haven't heard the half of it yet," she replied. "Let's go have our sauna."

She stepped forward and opened another door. The heat hit Michelle immediately.

Valerie said, "please don't tell me you take a sauna in a robe!" It was only then Michelle realised Valerie was naked, and she looked down at her body. Good boobs, enhanced perhaps, but good, big, firm. Nice arse too. Legs a little thick, and definitely a little bit of a belly, but in good shape.

Michelle laughed, and dropped her robe. "How silly of me!" she said and stepped inside.

The room was small, and well, a sauna, hot, steamy and seemingly empty. They sat next to each other on the bench. The warmth not overbearing, but definitely not something Michelle was used to. "I can see you are a bit overwhelmed" Valerie said, "but trust me, I both need a friend, and I think perhaps you do too. So, I went for some financial advice." She laughed and threw her head back. "I think that's where we ended up, didn't we?" and she laughed again.

Michelle smiled. "Yes, I suppose you are right."

"Well, he called me one afternoon. He said he had come up with another scheme that may be better for me in the event anything happened to Giles, and, because of the potential amount of money involved, he felt we should discuss it." Valerie smiled. "I wasn't entirely sure how true the excuse was, but I wasn't going to pass up the opportunity of meeting Jamie again, so we decided that Friday afternoon was a good plan."

"I got to his office around 12.30. He told me to make it about 1pm, but I was running early. Decided not to push it, and dressed well, even if the lace knickers, hold ups and lace bra underneath were just a little slutty! "To be honest, he had sounded professional on the phone, but I was just *hoping* for more, because I knew there was a glint, and, with Giles the way he was, I just needed *someone* to show some interest!" She laughed, "I may have been dressed to kill, but inside I was shitting myself!"

Michelle answered, "So did you think you would go for it if he came onto you? Or were you just testing him?" and she smiled, an almost guilty smile, thinking that she wished sometimes the guys she had "met" actually wanted her for her not just to fuck her.

Valerie smiled. "At the time Michelle, I was just flattered. I thought he wanted a little more, but I truly had no idea what would happen.

So, I duly sat in the waiting area, the girl on reception asked if I would like a coffee while I waited, and she buzzed his office." "Mrs Williams is here to see you" the voice on the other end sounded a little too bright for just a regular client.

"Oh excellent" came the reply, "I just have a couple of things to tidy up, and then would you show her to my office," Valerie smiled, a wistful, thoughtful smile, as if the memory had come flooding back hard. "So I sat patiently, and waited." "Anyway, within 5 minutes the south east Asian looking lady, pretty, mid-twenties I guess, said "follow me please""

"I did as I was told, my stomach was in knots, I had absolutely no idea what was going to happen, but the butterflies in my tummy told me I wanted something to happen! The Asian girl opened the door."

Jamie turned to me and smiled. "Thank you Jasmine," he said firmly, "would you kindly hold my calls, and ensure that the answer machine is on, you can now leave for the day."

"Thank you Mr Henderson," and with a smile to both Jamie and me, she turned and left.

As she shut the door he said to me, "Come in Mrs Williams," he grinned. "Why don't you take a seat, while I grab your file."

"The grin told me this wasn't just a business meeting, but I let him go over to a cabinet near the window. As he did so, he lowered the blind, and walked over to the other window, he lowered that blind too. I was now not so nervous anymore. But excited, and my stomach was performing somersaults, but more in anticipation than anything else."

Michelle smiled. She was jealous. It sounded romantic, not sordid like most of her "meets" had been. "You can't stop now," she said, "tell me more"!

Valerie grinned. "What do you want to know?"

Michelle looked slightly vexed. "I want to know it all!"

Valerie laughed out loud. "OK, OK!"

He said to me "would you like a drink?" and went over to the cabinet.

"I assumed he wasn't talking about coffee, and, as he opened it, I saw the spirits, and said, "I would love a gin!" As he poured the gin I took time to admire him. He wasn't super fit. But he was definitely very hot. He told me he would have a scotch and as he did he turned to me and smiled. I looked away a little embarrassed and could hear the liquid enter the glass. He said he had no ice. I replied "That's quite alright, I'm quite happy as it comes." He came back to the couch and handed me the drink which I took a big swig of quickly, I needed the Dutch courage. He sat next to me and smiled as he took a big gulp of his whiskey. He then put it on the table and leaned towards me, as he did so his hand rested on my knee and it felt a little tarty but I opened my legs slightly. He knew exactly what that meant and rode his hand up my thigh. I wanted him to touch me, it felt sexy, naughty, and a little dirty but I knew I wanted him, I wanted the attention I wanted to feel sexual and this man was making me feel all of those things. I had not felt this way in a long time, and I didn't give anything a second thought. As his hand found my knickers I willingly spread my legs wide and allowed him to press his fingers against the fabric and against my pussy. He stood up suddenly and I panicked that it may not be what he wanted. He smiled, took another swig of Scotch and knelt in front of me. My legs still spread, his hands walked up my thigh and he removed my underwear. It was horny, raw and sexual. He took off my knickers and his tongue played with me, licking and sucking and biting me as he finger fucked me, I was lost in the moment, I hadn't had this much attention in a long time and the pleasure was indescribable. It didn't take me long to orgasm and I genuinely came in his mouth."

"He stood up again as I lay there, spent, breathing heavily looking like a slut, with my skirt up, knickers off, legs spread and he smiled at me and said, "I think we should book a second appointment don't you?" I was almost too spent to reply but smiled at him as he drained his glass and unzipped his fly. I was now very nervous all of a sudden, I hadn't given a man a blowjob in probably 10 years and I was scared. He saw my hands shaking and looked down at me and smiled. Releasing the beast, he pushed it towards my mouth and I instinctively greeted it with my tongue. His cock was already wet with pre-cum and I hoped he could last and I wanted him to fuck me as I took him in my mouth he grew slightly and I smiled with pleasure. I may not have given a blowjob for a long time but I knew I was doing something right. He touched my head and pulled my mouth away. I looked disappointed and he knelt down and kissed me and at that moment, he laid me back and entered me. Instinctively I wrapped my legs around him, he felt amazing and it felt amazing to be desired, wanted and most of all fucked. I kissed him as he fucked me hard and I knew it wouldn't take long. I didn't need it to take long, I just needed him to come! Within what felt like a few minutes I heard him tell me, "I'm going to come," as he did so, I begged him, "come inside me," as I could feel my orgasm building just on the pleasure of what he was doing to me. As he exploded inside me I bit his shoulder hard to stop myself crying out and the orgasm swept over me. It was hot and sexual and wonderful. And that, my dear Michelle, is where it all began. After we had both orgasmed, he kissed me and

I said "I definitely think I need to come back for further discussions."

He got up and like a gentleman almost turned his back as I found my knickers. He pointed to a small door in the corner "the bathroom is in there if you need it."

I smiled back at him, kissed him again and said "I will be right back." "I remember that first time as clearly as if it was yesterday. Not because I fell in love with him but because he made me feel alive. I went to the bathroom, flushed. A little embarrassed to be honest, but thrilled inside! Couldn't think straight initially. I had my knickers in my hand and suddenly felt like a tart. Didn't care about Giles. More about me and my self-esteem. I washed my face over, (I hadn't worn much makeup, you know as well as me it's not my style!) And I slipped my panties on. I heard him moving around outside. And the nerves hit me again, shit! what if that was it? He just wanted a fuck and now I was no longer "needed". I pulled myself together. "Come on Valerie. If that's the case, you had a nice time and a bloody good orgasm and that hasn't happened in YEARS!"

While I was making myself presentable again, he asked, "Do you have to rush off?"

I hadn't thought about time. It was just after 2pm, "no, no" I said, trying to be nonchalant.

"Good," came the reply, "I have a table booked for a late lunch just around the corner if you fancy it. It's only 5 minutes."

I felt my face light up and my stomach churn again in a very good way. "Sounds perfect," I said, "just give me a minute."

"Take your time," he said. "I know them, if we are a little late it's fine."

I looked into the large mirror and smiled. This was a very good day. I smoothed my dress down, and as I stood, I could feel him inside me. My body shuddered, and I opened the door.

"He was dressed. The room is now immaculate. Curtains open, not fully, but enough for a little respite from the almost total darkness the black-out curtains had offered."

"Let's eat shall we?" he smiled.

"Lets," I said.

"He took my arm, and we left the room. He turned and locked it."

Looked at me and said, "perhaps I should have done that earlier!" And a deep laugh came from his mouth.

"I was a little shocked at the thought that anyone could have walked in! But I smiled too, and as we walked down the stairs, I felt really good inside, Michelle. Like I hadn't felt in years. No guilt, but just a thrill. A buzz. And I liked it. We went out into the street. He stopped and looked at me, he kissed me. And I can't describe the feeling. But the kiss was deep, and it felt like he meant it."

Michelle's mouth fell open. She was stunned. "And you remember all that detail?"

Valerie smiled. "I remember all that detail," she said, "because I fell for him. And for the last 13 years, he has been my lover, my friend, my soulmate, and the person I trust most in my life."

Michelle felt a pang of jealousy. Clearly this woman was much more complex than the cold hearted exterior she showed. But Michelle also had no idea why all this was coming out. She desperately wanted to ask, but also couldn't bring herself to in case she upset Valerie. So she sat, dumbfounded, bemused, intrigued.

Valerie looked at her. "You are thinking, why you, why now?" "Well," and she suddenly changed. Her persona became dark instantly, sad, she lowered her head. "My affair is coming to an end," and Michelle saw a tear.

Unsure how to react, Michelle blurted out, "why?" "How?"

Valerie looked up. Tears filled her eyes. And Michelle felt powerless to help. "He is dying," and she let the tears flow. They were real, and passionate, and Michelle felt heartbroken for her new friend. She said nothing as Valerie wept. Just held her close.

Eventually Valerie calmed down enough to look at Michelle and apologise. She said "I'm so sorry but I have no one else to talk to and quite honestly I think you're the only one I can trust. None of those other silly cows have a clue, they think I'm just some stuck-up cold bitch with no feelings which I guess sometimes is true."

Michelle looked at her and asked once again "I'm flattered you can trust me enough, I guess I just never expected it, why me?"

Valerie replied, "As I said to you, it's because you are not happy and I'm sure you're having an affair."

Michelle's face fell again. She looked at Valerie and said, "I'm not having an affair but yes there is something. Enough about me for now, what are you going to do Valerie?"

Valerie's eyes were still wet and she looked at Michelle and said, "I'm going to watch the man I love slip away from me."

Michelle had so many questions but she didn't feel it was right to ask any of them right now so she just hugged her friend and found herself saying, "well I'm here for you if that's what you need."

Valerie choked back more tears and said "I think that's exactly what we both need don't you?"

Michelle smiled cautiously, and nodded as she watched Valerie wipe her tears. She had a feeling this wasn't going to be the only Spa day they were going to have. Valerie looked up. "Had enough sauna?" she grinned. "Time for some food and perhaps a glass or two?"

Michelle couldn't believe the transformation. but she definitely wasn't going to say no! "Yes please," she said, and both ladies rose at the same time.

"Shower first," said Valerie, and pointed to 4 doors just along the corridor. "Take any one." Michelle did as she was told, and padded along the small dim corridor to the second door.

She opened it, and as she did, Valerie called "just put your robe on, we don't need to dress for lunch," and she grinned that wicked mischievous grin that Michelle had never seen her display in her "normal" life, but she was beginning to find out, this woman was *anything* but normal!

The shower room was just that. A super clean, super bright white shower room, with wine or burgundy coloured accents. Michelle smiled, Valerie has always liked her main bathroom, so perhaps there were things in common!

Michelle slipped out of her robe, and admired the clean chrome fittings and beautiful white marble tiles. She reached behind the glass and turned the shower on. Very powerful, and super soft water, Valerie had style. As she stepped into the almost fierce water, she smiled, and realised she was warming to Valerie, and perhaps she could trust her too. Michelle's life when she was young had meant she trusted no one easily, but she definitely felt she might allow herself to trust Valerie.

She washed her skin, the soft water feeling good against her naked body, she couldn't believe what today had brought. She was fairly sure there was a whole lot more, but for now, she decided, she would just embrace it, and enjoy. She let the water pound her head and almost massage her brain, it felt good, and she had felt like what had only been two minutes when the door opened from the other side, there was Valerie, grinning. "Come on woman, we have wine to drink!"

Michelle snapped back to reality, and smiled. "OK! Give me 2 mins."

Valerie closed the door, and as she left said, "along the corridor, second right, I will have the bottle open!"

Michelle turned the shower off, reached for her towel, and began to dry. She felt good. She realised she had perhaps discovered a real friend, yet Valerie was someone who she had never actually realised could be, and she was going to try to make sure she helped her as much as she could. As she slipped the robe on and opened the door, she looked back into the room. Her mind wandered, and she smiled, "bitch stole my colour ideas!" she laughed, and went to find Valerie.

As Michelle stepped out into a round almost entrance style hall, with a huge glass roof, she was greeted by another smartly dressed woman, who simply said "this way" and swung her arm to an opposing door. The network of doors and corridors had long since made Michelle confused, her sense of direction was never the best, and this place was all pastel shades and light oak doors seemingly everywhere, so she simply did as she was told.

She knocked, feeling a little foolish when the voice behind said, "Oh for Christ's sake, stop being so formal!" Valerie laughed as Michelle entered the room. "Come sit" she said, "I have wine, food, and enough stories to make your hair fall out, never mind curl!"

Michelle went over to the table and sat. She smiled as she did so, and couldn't resist a comment about the décor in the shower room. "So where did you come up with the colour scheme in the shower room?" she tried to hide the smile, but Valerie was already grinning.

"Oh, I have a friend who has very good taste in décor, shit taste in men really, but a bloody good interior designer!" and again she roared with laughter. A deep belly laugh, and Michelle finally felt relaxed. Whatever this very strange day was going to bring next, she was certain this woman was both someone she could trust, and also she figured that needed her too.

"You must give me her number," Michelle winked, "she sounds great!" and she too fell into laughter.

Valerie poured the wine, a cold clear light Chablis, and said, "so, how much do you want to know?"

Michelle thought for one moment, replied, "go for it."

Valerie drained her glass. And began to tell Michelle about the secret life she had been having with Jamie for the last 13 years. She told of holidays, brief, but beautiful to the Bahamas, of nights out at the theatre, of wonderful afternoons spent walking, of being fucked up the arse in a park on a drunken, hot horny evening!

All the time she talked, Michelle could see a real depth of love in the eyes of her friend, and after Valerie had been talking almost non-stop for 20 minutes, Michelle came out with the inevitable question. "So why the hell are you not together? Why didn't you leave Giles and go and be with this man that you so clearly love?"

Valerie smiled, "because my dear Michelle, it wasn't always like this. At the beginning, I had so much self-doubt. So much I was not willing to give, so much I feared that for probably 4 or 5 years, I just wanted the thrill. I needed to understand him, to find out the truth. To believe. Giles is an arsehole, but an arsehole who can afford a Bentley, buy me my Mercedes, and have a lifestyle that *any* woman would desire, in fact *any* person would desire."

Michelle nodded. "I can understand that," she said briefly.

Valerie continued, "so despite thinking I could be with this man forever and he was the man of my dreams, I was enjoying our time, and all the while finding out who he *really* was. Never mind the sharp suits, the nice office, and the Maserati. It turns out he was a thoroughly decent guy. Had been married; had always had a successful business, he came home one afternoon and she was screwing the gardener. He gave her another chance, but told her straight, if I catch you again, we are done. It's not difficult to work out, she couldn't behave, so they were done. He was honest enough to say he hadn't paid her enough attention while he was trying to get his business off the ground, and made the mistake of thinking a nice car, a couple of nice holidays, and a beautiful home fixed it all. Turns out she was a bit of a slut, and needed cock more than his cash. So she fucked others, In the end, he paid her off, and told her to fuck off!"

Michelle threw her head back and laughed! "So he never had another?"

"He had odd girls here and there, but nothing serious, he was too focussed on getting his business up and running."

Michelle said, "and then he went swimming!" and laughed again.

Valerie smiled wistfully, "and then he went swimming."

"So, after 4 or 5 years, why didn't you get together then? Clearly you two had a good thing going."

Valerie replied "that's where it gets *really* complicated." And her face fell again. "Because that's when he told me he had cancer. As you can imagine, it knocked me for six, because I was now ready to be with him. To give up my whole life. To have this man I trusted, and was deeply in love with. And he basically said no." A tear left her eye. "He told me he had been given 5 years max, and that he didn't want to waste a year with me trying to get a divorce and all of that, then another 6 months to arrange the wedding and stuff, then another 2 years of getting to know whether we could actually live with each other, then a year after that he could be gone!" She laughed through the tears. "He told me, let's just live for us as we are now. Let's have fun, let's party, let's have a ball, and when the time comes, there won't be two lots of heartache in your life."

Valerie exploded into tears again. Michelle stood from the table and walked around to comfort her friend. Sobbing, Valerie blurted, "he has days to live now." And she put her head close to Michelle. "He has left me a huge amount of money and I don't know what to do with it. He has left me his (new) Maserati! I was so angry, what the hell do I do with a bloody car?" And her persona changed a little. The eyes were still wet, but Valerie was cross, and also confused and grieving. It was a horrible mix and one she clearly wasn't coping with.

Michelle consoled Valerie. "I know somewhere we can store the car temporarily," she said and smiled at the thought of Charlie. She just hoped the signals were right and she could "pretend" to be a damsel in distress.

Valerie composed herself and apologised to Michelle. "Thank you" she said, "I guess I have no one else to let it out to, and I'm sick of crying to myself."

"Stop apologising," Michelle shot back, "I'm here as your friend. You are going through hell clearly, and if I can help I will."

''Thank you," Valerie smiled back. "I honestly don't know what I would do otherwise."

Suddenly, a knock at the door. The girls both looked a little surprised, before a woman opened the door and said, "shall I serve the food Mrs Williams?"

Valerie smiled. "That would be perfect" she beamed, almost trying too hard to cover the sadness. The woman left, and Valerie quickly took up the napkin and dabbed her face and eyes. "Oh and Michelle, if you breathe a word of this, which I know you won't, I wouldn't have told you otherwise, but I can promise you, you would regret it."

Michelle looked sternly, "I wouldn't do that!" she snapped.

Valerie looked up. "I'm sorry," she said. "I know you wouldn't but believe me, I don't need it getting out." As she finished the sentence, the door opened, and the food arrived.

Over the stunning lunch, consisting of more Chablis, a beautiful pate, cheeses, and selections of fruit and biscuits, the two women chatted. More small talk. The presence of the waiting staff made anything more in depth almost impossible, and much as Michelle wanted to know more and more, Valerie closed her down and chatted about the men, the golf club, went back over the lack of kids, anything except the thing that was troubling her most. Michelle understood. She didn't press anything, and simply enjoyed the company of a person who she had rarely seen in "real" life. It was both a breath of fresh air, yet still there was this nagging feeling of being slightly ashamed that she had misread her so badly. As they finished the meal, and finished the bottle, Valerie suggested that they relax in the "office". Michelle had absolutely no idea what she meant, but assumed it was both private, and had no waiting staff to disturb. The smartly dressed woman cleared the food and wine and asked, "will there be anything else Mrs Williams?"

"No thank you Angel," came the reply, "but I think Michelle and I will retire to the office for perhaps a little chill out time."

"Certainly," came the reply. Michelle couldn't be sure, but she detected just a hint that perhaps Angel knew a little more than she let on. She glanced at Valerie, who obviously saw that Michelle wasn't stupid.

"She has been with me for years," Valerie explained, "I wouldn't be without her," and she winked. Michelle smiled. At least she hadn't totally lost her judgement of character! "This way!" Valerie exclaimed and got up from the table. Michelle rose too, and followed Valerie into a very dimly lit, almost dark and unnoticeable corridor. Again the carpet beneath her feet was lush and deep, and she could only wonder at the cost, before the short walk stopped at yet another door. This time though, it was not

light oak. In fact, it was barely a door. "Welcome to the office,"
Valerie smiled, and she slid a picture to one side, exposing a small
control panel. With a touch of her finger, the door opened just a
little, and she instructed Michelle to push. As she did so, the door
swung open to reveal a dark room, oak trimmed, like a plush
gentlemen's club almost, with deep inviting sofas, and a chaise
longue. Valerie pushed Michelle inside and closed the door quickly.
"Only Angel and one or two others know about the office, and
that's the way I want it to stay."

Michelle nodded. "Does Giles know?"

Valerie laughed, "good God, no!" he may have paid for it,
but believe me, I'm pretty sure he has his own office, and not just
the one where he fucks that cheap little tart over the
photocopier!"

Michelle felt oddly embarrassed. "How the hell do you cope
with his "conquests?" she said.

Valerie snapped back, "same as you do!" Michelle looked
horrified. Valerie continued, " don't tell me you don't think Tommy
hasn't screwed others?"

Michelle felt embarrassed again. " Nnnn no!" she lied.

"Bullshit"

Michelle looked at Valerie. "OK, of course I know he has
fucked the dancers at the club. And probably Magda, that petite
blonde polish cleaner with the nice arse too."

"Exactly!" Valerie retorted, and you "cope" don't you?
With someone, or several, other cocks to ease the pain?"

Michelle was less surprised now. Sheepishly she said "yes,"
and almost immediately felt ashamed. Here was Valerie, at least if
she was cheating it was for love, and for one man. Michelle was
nothing more than a cheap slut who just needed the rush of sex to
get her high.

Valerie snapped again. "Well, I guess we are pretty similar
then?"

Michelle regained some composure. "Yes, perhaps, but you have love, and a man who is now going to be taken from you and there is nothing you can do about it."

"That's true" Valerie replied, "but God, it was a hell of a fantastic ride, in more ways than one!" and she laughed, the noise filled the room and the atmosphere relaxed a little.

Michelle asked, "So what is going to happen now with Jamie?"

"I am going to see him in hospital tomorrow, I am going to say goodbye," and the tears came once more. She sobbed. Deeply. Almost a harsh edge to her cries. Michelle let her be. She needed this out of her.

She looked around the room. A cabinet, a drink. She walked over, and saw the box of tissues, and returning to Valerie, placed them in front of her before going back to the cabinet. "Gin?" she asked. Valerie nodded and blew her nose loudly. "Do you have any ice?" Michelle asked.

"Over there in the corner," Valerie replied, "there is a small fridge and freezer. Don't put any tonic in mine please." Michelle placed 3 large cubes of ice in the tumbler and gave it to Valerie. She took a deep swig. More settled now, she began again. "He knows he has days, possibly even hours left. He can't really see me, but he can feel and hear. So tomorrow I will go to see him. Probably for the last time. He has made all the necessary arrangements, so when the inevitable happens, everything is taken care of." Michelle wanted to reply, but felt nothing would be appropriate. She looked at Valerie, and could see the sadness, as her friend wistfully went back to memories, fond memories, and she saw a faint smile.

"Where were you?" Michelle enquired.

Valerie smiled again. "I was with him at his office, making love, we did that a lot. We fucked a lot too!" And she laughed again, loudly, naughtily, and then her face fell again. "It's breaking my heart Michelle."

Michelle could see the hurt. "What will you do?"

Valerie straightened, and took a huge swing of Gin. "I am going to say goodbye to the man I love dearly, and then see where my life goes next. Now, let's have another drink!" Michelle smiled. This was going to be a long evening. Over the next couple of hours, Michelle let Valerie talk. She heard stories of love, of sex, of sin, debauchery but overall a deep caring for this man. And she felt jealous. She wanted to feel the same feelings Valerie had. But this wasn't the time to show jealousy, however, she knew that her friend had made her realise that the cheap sex she was having was definitely not what she wanted.

Valerie glanced up. It was now approaching 9pm. She figured Giles would be contacting her soon. She walked over to the "bar", picked up the phone on the wall, and dialled. Michelle heard her say, "we are ready to be collected soon," in a super slurred manner, and she quickly realised it was an act for her husband. "Yes, Michelle is as pissed as I am but we have had a lovely time!" and she smiled at Michelle and winked. "OK darling, see you in around an hour, and don't worry, I will use Barry."

She put down the receiver, and walked back to Michelle. "When he finally goes, I want you to come to the funeral with me," she looked at Michelle.

"He has no family?" she asked.

Valerie snarled "He has that bitch ex-wife sniffing around I think. But, other than a few friends, he has no one, except me, and I could do with some company."

Michelle nodded. "I will be there."

Valerie got up. "OK lady, we need to find clothes, pretend to be smashed, and get delivered home! And next time, it's *your* turn to tell all. But, you did say you might be able to hide the Maserati somewhere?" And she looked at Michelle, almost begging her to say yes.

Michelle smiled. Any excuse to see crooked smile nice arse. "I have an idea," she said, "leave it with me for a day, would you?"

Valerie smiled. "OK, as long as I can trust you, I might not want the bloody car, but I don't want to lose it either!"

Michelle reassured her it would be fine. And Valerie picked up the phone again. "Rita" she said, and Michelle's mind went back to her massage, and shuddered in a very pleasant way! "Could you get the changing rooms ready?" And she hung up. "Let's go," and she walked across the room, and opened the door, another corridor. "Second on the right," Valerie said, and Michelle walked along to the door. She looked back, and saw Valerie entering the first door. Michelle stopped, looked at Valerie, and she did exactly the same. Michelle mouthed, "thank you," and the warmth of the smile she received made her glow.

As the Mercedes pulled up outside the house, Michelle could see lights on, and the Bentley in the drive. The Aston was safely tucked up in the garage. She could hear laughter from the garden, and Valerie quickly realised Giles was enjoying Tommy's company too. And there was her car. Barry had brought it back safe and sound! "Shall we carry on?" Valerie laughed, and simply said to the driver, "thank you, Barry." And both ladies stepped out of the car.

The Mercedes left at speed, and Valerie reminded Michelle, "remember now, pissed!" Michelle took the advice, and wobbled a little along the drive, before getting to the door. Valerie laughed, "not now you silly cow, but when we get in!"

Michelle smiled, "oops!" and put the key in the lock. They stepped inside, and could hear the music. Not especially loud, but enough that Michelle could hear hillbilly rock n roll. "For Christ's sake," she muttered, and Valerie raised her eyebrows. "Not you too," she said, and they both laughed out loud!

As they went into the kitchen, the magnificent patio doors that spanned the whole of the back of the house were fully open, and the Sonos was playing loud enough to sound bloody good, even if the music was a matter of taste.

"Ladies!" bellowed Giles, and Tommy laughed. The girls smiled and began the "performance."

"Drink girls?" Tommy questioned.

"Just a coke please," Valarie slurred, and winked at Michelle.

"Me too baby," Michelle replied. Tommy looked a little disappointed, but saw Michelle swaying and decided it was probably a good idea.

As the evening carried on, it became clear the two men had no intention of slowing down, and pretty soon the talk of cars and golf meant the girls were yawning and saying, "we are going up."

The men looked around, "OK you lightweights!" and roared again.

As the ladies left, Michelle said, "turn that bloody awful music down a bit would you."

"OK babe," and she heard the volume lower.

"Christ, you have him trained," Valerie smiled. And the two ladies made the climb to the bedrooms. It had been a LONG day. As Valerie looked at Michelle on the landing, she too mouthed, "thank you" and with a final smile, they entered their rooms. It had indeed been a long

13 "THE MASERATI"

As the sun rose on a beautiful English morning, loud snores could be heard from the bedrooms but both women were up and awake. They smiled at the same time, as both came out of their respective bedrooms almost simultaneously. "Morning," they said in unison, and then fell about laughing like school kids.

Valerie looked at her phone. "No news," she said, but I need to get up there."

"I can drive you," Michelle responded.

Valerie looked back at her, "thanks, but I need to do this on my own," she said. "Would you drive me back home to get my car though?"

"Of course," Michelle replied, "how soon do you want to leave?"

Valerie answered, "before those two idiots wake up," and she nodded her head in the direction of the snores.

"I think they will be out for a while," Michelle said, "but sure, as soon as you want to go, let me know"

Valerie replied "I want to go as soon as I can really Michelle."

"Ok. Let's get ourselves sorted. How are you going to explain having to leave early?"

"Nails darling," Valerie smiled. "Had them done a couple of evenings ago." She proudly displayed immaculate nails. French manicure, very simple, but super elegant.

"Won't Giles notice?" Michelle asked.

Valerie laughed. "I haven't seen him for 2 days Michelle, he won't have a clue."

Michelle grinned. "OK!" With that, both women went back to their rooms. Michelle looked at her phone, it was already after 9am. She brushed her teeth vigorously, and grabbed clean knickers, and her sweatpants. They were all she needed for now. White trainers slipped on. And just a plain white t-shirt. She needed a bra really, but with the tracksuit jacket, she was confident she could get away with it.

Valerie appeared shortly after her on the landing. Looking immaculate as always, despite it being the same outfit she had worn the day before! "How the bloody hell do you do it?" Michelle questioned.

"I just have style dahhhling!" Valerie laughed and threw her head back as she made for the stairs. The snoring was as loud as ever. The two women crept out. Michelle grabbed her keys, and phone.

She dropped Valerie at her house. Whilst she had always thought Tommy and she had money, Valerie's was another level. A huge gated house! Beautiful oak gates. And a solid 6ft high but elegantly painted wall. "Just drop me here," Valerie asked, "I will use the side gate."

Michelle pulled into the entrance. "If you are sure."

Valerie smiled. "I'm sure" and as she opened the door, she leaned and kissed Michelle's cheek. "Thank you," she said quietly. "I will let you know how I get on." And with that, she got out of the car and walked towards the gate.

Michelle smiled. Thought to herself "strong lady" and pulled away. She lowered the roof as she drove, it may have been beautiful, but it wasn't super warm yet. She turned the music up, and the thought of Charlie came back. She was pretty sure her charms would be enough to ask him a favour, but it was a pretty big one really. Still. If he did want her the way she thought, he might at least think it was ok! It was naughty, but no worse in her head than some of the things she had done for the men she had met on those sites.

She pressed the accelerator harder and the Mercedes picked up and began to really move. Within twenty minutes she was

driving into the yard at SUMMER Autos. "Service with Sonshine."
Shit, it really was so cheesy!

She saw the Z4 immediately, and felt her stomach twist a
little. Why on *earth* did this happen every time? Charlie walked
out just as she pulled up. He smiled, that bloody crooked smile and
she couldn't help but smile back. "You haven't bent it again have
you?" he laughed.

"Very funny," she said and smiled. "No, I need a favour."

"*OOOOOOOOOOOOOOHHHHH a FAVOUR?*" He said loudly
and patronisingly, "you have only known me for five minutes, had a
job done free of charge, and now you want a favour too!"

Michelle looked at him. One of those stern, "I don't need
you taking the piss looks."

And he read it. "Sorry," he said, "are you OK?"

"I'm OK," she replied, "I just need to ask you if you have
any storage space around?" "Secure, discreet, storage space"

"If it's stolen I don't want it here!" he snapped. "You are
hot, but I am not into stolen cars."

Michelle smiled. She had him where she wanted him. "It's
not stolen, I guarantee it," she said. "It's for a friend. It won't be
for long, and I just need to help her out. You will earn well out of
it I assure you."

Charlie softened a little. "OK. Tell me more and I will think
about it."

"It's a very good friend of mine, she has been given a
present, and she doesn't quite know what to do with it. But she
can't tell her husband about it. And she winked."

Charlie smiled. "OK, and just what sort of present is it?"

"It's a Maserati Gran Turismo." Michelle didn't really know
what that was, but she knew enough to know Maserati equalled
expensive.

"Fuck me, that's one *HELL* of a present!" Charlie
exclaimed.

"He was a very generous man," Michelle laughed, "and now you see why she can't tell her old man."

"OK, OK, I think I get it, and to be honest, I don't want to know more. There is a barn where I have a few cars. It's dry, but a bit dusty, will that be alright?"

"How much is it going to cost?" Michelle asked.

"That drink," Charlie smiled. Figuring he had her where he wanted her now!

"You are on," Michelle looked at him, "but not around here OK."

"Deal," he grinned back at her. "And don't worry, it won't be at Tommy's club either." Michelle looked shocked. Charlie continued " if I'm going to play with fire, I definitely won't be stupid enough to do it in the fire station!" and he laughed again.

Michelle walked back to the car. "I need it collected too" she said, "and if you can do that discreetly, you will get another drink, and my email address, and with a naughty wink, she started the car and sped out of the drive. As she looked in her mirror she could see him watching her leave. He was hot!

She pulled over quickly after she had pulled out of the yard. Took out her phone, and texted Valerie. "The car is sorted." Valerie replied simply. "Thank you."

Michelle could almost feel the sadness in the text. She had no idea what was going on with the situation with Jamie. But she could feel it wasn't good. She drove home slowly. Her mind wandered in and out of all that had gone on over the last few days. Valerie. Charlie. Jamie. Massage – Oh my God, the massage!

As she swung the Mercedes into the drive, she saw the Bentley smiling back at her. She raised her eyebrows, great, Giles was still here! She opened the front door and heard showers running. Good she thought, at least they are awake. And she walked into the kitchen. They would need food: bacon, eggs, and beans. The full works. If nothing else it would take their mind off

Valerie and where she was. Michelle was a good liar, she had to be to do what she was doing, but this was another level.

She shouted up. "BREAKFAST BOYS?"

She heard the muffled, "PLEASE" in two different voices. She took the frying pans from the overhead rail and began to be a chef. Michelle threw the items into the two large frying pans. The sizzle made her jump, her mind clearly with Valerie rather than what she was doing, but the immediate smell wafting around the house provoked a "that's my girl!" from upstairs, and she smiled. Tommy at least appreciated her sometimes, even if he had changed beyond recognition over the years, the money, power, and she was pretty sure substances and booze had taken its toll.

Giles boomed back, "at a girl Michelle!" and she smiled again. She glanced at her phone. Nothing. She only wished that the old phrase no news is good news could be true. Despite the fact she had always thought a little as though Valerie was not really a person she wanted to get to know, she had a new found respect and admiration for her, and couldn't imagine what she was going through. Michelle snapped back to reality as Tommy shouted, "Ten minutes babe?"

"OK!" she retorted, and cracked the eggs. Toast and beans soon, and hopefully not too many questions as to where Valerie was.

Tommy appeared first. Actually looking remarkably good considering the amount of booze she assumed he had consumed. Funny how he never seemed to be so good when he came back from the club. Giles followed shortly after, smiling and commenting "what a woman you have Tommy" as he eyed the frying pans. "Cheeky to ask, but any chance of coffee my sexy Michelle?" Michelle smiled and went a little red, she had a bad experience with a smarmy fat man from the site, and Giles always reminded her of that awful "meet".

"Coming up," she smiled.

He grinned back, "two sugars would you, there's a love."

Michelle nodded and pressed the button on the Gaggia. "Coming right up."

"Make that two," Tommy responded, and he and Giles laughed like two naughty school boys.

"And where pray tell is my wife?" Giles enquired.

Michelle looked at him and smiled. "Making herself beautiful for you," she laughed. Giles looked slightly puzzled. Michelle answered, "she has gone to get her nails and eyebrows done."

"Oh right, good show!" Giles laughed, "can't have her looking anything else than perfect!" and he roared with laughter.

"You boys go and sit down, I will bring the breakfast over." As she said it, her phone lit up. She glanced, perhaps a little too quickly, but both men were making their way to the dining room. Michelle was desperate to see what the message was. But she knew it would arouse too much suspicion. Her stomach didn't feel too good about this. She put the full English on the plates. Sausages: bacon, scrambled eggs, beans, tomatoes, mushrooms and toast. Even she had to admit, it looked bloody good. As she carried the plates over, she called out "breakfast is served!" and was greeted by two massive cheers!

"Are you not eating?" Tommy asked.

"Oh, I'm just going to have some toast" Michelle replied. "I'm not super hungry like you boys!" And with that, she returned to the kitchen. Quickly grabbing her phone, she opened the message.

It was from Valerie, and it said very simply, "he has gone."

Michelle felt the euphoria of the breakfast delivery drain away immediately. She typed "Do you want me to come?"

"No, no, just keep Giles at bay for me, I need some time."

"OK, I will make sure I do that."

"Thank you."

And with that, Michelle felt the grief and knew there was no more to say.

She pushed the toaster down, and felt empty, just hollow. This whirlwind of friendship was both wonderful and bafflingly difficult in such a short space of time. But right now, she knew that Valerie had both horrific grief, and also an inner peace for the man she clearly had loved so deeply. She heard laughter from the dining room, and a shout, "more coffee babe!"

She replied "just coming, same again?"

"Yes please," they chorused. She smiled. OK Michelle, time to make sure Valerie gets the time she needs. She opened one of the cupboards near the sink, a secret stash of booze that was hardly secret, and opened the rum. A decent splash of Morgan's Spiced in both mugs should start the ball rolling. She looked at the clock. It was after 11, so that was the perfect reply. She carried the mugs into the dining room, and smiled.

Giles took a sip, and looked up. "What did you put in there, you naughty girl!"

Tommy looked up, and tasted his coffee. "Rum!" he exclaimed. "A bit early isn't it?"

Michelle was ready for him, "it's after 11 you lazy buggers!" she said and laughed as she watched Giles take another gulp.

"I'm not complaining," he beamed.

"Neither am I" replied Tommy, and she knew then that Valerie had all the time in the world.

"What are your plans for the day?" She looked at her husband. Knowing damn well it would either be the club, or the golf club, but probably both.

"I have to pop into the club, and then Giles and I thought we might have a round if that's OK?"

"Of course it is!" Michelle went back into the kitchen. She smiled. They had already forgotten Valerie wasn't around.

She texted Valerie, "take your time." And went back to the dining room. "Wow, you needed that!" she exclaimed. Looking down at two clean plates.

Giles replied, "you are a star Michelle," and winked at Tommy. "You are a lucky man Tommy."

Tommy looked at Michelle, and his expression worried her slightly, "I think she is the lucky one," he said and threw his head back with laughter. "Only joking baby, I know I am," he said. But the menace in his voice was unmistakable. Michelle shuddered inside. She knew that Tommy had always made her feel he had "saved" her, and, after he had spoken, he looked at Giles, and with the smile he got back from the fat, balding, round faced man at the other side of the table, Michelle knew Giles felt the same.

She smiled. "Oh I *know* how lucky I am," she replied, in her mind the next sentence would be "because Tommy never lets me forget it," but she said nothing. Being careful not to sound too sarcastic, she fluttered her eyelids at her husband, who was either too stupid, or perhaps was too pleased with himself for "putting her in her place" and he smiled back a genuine smile.

Michelle collected the plates, and the mugs, and walked out to the kitchen. Giles called, "thanks Michelle, that was delicious!"

"You are too kind," she replied as she left the room. She could hear muffled laughter and wondered exactly what the topic of conversation was now.

Though frankly she couldn't care less. All her mind was on was Valerie and how she must be feeling. "I'm going to the club Michelle," Tommy's voice rang out. "Giles is driving, he doesn't like getting in and out of my car!" and the laughter broke out again.

"OK," she replied. The relief in her voice perhaps a little too obvious, but the men hadn't noticed at all. She heard the door close, and the Bentley started.

It had all been a bit of a whirlwind. The morning and the evening before. The thoughts of Valerie. Michelle's head felt ready to explode, but she had to focus. She picked up her phone, sent the text "The boys have left for Tommy's club, then out for golf. You have as much time as you need I hope." Michelle looked at the words she had typed. They felt cold, and she regretted it immediately.

But the reply came back almost instantly. "Thank you for all your help."

Michelle decided not to push things. She typed back "It's not a problem. I know you would do the same." And she left it there. Michelle suddenly felt a bit empty. So she decided on a hot bath, and complete relaxation would be the best thing. She walked up the stairs, and sighed. Thankfully, the whirlwind of the last couple of days had at least slowed down.

And just for a moment, she thought of the site. It hadn't even crossed her mind for the last few days, and she looked down at her phone. She opened the phone, and was about to click on the site, when a text dropped. She smiled. It read. "I have cleared a space in the barn."

She decided a shower would be better. And then, as the men were out, and would be for a while, she might need to go and see her mechanic! She bounded along the landing. Stripping off her sweats as she did. A shower, and off to see Charlie would be just what she needed!

As she towelled her hair semi dry, she looked in the mirror. She decided she didn't need to go all out, but a skirt was definitely on the cards. It was sunny and warm. She was going to make the most both of the day, and Charlie's interest in her. A few minutes later she was dressed. Short ish denim skirt, off the shoulder white top, lace bra and matching thong. Her white trainers clashed a little, but heels definitely didn't fit today. She applied a little lip gloss, and a squeeze of Jean Paul Gaultier, and she was ready to go!

She locked the front door, dropped the roof on the car, lowered the shoulders on her top a little and sent a text.

"I'm on my way over if that's OK. Just want to check out where you will be keeping my friend's car!"

Almost as soon as she had pushed "send" a smiling face emoji appeared, and she slipped the car into drive and swung out of the driveway. This was going to be a fun afternoon!

She pulled into the stables and saw the BMW and once again felt her stomach turn just a little, no matter how many times she had seen it, she couldn't help herself. As she looked down at her legs, she wondered if the skirt was a touch *too* short, but hell, it was done now. She parked next to his car, and looked around before she got out. It was pretty quiet, she could hear the horses around the other side of the farm, but the outbuildings where SUMMER Autos stood seemed pretty empty. She found herself muttering, "bloody typical" when she heard a muffled crash and "bollocks!" She laughed as she immediately recognised Charlie's voice. The swearing continued as she wandered inside the workshop. And inside and outwardly also, she couldn't help but keep smiling as the voice got louder.

"Fucking piece of shit," "I will bloody murder that son of mine," and other expletives were coming from under a rather dilapidated old car. She could see Charlie's legs sticking out from the side and could most certainly tell he wasn't in the best of moods. She decided to carry on anyway, and see if she might cheer him up!

Michelle called out, "Hello!" in her best French accent, just as another barrage of swearing began to erupt from the depths of the car.

A thud, then "FUCKING HELL!" along with bollocks, shit, wanker and fucking cars. Michelle laughed, this time out loud, as she watched the legs struggle from under the vehicle.

"Would you like me to pull?" she asked a little sarcastically.

"Er, yes please," came the reply. Much calmer now he had realised who it was. She knelt, purposely revealing as much thigh as she dared, and grabbed at his jeans. She pulled, reasonably hard, and was surprised to find Charlie slid out easily, on some sort of matting. The speed wasn't something she had gambled on, and she fell backwards, and landed on her arse, with what was left of her modesty on display. Or at the very least, Charlie was in absolutely no doubt what colour and style of underwear she was wearing! She felt her face go red, and didn't quite know what to say. Charlie smiled, saw her embarrassment, and winked "very nice," as he pulled himself up, then offered his hand to help her up from the floor. Michelle dusted herself down, and looked down at her hands. They were covered in grease now, after Charlie had "helped" her up!

"Look at the state of my hands!" she exclaimed.

It was his turn to laugh as he waved his filthy hands in her face and said, "oh be quiet woman!" like a 16 year old school kid might!

Michelle found herself laughing and reaching out to punch him softly on the arm. "Can I please wash my hands?" she questioned.

"Of course, go up those stairs, there is a loo and a little shower room. He smiled as he took off his oil and grease stained t-shirt.

"What *is* that smell?" Michelle asked.

"Cats piss?" was the reply.

"YES!" she said abruptly.

"That's the joys of gearbox oil," he laughed, "hence the shirt has to go, you can't get rid of the bloody smell."

"Oh, right" she replied, as she walked up the narrow staircase. Only when she got to the top of the stairs did she turn to see Charlie watching her and she quickly figured out he had enjoyed another view of her panties as she had climbed them. "Did you like the view?" she smiled.

"Oh hell yes, I liked the view!" he smiled back, as she closed the door to the small bathroom.

"Well, I hope you won't be looking up my skirt when I come out of here!" she laughed.

"Wouldn't dream of it,'' he replied with a grin.

When she came out of the bathroom and opened the door she looked down the narrow staircase, and to her surprise he really wasn't there waiting for her. Michelle felt a little put out by this, and just for a moment, she wondered if she had mis-read the signals Charlie had been giving her. As she got to the bottom of the stairs, he came out of the office underneath and smiled, "all clean now?"

"Yes, no thanks to you," Michelle replied. "So come on, where is this barn and how safe is it?"

"Patience woman!" he smiled at her. "Can I at least get changed? I still stink of cat piss, and as an aftershave, it's not exactly refreshing is it!"

Michelle pulled one of those "if you *must*," faces and replied simply, "be quick." As she did so, she felt her phone vibrate and quickly took it out of her pocket. Charlie was still staring at her, admiring how she was dressed. "WELL GO THEN!"

Charlie turned and ran up the stairs. "Yes miss," he shouted, laughing, as Michelle thought, he really does have a nice arse.

She looked back at her phone. Valerie. Bloody hell, she had forgotten. She had been so selfish she had completely forgotten where she was.

The text read, "all OK here, I am going to help with some information and stuff. Feeling ok actually. Be back as soon as I can."

Michelle replied, "no rush, I am sorting the car."

A simple "thanks," came back. Michelle smiled.

At least she knew Valerie was as safe and ok as she could be. It was then she noticed the sound of water running, and she grinned. One of those naughty, "I have a plan," type grins. She crept up the stairs. And hoped the bathroom door wasn't locked. The shower was running, and clearly hot judging by the amount of steam. But she could definitely make out his body. He was trying to tense and show off his "six pack." To whom she had no idea, but she wasn't complaining one bit. He had no idea she was there, and she was enjoying him soaping his body. She had no idea why this man had something she wanted, but he most definitely did. Charlie rinsed the soap from his body, and reached forward and turned the shower off. He turned and felt for his towel, without yet opening his eyes. "Bollocks!" he exclaimed, "where the bloody hell is it?"

As he opened his eyes, he saw Michelle proudly holding the towel. "Did you want this?" she stood, legs slightly apart. Shoulders back, her "attitude" pose.

"Are you going to give it to me?" he grinned. That bloody crooked smile.

"Oh, you have no idea what I would like to give you!" she said, and her eyes wandered down his body to his cock.

He grinned and looked down too. "I think I can guess," he said. "Why don't you pass me the towel, and we can talk about it?" With that, he stepped out of the shower, and locked the door. She knew now that she was going to let him have her. And for the first time in years, it was something she both wanted and *needed*. She held out her arm, with the towel draped over it, and could see he was already getting aroused. He took the towel, but didn't cover his modesty, rather used it to towel dry his hair and face. As he did so she stepped forward and touched his body. He wrapped the towel around her, and pulled her close to him. As their lips met, a confusing feeling came over him, and he wasn't quite sure he was doing the right thing, after all she was the wife of one of the "big boys," but, much as Michelle felt, there was *something* about this woman. Their tongues met in each other's mouths. And she grabbed his now hard cock. As she did so, there was a sound of a large engine outside. She dropped to her knees, wanting his hardness in her mouth. Charlie looked down at her, and mouthed "Be quiet, it's Callum," his mind over and over repeating, bollocks as he did so!

Michelle smiled, and stood up, but not before allowing her tongue to run the length of his shaft, "best get dressed then, Dad!" she said sarcastically as Charlie unlocked the door.

He heard the heavy footsteps of Callum coming up the staircase shouting "FATHER, where the fuck are you? Come and see this!"

Charlie shouted, "I'M COVERED IN BLOODY GEARBOX OIL!"

Callum laughed back at him, and replied, "fair enough, see you in five! Oh, and by the way, that fit bird must be at the stables, her Merc is outside" Michelle grinned. Charlie grinned.

She listened at the door, waited till she was pretty sure he had gone, and said, "maybe next time?"

Charlie looked crestfallen. "You can count on it," he said, and grabbed at his boxers. "I can only apologise,"

Michelle smiled. "Don't," she said, "it felt good, and besides, I now *know* how you feel." With that, she padded softly out of the door, praying she wouldn't bump into his son. Charlie was *fuming*. Shit, shit, shit! His frustrations meant he found it impossible to dress himself properly, and he battled with his socks! Finally suitably decent, he opened the door, and prepared himself for Callum. When he reached the bottom of the stairs, he could hear voices. *Double shit!* It was her, and Callum. He walked through the workshop and rounded the corner to see his son leaning on a Dodge Challenger, and laughing with Michelle. They seemed relaxed, so he let his shoulders drop a little and walked towards them.

"There you are old man!"

"Watch it you cheeky little shit!" he smiled, and turned to Michelle. "Sorry to keep you waiting"

She smiled, enjoying seeing him a little uncomfortable. Said, "that's ok, young Callum here has been telling me about his new toy." Charlie didn't quite know how to react. Did Callum know anything, did he see Michelle coming down the stairs. She picked up on it, and saved him. "While I was waiting for you I popped round to the stables to see Marianne, When I came back, Callum was here showing off!"

Charlie smiled appreciatively, "oh right OK" he blurted, "well, shall we go and see the barn where I think the car would be safest?"

Callum, clearly confused, said "what car?"

"Oh, Michelle has asked if we can look after a friend's car for a while. There has been a bereavement, and she just needs a little time to sort everything. Oh, and we have to go and collect it too."

Callum sighed, said, "please don't tell me it's aunty Anne's Fiesta?"

Charlie turned, smiled, and said, "It's a Mazzer."

"Fuck!" came the reply. "What one."

"Gran Turismo."

"Fuck again!" Callum laughed. "Shall I go now with the truck?"

"Let's make sure the barn is suitable," Charlie replied, as Michelle laughed.

Callum followed them. Eager now to learn more. "Is it the V8?" he asked.

Michelle laughed again. "I don't even know what colour it is, but I do know it belongs to a special friend of mine who has just lost the man she loves, and she wants right now to have some time to just know the car is OK," she said firmly.

"I'm sorry," Callum understood what she was saying. "I wasn't thinking, please accept my apologies, and tell your friend I'm sorry for her loss."

"Thank you, I will," she replied as they entered the simply huge barn! It had been quite a walk, but with the chat she hadn't noticed. As her eyes accustomed to the dimly lit building, she saw dozens of cars, and knew some, though not all. "Who owns all of these?" she gasped.

" Er, we do, well, most of them anyway."

Michelle was shocked. "There must be 50," she said.

"62, came the reply, and we reckon we have room for another 2 or 3!" Both men laughed like children.

She wanted to be cross again, but loved the dynamic between them. "So, this is where you will keep it?" she asked.

"Yes" Charlie replied, "as long as you think it's suitable."

" As long as the mice and things don't get in here and eat everything," she said sternly.

" Do you think I would keep a Mk1 RS2000 with a price tag of around 50 grand in here if it did?" he snapped back, and she saw he could definitely give as good as he got.

She liked that. "Then it's perfect," she smiled. "I will give you a ring if I may, as soon as I know the details?"

"No problem," Charlie replied, the glint had returned. "I'm sure we can come to an arrangement regarding the storage," and he smiled.

She returned it, and said simply, "I'm sure."

They walked back towards the office, Charlie, made sure the barn was locked, and, as she got to her car, Callum went back to the Challenger and got in it. "Listen," he shouted, and revved the menacing black machine hard as Michelle got into her car.

"I better go before he pisses off all the horse owners," Charlie explained.

Michelle smiled, "I will be in touch," she smiled, "and perhaps we can finish what we started too." And she grinned as she slipped the Mercedes into reverse, swung the car around, and she disappeared out of the farm.

Just as the car turned out of the drive, the huge rumble of the Challenger made him spin around. "Callum!" he shouted, and ran over to the car. Leaning in through the window he looked at his son, "cut it out, the bloody horses will go ape shit, and so will Jo.''

Callum looked at his dad. "I know," he said, "but it got your attention, so now you are here, open the bonnet and check out this thing." Charlie smiled. They needed to go out for a pint, he needed to talk to his son.

After looking around the car, Charlie questioned his son. "What is this for, a customer?"

"Yeah, he asked me to look out for one. And well, here it is. I am only getting a finder's fee, but he said up to a grand. So I figured why not, I already knew Billy had this up for sale. Right colour, right spec, easy money."

"Nice," was Charlie's answer. "So who is it for?"

"Bloke called Tommy, he owns a club in town, wants it for outside, to promote the place, and make a noise,"

Charlie smiled. You couldn't make this up. "OK, so what is it, full valet and then drop it off?"

"Pretty much," Callum replied, and threw the wet sponge at his Dad. "Come on old man, let's earn some easy money."

Charlie grinned, "come on then!"

14 "HOT HARD AND HORNY"

As the black Challenger pulled up outside the club, Charlie couldn't help but feel uneasy. He knew his son was a little sod, and had definitely been into some things he shouldn't have, but his stomach turned a little when Tommy came out to look at the car. Charlie didn't acknowledge him, and watched his son show Tommy all the features of the car, and, when he revved it hard, and Tommy's face grinned, Charlie knew the deal was done. The two men shook hands, and Callum made his way back to Charlie's car. He got in, smiling, "sorted" he grinned, "£500 for driving it here."

Charlie looked at his son. "Good," he said. "You can buy me that pint then."

Callum looked puzzled at Charlie's tone. "You OK old man?"

"I'm not sure," he replied, "but let's get back home, and once we are changed, you can take the "old man" to the pub and help me find out."

The two men met back at the yard at around 8. Both were looking smart: jeans, shirt, shoes. They laughed, both knowing they always made an effort when it wasn't work.

The pub was only a short walk, it was a small, intimate, typical English pub with low ceilings, everyone knowing everyone. As they walked in, the barmaid, Sam, flashed her fake smile, and pushed her bra up a little. "Usual?" she shouted across.

"Please!" Charlie answered, and they saw a small alcove where they could chat. Charlie pointed, and Sam gave him the thumbs up.

Callum sat down and said, "come on then old man, what's up?" As Charlie was about to open his mouth, Sam appeared with the beers.

She smiled provocatively at Callum, and made sure he saw her cleavage as she said, "here you go boys," and teetered off back to the bar.

"She definitely has the hots for you," Charlie laughed.

Callum grinned. "Never mind me, what's up with you?"

"Well," Charlie began, "you know the hot bird with the Merc, the one who you got the dent out for?"

Charlie looked at his dad, "the one with the dodgy Maserati?"

"Yup, that's the one, well, you just delivered a black Challenger to her old man."

Callum looked at his dad. "Oh shit!" was the simple reply.

"Oh shit indeed!" Charlie answered. "Thing is mate, she is the first one in a *long* time that I thought I could ..."

"Oh father, you just met her!"

"I know, Charlie retorted, and that's why I know I like her. Coz I dunno mate, there is just *something,* ya know?"

"I will always cover your arse dad, you know that, just for fucks sake be careful with who you are dealing with."

"Another one?" Charlie smiled. "You can go to the bar, she likes you, and you get served quicker!"

Callum smiled. "She does more than like me!" and he went off to the bar.

The rest of the evening was spent drinking, talking cars, talking, women, and doing what fathers and sons do. But Callum knew deep down that his dad was playing with fire, and Charlie knew it too.

A few days later, when everything seemed to have calmed, Charlie pulled into the yard.

As he did so, his phone pinged and he saw it was Michelle. "Any chance you can pick up my friends' car today?"

As he stopped the car he replied simply, "Gimme five."

"Callum!" Charlie shouted as he went into the office, "are you using the truck today?"

"No old man!" came the laughed reply, "she is all yours!"

"Thanks mate, be back soon," Charlie grinned as he typed the reply.

"Where is it, and what time?"

"It's in town. An underground carpark. I need to meet my friend there. Chesil Street."

"POSH!" he typed, and laughed as he did so. "An hour?"

She replied, "See you then, and *don't* ask any questions, OK?"

"No problem." He grinned again. And went to check the truck, before going back into the workshop. The journey would only be 30 mins or so. "Callum," he shouted.

"What?" came the muffled reply.

"Are you under that bloody Dolomite?"

"YES!" Charlie stood next to the pair of legs, and explained he was leaving to pick up the Maserati.

"Cool," came the reply. "Take a cover from the barn, you will need a big cover for that!"

"OK, thanks mate." As he started the truck, he felt the pang of excitement. What the *hell* had this woman done to him?

When he arrived, he saw the Mercedes, and felt the pang again. As he parked the truck, he saw the two women step out of the car and walk towards him. Michelle said, "can you drive it out and then put it on the truck? I don't want to be seen in it." The other woman looked a little upset, and Charlie didn't offer any conversation.

"No problem, do you have the key?" The other woman handed it to him. As she did so she mouthed, "thank you" and walked back to the Mercedes.

Michelle quickly spoke. "Please take care of it. That poor cow has just lost the man she loved, and she really can't bear the thought of any of it at present."

"When is the funeral?" Charlie asked.

"Two days' time," Michelle looked deep into his eyes. "Perhaps then she can begin to think straight."

"The car will be safe with me," he replied. I will ring you and let you know when I am back."

"Thank you," she smiled, and walked towards him and kissed him lightly on the cheek. As she did so, she whispered, "I will come by later to check if it's safe," and she winked as she turned on her heel and made her way back to the car.

He grinned, and walked towards the entrance. Smiling, he pushed the fob, and saw the indicators flash on a beautiful black Maserati. He slid inside, pushed the button, and the engine roared into life. He eased the car out of its prison, into the sunlight, and carefully drove it onto the back of the recovery lorry. Once covered, he began his journey back to the yard. As he did so. His phone lit up. "Thank you." He looked around, and saw the Mercedes leave. He smiled and realised he was being tested. At least she now knew he was as good as his word. He turned up the stereo, and drove carefully back home.

When he got back he found the workshop deserted and a note saying, "had enough, called it a day"

He smiled. Callum had clearly had a bad day. He thought it best to leave it a while, let him calm down. He went back outside, and uncovered the car. It really was spectacularly pretty. He muttered, "lucky lady."

As he reversed it down the truck, he noticed the Mercedes slip into the yard. He grinned and carried on, played it cool. Watched Michelle get out, and admired the legs, the Nikes' and the thought of that body. As he selected drive, and pointed the car towards the barn at the end of the lane he saw her wave. He stopped, and she got in. As she did so, her skirt rode up and her thighs looked good. She saw him admire, and smiled. "I just wanted to say thank you in person,'' she smiled, and reached across to his thigh.

He looked at her, said, ''would you like to help me put it in?'' and grinned a cheesy naughty grin.

As she reached his cock, she smiled, "I think I should don't you? After all, Callum is not here, so we can't be disturbed now."

He smiled again. He wasn't sure if Michelle had put him up to leaving, or she had just seen the note, but it didn't matter. She was hot, he fancied her, she fancied him, and he was going to make damn sure he had her. The car slipped into the barn, Charlie carefully ensuring it was tucked out of the way. He raised the window, and got out of the car, "stay there," he said, "whilst I lock the door."

She smiled. "Don't tell me what to do," she said. He laughed and went to the barn door.

When he returned, Michelle was out of the car, and as he walked over, she carefully rested herself on the bonnet. "So," she said, "what now?"

As she finished the sentence he kissed her, hard and urgent. Her mouth responded in the same way. Biting, deep sensual kissing. Tongues clashing, and his hands between her legs. She parted them and his fingers found her knickers. She bit his lip as he slipped his fingers inside her panties and gasped as he entered her with his finger. Her pussy wet, expectant. She hung onto his shoulder and moaned softly as another went inside her. Fingers fucking her hard as she bit his shoulder. It was hot and hard and horny. "I want you to fuck me," she gasped. And he did as he was asked. She laid back onto the car, and he removed her lace panties. She unzipped his cock, he was so hard. She wanted to taste it. But he pushed her back and entered her. Hard, swift and urgent. She screamed, as the orgasm came over her. Wrapping her legs around him, she ordered him to fuck her harder. As he did so, he knew his own orgasm wouldn't be far away. He hadn't felt this good with a woman in a long time. She held onto him as her body shuddered. "shit!" she exclaimed. "I'm coming!" As her body shook he felt his cock explode inside her. He moaned loudly and held onto her tightly. His cock twitching inside her, and her pussy gripping him as the climax became one. They lay gently together. It had lasted less than five minutes probably. But they both knew it was a very special feeling that had swept over them.

He stood up. Semi hard still, and covered in her wetness. She sat up, and slowly lowered her mouth. "I want to taste you." And she looked at him as she took him in her mouth.

He looked down. "You are a naughty lady," he smiled.

She let him go. "I can be," she said. "Now, pass me my knickers please!" she laughed. He did as he was told. She definitely felt a little shy now, but slipped them over her trainers and up her thighs. He watched intently. She looked back at him. "I have to go, but..."

"But?" he enquired.

"But can I come back?" she smiled at him. As he shut the door and heard her feet along the gravel, he knew then and there his world was about to change. Forever.

15 "THE FUNERAL"

As the black Mercedes arrived, Michelle felt relieved. All the hard work of the last 2 days had paid off. Both men had been given the same story. An old school friend of Valerie's had suddenly been taken ill. The fact that Giles had never heard Valerie mention Janey, seemed to have passed the man by. Valerie was distraught, as it suddenly meant she had realised her own "mortality" and she had taken it badly. Michelle was needed at the funeral as support for her, as, because Michelle didn't know Janey, she could be detached, and just be there for Valerie, without emotion. Giles would be "far too busy" to attend and Valerie didn't want to put him out, so Michelle would do perfectly. Valerie stepped out of the house. She looked suitably immaculate. Knee length black dress, chiffon attached to a small hat, placed on one side of her head, and the material covering her face like a veil. She looked up, saw Michelle, and managed a smile through her blood red lips. "Thank you for being here," she said, as the Mercedes door was held open for her.

She climbed in, and beckoned Michelle to do the same. The door was closed for them, and with a whisper, it left the house. They sat in silence. Neither woman really knew what to say, but eventually, Michelle managed, "do you have any idea who will be there?"

Valerie looked back. "I would imagine his bitch ex, and a few colleagues, and of course, us, but to be honest Michelle. I have no idea." Michelle sat again in silence. Valerie asked, "do you have a handkerchief?"

"You didn't bring one?" she replied.

"I brought three, Valarie laughed, you know what I am like, and I know how scatty you can be."

Michelle went red, and she mouthed, "thank you, I didn't remember!" Both women smiled. And then silence.

They had been driving for around 45 minutes, and Michelle had no idea where she was now, but it was miles out of town, and she didn't recognise the area. Just as she was about to ask the question, the car turned left, and she saw the church. "He grew up here," said Valerie, seeing Michelle look puzzled.

"Oh, I see" she replied, despite not really understanding the significance.

The door opened, and the two women stepped out. They made their way into the doorway of the church. There, also in the doorway, was a tall woman, slightly overweight perhaps, and definitely underdressed. Michelle said nothing, but guessed this was the ex-wife. The woman eyed them up and down, but said nothing. As Michelle turned, the hearse came into view. The coffin was beautiful. The flowers displayed all around it were immaculate. And on the coffin, the most stunning bouquet of red roses. "They are mine," said Valerie, and Michelle heard the voice falter. She saw Valerie's face drop, and realised it was now time to be her friend. There were only 3 other people there. All men and all well dressed, and, as Michelle found out, all associates who had known him over the years. Jonny seemed to be the closest to him, and he was quite chatty. Michelle found out that Jamie had been distraught when his marriage initially split up, and that in the last few years of his life, he seemed to have been much happier, and certainly brighter. She discovered that Jonny had known Jamie since college, and they had always been close but, with their lives going in different directions, he had lost touch a little over the last 5 years. Michelle smiled. Jamie really was a lone character, and, it seemed, that was just the way he liked it.

The doors to the church opened, and they made their way in. Michelle sticking close to Valerie. They slipped into the pews at the back of the church, and Michelle couldn't help thinking that the small congregation didn't seem right for what Valerie had described as such a well-liked man. Valerie said nothing, she seemed lost. And Michelle could only hold her arm and say, "I'm here ok"

"Thank you" she replied weakly.

As the coffin came in, Valerie couldn't hold back her tears, she sobbed. And Michelle was slightly shocked at how deeply this woman was openly displaying her feelings of love for this man. She held her hand tightly, as the small congregation looked at Valerie and were clearly a little puzzled at the woman in the black dress. Valerie didn't care, she could finally let out all the emotions that had been building and growing in her. And she didn't care at all who saw it. Michelle watched the short skirted, fake tanned ex-wife Gemma looking over. As the service ended, Michelle couldn't wait to get Valerie away. She had a very definite feeling that Gemma wanted to do more than have a nice friendly chat. Valerie had at least regained some composure, and, as the doors opened, Michelle was glad they had chosen the back of the church to stand.

As they made their way outside, Michelle took Valerie's arm, and pulled her gently towards the car. They reached it, and Michelle opened the door. She ushered Valerie inside, then closed the door saying, "stay there" as she did so. She strode back towards the church, a purposeful almost angry walk. She needed to thank Jonny for his kind words, and also to say goodbye but was very conscious that Gemma, Jamie's ex-wife, had not stopped looking at them both, and Michelle figured she wanted at the very least to cause some sort of scene.

As she walked up to Jonny, and began to convey her emotions, a voice said, "so you are the fucking bitch he was screwing are you?" Michelle finished her conversation with Jonny, smiled and shook his hand.

She turned to Gemma. Walked past her, deliberately getting as close as possible. When she had got a step or two past, she turned. Looking into Gemma's eyes she replied, "even if I was, which I am not, I wouldn't give a low class, orange skinned, slut like you the satisfaction of saying yes. It's over, Jamie is gone. You have nothing, so stay away, and, if you decide you want to make any trouble, rest assured …" Michelle took a step closer, paused, then took hold of Gemma's hair, and looked her eye to eye, "you have no fucking idea who you would be messing with." And she turned around and walked to the car.

Gemma screamed, "*don't you fucking threaten me bitch.*"

Michelle smiled. Opened the door, got in, and closed it. She lowered the window, told Barry to "step on it," and gave the finger to Gemma as the Mercedes left the cemetery.

"I need a drink," Valerie said. "Barry, find me a pub, nowhere near home please." Barry had been Valarie's driver for a long time. They had a bond and friendship that she adored, and he respected, and one which they both knew was beyond anything that a "normal" employer/employee relationship could be.

After a short drive, they pulled into a small, quaint typically English pub. Just gone 12, thankfully it was open. "Get 40 winks," Valerie smiled as she motioned to Michelle, "let's have a drink." The two ladies entered the bar, which was totally empty, save for the barman. "GOOD AFTERNOON, JUST!" he boomed. "What can I get you both?" came in a slightly softer tone as he saw the black dresses, gloves, and figured it had been a funeral rather than a day out.

"Two large pink gin and tonics please," Michelle said. "Would you be kind enough to bring them to the garden, it's been a bit of a tough day?"

The barman looked a little put out, but Michelle looked around the empty bar, and he smiled. "No problem ladies." They stepped out into the sunlight, and Michelle looked for the furthest table from the pub, led Valerie to it, and instructed her to sit. Shortly after, the smiling barman came over, dropped the drinks and said "I don't do this for everyone you know!" He laughed as he bustled back to the bar.

Michelle and Valerie sat in silence. Val took a huge swing of her drink. Said, "well, that's that then," trying desperately to be "matter of fact" yet failing miserably.

Michelle replied, "I'm not so sure."

Valerie looked at her hard, "what do you mean?"

"Something tells me we haven't heard the last of the class act that is Jamie's ex-wife I fear"

Valerie smiled, "you think I'm worried about her?"

Michelle considered her answer. "I don't think you have anything to worry about, but, you don't need any waves at home either, and, if that woman showed me anything just now, it's that she has both jealousy and anger in her. And that's a dangerous mix sometimes."

Valerie's smile fell a little. "Yes, I suppose you are right," she sighed. "We will just have to wait and see." Michelle wanted to ask more about Jamie, but she could see Valerie just needed to release, to chill, to "come down", so they made small talk. The weather, what the boys might be up to. How grateful Valerie was for Michelle being there. How wonderful Barry was.

Michelle then blurted out, "I fucked Charlie Summer a few days ago."

Valerie spat her gin. She laughed. Said, "well I thought I had some secrets," and laughed again.

Michelle wasn't sure if the laughter was good, but she carried on. "I like him, and it's ridiculous because all I did was hit his car."

Valerie stopped laughing. "Ok," she said, "your turn - tell!"

As Michelle started to say, "well, I was driving out of town, and I wasn't paying attention" Valerie shook her head, "I don't mean about him, I mean *tell*"

Michelle's face fell, she knew what Valerie meant. And that wasn't something that filled her with joy. "Shit Valerie, *don't* judge me OK!" she said. "It started about 4 years ago, Tommy had been getting worse. Aggressive, moods, and I don't know, just something different. But he wasn't the same man I met 20 years ago. And I was, and I still am, a little scared of him, and what he might be capable of."

Valerie saw a hint of fear in Michelle's eyes. "So?" she prompted. "What happened?"

"Websites happened." Michelle looked at the ground, ashamed, the memories all too vivid. "I typed in married women feeling lonely one day, and well, I knew there were websites for everything, but I had no idea it was so easy." Valerie laughed again. Michelle continued. "So I signed up for one called Secret Sins, and opened my account. And that was it. It was just easy."

Valerie looked at her. "Sex you mean?"

"Yes," Michelle looked ashamed again. "I quickly became addicted. So much so that it got to the stage that I didn't especially care about what they looked like, I just wanted to get dressed up, and feel desired. Tommy often wanted to fuck me, but I was never allowed to enjoy it anymore. It was about him *only*. He would fuck me, come, then get off and sleep. It was like an animal. Just needed his satisfaction and then he was done. I began to enjoy being a slut. It meant I was in control. And to be honest, there were hundreds of guys for each woman, so it was just easy!" Valerie didn't look shocked. "I guess I have slept with dozens of guys. Fat, thin, short, tall, ugly, handsome. It started as I want a "type" and pretty soon became, I want a fuck." Valerie could hear the shame. "Until a few weeks ago," Michelle concluded.

"When you hit his car?" Valerie asked.

"Yes, I was on my way to a "meet" and I didn't pay enough attention and hit Charlie's car. He was nice, he definitely was interested in me, and I was flattered. He was the first man in a long time I felt was enjoying me for me and my looks, not the fact I was naked on a bed and showing them all I had," Michelle smiled. "Anyway, he gave me his number, and even though I carried on and went through with the meet, I felt physically sick when I got home. So much so that I puked at the thought of the guy I had just been with."

Valerie stopped her. "Let me get another," she said, and Michelle felt she could probably do with one.

"OK, will Barry be alright?" Valerie laughed, "he will be asleep bless him, he gets a bit tired," and she disappeared into the pub. Michelle thought hard. Much like Valerie before, it all seemed to have come out so quickly, but she felt she could trust Valerie 100% and she definitely needed an ear to at least give her some advice and guidance.

Valerie came back with the drinks. Michelle continued, "so since I hit his car, I haven't been back on the site. And I hadn't actually realised that until just now."

Valerie interrupted, "so, you fucked him?" she laughed.

"Yes," Michelle went red. "It was kind of me being what I have been for the last few years, me in control, doing what I do I suppose, being a slut," her head fell. "But it just feels like I like him. And, if I am honest, I think he likes me." Her turn to take a big gulp of gin. She began to share a few of the details of the crash, and the fact that Jamie's car was now safely tucked away in Charlie's barn.

Valerie drained her glass, and said, "I think we best get back."

They made their way back to the car. As they did, Valerie said, "whatever you do, I will have your back ok, but, *Do not* be stupid! We live in a small village. The women *all* know Charlie, and most would like a piece of him. The men have no clue, as far as they are concerned, he is nothing but a small-time garage, but just be careful."

Michelle smiled. "I will be careful," she replied.

Valerie tapped on the window. "WAKEY, WAKEY!" she shouted. Barry woke up with a start. Valerie laughed, and, as Barry started the car, she felt a huge sense of relief. It had been a very emotional day. But perhaps not in the way she could ever have dreamed.

16 "THE AFFAIR BEGINS"

And so began the affair that Michelle had been dreaming of. It started with Charlie parking just around the corner and waiting for Tommy to leave.

Almost immediately afterwards her phone pinged and she looked to see the WhatsApp message, "are you alone?"

She replied, "Yes, but it's not safe here."

To which he said, "I am outside, do you fancy a drive?"

She knew that Tommy was away for the whole day, he was going to London for some important business deal but equally, as Valerie had reminded her it was a small place, and she had to be careful. She could hardly contain her excitement. She replied, "give me 10 minutes."

She made a call to Valerie. "I need to not be found for the day," she said excitedly.

Valerie smiled, "I assume you have a date with your mechanic?"

Michelle laughed, "I'm not sure it's a date, in fact I'm not sure what is, all I know is I want to go and I don't want anything in the way to stop me."

Valerie replied, "don't worry, your secret's safe with me, I will make sure that if the boys appear I will drop you a text to let you know." Even though she had only known this man for a short amount of time Michelle knew she wanted to know him better. She quickly threw on some clothes and as it was still warm make sure that her legs were on display. She had already shaved the night before. With a smile as she looked in the mirror, the denim skirt and trainers, along with the off the shoulder top would do just fine today. She bounced down the stairs, and set the alarm.

As she closed the front door dropped a text back, "where are you?" and as he did so the Z4 came into view. She frantically beckoned him to go past. "Not here!" she sent another text. Charlie carried on driving past the house. She went to the Mercedes and sent the final text, "I will follow you, we need to hide my car somewhere," he grinned and waited just around the corner for her to pull out of the driveway. With a few short twists and turns they found the car park where her car would be safe enough, and she climbed into the BMW.

He grinned. "Hello, my sexy French seat cover," she looked back at him.

"What did you just call me?"

"My sexy French seat cover," and he laughed out loud. "Where to madame?"

She looks back at him, "I don't care let's just get the hell out of here."

"So where are we going?" she asked.

He replied, "do you fancy fish-and-chips?"

She looked a little disappointed. "Not exactly romantic," she laughed.

He smiled again, "do you fancy fish-and-chips at the beach?"

She smiled. "Are you always this crazy?"

"Only if I have someone to be crazy with," he replied. It took around 20 minutes to get to the motorway. As they drove they talked. He asked why she had no kids, she answered that she'd just never got round to it. She asked questions about his son and their relationship. He confessed to having another son who now lived in America and they had a difficult relationship for a time. Although they were on a voyage of discovery already it felt like they had known each other for years and Michelle was in a very happy place as the car hit the motorway. She put her shades on, turned the music up and Charlie put his foot down and let the powerful BMW Z4 have its head. It took around an hour and a half to get to Brighton, and, by the time they found somewhere to park it was probably 2 hours into the day. She had never felt so free and it was wonderful to talk to another human being on the same level. To laugh, to share some passions, to be infuriated by his love for country music something which she sincerely hoped would change but already she liked this man very much as they walked along the pier arm in arm. It felt natural, not forced, and certainly wasn't about sex, like all of the men she had met in her recent past. As they walked into the amusements, Michelle looked at the grab machines everywhere, looked at Charlie, and said, "can I have a souvenir?"

He had always been competitive, and this was no different, so he immediately took up the challenge, and soon began to wish he hadn't. Despite grabbing a few of the furry toys, none of them had fallen into the winners bay. It was probably 15 pounds into feeding the machine he suddenly managed to capture a small furry cat. Michelle squealed with excitement and Charlie laughed as the small furry animal dropped into the winner's enclosure and he collected it and handed it to her. "Just for you," he looked into her eyes and couldn't help kissing her. Whatever this woman had done to him he was enjoying the feelings too and was certain that despite the fact it was going to be very difficult, he wanted to see more of her.

They went to the beach and searched out a small fish-and-chips stall. Taking them to the beach, wrapped in paper and covered in salt and vinegar, it brought back memories of her childhood in France. She looked at him and said, "maybe this is romantic, I haven't felt like this in a long time."

He looked back. "I have no idea where this came from Michelle, and I should never be happy with somebody hitting my car, but the truth is I'm very glad you drove into me that day." He looked her up and down, said, "you look fantastic!"

Michelle smiled, "why thank you," she said, "are you trying to charm me a little perhaps?"

He replied, "I might be," and kissed her again. Her mouth tasting of salty chips he softly licked her lips and put his hands on her arse, squeezing gently. "You're a very attractive lady Michelle."

She blushed, and didn't quite know how to return the compliment, so simply said, "I need to lose a few pounds."

He replied, "You look just perfect to me, I would be quite happy for you to stay as you are." They sat on the stones, and ate the food in near silence.

"Can I have a coke? Zero please!" she asked.

"No problem," he said, anything else?"

She shook her head, and her curls caught the breeze. He finished his chips, and stood up and went back to the stall. When he returned, Michelle had finished her food too, and as he screwed up his paper she said, "don't you dare just chuck that!"

"I wasn't going to," he smiled, but I *guarantee* I can get it in the bin from here."

There was a glint in his eye. Michelle took up the challenge. Screwed her paper up and aimed. She failed miserably, and he laughed and fell back onto the stones before she whacked him and said, "come on then Mr know it all!"

He knelt up, screwed his paper up, and very carefully took aim and threw. It fell into the open mouth of the bin, and he raised both his arms smiling and saying, "oh yes!" She jumped on him, and like two teenagers would tease each other for not being able to throw the wrapping in first time, fell onto the stones in an embrace.

As the sun beat down Michelle sat up and simply sat on the stones, knees raised. "I just want to listen to the sea," she said. "My early childhood was near the sea and I love it more than anything else," she shook her curls, lifted her glasses and looked out to see just to absorb the waves and the sight and sounds. As she did so Charlie lay next to her, he couldn't look at the sea he was too wrapped up in looking at Michelle. She turned to kiss him, and as she did so he put his arms around her. He felt strong, safe and she enjoyed his touch. Very quickly she realised that if this man wanted her she had no need for websites anymore, because she wanted him and the feelings he was giving her.

As the day wore on she began to understand that they had a great deal in common, certainly from their childhood and their upbringing. His mother had never been around, always enjoying the next man and he had left home at a young age, and fought hard to make his business successful. He liked living under the radar, and apart from his ex-wife, he had not really had any serious relationships. His ex had given him his best friend, his son Callum and he was extremely proud of the way they had grown what they have as a business and as a father and son relationship. And he had made sure no one was going to come between that, *but* ... He couldn't get enough of this sexy French woman. She was utterly charming, very attractive and he was sure he wanted more and more of her.

They were lost in each other despite the hustle and bustle of the sea resort, when her phone pinged. She looked at him and said, "I'm sorry I have to check this." She opened the message from Valerie and already knew what it would say. She looked at Charlie, "I need to get back. I'm so sorry I didn't plan this at all well, and I need to be back before he gets home." She kissed him gently and said, "With better planning can we do it again?"

"I would like that very much," he said and returned the kiss. "I guess we better get back to the car" As they walked along arm-in-arm it was as if they had been a couple for years, and thought nothing of pointing out strange people. The odd haircuts, the huge beer bellies. They laughed and she gave him a hard time about his country music. He told her "wait until you hear my rock and roll!" as she raised her eyes to the heavens there were definitely some things she didn't like about this man, but if she had to suffer rock and roll and country in order to feel so alive she figured she could do that. They drove back with the music on his hand resting on her knee and hers returning the compliment.

She suddenly realised that there was nothing sexual about today, it was an experience of learning about a man who in a very short space of time had become very important to her. And what she was learning, she was liking very much indeed.

Her phone pinged again and she looked down the message. It read, "you probably have an hour."

"Charlie?" she enquired. "Will we be back in an hour?" he put his foot down and she felt the car leap forward.

He looked at her and smiled, "anything for you princess."

As he dropped her at her car, they kissed. A deep and passionate embrace, one which she felt deep inside her. "One thing," she said abruptly. "You can only contact me via dial chat, do you have it?" He looked puzzled, she smiles, "Oh my God, I forgot you're a mechanic!" She laughed, "download dial chat - D-I-A-L C-H-A-T," she spelt it out slowly for him. "Have a look in your app store, download it, and find me!" She quickly went into her bag and scribbled down her dial chat address. "I have to go!" and she kissed him on the cheek. "Thank you for the most wonderful day."

She started her car and sped out of the car park. Charlie was left standing smiling, his head confused. He hadn't felt this way in a very long time, and he wanted this woman to stick around.

17 "NIKKI"

She pulled into the drive, and with a huge sense of relief she could see that Tommy's car was not around. Now all she had to do was make it look like she had been at home for ages! She rushed indoors, quickly poured a glass of wine and made sure that the stereo was on and turned up, opening the patio doors to let the last of the warmth in. She kicked off her shoes and sat in the garden. R&B was her favourite and she was enjoying the sounds of Usher when, after about 15 minutes she heard the Aston. Why was the bloody thing so loud? She smiled and checked her phone. Nothing on dial chat from Charlie, but there were lots of messages from men that wanted to fuck her, however, sadly none from a man she would desperately like to hear from again. She smiled, he was just a mechanic, he probably didn't even know what dial chat was unless he was talking to a car that wouldn't start! She drained her glass and poured another, just as Tommy opened the door. She smiled sweetly, "hello baby how was your day?"

He grinned, "let's just say it was very productive, pour me a drink!"

She was very pleased to see he was alone. At least she wouldn't have to suffer pretending to like Giles as well. "Have you eaten?" she asked.

"Yes, had a fabulous lunch" he said.

"Do you want anything now?" she asked.

"No, no, just the TV and a drink." She poured a rum with several cubes of ice and went into the living room where he was sitting just about to turn on the TV. He closed the door "I want to catch up on the cricket," he said as she smiled again.

"Ok! Are you OK if I still listen to some music?"

"Sure," he replied, "just not too heavy on that R&B shit you listen to."

She laughed, "OK, I will make sure it's not too loud and not too heavy for you."

He thanked her, "I know I don't have to listen too much to the cricket, but I like to hear some of the comments."

Michelle left the bottle of rum on the small table, "don't spill it!" She looked around the room at the immaculately pale furnishings.

"I won't," he said and she left the room. She crossed the kitchen and went out into the garden, pouring another glass of wine as she went. She could never quite work out what mood Tommy would be in. Right now he was as normal as could be. Yet like a switch he could change. She had no idea if Charlie would ever contact her again, but she was praying he would.

He pulled into the small cottage drive and found himself smiling for no reason other than the day he had spent with a very attractive woman. His mind was totally confused. He fancied her very much, but he knew it was a mistake, she was involved, indeed married, to a club owner whose reputation, well, let's just say he didn't suffer fools gladly. He wasn't especially worried for himself, more that he was worried for her. Tommy had a reputation for dealing with things in an ugly way but he couldn't put his finger on quite why, he just knew he wanted to see her again. The small piece of paper with the scribbled writing giving him her dial chat contact details was still in his hand. He had no real idea what he was doing but as he opened the door to the cottage and looked around he smiled again to himself. It had been a good day. He slipped off his shoes and went to the kitchen. "I need a drink," he said out loud.

As he did so a voice from the living room said, "I will have a wine."

At that moment he came crashing back to reality realising his ex-girlfriend was still there. If he thought that the situation with Tommy and Michelle was difficult, having his ex-girlfriend living with him since her house had been burned down was even more so! He sighed, grabbed the cider, poured a glass of pinot grigio and went to the living room. "How was your day?" Nikki said.

"It was OK," he smiled. "I didn't do much, I had a couple of things to catch up on," and he walked out into the garden. At the bottom of the garden was a large 4 car garage which he had built himself. It contained every mechanical and electrical device anyone could ever need. As he threw the door open, he turned on the TV, and muted the sound. He wanted to catch up with the cricket but he didn't really care for the commentary so decided that this evening was a rock and roll evening and shouted to the speaker, "ALEXA, play Elvis Presley." He took a large gulp from the can of cider, as the speakers began to play "Little Sister." Charlie sunk into the comfy armchair and allowed himself a smile. He turned to the right and saw his 3 favourite cars looking back at him. He was very aware that life had been kind to him, but he had worked bloody hard for what he had. He took out his phone and opened the apps store and searched for dial chat. Whatever the future held, he decided he wanted Michelle in it.

She had forgotten to put her phone on silent. The tiny "ping" alerted her, remarkably, she was just between songs when the message arrived, or she would never have heard it. Tommy was deep in pundit mode watching the cricket, shouting absurd instructions and telling each player why he was either, "so shit you don't deserve to play for England," or, "fucking top drawer." So she opened her phone. Dial Chat, shit! Another bloody guy from the website. She opened it, a name she didn't know. As she clicked on "Summertime Blues'' she saw Charlie. She couldn't help but grin. Shit! She quickly muted the chat.

The message read, "Hello Princess."

She replied, "Hi. So you managed it then?"

"I managed it!"

"Tommy is around, so I can't talk now. But I'm very glad you did."

"No worries. I'm still learning this, OK!"

She smiled again. "Even you should be able to work Dial Chat!" and she closed her phone.

She gasped, and poured wine. God, he was nice! Tommy came out about an hour later. "I'm going to shower," he said. "I thought I would go to the club, see if the new car is pulling in the customers. Do you want to come?"

"Not really," Michelle replied, "I thought I might have a bath and just chill."

"Suit yourself," he snapped. The mood was darker already. Yet he bounced up the stairs. What the *hell* was making him so happy? Michelle questioned in her mind. Truth was, she didn't care, she had other things on her mind. And the last place she wanted to be was the club. She had loved singing there, but, as Tommy got richer, and the club changed from a cabaret style to a full on nightclub, she had wanted to keep away. It was no longer intimate and "cool", just a noisy club with brash clientele and a slightly dodgy reputation. But it made money, *huge* money! And Michelle wasn't quite sure all of it was legitimate, but she couldn't care less. It paid for a very nice lifestyle, and she would take all of that.

He came back down around 20 minutes later. Suit on. Shirt. Shiny shoes. "You look very smart," she commented.

"Business!" he barked, and he grabbed his keys and phone and marched out of the door. She couldn't explain why, but she felt uneasy, even if he was in a bad mood he didn't usually behave so angrily. The Aston roared away, wheels spinning, and she knew something was wrong. But had no idea what.

All she had on her mind right now was that she needed to tidy up her Dial Chat account, and contact Charlie. She opened her phone and began to delete contacts from Dial Chat. An hour later, she was still doing it. She slowly realised what a slut she had become. Even if she hadn't fucked anywhere near all of them, she felt more than a pinch of shame as she looked at the list. When she had finished, she couldn't explain it, but she felt clean. She decided she needed to delete the website too. She needed the laptop for that. And it always made her a little nervous. She opened it. And quickly went to her log in. She couldn't resist opening her message box. There were dozens, from "fancy a fuck" to long prose asking her likes and dislikes.

She scrolled down. "Delete account". She stopped, and changed her mind. "Hide profile," she selected instead. Just in case she was wrong about Charlie. She knew now that dial chat would probably go mad. Or at least she would be bloody disappointed if it didn't.

She typed, "are you alone?" and pushed send.

Charlie was enjoying a new rum now. His Man Cave had become his place of rest since Nikki had appeared. He turned the music up, picked up his phone, and saw the message. "Sort of," he replied.

Michelle answered, "Can we meet?"

Bollocks! He knew he couldn't drive now. He replied. "I have had a few beers, I can't drive, I'm sorry."

Oh crap. She felt let down. Replied, "Of course, let's make it another time."

He answered, "I'd like that."

She threw her phone. Balls! Had she misread all of it? Was he suddenly not keen? Had he just enjoyed the fuck and thought she was cheap?

She banged her fist on the couch and was angry with herself. She went upstairs and began to run the bath. She stripped, and looked in the mirror. She definitely needed to lose a few pounds. She took the glass of wine, and stepped into the bath. Deep and full with bubbles, she sunk down into it. Feeling better, she allowed herself to relax. She would just enjoy it too. And if Charlie wanted to see her again, he could make the first move! She went to bed with that thought on her mind. But she knew in her mind, if he didn't, she would.

Over the next week or so, they exchanged a few brief messages. He seemed to be totally unfazed. She was feeling a bit stupid. But she was happy they at least were chatting. At the same time, Tommy seemed to be getting more and more angry. Despite the club booming, he was agitated, and spent less and less time at home. Michelle called Valerie, she needed to talk.

They arranged coffee at a garden centre, well out of town. A nice walk if they wanted it too. And discreet enough to not be overheard. Michelle asked how Valerie was. She said she was doing fine. That Jamie's estate was split between his 3 friends mainly. No house, so just the business. And they had all been at school and then uni together. She had the car. And now all she had were memories that she would be able to smile at for the rest of her life. They arranged to meet the next day at 11am. Valerie wanted to know all the gossip!

Michelle asked, "How is Giles?"

Valerie replied, "awkward, but let's talk tomorrow."

Michelle dressed. And kept out of Tommy's way, as she left the house, telling him she was going for coffee with Valerie. That at least made him calm a little.

"Good, I am with Giles today."

Michelle got in the car, tapped in the postcode, and reversed out of the drive. It was around 30 minutes' drive. Valerie's car was already there. Michelle felt better seeing the car, and went straight to the café. She sat and sighed.

Valerie asked. "What's up?" Michelle told all. About the sex with Charlie. About her taking control and almost demanding he fuck her. About him then not being in contact so much. And about Tommy being so agitated. It kind of all poured out and then she stopped, breathless.

Valerie took it all in. Laughed out loud. And said, "ok, which bit should I reply to first?" She looked at Michelle. "Giles and Tommy are up to something. I don't know what, but it's some sort of business deal. And until it all goes off smoothly, take advantage of him not being around. I know I am with Giles not being there!" She gave a wink.

Michelle looked shocked, "You don't have another man do you!"

Valerie laughed again! "*Shit no!* but I'm back swimming!"

Michelle smiled. "Be careful of your locker key!"

And it was her turn to laugh. "As for Charlie, what do you want to do?"

"I want him to want me!" Michelle burst out.

"Then make him," Valerie retorted. "I will book you both a spa day, *if* you can trust him."

Michelle looked at her. "He has your car, he has definitely had me, I *know* I can trust him!"

"OK," Valerie smiled. "Then tell him you are having a spa, and have a spare ticket." She sipped the last of her coffee.

"You think that's a good idea?" Michelle asked.

"Why not?" It will give you a chance to have some time, I can say you are spending it with me, and I will be around in case anything goes wrong."

Michelle smiled, she remembered Rita. The spa day had been a *very* good experience for her. She just hoped Rita wouldn't be the one giving Charlie the massage! "OK, I will do that, thank you Valerie."

Valerie looked at her sternly. "I told you at the start, if you fuck it up, you are on your own, but, as long as you are careful, I will help any way I can."

Michelle took out her phone. "You think I should message him now? When do I say the booking is for?"

"He works hard, and will have to plan. But the spa is much quieter Monday/Tuesday. So I would suggest early next week. Give him the chance to put things in place." And give Giles and Tommy time to either calm down or not bloody care coz they have too much on their mind." Valerie smiled. "You have been doing this a lot Michelle, don't tell me you don't know how."

Michelle went red. "I have, but it's just been a fuck," she said, and shocked herself at the expression. "Shit, I have been so cheap!"

Valerie smiled. "You have you slut, now get yourself some bloody self-respect back, and if nothing else, at least enjoy one man and what that might give you!"

Michelle's face went red. She knew Valerie was right. And she wanted it to happen. She just couldn't be certain yet that Charlie was that man. Valerie had 13 years with a man who clearly loved her, and she loved him. Michelle knew she wanted to feel the same way about Charlie. And, if she didn't try, she would never know. She opened her phone. Dial Chat. And sent Charlie the message, she just had to wait now. The girls chatted, Giles had been very jumpy and Tommy the same. They had been together a lot. And both women were pretty convinced that it was definitely not something they needed to know about. Yet in the back of their mind, whether it was legal was pretty doubtful too. It made them both feel uncomfortable. Caught between a rock and a hard place. Say nothing, do nothing. But all the time doubting and wondering. It was an uneasy mix. Especially as they both knew it involved the nightclub, and probably the golf club too.

Instead they ordered a wine and, as it arrived, Michelle checked her phone. And saw the Dial Chat message. "What time?"

Michelle choked on her wine, and as she did so, she showed Valerie the screen.

"Tell him the car will pick him up at 10.00 am. And to dress at least respectably, we don't want any overalls!"

Michelle laughed. "OK," and she typed the message, just as Valerie had asked.

"It's a date," came the reply.

Michelle grinned like a child. "So what now for you Valerie? Now the dust has settled?"

Valerie looked wistfully out of the window. "I have no idea Michelle, but whatever it is, I'm going to make damn sure I enjoy it." The morning slipped away as the two ladies chatted. About their men, about what on earth was going on, about the weather, about shoes, before Valerie said, "I want to drive the car!"

Michelle was taken by surprise. "Er, OK, sure, when?"

"Now!" she said.

"Shit!" Michelle expleted. "OK, let me make sure he is there." She dialled.

"Hello sexy French lady." Valerie laughed, "oh, you are not alone!"

Michelle laughed too, "no, I'm not alone," she smiled. "I have a friend with me, who would like to come drive the Maserati you are storing."

"Really?" came the reply.

"REALLY!" Valerie shouted in the background.

"OK, OK! give me 30 mins to shift a few things about."

"No problem," Michelle returned, "see you then."

45 minutes later, they followed one another into the yard. There before them was the beautiful Maserati. Valerie took a deep breath before getting out. Michelle walked to her, sensing her unease, she offered her arm and Valerie took it gladly. Charlie appeared, a little greasy and also a little uneasy. "Good afternoon ladies," he chirped. Michelle grinned like a school girl.

Valerie replied, "good afternoon Charlie, I've heard a lot about you," and smiled.

"All good I hope!" He barked back, and laughed.

"I will be the judge of that," she smiled. "So, can you take me for a drive?"

Michelle looked a little concerned. "There are only two seats," she said puzzled.

"I know" replied Valerie, "I just want to feel a little piece of Jamie, and I want a little chat with Master mechanic here!"

Michelle didn't quite know what to do, she hadn't bargained for anything like this and it had taken her by surprise.

"You can wait in the upstairs office," he said.

"I might go see the horses," Michelle answered back, and she wandered off to the other side of the farm.

Valerie climbed into the passenger seat, "let's see what this thing can do shall we?" Valerie beamed.

"Fasten your seatbelt!" Charlie laughed, as he started the car. The noise of the V8 engine was just thrilling, and Valerie smiled and pictured Jamie there, foot down, sunglasses on.

"Just don't crash," she said, and closed the door. Charlie pulled out of the yard, put his foot down hard, and as Valerie sunk into the seat, she closed her eyes, and allowed herself deep thoughts of the man she had loved and lost. When she opened them again, she looked at Charlie. "I don't know if you know who that woman is," she said, "but are you sure you want to get involved?"

Charlie looked back, slowing as he took his eyes off the road. "I'm sure," he said softly.

"Then don't fuck it up, because if you do, you will have one *hell* of a repercussion," she snapped.

He heard the threatening tone. "I won't fuck it up," he returned.

"Good, then be ready at 10 on Tuesday, and my car will collect you, *but*, whatever happens that day, if you breathe a word, it won't just be Tommy that needs a word with you."

Charlie felt a little uncomfortable. "I won't say a word," he replied.

"Good!" Valerie paused, "then we understand each other. Now, let me get behind that wheel."

They pulled back into the yard. Valerie exhilarated from the sheer performance the car had to offer. "What would we get for this?" she enquired.

Charlie looked at the miles, less than 10,000. "I reckon around 70 grand," he said.

"Sell it," she replied.

"OK!" he looked puzzled. Michelle had heard the car and was coming back. "Are you sure?" he said.

"Never been more sure," she replied. And they stepped out of the car.

"Was the drive good?" Michelle asked.

Valerie smiled, "it was fabulous, I think Charlie and I understand each other perfectly now, and it was wonderful to drive the car for the first and last time!"

Michelle inquired, "why last time?"

"Because I just needed to feel what he felt when he drove it, and now I have, that memory is all I need. I have asked Charlie to sell the car for me and I will make a donation to charities with the money," she paused for breath, "it's a bit cheesy but what do I need more money for?" And with that, Valerie said, "I will leave you two to it, see you on Tuesday Charlie!" and as she did so the black Mercedes pulled into the yard in a hurry.

Michelle was a bit taken aback as was Charlie. "What are you going to do?"

"I will put the word out," he said "and try to get the best price I can. Is she serious about not wanting 70 grand?" Charlie still had no idea who this woman was.

"I don't think it's the 70 grand," Michelle said. "I think it is the memory of what that 70 grand represents."

"Fair enough," Charlie said. "I will do what I can. Now do you want to come to the barn to help me put it away?" he grinned.

"No" she said, "I'm going to make you wait. I will see you on Tuesday too." and she got in her car, smiled at him, and slowly left the yard making sure he stared at her until he could no longer see her.

She grinned as she pulled out and waved, watching him with his feeble wave acknowledging her. She laughed, and hoped that she had him exactly where she wanted, but she knew that on Tuesday it was going to be a whole different level. It would make them complete, and inside her stomach she couldn't wait. She already could feel the butterflies! She had no idea why Valerie had really wanted to take the car out alone with Charlie but whatever the reason, all she wanted now was Tuesday to hurry up and come around. Much as the sex had been good, it had been swift and there had been no intimacy, and she had already decided that the next time they had each other, she wanted it to be intimate, she wanted it to be close, she wanted it to be special in her mind if nothing else. She was sick of cheap fucks and seedy hotels and websites and Valerie had already told her, "To get yourself some self-respect," and for the first time, she felt that she might actually have some. If she was going to do it again she was going to make sure she did it her way but also that she felt that this may lead to a love affair rather than the cheap fucks she had before. She drove home slowly knowing that Tommy would not be back yet, and her mind was already planning what it was she wanted to happen on Tuesday.

18 "CHARLIES SPA DAY"

The black Mercedes pulled up at Charlie's address at precisely 10:00 am He was ready. New jeans, crisp white shirt, loafers and to be honest not much else. He knew he smelled good and he thought he looked good and he just hoped that it was all going to be worthwhile.

The driver opened the door, smiled, and said, "hello sir, I'm Barry."

"Hello Barry, pleased to meet you," replied Charlie and got into the back.

Barry closed the door and they headed off. "It will be almost an hour," Barry said, "I have to take a couple of detours."

"That's no problem Barry, you take your time." And Charlie settled into the comfortable leather seat and wondered what today held.

Tommy had already left. Whatever the deal might be that he and Giles were planning, it was definitely not fulfilled yet, and his mood was as dark as it had ever been. Michelle smiled, she didn't care, but between herself and Valerie, they had already told the boys that there was going to be a spa day for them.

Giles simply questioned, "again?"

To which Valerie replied "*again* Giles!" he didn't ask anymore.

He knew better than to have a difference of opinion with his wife over a spa day so he simply said, "no problem, enjoy ladies."

Tommy couldn't care less, his mood much darker than Giles. He knew that if this deal didn't come off, he could have some very expensive explaining to do, so when Michelle said she was having a spa day his response was simply, "whatever."

On that Tuesday morning he had left early, Michelle had simply waited by the window until the black Mercedes arrived. With his blacked out windows there was no danger of anybody seeing anyone inside. She was dressed casually, heels, and a cream outfit. She set the alarm, and locked the front door. Walking towards the car she couldn't contain her excitement and sincerely hoped he had not worn his overalls!

Barry got out of the car, "Good morning miss," he smiled.

She returned the smile, "Good morning Barry, good to see you!"

"You too," he said as she got into the car and he closed the door. As they left Charlie and Michelle looked at each other, grinned and giggled like schoolchildren. It would be about a 30 minute drive so they began to talk. About their early childhood. Michelle explained a little but not in too much detail, that she had had a tough beginning. Charlie could sympathise. The beginning of his life had been much the same. Perhaps not with drugs, but certainly he had been pushed from pillar to post and never feeling like he belonged. He explained he was proud of his success and even though people figured he was just a small time mechanic, with what he had learned and amassed over the years certainly what was in the barn was more than enough for his retirement fund.

Michelle laughed. "Do you plan on retiring then?"

He laughed, "I wouldn't know what to do with myself," he replied, "what on earth would I want to retire for?"

She looked at him teasingly and said, "I could give you a few reasons," he laughed again and wondered just how serious that statement was. Shortly, they arrived. Barry ensured the car was parked carefully behind the regular car parks through an entrance that only Barry could know.

He opened the door and escorted them out. "Follow me," he said and they duly did so.

Rounding two corners before coming to a small oak door barely noticeable he tapped 3 times on it and Michelle saw Rita open the door.

She smiled, and whispered, "Good afternoon, I am pleased to be your guide for your experience day, Michelle," she winked. "Come in, let me make you comfortable."

Michelle smiled back. She had a flashback to her last experience with Rita, and decided perhaps Charlie might just enjoy that a little too much. "Thank you," Michelle returned, and duly followed. Charlie close behind, somewhat puzzled, but happy to go with whatever the day held in store.

They soon arrived at the same changing area Michelle had enjoyed a few weeks ago. Rita turned to them. "If you would like to step inside and change, we can begin the experience."

Charlie looked confused. Michelle simply said, "go in, get changed, and I will see you on the other side of the door." He did as he was told. And enjoyed the same admiration for the fine furnishings and products contained behind the door.

He could hear Michelle on the other side of the wall. "I guess we just have the dressing gown on?" he tried to whisper but needed to be a little loud for her to hear.

He heard her laugh. "YES!"

He smiled, and stripped. He saw himself in the mirror, he needed to lose a stone. He sucked his stomach in, tensed his arms and said quietly, "not too bad for 52." He put on the gown and opened the other door. They stepped out simultaneously and smiled at each other.

"This way," Rita instructed. They followed in silence. Shortly, they arrived at the door Michelle thought she remembered. Rita opened the door, and said, "your masseuse will be with you shortly." She looked at Michelle winked and whispered, "don't worry, it's not the full massage you had," and she left the room. Shortly after, a man and a woman appeared. They introduced themselves and asked that their guests remove their gowns and lay on the benches. Charlie slipped his gown off, and Michelle smiled. Charlie went red and looked shy. Michelle laughed. And they lay down to allow the 2 people to do their job.

It was beautiful; relaxed, warm and soft. The pair of them did not want to talk too much, they just wanted to enjoy the feeling, and the feelings. It was 20 mins of pure bliss.

The two masseuses then instructed them to dress and to follow Rita.

She led them to the sauna room. "I can assure you, I have strict instructions not to let you be disturbed," she smiled.

"Excellent," replied Charlie. And he held the door for Michelle.

They entered the door, and Michelle quickly stripped and stood naked in front of Charlie. She undid the belt on his robe and kissed him. A deep and passionate urgent kiss saying, "I have wanted this ever since I first met you and I hope you feel the same." He slipped the robe from his shoulders and let it fall to the floor. This was not a time for sex but it was a time for sensual exploration and enjoying each other's bodies with a mutual admiration. They sat quietly for a few moments, before slowly beginning to reveal some more of their respective pasts, and hopefully what they both agreed would be some sort of very dangerous future. Michelle told him more about her childhood, not in detail but enough for him to know and understand that this was a woman who needed to be cared for, she needed to be nurtured and loved and made to feel special, and clearly that was something that she had definitely not been made to feel, certainly in the last few years. She didn't feel it was appropriate to mention the sites yet but she confessed to having had a few men throughout her marriage. More because of the change in her husband and the fact that he no longer saw her as desirable but purely as an object to fulfil himself with whenever the urge took him. In turn Charlie explained that his childhood had been in some ways similar to hers, there had been many homes and many "uncles". None of which were his father who he had never known. He didn't resent that but he knew that he wanted to be the best father to Callum that he possibly could. From a very young age he had set out a goal to try and achieve at least some sort of security, both financial and mental, which would allow him, if he ever did have a kid to make sure that that child was looked after for life, in a way that he had never could have been. He asked if she regretted not having children. She said no she had never really been the maternal type and she felt that in particular with her lifestyle and certainly with Tommy the way he was there was no room for a child in her life. As they talked it became blindingly obvious that there were many similarities between the two of them in their upbringing, and to a degree in their outlook.

She asked what happened with Callum's mother and Charlie told her that he and Marina simply grew apart. She wanted different things from life and in particular, when he was building up his business he was never around. He understood now that the pressure she had been under with a young child had been too much, and he was man enough to admit that he had not been there enough to give her the support she needed. In the end she had enough and he came home one day late to find a note saying, "I can't do this anymore. I have taken the baby and I am back at my mum's. I'm sorry and I hope you understand." At the time he had been completely devastated, and they had talked and agreed that certainly for a short term it may be best for them to part. That short term turned into 17 years, during which he had grown to have a really beautiful relationship with his son that now allowed a flourishing business, a wonderful friendship, and also the pride that his child would be able to take over what small empire he had built, and if Callum ever did have a child the same security would be there. Charlie was proud of that, and Michelle was fairly sure it was nothing like the depth of involvement in the Underworld that Tommy had. After around 30 minutes they had both had enough and went to get their robes. After knocking on the door, it was opened immediately by Rita. If Michelle didn't know better she would have sworn Rita had been standing guard.

She smiled "I hope you feel relaxed," she said, "lunch is laid on in 30 minutes, I will escort you to the green room."

Charlie looked puzzled. "Do we have to get dressed?" he asked.

Michelle laughed. "No, just relax!" she said, "and enjoy the experience."

Charlie questioned, "how do you know so much about this?" as he looked puzzled again.

Michelle winked, looked at Rita and said, "it's not what you know!"

Charlie decided it was best not to ask any more, but simply to go along for what seemed like a really rather wonderful ride and just enjoy it and embrace it. As they reached the green room with its comfortable chairs, oak panelling, and dim lighting he smiled. Deciding not to ask any more questions was *definitely* the right thing to do.

He let his shoulders slouch slightly and Rita sensed the relief in his body. "Would you two like a drink before lunch?" she enquired.

"I will have a gin and tonic please Rita," said Michelle.

And Charlie returned, "Rum for me, just ice thank you." As they sat with a soft gentle music background they continued the chat. Neither of them really wanting to go too deep, because with both of them knowing that they wanted each other sexually very badly, this didn't seem the time or the place to take the conversation either too deep, or too sexual!

Rita looked at the clock. It was now just after one, "lunch will be at 1:30," she said. "Please enjoy," and she left the room.

Charlie sat opposite Michelle, the two of them almost teasing each other sitting with their legs apart and showing each other they were naked under the robes. Yet knowing that right now was not the time to take anything further.

So they talked, they drank and they slowly enjoyed each other's company, before Rita re-entered the room. "If you would like to follow me," she said, "lunch is served."

They enjoyed a similar spread to that which Michelle had already found was so delicious the day she had come here with Valerie. The conversation was now lighter and they talked about aspirations, about her singing. She even managed a few bars. Preacher Man was always her go-to song, easy to sing acapella and one that she was very comfortable with singing. He clapped in admiration and was genuinely surprised at how good this lady's talent was. He had no such talent and told her so, showing off his gnarled hands, the grime deep in his fingertips.
She touched them "working hands," she said, "honest hands."

"I don't know about that," he laughed. "I don't do much of the work anymore, Callum is the main man." He told her how proud he was of young son, his abilities, his mechanical knowledge, his cheeky chappy outlook on life. The same one he had always been trying to keep but had at times struggled when he felt he had let himself and his son down.

She couldn't help but enjoy this wonderfully endearing man and as lunch came to an end Rita appeared once more and said, "perhaps you would like to retire to somewhere quieter?" and she smiled at Michelle. "We have a couple of guest rooms available, and perhaps you would like to take a small nap, though I am imagining you may only need one room."

Michelle returned the smile and said, "yes, just one room will be fine, thank you."

They closed the door and finally - they were alone. Michelle once again took control and undid his robe. This time she let it fall to the floor and knelt down, taking his cock into her mouth. She had wanted this, and she wanted it to be perfect. She felt him swell as her warm mouth and tongue performed its magic and she was pleased, but she knew that she wanted him inside of her. She teased him. Licking, biting using all of the tricks that she had learned from the sites, yet not feeling cheap or trashy this time but a genuine want to make love to this man.

He looked down at her, lifted her head and said "stop!" "Take it slow, and kiss me Michelle, I want to make love to you." She did as he asked and stood to receive his tongue into her mouth and his strong hands undid her robe. It fell to the floor and their naked bodies embraced. Very slowly he guided her to the bed and for the next 2 hours they explored each other everywhere. He lay on top of her. Her mind raced at the thought of what she wanted him to do, but he refused to be told now. "It's my turn," he said firmly. He kissed her. Gently, his tongue explored her mouth as his hands massaged her breasts and teased her nipples erect. He bit her top lip, and she closed her eyes as his body moved down hers.

Biting softly at her neck, he lowered himself to the floor, on his knees, and encircled her nipples with his mouth. Biting them in turn, she moaned with pleasure, and took a deep breath to relax. This was beautiful, and she wanted to enjoy every moment. She gave herself to him, in a way she had not done in a very long time, and, now relaxed, her body *ached* for his touch everywhere. He kissed lower, his hot breath on her belly. She put her hands on his head. And began to push it down, spreading her legs wider as his tongue flicked across her wet lips. She wanted his tongue on her clit, and he responded by softly sucking it between his teeth as he slid two fingers inside her.

She arched her back, and moaned louder. He bit her clitoris and she shuddered as he pushed deeper. "Fuck me Charlie, please!" he ignored her, and enjoyed her getting wetter as his tongue and fingers pleasured her. She wanted to orgasm, and begged him again, fuck me please." He kissed her, looked lovingly into her eyes as he entered her. She kissed him and wrapped her legs around him, feeling skin on skin. She gasped as he went inside her, and her nails dug into his back. She moaned softly as he moved back and forth. Enjoying teasing her now, pulling his shaft out of her almost completely, looking at her experiencing pleasure, seeing her eyes closed and then pushing deep into her and hearing her moan louder as he moved faster. She was close to orgasm, and asked him softly, "make me come." His mind lost focus, he couldn't hold back and began to fuck her a little more frantically. She screamed, a soft, gentle, loving scream and told him, "I'm going to come." As she did so, his mind exploded, and he could no longer hold back, he put his hands under her arse, lifted her buttocks and could feel the orgasm begin.

As she screamed louder, harder and more urgently, her orgasm swept over her, he convulsed and could feel his cock pulse as he reached climax. Without thinking, he held her tightly and whispered, "I love you."

She gripped his naked body tighter than she could ever remember doing before, and replied, "I love you." Even though it had only been a short time they had known each other, both of them had never climbed to the heights of pleasure they had both just experienced.

He raised himself, and looked into her eyes as they opened. "Are you OK?" he smiled.

"No" she replied."

He looked crestfallen, "what's wrong?"

She smiled, a deep, naughty smile, and whispered, "I'm fucked!"

He laughed, "you and me both princess!" and he moved to lay next to her. Their bodies glistened with sweat. Spent. Feeling high on the orgasms, but also high on the simple feeling of being wanted.

"Did you mean it?" she asked curiously.

"Mean it?" he looked puzzled but knew full well what she meant.

"Don't bullshit me that's all" she snapped.

"Michelle, you are remarkable," his tone soft, as he brushed her curls to one side. "And if I can be in love with someone after only a few weeks, then yes, I love you."

She blushed. "I'm definitely *not* remarkable, in fact I'm nothing but a cheap slut," and she grabbed him and let the tears run from her without holding back. Charlie had no idea what was happening, but he could suddenly feel a desperate sadness both for and coming from this lady. He held her tight, and let her tears flow. Saying nothing, he simply showed her the affection she craved, and let Michelle cry until she was done crying. He decided not to ask too many questions just yet, but instead looked around for a drink. He saw the decanter, clear liquid in it, and assumed either vodka or gin. He laid her head on the pillow as she sighed, and walked to the other side of the bed.

The chink of ice made her sit up. She looked genuinely sad, and weakly nodded, "yes please."

Charlie found a small fridge. The room was quite beautiful. Clean crisp white everywhere. The odd dark blue accent. But above all, it felt expensive. He took out two large ice cubes. Poured a large measure into each tumbler, and came back to the bed. "Here you go princess," and he softly wiped her tears.

"Can I have a tissue please?" she asked meekly. He went to the bathroom, Michelle couldn't help but smile. He had a really nice arse! He returned with a handful of toilet tissue. She blew her nose noisily. Embarrassed, she apologised.

"Don't be sorry," he said, "you want to talk?"

She shook her head. "Another time, please," she mumbled.

"No worries" and he opened the bed clothes. "I think you could probably do with a chill."

She smiled. A lost, empty smile. "Thank you," and she moved under the duvet.

He got in beside her. And as she lay, he cradled her and kissed her neck gently. "Take it easy," he whispered. She didn't hear him. Her arm wrapped around him, and she was asleep almost instantly. He lay down, wrapped her in him, felt the warmth. And closed his eyes. He wasn't certain it was love, but it felt more special than he had felt in a time too long to remember.

The small ornate telephone buzzed gently. He picked it up. A voice said, "it's Rita, Valerie has asked me to inform you it's approaching 4pm and she feels for safety that perhaps your visit should be coming to an end."

Charlie sat upright. "Yes, of course," he coughed.

"The car will be ready in 30 minutes. I would suggest you both are ready to meet it."

And the phone went silent. Charlie didn't panic, he looked down at Michelle. She looked peaceful, beautiful. And he knew he wanted *much* more of her. Softly he stroked her hair as she moaned and tossed her head. "Time to wake up princess, the party is over for now." Michelle opened her eyes. She couldn't focus properly, but she saw Charlie and smiled. "Hello sleepy head," he smiled. "We have 30 minutes to get ready, Rita called, it's just after 4!" And he laughed. "So much for an all afternoon sex session!"

Playfully he slapped her arse. "Stop it!" she squealed. "Shit, 4pm!"

"Don't panic princess, we just have to get dressed."
Michelle composed herself. He was right of course. She threw
back the covers. He admired her naked body. She became
conscious of him looking. "You are delicious," he said, and bent to
kiss her before retrieving his clothes.

"Pass mine would you?" she asked. He did as he was asked.

Within 15 minutes, they were both dressed, and Michelle
was brushing her hair as the knock on the door came.
"Michelle," said the voice of Rita, "the car is here."
As they left the room they both still felt slightly dazed,
as they followed Rita. Barry greeted them with a smile. As they
left, Valerie watched from the window at them holding hands. She
smiled. Perhaps.
Charlie stepped out of the Mercedes, and looked back as
Michelle smiled and waved. He blew a kiss. "Speak soon princess."
She raised the window, and Barry accelerated away.
Charlie opened the front door. Music blaring, Nikki dancing
around the kitchen was the last thing he needed.
She looked up and smiled. "I'm going to the pub," he said.
She put her thumb up. He left as soon as he had walked in.
He took out his phone. "Fancy a pint?"
The reply was almost instant. "I will get them in."
He smiled. Callum must have had a bad day. "See you in
ten." Another thumbs up. But this time, one he didn't mind seeing.

19 "MICHELLES CONFESSION"

Michelle got home to find the Aston not back yet. A huge relief enveloped her as she swept in. Her peace was shattered all too quickly as she heard the Aston, angry, hard and approaching fast. She quickly kicked off her shoes. Poured wine, and flicked on the TV.

Tommy threw the front door open, it crashed loudly, and Michelle jumped. "I've DONE IT!" he bellowed.

She looked confused. "Done what baby?" Trying to gauge his mood.

He smiled. It was a menacing, deep, powerful smile. "The biggest fucking deal this place has ever seen." And his head fell back as he roared with laughter. "Get me a drink, Giles and Valerie will be here around 7, I want a decent takeaway from that Indian place and plenty of good wine, it's time to CELEBRATE!"

Michelle smiled, and threw her arms around him. "I'm so pleased for you!" she said through a fake smile. She knew full well, and with some trepidation, that this deal wasn't anything to do with business. Whatever it was, was dark, dangerous, and she didn't like it one bit.

She poured the wine and gave him the glass. He drained it, and shouted, "I'm going for a shower." He ran up the stairs. As he did so her phone lit up.

"Don't worry, you were with me all day, OK."

Michelle grinned. A simple reply. "Thank you, see you at 7."

She sent another message, via Dial Chat. Another simple thing. "Thank you."

The reply didn't come immediately. She checked back, and couldn't stop looking at her phone, when she heard, "Your turn!" from upstairs. She froze.

And suddenly the response came. "I loved it. I love your company, I love your story, and I could fall in love with you. I know you can't talk. But message when you can. X"

Her heart warmed. She sent one more. "I could fall too," and closed the phone.

7pm arrived. Valerie rang the bell, and, as Michelle opened the door to make sure she greeted her, Valerie simply said, "I hope you enjoyed, not a word now, they are too full of themselves." And she swept into the lobby, Giles followed, little out of breath.

He kissed Michelle on the hand, saying, "you look divine," and waddled after his wife.

Tommy boomed "HELLO GILES YOU OLD DEVIL!" and belly laughed like a comedian laughing at his own joke. "And how is the lovely Valerie?" he said sarcastically.

"Perfectly wonderful," she returned, and shot him a glare.

Tommy laughed again, "get the wine would you Michelle," as he ushered the guests to the dining room.

Michelle muttered, "what am I a fucking waitress?" as she heard Giles join the laughter. It was going to be a *long* night. She saw her phone and opened Dial Chat.

"I have company tonight, but I'm thinking of you." And she replaced it on the side. It lit up immediately.

"Where is that bloody wine woman?" Tommy laughed.

"Coming baby!" and she chinked the glasses.

She opened her phone again. Read the message, "Be safe, I'm still here." She smiled. Felt a warmth inside her, and carried the wine into the room. As the evening wore on, Michelle got less and less interested. Valerie could see it too. And, after the takeaway had been demolished by the men, and picked at by the women, Valerie suggested the men retire to the den and chat "men chat."

The two men, full of both themselves, and Indian food, readily agreed, and Valerie ordered, "Michelle, get the rum, and the scotch, let's let these hot shots chew the fat, whilst we watch a girly movie." She winked. Both men missed the point completely and wandered off to the cinema room, which Tommy had dubbed the "den".

Michelle once again became a waitress, but this time couldn't wait to deliver her cargo. She smiled as she dropped the bottles and two crystal tumblers. "The ice is in the bucket," she announced, and closed the door as the two men whooped with laughter.

She went back to the living room. "Shut the door,'' Valerie demanded, "and tell me all."

Michelle said, "Well, you know we came to the spa."

"No, you silly cow," Valerie laughed, "tell me *all*"

Michelle went red, she hung her head. "I will tell you what I think you need to know. I can't tell all, because the truth is, I can't remember them all, and if I did, I think I would be physically sick." She drained her glass, "I need another bottle." Valerie looked at her friend and wondered just how deep things had got for Michelle. She was about to find out. Michelle came back from the kitchen. A Sauvignon and a Rose Pinot. "OK," she stated. "Don't judge me." And for the next 2 hours or so, she told all, or at least all she could remember. Told of debauched afternoons, with men, sometimes 2 or 3 men. Of being an unpaid whore. Of feeling so low about herself once it was over she had showered and scrubbed her skin till it was red. But, of the absolute high she had got the more she did it. The further and deeper her sleaze got, the more she liked it. Yet, slowly, she had realised it was nothing more than an addiction. The same as Tommy had with cocaine. (Yes she knew, but she didn't care.) All the time, Valerie barely spoke. She nodded now and again. She shook her head. She looked shocked.

But she didn't interrupt. When finally Michelle described the sweat smelling last encounter in detail, she burst into tears.

Valerie held her and passed her a tissue. "Wow!" was her response. "No wonder you could cope with Jamie and what I told you." She looked at her friend. "What now? What about Charlie?" What about Tommy?"

Michelle looked at her friend. "I just don't know," she said. "We made love today, and I told him I loved him."

Valerie choked on her wine, "you did what!" she exclaimed.

"I know, I know, OK!" Michelle hung her head, then smiled, "but he said the same thing."

Valerie spat her wine out. "What the fuck!"

Michelle laughed. "Do you mind, that wine was bloody expensive!" and she grinned. "I know it isn't love" she went on, "but it's a feeling. It's a common need to feel something for a person. *He* felt it too. And I guess it came out as "I love you"" She took out her phone. As she did so, the door to the den opened, and Michelle froze.

"Need a piss!" came a slurred lazy voice.

"Are you OK baby?" she shrieked.

"MMMMMMMM" came the response.

She smiled, turned to Valerie, and said, "It won't be long till they are asleep."

"I'm not bloody surprised, she returned, "it's gone eleven, and they have done nothing but drink!" They both made small talk until Tommy closed the door to the den again. Michelle showed Valerie the Dial Chat messages. Valerie looked and smiled. "So woman, what now?"

Michelle shot her a glance. "Now," she said boldly "now I see how much he is full of bullshit, or if he *really* means it."

Valerie thought for a moment. "Isn't it all a bit sudden?" she remarked, with more than an element of doubt in her voice.

"YES!" Michelle shrieked again.

Valerie laughed, "you always squeak when you get het up."

Michelle went red, she knew she was right, but she continued in her high pitched squeak "of *course* it's too soon, too sudden, and too much, but I *desperately* need to break the awful cycle of cheap shit slut sex, and at least if I'm going to have another man, I want it to be just one, and I think he wants just one woman too."

Valerie looked more serious. "You know he has a son, and an ex, and has been alone a long time."

"How do you know so much about him?" Michelle asked.

"You don't think I was going to give a seventy grand Maserati to just anyone do you!" she grinned, "I had him checked out."

"You bitch," Michelle laughed, "you sly cow!"

Valerie enjoyed the banter, "I may be a sly cow, but ..." she paused, partly for effect, and partly because she wasn't quite sure if she should say too much just yet.

"But?" Michelle asked.

"But you could do an awful lot worse."

"What does that mean?" Michelle didn't understand.

"He is very sound that's all," Valerie smiled. "We don't all have to drive an Aston Martin to *show* people how wealthy we are," and she winked. "He has worked hard, and is a very shrewd businessman by all accounts"

Michelle still didn't quite understand. "How do you know all this?"

"I have my sources," Valerie said, "and I just want you to be OK."

"Thank you," she returned. "Truth is, he is a nice guy, that's all, and I haven't *had* to fuck him, I *wanted* to." I could quit that shit website right now. And it's not for love, it's because he makes me feel good about myself."

"So quit, *now,*" and Valerie picked up Michelle's phone and handed it to her. "Do it now!"

A sudden panic came over Michelle. "*Really?*" she said. "*Really,*" Valerie said with a steely tone. Michelle opened her phone. Within seconds she had loaded the site. She clicked on her profile. "Let me see," Valerie said.

Michelle felt the shame once more.

She gave her phone to Valerie. "Shit girl, you certainly went for it didn't you!" as she flicked through the hundreds of photos, none showing Michelle's face, but definitely showing every other part of her body, and in detail. "How many guys have you fucked?" Valerie asked.

"I don't know," was the mumbled reply, "but it's too many." She took the phone back, and clicked, "delete account". With a final "are you sure?" she clicked yes, and Valerie saw her shoulders visibly drop.

"What was that for?" she asked. "Are you disappointed you have just quit?"

"NO!" Michelle barked back, "it's the fucking relief. Charlie may not end up being the answer, but, right now, between you and him, I *needed* to quit, and I can only do it with your help."

Valerie smiled. "I bet he knows nothing about it though."

Michelle reddened, "no, right now, he knows nothing," she looked embarrassed. "How do I tell a man I really like all that shit?"

"Slowly," came the measured response. "Give him time to absorb little bits. She looked at the clock. Midnight. "I am pretty sure those two won't be coming out of there now. Do you want to call it a night? Or are you OK?"

The truth was Michelle was both drained and buzzing. "I don't know that either," she laughed, today and the emotions have all been a bit of a whirlwind, and I haven't been able to think logically at all."

"Then you have your answer," Valerie smiled, "let's call it a night."

Michelle was relieved, yet also had so many thoughts running around her head. But she knew they could wait until morning. "I will get a couple of blankets for sleeping beauty and his partner," and she disappeared.

Valerie grabbed Michelle's phone. Shit, locked! She would need to know a little more before Michelle would give up her password. She was sure of that, but she definitely wanted to know more about Charlie, and that bloody website! Jamie may be gone, but her sex life had gone with it, and, whilst she wasn't planning on doing what Michelle had been doing, she could always use a nice hard cock once in a while! She smiled.

Michelle went to the den and returned. "Let's go to bed, we have all day tomorrow." The two women padded up the stairs. Valerie knew the guest room would be immaculate and said her goodnight to Michelle before retiring into bed. Michelle brushed her teeth, and was asleep almost as soon as her head hit the pillow. Valerie couldn't sleep, her mind was racing. She was pleased Michelle had quit the site. Having seen what she had been offering and displaying of herself, she couldn't be anything but pleased. But what now? It was all too much too soon it seemed. She closed her eyes on that thought. And wanted the morning to come.

The day dawned. Uncanny how the two women seemed to wake almost at the same time. And met on the landing.

"Coffee?" Michelle asked.

"*Of course!*" Valerie replied. "But first, what are you going to do about Charlie?"

Michelle was taken aback by the question. "*What?*" she replied, "Tommy might hear!"

Valerie laughed, "they were so smashed last night they won't be up for hours."

Michelle knew she was right, but it was a way of avoiding the question. "I don't know,'' she answered. "I like him. A lot!"

Valerie shot her a glance. "You hardly know him."

159

Michelle snapped, unintentionally really, but she felt defenceless, "how long had you known Jamie?" she barked.

"Calm down" Valerie smiled, "I'm just saying take it slow that's all."

"I'm sorry," Michelle replied, "I *know* I shouldn't be feeling anything, especially with all I have done in the last few years, but I *like* him, it just *feels* different," as she spoke, she could feel the tears building. They ran from her eyes. Not deep sobs, but more because she felt the shame of what she had been doing for the last few years.

Valerie looked at her. "Pull yourself together," she said. "He is a nice guy, and perhaps there may be something between you. But I honestly think right now, he has just made you see what a slut you have been."

Michelle began to argue, then her head fell, because she knew Valerie was right. "Yes,'' she mumbled. "That's pretty much it. I have seen me from a side I really don't like, and realised one *nice* guy is perhaps what I needed from the start."

Valerie looked at her, perhaps a little more sympathetically now. "I am not here to judge you, I'm here to listen and be your friend. I know how it feels to love another man, and I know how good it feels to be wanted and desired, so I can hardly judge you for fucking Charlie. But I can judge you for the other stuff! Have some respect for yourself. And I know Tommy is an arsehole who treats you like shit. But fucking random people doesn't fix that. Charlie might."

Michelle stopped crying and listened. She responded with a simple, "I know."

Valerie continued. "Then let things develop *slowly.*" Don't hang everything on him, but, *do* enjoy *just* him. And be very, very careful! Tommy is a violent angry man now, the drugs, the booze, and whatever deals he seems to have been doing have made sure of that. So don't overstep things until you are sure."

Michelle looked totally shell shocked.

"You don't *know?*" Valerie said.

"Of course I know," she replied. "I guess it's just the first time anyone has said it to me."

Valerie smiled. "It's a bit of a shock when you realise your husband is both a dealer and a user eh? Not that I know, Giles would never touch the stuff, but he enjoys having that power. Exploiting people's weaknesses. In Tommy he has both. Someone who can do all the deals and piss with the big boys, but also, he still has that weak side of him. To be desperate for the drugs." It was the first time the women had spoken openly.

"I know Tommy can't get off the coke, and I know about some of the deals, but I choose not to know about all of it. But, just lately, he has changed. His personality; he is more aggressive, more angry, more threatening. I'm just a little scared."

Valerie listened. "I guess I don't have that. Giles is a pussy with drugs. But he knows enough people to get violent in his own way over money especially." Just as she opened her mouth to continue, they both were startled by a massive yawn from the den.

"Bollocks!" Michelle exclaimed. "they are awake."

Valerie laughed, "time to be the doting wifey," she smirked. "Let's get coffee on, and lots of sugar."

A couple of hours later, as they both cleared away the breakfast and coffee chinaware, the men having gone into the garden, Valerie had time to say, "enjoy Charlie, just take it slow." Before Giles appeared booming, "come on Darling, this won't buy the baby a new bonnet!" and he leaned back as he roared with laughter. "See you for golf later today Tommy old boy!" Michelle saw the wink from Valerie as she closed the front door. Michelle smiled inside. Tommy was on the phone.

She opened Dial Chat. "Want to say hi this afternoon?"

The reply was instant. "What time?"

"2pm," she replied. "And bring the Maserati, it's more discreet."

Charlie grinned. How the hell she thought the Maserati was discreet he had no idea. "See you at two, meet me at the garage." "OK."

They both smiled.

Tommy ended the call. "Going for a bath," he said, "they are cleaning the Aston in 30 mins," and he walked up the stairs.

"OK baby," she muttered. All she could think of in her head was Charlie. She *knew* it was crazy, but she also knew she *felt* something. Something *much* deeper than the cheap sex she had been used to. Something she never really thought she had needed, but that, having experienced the feeling, she both wanted and craved in equal measure.

Opening her phone, Dial Chat, "I can't wait to see you. Can we just drive?" She closed the phone again.

She knew Tommy was so precious about the bloody Aston that he wouldn't be long. Sure enough, he shouted, "don't let them start without me there!"

"I won't!" promised Michelle.

She opened her phone. "Sure. We can just drive, I'd like that," she smiled.

Shit, she must stop doing that, Tommy would see her one day she was sure of that! "See you at two" and she closed the phone.

Tommy came down, just as the van pulled into the drive. Her husband still knew how to dress; shorts, cream, tailored, a dark blue shirt, and blue boat shoes. He opened the door, saw the driver, and smiled. "Joe my old son, at least she will get a proper job today!" and he shook the hand of a scrawny young individual.

"I will make sure of that sir," he replied.

"Call me Tommy," he said, "want a coffee?"

"That would be great, one sugar please."

Tommy turned, "Michelle, make two coffee's, white with one please!"

"OK baby," she tried to mask her feeling of being used as she did his bidding. She knew she was just bitching about him. But it made her all the more determined to make today happen with Charlie. She returned with the drinks, handed them to her husband, and said, "I'm going for a bath."

Tommy wasn't listening. He was deep in discussion with scrawny Joe about what he wanted from the clean. She heard, "I know it won't be perfect, I'm on a time limit today."

"No problem er, Tommy. Leave it to me." And the two men chatted about cars as Joe got to work.

The sun was warm, Tommy was out to impress, and she dreaded the question asking her if she would come to the club. She knew she would have to go, but later, when they had finished. She had at least 4 hours alone. As she got out of the bath, she realised how long she had been in there. She heard Tommy saying goodbye to scrawny Joe. And the water was cold. Shit, how long had she slept!

Tommy closed the door. "Michelle!" he boomed.

"Just getting out," she replied. Her voice was shaky, she was freezing!

Quickly wrapping herself up in her dressing gown, she let the water out, as he opened the door. "I am off to the club, are you coming?"

"No thanks, she replied, "but I will come down later if that's ok?"

"Whatever," he snapped. He knew she didn't much care for the club. But he wanted his "prize" there.

"Good luck," she mumbled.

"Thanks," he said as he slammed the door. She heard the car start. No matter how many times she heard it, it was so loud. She smiled.

Found her phone, and typed, "Thirty mins."

Instantly, "OK."

And she immediately felt warm and the pang of butterflies in her stomach. Thirty minutes later she was standing just around the corner from the small village garage. Certainly not dressed to kill. Just dressed to talk. She heard the car long before she saw it, and began to realise a Maserati may not be as discreet as she perhaps needed. Charlie swung into the small gateway and she jumped in. "Let's go," she said and pulled her cap down until, in a very short space of time, they had left the village and were heading north, well away from home, golf, and anything to do with the place. As they drove, she talked, she couldn't stop herself. She wasn't going to tell all. But she needed to let Charlie into what her home had become, Tommy especially. The anger, the fear she felt. And she began to let Charlie into her sordid past. Very slowly. But she figured if this man wanted her, he needed to know some. She had been planning the conversation almost since they had met. But knew she had to balance the truth, with keeping him at least interested. She just talked, fast, without structure and without balance. And as she built to tell Charlie about joining the website, both her mind and her eyes exploded. Charlie panicked. Michelle sobbed. Huge deep sobs of regret. She had opened the sex box, and now didn't want to say anymore.

Charlie found a lay-by and pulled over. He cradled her in his arms and let her cry. "Hey princess," he soothed, "where has all this come from?" Michelle could say nothing. Whilst her tears had stopped, her mind had not. And she was now fearful of what to do next. She sat. Silent. And gazed into space. Charlie didn't quite know what to do. "Are you ok?" he whispered.

"Yes," she said meekly. "Can we find a pub? I need a drink."

He smiled. Started the engine, "coming up princess!"

"Thank you."

Charlie floored the accelerator and the Maserati growled as he encouraged the beast to waken. Within a short space of time, and it seemed all too easily, Charlie pulled into a small but old fashioned country pub. He opened the door. "Sauvignon princess?" he smiled.

"Yes please, large!" "And can we eat?"

He laughed, "You want it all!" He smiled with his hands on his hips. "Go find a seat in the garden, I will bring you a wine, and we can see what they do.''

She looked up at him, and felt a warmth, a safety. "Thank you," she said again. And wandered into the garden as he stepped inside the low doorway. She was relieved to find the garden empty.

Making sure she chose a table furthest away, she sat and looked longingly at the door. Charlie appeared quite quickly, blinking into the sunlight. He carried the pint and the wine carefully and sat down. Michelle smiled and grabbed the glass. Taking a huge swig, Charlie saw her shoulders slump. And she smiled and said, "God I needed that."

He took a sip from his pint. "Gonna tell me what that was all about?" he questioned.

Michelle drained her glass. "Get me another, and I will explain as much as I can, and as much I feel comfortable to."

He looked at her, a little worried, picked up the glass, and said, "I will be back in a minute princess."

When he returned, Michelle was calmer and had composed herself. "OK, sit down," she demanded. "What I am about to tell you isn't pretty, but it is what it is." She slowly let Charlie have the full force of the last four years, the websites, the men, the sometimes awful experiences, the lows, the occasional highs too. And she hung her head in shame. "I need you to know who I was."

"Who you *were!*" he looked puzzled.

"Yes!" she almost screamed. "I don't want to be that person anymore. And I know us is a total whirlwind, but I feel a connection with you that has already led me to stop going onto the sites. I know it's crazy, and I know I behaved like a slut, but you must believe me. I don't want to be that person. I needed a reason to escape from all that crap. And I know I'm married, and I shouldn't even be here, but I don't love Tommy anymore. He is a monster and I just want to be me." She could feel herself get emotional again. And, whilst she fought it, the tears came.

Charlie sat quietly and took her into his arms. "Easy now princess," he said softly. "We all have a past, and have done things we are not proud of. Believe me, I have a closet that I don't want to open either."

She looked up at him. "I don't know how you do it?" she puzzled, "but I really love the fact you are still sitting here."

Charlie smiled. "Don't drink that one so fast woman, you will be smashed!"

Michelle smiled. "I know," she said as she took another swing of the wine. "so, I guess this is the part where you tell the slut to piss off and I never see you again."

Charlie smiled. "Why would I do that?" he said through a cheesy smile. "I have sex on a plate, who would turn that down!" And he laughed out loud.

"You bastard!" she smiled, seeing the fact he was joking, and hitting him gently on the arm.

"We all have a past princess," it was his turn to allow his face to fall.

"Tell me" she said immediately. The laughter ended suddenly for them both.

"My ex and I used to swing.'' He bowed his head as he said it.

Michelle choked on her wine. "Fuck!" she exclaimed, "I didn't see that coming."

Charlie sighed, "not many people know, it's hardly what you would announce at a dinner party is it?"

Michelle laughed, "unless all your keys are already in the bowl," she smirked.

He carried on. "It wasn't a hard and fast thing. My ex, Nikki and I were at a party one night, it was a long while after Marina and I had split. We both got pissed, and needed to have a play with each other. Went upstairs, found a bedroom, and went in. There was another couple in there, already at it. Nikki and I were too pissed and too horny to care, so we stripped and started to play on the floor. As it went on, the other couple joined us. And well, the rest is history." He hung his head in shame.

Michelle didn't know what to say. After all her revelations, she thought he would never want to see her again. Yet here she was, wondering if she actually wanted to see this man again. "What happened?" she enquired.

"We saw each other for a couple of years I guess. Nothing concrete, no love, but a good time and the odd night at a swingers club. Then she got deeper into it, wanted more. Had read a book called First Tango in Paris. Wanted gangbangs and more and more risk. I had had enough. So we split."

"WOW!" Michelle exclaimed. "I had no idea."

"I'm not exactly proud of it, and wouldn't go singing it from the rooftops."

Michelle laughed. "I would love to see that," she beamed.

He felt better it was out. Managed a weak smile, and said, "well, you know it all now."

"As do you," she returned. "The question is, where do we go from here?"

They spent another hour or so making small talk. Walking on eggshells about their sexual past. Like boxers dancing around each other, neither one ready to land a punch. She said "I'm really sorry, I have to get back soon. He is expecting me at the club. Some bloody important "do" that, to be honest, I could do without, but he will want his trophy there."

"No problem," Charlie replied. He finished his pint, and said, "your carriage awaits princess!"

They drove back in almost silence. It had been an afternoon of revelations, and one that both would need some time to process and understand. Charlie felt it best not to admit Nikki was currently residing under his roof since her flat caught fire. They arrived back at the small lane near the garage.

She kissed him on the cheek. "Thank you for a wonderful afternoon," she said.

"My pleasure" he returned. And they parted. It seemed almost an anti-climax to end the day on such a low note. He drove back home, fast and angry. Needing to use the car to get the emotions out of him. She walked back home. Head down. Lost in thought. Wondering what on earth the next day would bring.

20 "DON'T SET THE FUCKING ALARM OFF"

As the late summer approached, Tommy became deeper and deeper involved with the club. Both the golf club with Giles, and his own club. Staying nights and coming home in a strange state. More abusive, yet also more attentive. Depending Michelle assumed, on what he had taken or drunk the night before. She felt more scared of him, and was never entirely sure how he would be. Not that he seemed to care. He seemed to have an ability to switch on a "persona" that meant he came across as the loud and brash Tommy everyone knew. A laugh, always life and soul. Yet with a dark side that only she saw, (and she assumed his enemies did too) he could be a vicious and angry man when provoked. The man she had fallen in love with had long disappeared, and she couldn't talk to him about it, and neither did she want to. He had come close to beating her once, when she mentioned the drugs, she had never done it again. And now, with Charlie in her life, and her own addiction to sex slowly fading into the background, she vowed that somehow, either with or without Charlie, she was not going to spend the next 20 years of her life with a monster.

"I won't be back for a few days," he bellowed. "Giles and I have some stuff to attend to in Brazil. I didn't think you would want to come, business and all that, and Valerie definitely wasn't interested in coming, so Giles thought maybe you two could use the house on the coast?"

She hated being told what to do! "OK," Michelle mumbled, "that sounds nice." Trying desperately not to sound relieved he was going, and also excited for a potential to have some time with Charlie.

"Giles is picking me up at 3. Plane is at 7."

Michelle beamed as she stepped into the garden. She looked at the time, it was midday. Perfect. "I'm going to pack," he shouted.

She didn't respond. Her phone was already in her hand. "Is it true?" She sent a short message to Valerie.

Instantly the answer "Giles is packing now!"

"What do we do?" Michelle's fingers ran across the screen expertly.

"I know *who* you want to do!" came the sarcastic answer.

"Too bloody right!" was the message she sent back. "But the men expect us to stay at the house in Littlehampton?"

"Leave it with me" Valerie sent back. "I am sure we can make something happen for the both of us."

Michelle fell back against the fence and took a deep breath of the warm summer air. Tommy looked out of the window. He opened it and bellowed, "ARE YOU OK?"

Michelle jumped. Looking up she said "I'm fine, why?"

"I thought I saw you fall," he enquired.

"Oh no," she said, "I just took a deep breath of the beautiful air and it made my head rush a little!"

He smiled, thinking of his own rush last night. That hot little cleaner did have a great arse, but she gave an even better blow job. "OK," he replied, "take it easy."

The next couple of hours dragged. Eventually Michelle heard the Bentley pull into the drive. Tommy almost ran to the door. Michelle had never seen him quite so animated. She had no idea why, and didn't care, she just wanted him gone. He carried the small black case, and another larger one. He turned, kissed her cheek, and said, "now be a good girl while I am away," and without a look back, he climbed into the car.

She closed the door, and for the second time that day, took a huge breath. Almost immediately her phone lit up. "I'm coming over," Michelle smiled. Valerie had wasted no time. As they enjoyed a Chinese and bottle of wine, the two women chatted. A friendly chat really. Getting to know each other a little more. And without too much thought for both their slightly sordid recent pasts. Eventually, the subject got to the house on the coast. "I will give you the keys," Valerie said. "But, you will only have one day before I will come down. I can hide the CCTV for a day, but after that, if Giles checks, I will need to be around."

"You would do that for me?" Michelle asked.

"Of course I would," she replied, "you have helped me."

Michelle blushed. "I am sorry you know," she said and looked down, "I have no idea how we got here, but I'm also very sorry I misjudged you so badly"

Valerie laughed out loud. "You mean you always thought I was some stuck up cow who had no time for anyone?"

Michelle smiled. "Yes I guess that's it."

Valerie laughed again. "I like to keep a distance. It means I can watch and take it all in. Unfortunately, (don't take that the wrong way) you caught me with my guard down. And I guess I needed a friend, but didn't realise it until that moment."

Michelle smiled. "And of course, you thought I was having an affair, so you could talk to me."

"You were having a lot more than an affair," Valerie laughed, "but perhaps now is your time."

"Perhaps," Michelle replied wistfully. "What do you think the boys are up to?" Michelle enquired.

"I don't want to know," Valerie replied.

"Neither do I," they laughed and chatted as the evening wore on.

Michelle sent a Dial Chat. "I have a friend who has let me use her house for tomorrow, just us two, but we *only* have 24hrs, can you make it?"

Valerie smiled. "I can see the feelings when you type," she commented.

Michelle blushed. "I like him," she said.

"I can see."

The phone lit up. "It's a bit short notice!" Michelle felt deflated. "Let me move a few things if I can."

"Bollocks!" Michelle said out loud.

Valerie took the phone. She read what Charlie had written. She smiled. "He will be there."

Michelle looked surprised. "How do you know?"

"Because who the hell can move things around at seven pm for the next day?"

Michelle smiled. "You have a point, he is a bastard!" she laughed.

As she did, the Dial Chat came back, "what time?"

"Five am!"

And immediately, "shit really?"

She laughed again. "Really!" "See you at five!"

Valerie smiled too. "Well it's time I wasn't here," she said. "You need a good night's sleep and these," and she rummaged in her bag and produced a set of keys and a fob. "Just touch the fob on the panel as you go in, same to leave. You have all day tomorrow, and tomorrow night. I will be there the following morning, so make the most of it!" And she grabbed her jacket and got up to leave.

As she did, Michelle stood and her eyes filled with tears. "Thank you!" she blubbed.

"Oh pull yourself together woman," Valerie smiled. "Enjoy, and don't set the fucking alarm off!" And she closed the front door, she felt good inside. She had experienced a wonderful time for the last thirteen years. Perhaps it was time for Michelle to feel something similar.

Michelle was awake from four. Her heart was racing, her mind racing even faster. She rushed around checking and changing outfits, selecting knickers, deselecting shoes. Her phoned pinged.

The message read, "good luck!"

Michelle stopped, she smiled and replied. "Thank you!" and looked around.

She needed little in the way of clothing. Throwing a few things in a bag, she set the alarm, and left the house. Within a few minutes she was around the corner from the small garage. No David there at 4.45am, she smiled to herself, she liked David. As she looked up, she heard an engine, but saw nothing. Then the soft glow of a car's lights, not bright like head lights. The Z4 appeared and she opened the door. "The boot is open," she smiled, threw her bag in the boot, and got in. Charlie grinned and kissed her.

"Not here" she snapped.

"Who the fuck is going to see us at 5am!" he laughed.

He had a point, but she wasn't going to let him know that. "That's not the point and you know it," she smiled as the words came out. Trying to keep a straight face had proved impossible.

Charlie grinned. "So where are we going at this ungodly hour princess."

"Don't laugh," she said, "Littlehampton!"

Charlie did indeed laugh. "Hardly St Tropez is it?" He beamed.

"No," she said, "but it's free, it's quiet, and it's ours for today and tonight so be grateful!"

"I am!" he said, and pressed the pedal a little harder. As they drove, they talked. About his love of country, rock n roll, and generally being an "old git" as he described himself. She opened up even more about her younger self. Telling him that singing had been her only love.

And treating him to a few songs as they drove. As they approached the coast, Charlie pulled into a lay-by.

"What's wrong?" Michelle enquired.

"Nothing is wrong princess," he replied, "but just look at that sunrise!"

Michelle turned, and was taken by surprise at the sheer beauty. She enjoyed nature, but since her "crazy" time had started, she had paid so little attention to anything, let alone nature. "It's beautiful," she said softly.

As she did so, he put his arms around her and kissed her neck. "Cheesy, but you are too."

She snuggled in to the warmth. "You old smoothie," she smiled.

Charlie said, "let me take a photo of you with the sunrise." She put on her best model pose, and pouted. "Not like that!" he laughed.

"More attitude dahhhling?"

He threw his head back laughing, "oh yes baby, he played along, "work it!" He took a few shots.

Then she stole his phone, and shouted, "Oh MY GOD I look so old!"

He took the phone back, flicked through the ten or so pics, and showed her the one natural photo. "You look stunning," he said.

"Thank you," she looked down, feeling a little embarrassed.

He continued, "I love your curls, and I love your smile." Michelle went red. "I love your arse too," he winked.

She slapped him playfully on the arm. "Well, get me to the seaside and then I might let you see some more!" she squealed excitedly. They got back into the car, and despite the cold, Charlie decided to lower the roof. She looked at him, incredulous. "*Are you serious!*"

He smiled. Flicked the heated seats on, and smiled at her again, "yup, I sure am!" She could feel her backside warming as they drove. It was cold around her shoulders, but she was at peace with both herself and the situation. They laughed, and as the sea got closer, they both took a little time to just enjoy the view. They swung into the secluded driveway. After two or three hundred yards, it opened out into a courtyard revealing a relatively small bungalow. Looking a little ramshackle, but with new windows, doors, and roof. "Is this the place?" Charlie asked.

"Don't be fooled by the outside," Michelle smiled. She opened the door, clicked the fob on the panel, and silenced the alarm. The outside of the house displayed nothing of the beautiful interior. Michelle had never been here before, but she had spoken to Valerie about it on the odd occasion when the men had "gone to the coast." Valerie had told her that inside it was immaculate. Giles liked to keep the outside a little low key, it meant no one was interested in the place, she was right. It had 3 bedrooms, all en-suite. An open plan kitchen, and a beautiful living room. The open fire was no longer in use, Giles didn't want the attention, but there was an electric fire looking like a log fire in its place.

Charlie smiled. "This is a bit of alright!"

Michelle grinned. "You have such a way with words," she laughed.

He stood in front of her. "I do," he said, "I really like you Michelle." And he leaned forward and kissed her, gently, and softly. With a warmth that she could *feel*. She allowed herself to fall into his arms. They stood, just enjoying the peace and the comfort and warmth of each other. Slowly, they kissed again. Their tongues and hands suddenly becoming urgent and wanting to explore each other. They had barely got inside, and the realisation slowly dawned. Charlie pulled away. "There is no need to rush," he said, "we have all day and night!"

Michelle glared at him. "We do," she said sternly.

"But I want you now, *and* all day and all night!" And she grabbed his hand and led him off to the nearest door. Living room. Bollocks! She tried another door. Spacious bedroom, perfect! "Come here you delicious man."

Charlie smiled. "OK, if you insist," he said with a tongue-in-cheek dour tone. He rolled his eyes into his head.

She bit his neck, and undid his jeans. "Make love to me Charlie, please." And she kissed him as she released him.

He stopped her. "My turn princess," and kissed her mouth. She felt fuzzy inside. And he slowly stripped her. Taking her naked body in his arms, he carried her to the bed. He gently laid her down, and began to undress. She watched him intently. He was hard now. And despite his age, his slight beer belly, his body looked good. He climbed in beside her. She moved to lay her head on his chest. And they lay. Quiet. Soft warm flesh against one another. He held her tight. And they began to explore. A new slow, sensual voyage of discovery, without interruption, or time restrictions. It became a sensual meeting of mind and body that took them both to the edge of sexual pleasure. They simply allowed themselves to let go and just become one. It was a heady mix of sex, urgent raw exploiting of bodies, his cock fucking her mouth so hard she almost choked, yet also a tenderness when he entered her and made love to her so softly and gently she lost her mind, and as her orgasm came, she simply forgot where she was. It was something so powerful she couldn't speak, she simply let herself be carried on the wave of sexual pleasure. Charlie held her as her body convulsed and he gently kissed her neck. "You ok princess?"

She could barely speak. "I'm ok," she said breathlessly.

"Rest now," he said in a soft tone. She wanted to argue. To insist he let her pleasure him to orgasm, but her body and mind felt spent. As he lay down, she put her head on his chest. And gently she closed her eyes. It was beautiful, something she had rarely experienced in life. And this man made her feel amazing. She liked the feeling a lot. She liked him a lot. She ... did she? Her mind pondered love as her eyes closed, soon she fell into sleep. And he softly played with her hair. She felt safe. Warm, pleasured, *loved*. He watched her sleep. His mind also racing. He knew that what he felt for this woman was dangerous. She was married; married to a man who had a nasty reputation depending on who you believed. But despite all of that, he liked her. He *really* liked her. He moved his arm. Cradled her gently, and slowly allowed himself to fall into sleep. As he drifted off, he glanced at the clock, it was barely 10am. He smiled. They had all day, and all night. It was a good feeling. He kissed her neck, and closed his eyes.

She woke up with a start. Just a little unfamiliar with her surroundings. It quickly all came back and she smiled thinking of the pleasure. She looked at him and he softly snored. Relaxed. She got out of bed as quietly as she could. Needing to pee, naked she padded out of the room. After she had relieved herself, she came back.   Only to find Charlie awake and smiling. "Hello princess," he beamed.

"Hello you," she replied. And suddenly felt self-conscious.

He looked at her naked body. "God you are gorgeous" he exclaimed.

And as she sat next to him he ran his hands over her smooth skin. "So, what do we do now?" she enquired.

"Now we have lunch," he replied. "I want a pint and something to eat!"

She raised her eyes. "OK," she laughed, "come on!" and she moved to recover her clothes.

"Then I want afters," he grinned.

"Only if you are a good boy," she returned.

They got into the car. Charlie set the sat nav, and within 10 minutes they were in the little town. With its harbour, and beautiful boutiques, fine restaurants, and bustling community, it was perfect to have a little "life" but be far enough away for no one to look at them. She held his arm as they stepped into the nicely presented restaurant. "Table for two?" Charlie enquired.

"Certainly sir," and they were ushered to a vacant table near the window. The waiter pulled back the chair and Michelle sat. "Can I get you something to drink?" the small man with a pointy nose enquired.

"Can I have the wine list please?" Charlie asked.

"Certainly sir," and off he went.

Charlie sat. "This is nice," he observed.

Michelle laughed. "*Nice!*" she exclaimed.

"Yeah, *nice,*" he laughed. And as he did so, the waiter returned. Charlie picked a light Pinot Grigio, and they studied the menu. Crab and chilli linguine, and a sea bass for her.

"At least we will both have fishy breath," she laughed. Charlie smiled, he felt good. Michelle looked good. And he told her so. She blushed. "Thank you." And for the next couple of hours, they laughed, they ate, they smiled, they drank, and they learned more about the person they were with. She quizzed him discreetly over the swinging. And what happened to the woman it had all started with.

He took a big swig of wine. "OK, he said, "I need to tell you something."

Michelle looked panicked. "*What is it?*" she breathed.

"I have a house guest right now." Michelle glared. She guessed what was coming next. "It's my ex, Nikki."

Michelle almost spat out her wine. Despite the fact she had a feeling what he was going to say, hearing it was still pretty rubbish. "OK," she said with a stare that would have made many lesser men wither, "tell me all."
Charlie decided there wasn't much point in covering anything up. So he let Michelle have all the truth. That she had organised a party at her flat for 4 couples. Sex, drugs and debauchery. However, it had gotten a little out of hand, and the candles she had used for both setting the mood and for lighting had actually set fire to the curtains, and the resulting blaze had left her temporarily homeless, not to mention eight people in the street naked that afternoon. She had no one else to turn to, so had asked if she could stay. Just until all the fuss had died down. Turned out two of the couples were not married to each other, and the resulting local paper photos meant she had to hide for fear of repercussions. Michelle didn't know whether to laugh or cry. But she was going to make him squirm just a little now.

Charlie looked down at his plate. "I know I should have told you. But what could I say?"

Michelle smiled. "You could have said what you just did." He looked crestfallen, she was right, of course. The one thing he had promised was no lies. He looked up, to see Michelle almost laughing. "It must have caused some shit!" she couldn't hold back anymore. Her shoulders chuckled and she gave him the most beautiful smile.

Without thinking he said "I adore your smile Michelle." She smiled even more broadly and he couldn't help it, he did the same, and they both had a quiet chuckle at the ridiculous situation his ex had found herself in. Pulling herself together Michelle asked, "so when will she be leaving?"

"Not soon enough," Charlie replied. "I can't wait to get rid of her I just don't know when her builders will be finished, she seems to think she's staying for ever and that's definitely not the case!"

"Too bloody right she is not!" said Michelle, "I want my claws in you and you have a house full of the ex girlfriend!" she continued, "we can't always come to Valerie's holiday home so what do we do Charlie because I can't stop seeing you and I want time with you?"

He smiled, "I will do my best to get rid of her I promise. For the short term I'm sure we can find a hotel and we can make this work. I want to keep seeing you Michelle," He looked up and beckoned the waiter, "can we have the bill please?" It duly arrived and he took her hand after handing over his card. He paid for the meal, left a tip, gave a compliment to the front of house and they went back to the car. "What would you like to do?" Charlie asked.

She said, "I'd like to walk with you, arm-in-arm and just take some time to enjoy each other."

"We can do that Princess," he smiled, and as they closed the doors he lowered the roof. "To the beach?" he questioned.

"To the beach!" she replied. A short drive later they were indeed walking arm-in-arm, both of them unsure as to which direction to take the conversation.

Charlie plucked up the courage to ask, "why me?"

She replied, "it's simple, I like you," she answered. "Why me?" she asked.

He said, "pretty much the same reasons. I never knew I liked you until you crashed into my car and at the same time Michelle you came into my life. And yes, I know you are married, I know who your husband is and I know what your husband does. For sure I know I'm playing with fire, but I also know I can't stop right now but I fully understand if you think it's too risky for you. All I can tell you is I'm not looking for just a bit of fun, I want to enjoy you and I know we talked about love but the truth is I genuinely feel something for you in a very short space of time." He took a deep breath.

She blushed and shivered slightly as the sun hid behind the clouds that had built in the sky. It turned a little colder and she could do nothing more than smile at the man whose company she was enjoying greatly. "I want to see more of you too Charlie, I

know this isn't going to be easy and I don't know where it's going, but I know right now that I
want to enjoy you and embrace wherever our journey takes us."
They did a big loop of the sand, before stopping at a small shop. The typical seaside "shit shop" as Charlie described it which sold everything from sticks of rock to fridge magnets but crucially tonight had a bottle of cheap white wine.

Charlie grabbed a white and a rosé. "Shall we go home princess?" He smiled.

"Yes, let's do that," she said and returned his beaming face. They made their way back to the car and within a short time were opening the front door.

As Michelle let herself in, her phone lit up. She glanced down, a message from Valerie.

"I hope all is OK, remember you only have tonight."

Michelle replied back, "everything is perfect and trust me I only need tonight."

The simple reply came back. "Enjoy girl" and the rest of the evening was spent doing a crossword, talking, laughing.

Michelle wanted to know more about Nikki. Charlie assured her there was nothing more to know. Michelle told him in no uncertain terms, "you need to get rid of that woman."

"I know," he replied, "trust me I will work on it and make it happen."

As the wine went down, the smiles went up, and as the darkness arrived Michelle kissed Charlie and said, "take me to bed."

They woke the next morning to a clear bright crisp summer's day. Michelle had already been up and had made coffee, and she brought it to Charlie with a smile and stood in front of him in a tiny house coat. He smiled, "you look stunning," he commented.

She blushed and said, "would you like some breakfast?"

He smiled a naughty mischievous smile. "What time is Valerie coming?"

She replied, "I have already had a text from her. She's on her way and will be here in about an hour."

Charlie grinned like a naughty school boy and said, "come and undo that coat, we have an hour!" They spent the next hour enjoying each other one last time until the realisation hit that Charlie would now have to leave and that for the next day or two there would be less contact. After they had both showered and dressed they heard the car pull into the drive. Charlie kissed Michelle softly and whispered gently into her ear, "I do love you so. I will see you in a few days."

Michelle fought back the tears. "I love you too Charlie, drive safely."

Charlie opened the door and greeted Valerie with a smile. "Have a great time ladies!" and he got into his car and pulled out of the drive.

Valerie stepped inside and as she did so she saw Michelle's tears. "OK, girl," she said, "it's time for some girly love now, make me a coffee and tell me all!"

She saw Michelle had her phone open and saw the hearts she was sending to Charlie. Michelle then put her phone to the side and said, "one sugar right?" as she went into the kitchen. Valerie picked up the phone, quickly browsed the Internet and looked at the history. As luck would have it she hadn't deleted it all, and there was the sex site that Valerie had decided she needed to explore. Michelle came back unexpectedly, "what are you doing?" she asked Valerie.

Valerie looked flushed. "I want you to tell me more about the site,"

Michelle laughed. "You don't really want to go there do you?"

Valerie looked at her. "I need it Michelle, I need something to help me cope."

Michelle couldn't hide her displeasure. But, as Valerie had said, she was big enough and ugly enough to know what she was doing. So, over the next hour Michelle helped Valerie create her account. "Pippa123" and told her "for a few days at least, don't put any photos up. Otherwise you will be inundated with idiots who just want to collect pictures." Michelle told her to create a fake email address and Valerie had her profile. Michelle kept trying to persuade her this wasn't the best way to deal with grief, but Valerie was insistent. She just needed her mind taken away from Jamie. Michelle told her she would be there to help and guide her. And it was done. The two women no longer talked about the sex site.

They decided that breakfast would be in town. Neither of them were going to cook this morning. So Valerie drove into the small town and they found a cafe overlooking the harbour.

"OK, so what's your next move?" Valerie asked Michelle.

"I have no idea," Michelle replied, "but I know I like him. I know I *more* than like him. Valerie, what am I going to do?"

"Well," Valerie smiled, "first of all, I assume he doesn't have a life threatening disease so if you really do like each other that much you need to decide what your long distance future may be, or, if it's just sex, enjoy it for what it is."

Michelle looked back at her friend and knew she was right, "I want him long term." Michelle replied.

Valerie said, "then you need to put some plans in place, *both* of you." Michelle then began to explain the bizarre story of Charlie's ex-girlfriend currently living with him and the reasons why. Valerie could do nothing but laugh, at just how ridiculous it sounded.

The weekend carried on in a similar vein, both women just enjoying each other's company. Sharing stories, talking about old times for Valerie with Jamie, and touching briefly on the subject of the site and what Valerie expected to get out of it. Michelle was still certain this was not a good idea but she was happy to support Valerie if that was what she wanted. After all she had been so kind to her. The subject inevitably drew back to their respective husbands, and also to Charlie. Michelle already knew she was in too deep, but she believed that Charlie felt the same and right now despite all of her luxuries, the only thing she had in her mind was making the most of her time with the man whose car she had hit! Valerie's own mind was still in turmoil but she was happy to see that Michelle could at least perhaps have some of the happiness. The same sort of feelings she had felt for those short wonderful years before Jamie had so sadly been taken from her. They ate, they drank, they enjoyed the beach, they enjoyed each other's company, and they even discussed what they would do If anything went wrong. The subject turned to what would happen if their husbands ever got caught.

Michelle piped up, "I think we should do a Thelma and Louise, just get in the car, pack a bag maybe go to the airport and run away! Take their money with us!"

Valerie laughed. "You don't think people would look for them or look for us?"

"I don't know," Michelle said, "it's just a pipe dream." And on the final evening sitting on the terrace with a glass of wine they both agreed that if ever that situation arose they would do exactly that. They chinked glasses for the last time that day and both went to bed smiling and in a good place.

Valerie opened her phone and opened the sex site. It was the first time she had actually gone back on the site since Michelle had helped her to create her profile. She just wanted to look, understand and observe. Valerie was an intelligent woman and certainly didn't need too much help navigating the rather basic and rather graphic site with its pictures and descriptions. She quickly realised she could narrow down her search by area and decided she would take a photo then and there. No face, so she posed as sexily as she thought she could, set the timer and took the photo. She was lying on the bed naked except for a thong. She bent her feet, pointed her toes, elegantly painted of course, and all you could see was up to her neck. She didn't bother opening any of the messages she saw. She had dozens already. She would come back to them, but for now some sleep and the prospect of a drive home in the morning.

The two women arrived home after a smooth and uneventful journey. Valerie dropped Michelle off, and as she entered the house she felt a huge sense of relief. She checked her phone, it was only just after 11am. Perfect. Tommy was not due back in the country until late afternoon, so she opened her Dial Chat and sent a message. "I'm back, how are you?" With that, she decided to unpack, put on her sweatpants and just chill. It had been a wonderful weekend with both her lover and what she had discovered was a very good friend.

The reply came back. "Hope you had a great time, I am at the garage, Callum needs a hand."

Michelle felt strangely disappointed but realised that this was her life now. If she needed any thrills that Charlie couldn't provide she was sure that with Valerie back on the site, her stories would be enough to make them a reality! She put the clothes in the machine, generally made sure the house was tidy, and then decided to go and see Charlie. As she got to the stables, the familiar feeling inside her stomach of joy, a little fear, a little nervous. This man had definitely kept on taking her by surprise and genuinely had taken her heart and her mind and right now she needed just a little piece of him before Tommy returned. She could hear the noise in the garage, stuck her head around a corner, tapped gently on the door and said, "shall I make a cup of tea?"

Both men smiled. Charlie turned, "that would be delicious!" he said "as are you."

Callum tutted, "you are so cheesy old man, how's the Challenger?" Callum shouted out.

Michelle returned "I'm not sure, Tommy seems to love it, and it's definitely pulling in the crowds at the club."

"Excellent!" came the reply from the depths of the car and Michelle walked up the stairs to the small office. Charlie couldn't resist looking at her arse and wolf whistling as she went. She smiled but didn't turn around. This was a very good feeling, one that she was enjoying very much, and one that she didn't want to lose. She spent no more than an hour there, there was nothing sexual. No intimacy other than a kiss on the cheek good-bye, as she knew she would have to be home and ready for Tommy. She parked the car, opened all the windows and doors, the sun was now warm, the day in the mid-seventies.

She hadn't heard from Tommy the whole time he had been away and neither did she expect to when suddenly there was a ping on her phone.

"We took an earlier flight, I will be home in 30 minutes."

It sounded like it was a warning, at least that's the way she read it, but she wasn't worried. She poured a glass of wine. In fact, the one thing she knew already in her head was that if the time came, she would leave Tommy. He had been good to her and the beginning of their relationship had been a bit of a car crash but living on the edge of excitement and thrills. But, as time had gone on, the drugs, the deal's, the money and the power had turned him into the monster she now lived with. And one that she no longer wished to.

She had thought long and hard about Valerie and the relationship she had had with Jamie. She felt genuinely sorry for her friend but was determined that if the love she was feeling for Charlie is anything like as deep as it was the love Valerie had told her she had for Jamie, then she would grab the opportunity with both hands. Of course, this all depended on Charlie actually wanting the same thing. But the first thing he had to do was get rid of that bloody woman living in his house. She decided that over the next week or so she would make a plan to knock on Charlie's door. She smiled a wry smile, and as she did, she heard the car swing into the driveway. Her mood sank just a little as she knew her husband was home.

Tommy came swinging through the door, it crashed against the side wall and he almost fell into the house. Even from where she sat she could see he was drunk but it seemed a happy drunk. He looked at her with an expression of satisfaction and just a little malice. "I think we are one of the big boys now!" he gloated. "Pour me a drink would you, I'm going to have a quick wash and then let's get some food in."

She raised her eyes, "no problem honey, do you want rum?"

He turned, "of course I want rum!" he snapped, and he went upstairs with his suitcase.

Michelle sighed. It was going to be a long night. When he came back down, Michelle failed to notice his demeanour straight away. It didn't take her long to see that he was charged up, she assumed whatever he had taken in the bathroom had certainly made him come to life. She hated the thought of the drugs in the house. It had always been an unwritten rule. But tonight he had most definitely taken something. She was unsure how to react, or indeed how he was going to react. She handed him the rum. "Where is the bloody ice?" he glared at her.

She looked back at him. She was now fully aware that tonight was probably not going to end well. "I'm sorry," she said sheepishly.

"You will be," he mumbled, just loud enough for her to hear.

She snapped back, "*what* did you just say to me?"

The next thing she knew, she hit the floor. Tommy's powerful arm had come from nowhere, and, though he hadn't really made too much contact, the force had been enough for him to knock her down.

"DON'T YOU FUCKING DARE SPEAK TO ME LIKE THAT," he boomed at her. "KNOW YOUR FUCKING PLACE!" He took the rum, and left the kitchen.

Michelle wanted to cry, but her pride forced her not to. There was *no way* she would let him see what he was doing to her. She opened the fridge, took out a bottle of wine, and went into the garden.

She heard him shouting, but couldn't care less what he was saying. She mumbled under her breath, "fuck off Tommy." And curled up under the Gazebo and opened the bottle. She sunk the first glass, cold and crisp. She felt better. She could no longer hear Tommy.

She took out her phone. Dial Chat. Sent, "I hope you are ok." She put the phone down. She had made sure she could see the whole of the house, and would be able to put it away if she needed to.

She sent another, this time WhatsApp, to Valerie. "He fucking hit me!"

And received an instant reply. "What the hell? Do you want me to come over?"

"No, no, it's OK, I'm fine. But I'm not taking much more of this."

"If it's any consolation, Giles is being an arsehole too," though he knows better than to touch me."

Michelle suddenly felt the tears. Dial Chat. "I'm good princess, just having a pint with Callum." Michelle smiled. How she longed to be there.

She replied to Valerie. "I don't know what to do." As she did so. She heard the Aston roar. Shit, he definitely shouldn't be driving! "Tommy has gone out."

The instant reply, "So has Giles. I'm coming over."

21 "ENRIQUE"

Michelle replied to Charlie. A simple, "enjoy!" The smiley face emoji came back, along with a beer glass. She laughed out loud.

Just then the WhatsApp "I'm here." Michelle almost ran to the door. She opened it to find Valerie smiling.

"Hello you," she greeted her with a smile. "I guess they have gone out together, are you hungry?" Michelle asked.

"I'm starving," Michelle smiled.

"Fancy a kebab?" she almost laughed as she said it, realising a kebab probably wasn't Valerie's idea of fun.

"Doner please," was the reply, "with garlic mayo!"

Michelle turned, "you are just full of surprises!" she laughed. And poured a cold glass of wine as she did so. They both took a big gulp. And then, suddenly and without warning, Michelle burst into tears. She sobbed as Valerie put her wine down and consoled her. "I can't take this," she managed to blurt out.

Valerie understood only too well what she was going through. Valerie wiped her tears. "Then you need to get your arse in gear with Charlie and make some sort of plan, Michelle. Because, from where I am sitting, Tommy isn't going to get any better, and, if the pair of them get much deeper, they will only get worse." Michelle looked at her. She knew she was right. It might take some time. But somehow, she needed to be free of Tommy. Of the drugs, of the dangers. And not for the first time in her life, she genuinely felt a little scared of him.

The doorbell rang. And within a minute, chips, kebabs, and assorted condiments were scattered across the kitchen. Coupled with another bottle of pinot grigio, the two women began to laugh and relax. The pent up energy of Tommy's actions finally releasing from Michelle's mind. And Valerie being brave enough to admit to Michelle that the sex site had turned her on a lot. Since she had met Jamie her sex drive had gone into orbit, and she needed to fulfil her desires. Whether virtual or real remained to be seen, but, as the wine went down, she opened her phone. And as the evening wore on, the two girls laughed at small cocks, fat men, and seemingly sex gods, all who seemed to be desperate to meet! Michelle told Valerie to take it slow. And to expect that she would see plenty of photos of men, who if she ever met them, would be at least ten kg heavier, and a whole lot uglier! She tried to advise her *not* to just meet and fuck. But she knew in her mind that she had done so, many times, and the more she thought of it, the less she liked herself. Valerie smiled, they both laughed, and teased and enjoyed a naughty, drunken evening with neither of their husbands entering their minds. They chatted to a few guys, and both women by the end of the night were definitely feeling hot under the collar and horny!

As they climbed the stairs, Michelle thanked her friend for the company.

Valerie smiled. "It's been my pleasure," she smiled, "now, get some sleep, I'm going to chat to Enrique!" and a wicked grin appeared on her face, as she entered the guest room.

Michelle laughed. She had needed it tonight. And, right now, had a plan in her head to see just how much Charlie really wanted something out of this. She went to sleep feeling that somehow, her life was going to change, and she couldn't right now be sure if it would be for the better or worse.

Valerie was still asleep when Michelle woke. Michelle guessed "Enrique" must have kept her interest late into the night. She smiled. Remembering her addiction to the site and all it had to offer. Good or bad by the end, she had just wanted sex. And it had become dangerously close to not mattering how she got it. She needed to make sure Valerie didn't fall into the same trap. If she regretted nothing else, she hated the fact she had lost all her self-respect. And she could *feel* that, with Charlie at least, despite the fact she had probably behaved like a slut, he had a depth to him that she had honestly never felt before. She *liked* him. And it seemed he liked her. Love at first sight was *so* corny. But, despite the fact she didn't like the expression, it's kind of how she felt.

She went downstairs. Her mind had not even noticed that Tommy had not come home last night. As she went into the kitchen and opened curtains around the downstairs, she heard the Aston Martin pull into the drive.

As it did so, Valerie came down yawning. "This should be interesting," she said and grinned at Michelle.

Tommy opened the door. As he came in Valerie tapped her watch. Michelle looked horrified, but Valerie clearly was not afraid of Tommy. "What time do you call this!" she laughed.

"*Who the fuck do you think you are to ask me?*" he snapped.

Michelle looked at Valerie. She smiled. "I'm the fucking wife of the man who bankrolls you, you jumped up little prick. And don't you dare forget it!" The voice was harsh. Menacing.

Michelle fought the smile.

Tommy walked up to Valerie and smiled. *"Of course,"* he said, and, pushing past her said, *"I'm going to bed,"* to no one in particular.

Once Michelle heard the bedroom door shut she burst out laughing. *"Shit,* Valerie, you are brave."

"I'm not brave," she replied. "He needs a few home truths, and I am probably the only one who can give them to him. But I have to say, it felt *good!"* and she laughed too. Then her face hardened. "Don't you dare let that man touch you again. Giles may be the brains and not the muscle, but I won't take any shit from him, or Tommy, and neither will you!"

Michelle was amazed. Valerie was so strong, and she could feel the strength coming back in her too. "I won't let him touch me again," she said.

"And I suggest you ask Charlie what he intends, coz if you don't, I will!" and she laughed again. Michelle wanted to know too. She *needed* to know.

Over breakfast, Valerie confessed she had planned to meet Enrique in a couple of days. "Just for coffee," she smiled.

"Just make sure it's for coffee," Michelle replied. "Please take your time. It's a bloody lottery with these sites, and I want to make sure you are OK."

Valerie assured her she would be fine. Michelle was pretty sure she would too, after what she had seen that morning. "Right," said Valerie, "time for me to get home and see what my useless husband has to say for himself." Michelle smiled. "Don't take any of his shit!" Valerie pointed her finger as the words came out of her mouth to emphasise the point. "Coz believe me, if you do, he will use it against you." And she drained her coffee cup and grabbed her coat. "See you soon" she waved as she left, "and make sure you chat to that delicious man!" and she practically ran to her car.

Michelle closed the door. She went back to the kitchen, and could feel the anger and tears in her throat. *Why* couldn't she be strong enough to do what Valerie had just done? Why was she so weak? She crept upstairs, she could hear the snores long before she got to the top. She decided she would go back downstairs, have another coffee, and Dial Chat Charlie to tell him what had happened. She flicked on the coffee maker, and reached for her phone. She opened Dial Chat. And there were at least 15 messages. All from men she had either met or chatted too.

But the only one she wanted to read was from Charlie. It simply read, "Hello Princess."

She smiled, and her eyes welled with tears. She had no idea what she was going to do. But, if he wanted her, she was going to make damn sure it involved him.

She replied. "Hello my sexy mechanic". She waited, the message was delivered. She slowly worked her way through the others, deleting and blocking each sender. She no longer wanted to be reminded of her recent past. Whatever the future held. It did not include anything to do with a sex site. As she deleted each contact, she almost felt "cleaner" and better inside.

The reply from Charlie was not the one she wanted. "How are you Princess? Hope all is ok. Can we say hi?"

She knew that Tommy would be asleep for a while yet. "Yes," she answered, "I will come to you, give me half an hour. I won't be looking my best I am afraid."

The answer; "I don't give a shit, I just want to see you!"

She grinned. "OK," and with that, she crept up to the back spare room. She always kept a few clothes in there, just in case Tommy was sleeping and she needed to escape. She thought briefly about some of the meets she had been to, and shuddered. It wasn't something she was proud of, and she was pretty certain she could never tell Charlie all. But for now, she needed to see him, and at the very least tell him what had happened and see his reaction.

She clicked the front door shut gently and got into the car. Slowly she drove out of the driveway and made her way to the stables and to Charlie. Her heart was in her mouth, and she drove as carefully as her racing mind would let her. As she pulled in, she saw the Z4 and her heart skipped. No matter that it had only been a few months, she liked this man very much, and her anticipation at seeing him was something she could barely contain. She saw the old Escort pull out of the barn, shining. It was hardly her thing, but it was definitely in beautiful condition.

"Hello Michelle," the voice from the driver's seat belonged to Callum. Beaming he smiled at her.

"Hello Callum," she returned, going slightly red.

"Dad is inside," he said, "must dash, got this to deliver!" and he sped out of the yard. She smiled. He was so full of energy. She could understand why Charlie was proud of his son. She pushed the door open.

Charlie was on the phone. "Why the fuck didn't you tell me it would be another week?" He looked up and smiled, that crooked, warm smile. Holding up one finger, he mouthed, "one minute!" and pointed to the receiver.

She smiled back. Pointing to the coffee cup, he raised his thumb. She grinned, and walked up the narrow wooden staircase. She *knew* he would be looking up her skirt, just as he had done the first time. She felt good inside. As the door closed, she could hear more raised voices, and guessed Charlie wasn't too happy with whoever was on the phone. She waited in the small office. After a few minutes, she heard the phone slam down, and "wankers!" came out of Charlie's mouth. She smiled to herself. She had never heard him angry. He stomped up the wooden staircase.

As he opened the door, she smiled and said, "your coffee sir."

He broke into a grin. "Why thank you!" he exclaimed. "This is a very lovely surprise!"

Michelle went red. And kissed Charlie deeply. "WOW!" he said. "You can come over anytime!" and he laughed a little.

Michelle smiled, but Charlie quickly picked up on the fact she wasn't quite herself. "What's wrong Princess?" he said quizzically.

Michelle looked at him. "How do you *know*?" she asked.

Charlie looked confused. "How do I know what?" he replied.

"How do you *know* there is something wrong?" Charlie didn't understand, but Michelle had already realised this meant he *liked* her. He noticed. She had tried hard to conceal what she was feeling, but Charlie was either a great judge of people, or he really *was* into her.

"You just don't seem yourself princess, I hope I haven't done anything to upset you?"

Michelle laughed, and spilled her coffee, "*Christ no!*" she squealed, and the tears began. She put down her coffee, and wrapped her arms around him. Charlie was still none the wiser about what had happened, and he stood a little helpless as he tried to put down his coffee cup and at least hold her. His cup missed the desk, and hit the floor. He wrapped his arms around Michelle and just held her. Still oblivious to what might be wrong. As the cup hit the floor it startled Michelle and Charlie felt her jump. She stood up, her eyes wet with tears, and said meekly, "I'm sorry."

He looked back, feeling a little helpless. "What did I do princess?" he asked.

"It's not you," she sobbed, "though you being so lovely doesn't help!"

Charlie was bemused. "For fucks sake woman, will you tell me!" he shrieked. "I have no bloody idea what's going on!"

Michelle laughed. A nervous, shy laugh. "Clean up the coffee first and sit down," she said. "I will tell you all, but you have to give *me* some answers too."

They both bent down to pick up the broken pieces of the cup. Thankfully, there wasn't much coffee in it. They looked into each other's eyes, and kissed. It felt *so* good to Michelle, and she dropped the pieces of the cup and held Charlie. He could only do the same. And with a deep and meaningful squeeze, he took her in his arms. They both knew this wasn't sexual, but just an expression of two people who were enjoying the feeling of being together.

The kiss seemed to last an age, before Charlie said, "OK, enough, what the hell has happened?"

Michelle sat down on the small couch in the corner. Charlie had told her he had slept here many times, and briefly it had almost been his home when times had been tough. She didn't like to think who else may have slept here, but she was pretty sure, if life went the way she wanted, the couch would be going! She began to describe the events of the night before. Charlie's fists began to clench, she could see he was boiling slowly inside.

When she finished her story, Charlie was seething. "I want to flatten him," he said. His hands on his head, like his brain was hurting.

"You can't do anything," Michelle said. "Please, for my sake, do nothing. But ..." She paused.

Charlie looked puzzled again "BUT?" he questioned.

"I need to know what you feel for me," she asked. "I need to know if this is all real, or you just want to fuck me?"

Charlie sat down on the edge of the desk. "Michelle," he began. "Ever since you hit my car all those months ago, I have done nothing but have you in my mind. Please don't ask me to explain it, because I can't, but I find you simply wonderful. I enjoy your company, your craziness, your naughtiness, your vulnerability, and most of all, I enjoy *you*. I told you before. I know you are married.

I know who your husband is, and I know *what* he is. But I also see you are unhappy. And, after what you just told me, I can only imagine that is at least some of your unhappiness. You make me happy. And I hope I make you happy. I love the times we have had, and, if life was different, I would love nothing more than to give us a shot." He drew a massive breath. Then said. "Shit, I guess that's really *not* what you wanted to hear, but it *is* the truth!"

Michelle looked at him with wet eyes. "You have *no* idea how happy you just made me." she said. "now come here and fuck me you sexy man." She smiled, and lay back. Kicked off her trainers, opened her legs, and she hitched up her skirt. "Come and make love to me."

Charlie grinned like a school boy and pulled off his t-shirt, he knelt down. And slipped off Michelle's panties. He kissed her inner thighs. Softly biting them. Ever closer to her soft naked pussy. As his mouth reached her clit, and his tongue gently touched it, Michelle shuddered. She put her hands on his head. "Taste me," she said softly.

Charlie didn't need to be asked twice. He pushed her legs wider apart, and began to use his tongue, inside her, and over her clitoris. Her hands massaged his head and her body writhed gently with the pleasure she was feeling. The emotions of the night before, and the relief at being able to both tell the man she adored, and also him confirming his adoration for her, meant she knew she was in the right place, with the right man, and he was most *definitely* doing the right things. She could feel the orgasm building much quicker than she had anticipated. She forced his head. "Bite me," she instructed. He softly bit her clitoris, and she exploded. Her head tossed from side to side, she could feel her pussy soak, and she could do nothing except ask for more. Charlie licked and teased her as he undid his jeans. He moved up her body, and kissed her. Michelle could taste her juices on his lips, and kissed him hard as his cock entered her. She wrapped her legs around him, sucked his tongue, and dug her nails into his skin as he pushed himself all the way in. Slowly, Charlie took control. Kissing her passionately as he slowly moved himself inside her. He held her and Michelle could feel this man meant what he was doing! He wasn't fucking her like the sordid meets she had had previously. He was making love to her. And she wanted it, she wanted him. She gripped him tighter. He fucked her a little faster now. She was going to come again. The rhythm ensuring her clit was stimulated as he went in each time. She bit his ear and whispered, "I love you," as the orgasm swept over her. He shuddered, at the same moment and let out a cry of ecstasy. They lay quietly. He was heavy on her. But she enjoyed the feeling of closeness. And held him tight.

He looked into her eyes. "I love you too Michelle," he said softly. "The question is, what the *hell* do we do about it?"

"Right now, I don't know," she said, "but, if you are really serious, and can give us a little time, then I will put things in place to allow me to be free from Tommy. I can't carry on living the way I am, but I needed to know you want me and are prepared to be with me."

Charlie rested himself on his strong arms. "I'm prepared to wait," he said with a smile. And slowly he stood up. As he did so, Michelle couldn't resist kissing the tip of his cock. "Are you sure you don't only want me for my cock?" he smiled at her. She went to bite him, but he swiftly moved his manhood to ensure no teeth made contact.

She looked up. "Is that *really* what you think?" She looked incredulous.

"No princess, I don't," he said softly, "but I bet it helps!"

She slapped his leg and exclaimed, "pass me my knickers you bastard!"

As they both dressed, Charlie was looking at her the whole time. "I will wait," he said again, "just don't make me wait too long."

Michelle replied, "please don't pressure me, that's all I ask."

"I won't" he said.

"Thank you." Michelle stood up and straightened her skirt. Smoothing it down she said. "I don't just want your cock Charlie. I love you. And I know it's all been a whirlwind, and *definitely* not what I thought I ever wanted, but just to have you in my life makes it better."

Her mind went back to Valerie, and the feelings she had for Jamie. She knew this felt right, felt good.

"I know," Charlie responded. "It's the same for me. We met by pure fate, and, though I wasn't looking for *anything* let alone love, it looks like I found it. And I don't want to let it go."

Michelle looked at the clock. "I have to get back," she said as her head fell.

He picked up her chin. "Be safe for now princess," he smiled, knelt and kissed her forehead. "Go, before there are more awkward questions to answer."

She mouthed, "I'm sorry," as Charlie put his finger to her mouth.

"Stop it," he said, "it won't be forever, now get going."
And he pulled her up into his arms. Kissed her deeply, and then pushed her playfully towards the door. She smiled, but he could see the tear in her eye. "Soon Princess," he whispered. And she slipped out of the door.

22 "VALERIE AND THE HOTEL"

Just as Michelle was leaving, Valerie was knocking on the door of Charlie's house. Michelle had told her about Charlie's ex-girlfriend, and, being the sort of woman Valerie was, she didn't like the idea one bit. She neither trusted Charlie fully yet, nor did the presence of his ex living there make her mind any clearer. She wanted to know all about this man, and more importantly, this woman that was living with her friend's lover. She knew Charlie wasn't home, Michelle had let her know she was going to see him, and that he was at work. She had no idea if the ex-girlfriend worked, but she was taking a chance. As she approached the door, she could hear the music. Loud and heavy. Not to her taste at all. Still, each to their own. She banged on the door. After what seemed like an eternity, she banged again. The music was so bloody loud she figured that whoever was in there would never be able to hear her. Just as she was about to leave, she noticed the door was one of those old-fashioned farmhouse type things. She tried the handle. Of course, it would be locked, wouldn't it? She smiled gently to herself. It wasn't locked, the door opened and almost immediately you went into the kitchen. Valerie knew she wasn't going to be staying long. The noise was one thing, but what she saw was enough. She calmly took out her phone and raised it. Clicked a couple of photos and closed the door. Nikki was not only staying there, but she was either enjoying Charlie's cocaine, or she was a junkie abusing his hospitality. Either way, Valerie was going to find out, and, for the sake of Michelle, she hoped to god it was the latter.

Michelle got home to find Tommy still asleep, the relief was unimaginable. She took out her phone.

As she did, it rang. "Are you home?" the voice of Valerie in her ear.

"Yes," Michelle replied, "I have just walked in, what's wrong?"

"Perhaps nothing," Val returned, "but perhaps a lot. Is Tommy awake?"

"Not yet," Michelle said, her voice clearly showing signs of worry now. "What's wrong!" she exclaimed.

"I will be there in 20 mins, get something on and let's go for coffee," the line went dead.

Michelle was in a mild state of panic now. *Shit*, what on earth had happened! She looked at herself in the mirror. She could go out like this. She knew Valerie would be immaculate as always, but she didn't care. Around 15 minutes later, Michelle slipped out of the front door. She closed it as quietly as possible and made her way down the drive. Valerie was waiting. As the two women left, Tommy closed the curtain, and smiled. They had become real friends, the two girls, which could only be good for himself and Giles. He lay back down, smiled to himself, and, within seconds, he was back asleep.

"*What is it?*" Michelle shrieked. The level of panic in her voice notched up a little as Valerie drove to town.
"How well do you know Charlie?" she asked.

"Intimately!" Michelle replied. And laughed a little.

"I MEAN HOW WELL?" Val snapped back. "Have you talked, not just fucked?"

Michelle was shocked at the aggressive nature of the reply. "Yes we have talked, about many things" she replied.

"About drugs?" Val asked.

"A little I guess," Michelle said. "He told me he hated smoking, would never even touch a cigarette, so had never really touched weed or hash or anything like that. *Why?*" she asked again.

"What about anything harder?"

"No!" exclaimed Michelle. "He is pretty anti-drugs. Apparently, his son got mixed up in cocaine for a while, and when Charlie found out, he went ape shit. He doesn't mind if Callum has a hit on a night out, but when he found out he was close to getting involved with dealing, he went mad"

Valerie grinned. She was pleased for her friend. And relieved that the man Michelle had met, (and whom Valerie had made sure she had *thoroughly* checked out) was indeed the person she thought he was. Perhaps she could trust a little more now. She looked at Michelle, and said, "then I think he has a problem."

Michelle looked shocked. "What do you mean?" she gasped.

"Let's get to town, and I will explain. But I'm glad you told me what you did. It's now a question of what we do about her."

Michelle was totally confused. But didn't know what else to say. So they drove on in silence.

Around twenty minutes later, as Valerie was parking the car, Michelle asked, "do I want to know?"

Valerie looked at her. "*Yes*," she raised her voice to emphasise "you both want, and *need* to know."

They made their way swiftly to the coffee shop. This time, Valerie whispered in the owner's ear. He led them upstairs, informing them that the wine was in the usual place. Michelle looked puzzled.

"I told you before, Giles sometimes has his uses!" And Valerie laughed. When they reached the flat above, Valerie went to the kitchen, whilst Michelle sat awkwardly on the arm of the sofa. Valerie came back with 2 glasses.

"So" Michelle began.

She was cut short by Valerie thrusting a mobile phone into her space. Michelle focussed and could see a woman, slumped over a table, in a kitchen. Nice kitchen table. Old and rustic. The woman had blood running from her nose. Her hair is a mess. Her head was flat on the table. And a credit card, and a sprinkling of white powder covering a significant area of the table.

"What on earth!"

Valerie looked very pleased with herself. "I went to Charlie's house," she said. "I wanted to see just what this ex and he got up to. Turns out, she isn't very good at locking doors, nor snorting coke by the looks of things!" and she laughed again.

Michelle was dumbfounded. "I, I had no idea" she blurted.

"I don't think he does either," Valerie replied. "The question is, how and what do you do next?" Michelle didn't know what to say. Valerie then smiled, "I reckon I know where she got the coke don't you?"

Michelle nodded. She had never liked the fact that Charlie had her there, but he also was a decent man and she knew he was only helping a friend. Yet she could hardly confront him when she wasn't supposed to know.

She looked at Valerie. "That woman has to go," she said. Valerie nodded her agreement. They finished their coffee, and, over the next couple of weeks, Valerie made sure that Michelle was ok. And Michelle did likewise. They hadn't talked much about Valerie and the sex site, but Michelle had noticed she was a little more agitated and on edge over the last few days. Michelle had spent time with Charlie. And wanted to dig deeper into his past, she needed to know about the drugs especially. She already had an abusive drug using husband, she didn't need an addicted lover either! Thankfully Charlie had been able to reassure her that the only thing he sniffed was Vicks if he had a cold, and the only thing he liked smoked was fish!! That had made her smile, and she warmed even more to a man who fitted her, it seemed so well.

Michelle woke late, it was a wet and miserable Wednesday.

She heard Tommy shout, "see you tomorrow," and watched from the window as he left.

Glancing back at the clock, she saw it was after 10am! Jeez I definitely had too much wine. She smiled, thinking of all the naughty Dial Chat messages she had been exchanging the night before. She decided to send another, "hello you delicious man." She waited, smiling. And waited. And thought she had better get up. She needed to food shop, and it would be a big one this time. No little shop at the garage. She dressed casually. Unlike Valerie, she didn't really feel the need to be immaculate every time she went out. So leggings, no knickers and a top would do just fine. As she finished dressing her phone lit up. She smiled. But her face fell slightly when she saw it was Valerie.

"I'm off to meet Enrique, I need you to know the name of the hotel, the time, but I'm not giving you my room number!"

Michelle smiled weakly. She wanted to say "go for it girl" but it did nothing but bring back memories she didn't want to think about. "Be safe, and enjoy!" she wrote, and pushed send. Charlie hadn't responded so she figured he was busy, and got into the car. Shopping would be her "excitement" for the day! A couple of hours later, she was pulling back into the drive. She had no idea where Tommy had been going, but figured it was with Giles. So she was alone and could just vegetate. She packed away the shopping and as she did so, she checked dial chat.

"Hello Princess, how is your sexy French ass?"

She grinned and her whole body smiled. "Missing you," she typed. "My house is empty."

Charlie replied, "do you want to?"

Michelle thought, but it was just too dangerous. She had no idea where Tommy was, or if he would be coming back. "I wish I could," she typed, but maybe we can say hi?"

"My house is empty too!"

Michelle was a little taken aback. "Do you want to?" she answered.

"Hell yes!" came the reply.

She smiled. "See you in 30 mins"

As she drove to the address Charlie had given her, she wanted to stop grinning, but found she couldn't. Did this mean the ex-girlfriend had gone? She would find out all when she got there. She parked opposite the old but beautiful cottage. Admired it briefly, from its thatched roof, and white walls to the small garden and the ramshackle collection of plants. She didn't notice the state of the art CCTV or alarm, nor did she see how far the wall indicated the size of the back garden. Michelle almost ran across the road, and knocked loudly.

"Hello Princess!" she heard Charlie shout, "it's open. But make sure you lock it and bolt it when you come in!"

Michelle did as she had been asked. She looked around the open space. Definitely old. Rustic. And with that bloody table she had seen in photos only too recently. "Where are you?" she called.

Charlie replied, "follow the arrows." She looked to her left, and saw the wooden staircase, with post-it notes on every other one, and a note on the bottom step saying "This way please."

She smiled. Her mind became "naughty" and she did as the note said. She walked along the landing, before coming to a very old looking door. "Knock, knock," she laughed.

"Come in, Princess," he replied. She opened the door, Charlie was on the bed. The room was dark, save for a small light in one corner. Flowers filled the room. The curtains drawn, a heavy velvet curtain. The prosecco in an ice bucket. Charlie was naked and hard. She smiled. He looked at her. "Well, hello," and he stood to kiss her. A deep, loving kiss that she absorbed with all her body. His stiff cock touched her clothing and she wanted to be naked. She touched him as they kissed again. And he slipped her leggings down. She wasn't quite ready for him to pick her up, lay her on the bed and enter her as quickly as he did. She gasped and closed her eyes. Charlie pushed himself inside her. Slowly fucking her. Rhythmically, sensually. She loved that. He made sure she was soon on the brink of coming. As Michelle moaned beneath him, he took his cock out of her.

She lay there. "What's wrong Charlie?"

He smiled. "Absolutely nothing Princess, I just want to look at you."

Michelle wanted to be naked now. Skin on skin. She wanted to feel him again. She sat up, and took off her top and bra. As she did so, he teased himself into her mouth. Greedily she paid his delicious shaft attention. Taking him deep, and hearing the pleasure coming from Charlie's mouth. She lay back. "I want you to make me come," she demanded.

He lay down next to her. "you're in control," he smiled. "Come here and fuck me Michelle."

She slid softly down him. He filled her completely and she rode him. Cowgirl was definitely her favourite, and it didn't take long for her to build to her orgasm. "I'm going to come, Charlie," she said breathlessly.

"Come for me Princess," he held her hips and pressed harder. Making sure his cock was as deep as it could be. Michelle threw her head back as the orgasm swept over her. Shuddering and with real emotion she lay on Charlie and sobbed.

Tears of joy, she felt amazing. "I'm sorry," she blurted out, I just feel so perfect with you."

He held her. "I'm here Princess," he said, "and you feel pretty perfect too."

She sat up, and gasped as he went deeper. "*Shit!*" she said.

"What's wrong?" Charlie enquired, "are you ok?"

Michelle grinned, "you haven't come have you?"

Charlie went red. "No," he said, it was just about you today."

"Oh no it bloody isn't," she grinned. "You are going to come *my* way!" and she slipped herself off him. She patted the pillow, come rest your head here," she smiled. Charlie did as he was told. Michelle lay next to him. Kissed Charlie hard and took his cock in her hand. She lowered her head, took him in her mouth, and played. Licking his hardness. Rolling her tongue around, then taking him deep in her mouth.

He watched her. Smiling. "I want to come, you naughty girl."

"IN MY MOUTH!" she squealed. And Charlie exploded. His hot semen filled her mouth and she drank him. His body shuddered and he moaned loudly. She enjoyed teasing his cock head as the last remnants of his orgasm ended. She looked up.

"*Wow!*" he exclaimed.

She smiled. "Wine now?" And she stood up and poured two glasses. As she took a large drink her phone pinged, she must have forgotten to put it on silent.

"So where is your lodger?" she enquired, as she looked at the screen.

Two words. "HELP ME!" and it was from Valerie.

"Fuck!" Michelle looked at Charlie. "I need to make a phone call."

"Is everything ok?" he asked.

"I don't know yet" she replied. And she dialled Valerie. She didn't have to wait long for Valerie to answer. She could barely make out what Valerie was saying, but one word she understood *very* clearly was rape! "*Fuck!*" Michelle almost screamed. "Don't move. Just stay where you are," she said.

Charlie could hear the anger in her voice. "What's up princess?" He was naturally panicked.

"Long story," Michelle snapped, "but please Charlie, I'm begging for your help."

Charlie was slightly stunned. "Anything," he said.

"We need to go and get Valerie from a hotel. You can't ask why, just take me there, and help her. Please!"

Charlie nodded his head. Within ten minutes they were dressed and driving - fast! Michelle for once didn't care, she just knew she needed to get there. The drive seemed to take an age. They found the hotel, and Michelle breezed into the lobby. She didn't wait to see or talk to anyone, she found the lift, and headed up to floor seven. Charlie was right beside her, and she knew she needed him just in case. They reached the room, and knocked softly.

Michelle barked "Valerie?" and the door opened. The room was dark. Curtains pulled, and trashed. Chairs turned upside down. The bed linen all over the place. And Valerie ... Shivering, wrapped in a sheet, covered in blood.

Charlie shut the door, went into the bathroom whispering to Michelle, "sit with her," as he rinsed a towel under the shower.

As he came back, Valerie was sobbing onto Michelle's chest. She was shivering harder now.

"I will go down to the bar," Charlie said. As he passed the towel, and told Michelle to sooth her and clean as best she could.

"But this bastard will need to be caught," she questioned.

"I will come back, with a drink, something for the shock. For now, let's worry about Valerie, and then we can decide what to do."

Michelle looked at him. His eyes told her he was right, and she felt warmth for this man again. "OK," she whispered. And held Valerie a little tighter. It took a little more persuading than Charlie would have liked to get the barman to sell him a bottle of scotch and three large cokes, but the promise of doubling whatever the cost seemed to do the trick. When he arrived back at the room, Valerie was better. A little calmer. And ready to talk.

"He left a blindfold for me at reception," she told Michelle, as she took a swig of coke, "give me the bloody whiskey," she snapped."

"When you have some sugar in you," Charlie demanded, "you need it to counteract the shock."

Valerie knew he was right. She looked at Michelle. Smiled. And whispered "keep him."

Valerie downed the coke, and Charlie poured her a scotch. One for Michelle too.

As he began to clean up, Valerie continued, "I was so excited!" "I got to the door, listened before I knocked. I heard a voice say, "one minute," and then almost immediately, the door opened. I had my blindfold on, so I was led into the room. I felt hands on me immediately, and gasped. Suddenly I felt more hands on me. I tried to reach for my blindfold, but two hands held my arms. I have no idea how many were there, all I know is, one kept my arms held the whole time. And the others just used me. I felt sick. I was abused, and they didn't care. They laughed and passed me around. All the time I was held by "Enrique." And she broke down again.

"We need to call the police," said Michelle.

Valerie was still crying, but Charlie soon cut in. "And tell them what? That a respectable married woman came to a hotel to meet a man she had never met for sex?"

Michelle's head fell. "So what do we do?" she said "Look at her!"

Valerie looked up. "Charlie is right," she said softly. Almost resigned to what had happened. "I can't go to the police. I can't." Michelle knew he was right too.

"Did they hurt you?" Charlie asked. "Did they hit you?"

Valerie shook her head. "No, he was far too clever for that. Told them all to fuck me where ever they want, but no hands. No bruises."

And she hung her head shamefully. "Ok!" Charlie sounded somehow upbeat.

"How can you be so cool?" asked Michelle.

"We will talk," he said softly, "right now, let's get Valerie out of here as discreetly as possible and make sure there is no fuss."

Valerie went into the bathroom with Michelle. Threw up, and then came back into the room, naked. Charlie was a little shocked.

She said nothing, but got dressed. "Thank you both for coming," she croaked. "I know I don't need to say it, but not a word OK?" They both nodded. "I feel so stupid," she muttered.

Michelle felt it was her turn to hang her head. "I'm sorry," she said.

"What for?" Valerie enquired.

"For getting you into this shit."

Valerie laughed. "My darling Michelle" she said, "you may have opened the gate, it was I who decided to walk down the path."

They left the room, Charlie having tidied up as much as he could. They left the hotel without another word.

As they went to the car park, Michelle asked, "do you want me to come back with you?"

"No, I will be fine," Valerie replied. "Tommy and Giles are away on some golf do, so I have an empty house. It will give me time to think, and to get myself together."

Michelle smiled at her.

Charlie went over to Valerie. Gave her a friendly hug, and whispered, "send me his details," and he grinned.

"Thank you," Valerie mouthed as she slipped into her car. She sped off, and Michelle burst into tears.

Charlie put his arm around her. "It could have been you right?" he said softly.

"YES!" Michelle barked. "And I feel responsible."

Charlie hugged her. Kissed her head. "Don't worry Princess," he smiled, one way or another, "Enrique" will not know who or what he has messed with."

He led Michelle back to the car. "Tommy and Giles are away tonight." Can I stay?"

Charlie looked a little uncomfortable.

"Oh shit, Michelle said, I forgot she is still there!"

Charlie looked crestfallen. "I'm sorry," he said. "I am trying to get rid of her." "As he did so his phone lit up he smiled, "it's Nikki."

Michelle looked crestfallen, "what the fuck does she want?" she questioned.

Charlie held his phone up and she read the message. "You can lock the door tonight I won't be coming home."

She grinned, "so can I stay?"

"Bloody right you can stay!" he said as she grinned again. "Let's go home" and stopped almost as soon as he had said it.

Michelle smiled, took his arm, and said, "one day Charlie, we will."

Charlie put the Z4 into gear and drove as fast as he could. When they arrived back at his small country cottage he opened the door and as he did so he said to Michelle, "call Valerie, make sure she's OK."

She looked at him with loving eyes, "you are so thoughtful," she said.

He grinned, "I'm just wonderful," and he laughed. He opened the door and walked to the kitchen, he opened the fridge. Perfect, plenty of wine, plenty of beer and ice in the freezer, what more did he need?
As he came back into the living room he heard Michelle ending her call with, "I don't want you alone of course you can come over." Charlie looked downhearted.

Michelle saw his disappointment and as she ended the call she walked over to him.

Kissed him softly and said, "Giles is away tonight also, so I can't let her be on her own."

Charlie smiled, "of course you can't, and she is more than welcome, just don't say I didn't give you a house alone!" and he laughed loudly.

About an hour later the door knocked and Valerie arrived, Charlie opened the door with a simple greeting, "hello Valerie! Chinese or Indian?"

She smiled, "well that's a welcome! Chinese please, and can I thank you for your hospitality and your kindness today."

''It's nothing," he replied, "you're a friend of Michelle so you're a friend of mine." And he walked back into the kitchen shouting, "would you like wine Valerie?"

She acknowledged him with a smile as she poked her head around the corner, "yes please, she's a lucky girl to have you."

He grinned, "course she is, I'm amazing," he laughed.

She smiled, "don't push it," she said and took the wine.

"Michelle is in the living room," Charlie told her, and Valerie went off to go and see her friend. Charlie found plates and cutlery, set the plates to warm and dialled the number of his favourite Chinese restaurant. This was going to be a *long* evening and he figured he would need the food and the beer to get himself through.

The door knocked again about an hour later. As they sat enjoying the meal Michelle opened her mouth to speak. "I'm sorry," she said to Valerie.

Valerie told her once again, "don't be so stupid it's nothing to do with you, you gave me the idea, I chose to run with it." She smiled at Michelle. "I see now that this man," and she pointed to Charlie, "really does care for you and I know I have been stupid in trying to replace and "bury" Jamie too quickly. I miss him so much and it hurts more than I can explain. But I need somehow to rebuild myself."

Charlie said, "Anything we can do to help we will."

Valerie replied, "Right at this moment, I just need a friend, you are doing all you can and I love you both for it."

The evening passed without too much depth of conversation. Michelle tried to understand what had happened earlier in the day but Valerie did not want to talk about it and for once Charlie agreed it was probably just time to let her absorb it all.

As the evening came to a close Valerie said to both Charlie and Michelle, "do you think you can find a way to get away for a while?"

Michelle looked puzzled, "why do you ask?" she said.

"I have a friend who has a villa in Spain, it's very private, it's very safe, and Jamie and I spent some time there whenever we could get away."

Charlie looked to Michelle, "you know it's no problem for me, Callum is more than capable of running the business, so if you could escape for a short time then I'm more than happy to do so!"

Michelle smiled, "I need to find a way to be able to escape."

Valerie smiled. "I'm sure we can come up with something."

Charlie grinned like a child. "Yes please," he smiled.

Valerie then changed the tone. "I was stupid today," she snapped. "Michelle, please delete the account for me. I will give you passwords and stuff, but I can't face opening that bloody thing again." She took out her phone. Sent Michelle her log in details. And looked at them both with tears in her eyes. "Thank you," she smiled weakly. "Can I stay here tonight?"

Charlie looked at her. Strong she may be, but right now, she was vulnerable, and a little ashamed. "Of course you can. Use the guest room, upstairs, end of the corridor, and it's all yours."

She smiled. "Thank you again" and she left the room without another look.

Charlie sighed. "What a bloody day."

Michelle could do nothing but agree. "I need to delete Valerie's account," she said.

"Not quite so fast, if you don't mind. Just leave it there for a while. I want to find out more about this "Enrique"

Michelle was shocked. "What do you mean?" she enquired.

"Just leave the account there. Now you have her login details, just check in once in a while. Let's see exactly what he thinks he can get away with."
"Now," he smiled, "are you coming to bed or not?"

Michelle grinned. "Yes please" she smiled. "Take me to bed you sexy man." Charlie did as he was asked. Slowly leading her up the stairs. As they got into bed, she kissed him, and whispered "thank you" as he returned her kiss.

100 miles away, in a hotel, Nikki had just taken Tommy's cock into her mouth, as Giles started the recording ...

When they woke the next morning, Valerie had already left. There was a note in the kitchen. A simple "thank you," and underneath, "SPAIN!"

Michelle kissed Charlie. And as she closed the front door, she promised Charlie she would make it happen.

23 "SPAIN"

Charlie meanwhile, had made a note of Valerie's membership. He wasn't a violent man, but he had his moments. And his son was a big built and hot headed so and so, who didn't mind a fight if it was justified. And Charlie was pretty sure this was justified. He would find a way to deal with Enrique, and his cronies. But he might need his son's help.

Michelle felt warm inside. Despite what had happened to Valerie, and the fact she couldn't help feeling responsible, she was warm from the feelings of love and closeness she had with Charlie. She heard the Aston an hour or so later. She felt stronger. She couldn't explain it, but she knew that the bond and love between Charlie and her was more and more real, and she appreciated that she had long since lost that with Tommy. He came in. Sober, smiling. He walked to her.

Kissing her on the cheek, she mused, "you are in a good mood!"

He smiled. "I'm always in a good mood,'' he laughed, and his face scowled. "Why, do you have something to tell me that will put me in a bad mood?"

She wanted to respond with anger, but, for now, she would wait. The strength that Valerie and Charlie had given her wasn't quite ready to retaliate yet. "Of course not," she returned, "I'm just glad your trip was a good one."

Tommy smiled. "Oh it was good," he laughed. That same menacing laugh. And he took his small case upstairs.

Nikki got back to Charlie's place, to find it completely locked up. She had no idea why, but Charlie had locked both locks, on both doors, and she didn't have the key. She called his phone. "Why the fuck have you locked me out?" she snapped.

"Who the fuck are you to speak to me like that?" Charlie answered angrily.

"I'm sorry," she answered. "Nikki it's not working, you are going to have to find somewhere else to live."

She felt the hair on the back of her neck stand up, "why, got some tart you want to bring back have you?"

Charlie was boiling inside, both at her attitude, and the fact she had called Michelle a tart. He kept calm. "No," he said, "I just want my house and my life back. And you are not part of that, so find somewhere to live. I need my keys back by the end of the month." The line went dead. He knew she would be pissed off. But he had to get her out. He couldn't have his ex-girlfriend around anymore. He had other things of more pressing nature to deal with.

He got a text. "I will bring the keys back in an hour or so."

He replied. "Fine." He smiled.

Tommy smiled too. The flat was empty. He had used it as a shagging den for both he and Giles. But it had become an effort as it was well away from the village. He could rent it, but did not trust anyone, so his new front of house could supplement her wages a little more now. Rent on a flat, or a fuck at least once a week to pay the rent sounded a very good deal to him.

Once Nikki had moved out, which she did surprisingly quickly he thought, he invited Callum over. Boys night in he said. He would tell Callum about Enrique, and make sure his son was right behind him. At the same moment, Michelle was planning how to disappear for a few days. Tommy was in a decent mood. And about to go to the club, when she blurted out, "I think I might take a holiday with the girls."

He shouted, "you go for it," as he almost skipped down the steps to the Aston.

What the hell was going on? Michelle had no idea. But the truth was she couldn't care less.

And so, a week or so later, she had told Valerie she had it all arranged. Valerie had settled now, and was back to her usual self. She made sure the villa was free, and told Michelle she would need to organise a car. It had a pool, but was nowhere near the beach so she would have to drive. A week or so after that, she was at the airport. Barry had collected her, and Charlie. All the details had been finalised. Valerie had told Tommy and Giles that she would be going out with Michelle. She had no intention of going with them of course, she would go to Spain, but this time, she wouldn't be the third wheel! As the plane left the ground and Michelle wrapped her hand around Charlie's, she knew that this was what she wanted. That somehow, she had to find a way to leave. Because she could no longer cope with the feelings she had for Charlie. Nor the lack of feelings she had for Tommy. Valerie smiled. She was out on a later flight, and was meeting Anesh, a friend she had known for years. Who also happened to own not just the villa Michelle was staying in, but several around Spain. He had done some "business" with Giles, and they had enjoyed a few weekends on his amazing boat. But a deal had gone sour, and he and Giles no longer spoke. Valerie liked him, and he had always had a soft spot for her. She needed a little time out, and Anesh would be the man to give her that time. As Michelle and Charlie touched down, Valerie was boarding her own flight to Spain.

And Nikki was in Tommy's office, bent over the desk as she sucked Giles's cock and Tommy fucked her from behind. Her addiction to sex wasn't far behind her addiction to cocaine. And if she could use one to pay for the other, she figured it was the best of all worlds.

Charlie had already made sure the hire car was ready. The temperature was around 28 degrees as they found the Ford Focus. Sat nav ready, and with Charlie driving, he had already told Michelle he didn't trust her in a left hand drive, to which she had replied, "I'm bloody French!" He laughed, and took the keys anyway. Then promptly tried to change gear with the door handle. Michelle smirked. "Sure you want to drive?" she laughed.

"I will be fine!" he exclaimed, "I just need a minute to get used to it!" The sat nav told them it was almost an hour's drive. Altea Hills. Neither knew particularly the area, but neither of them cared. This was a time they could be totally alone, totally safe. And allow their feelings to spill out in front of whoever they wanted to. As they drove, and Michelle played around with the radio, she eventually found a station playing English music.

Just as she flicked the station on, "Billy Ray was a preacher's son" came out of the speakers. She smiled. And felt warm, as she held Charlie's hand and began to sing. Charlie watched and listened in awe. Michelle let her diva out, and sang the song with all her might. Charlie could feel the tears running down his face as she lost herself in the moment. When the song finished, Michelle came back to reality, and saw Charlie almost sobbing. "Shit!" she exclaimed, "was I that bad?"

Charlie gathered himself. "No Princess," he said softly, "you were amazing."

They drove on, and Michelle turned the radio down. "I used to be good,'' she said, and bowed her head. "I was the top billing at the club. 20 years ago it was a classy, upmarket place. Now it's nothing but a seedy nightclub doing drug deals and with semi naked women serving you drinks.''

Charlie was interested. "Tell me what happened?"

Michelle shook her head. "I don't really know," she said, "Tommy happened."

Charlie was a bit bewildered.

Michelle could see the look on his face. "I was the one who brought in the public. They came to see me sing. I was the top girl, the headline act. And I think he was jealous. So, slowly he introduced a "DJ" night. Telling me that I was amazing, but he thought I needed a night off, and we needed some different "faces" in the club. I was slowly pushed aside, and I see it now. At the time I thought, "aww, he is so thoughtful." Before long, I wasn't singing there at all anymore. He had a DJ every night, and the older clients just left. It was never old fashioned, but it was, I suppose, not what he needed for his deals and covering his arse." Michelle paused for breath, The passion building inside her. "Singing was the only thing I loved. I mean *really* loved. I knew I was good at it. And I enjoyed every minute. I let Tommy take control of me. And I didn't just stop singing. I lost who I was." It was her turn to have tears in her eyes. Charlie wanted to hug her, but he had to concentrate. He squeezed her hand tighter.

And as the sun began to set, they pulled into the driveway of a simply beautiful, typically Spanish, white painted Villa. High in the hills with amazing views. But the house itself was stunning. With its high round towers, and beautiful balconies, it was everything you would want in a Spanish Villa.

"Wow!" Charlie breathed.

"Wow indeed!" Michelle agreed. They went inside. And the theme continued. It was beautifully furnished. Amazingly appointed. And just perfect. As they closed the door.

Charlie put his arms around Michelle. "Sing to me," he asked.

She slapped his chest playfully. "Not tonight Josephine!" she laughed. "I'm tired. I want my bed. *But* ..." she stopped. "I will sing for you."

Charlie smiled. "I'm going to hold you to that.''

They went to the bedroom. A simply *huge* bed greeted them, with a similarly large en-suite. As Michelle brushed her teeth, Charlie turned down the bed. And they softly held each other, as Charlie kissed her gently. "Goodnight princess." The next week was idyllic. Michelle had made sure Valerie was ok. Anesh wasn't a sexual friend at all, (he was gay for a start!) and the two women had only had to make sure they were booked on the same flight home, which also included Charlie. So for the next 5 days, Michelle and Charlie simply enjoyed one another. From the walk around the market, where Charlie insisted on buying a ridiculous straw hat that Michelle hated to admit *did* suit him and make look even more attractive, and she was taken by the shocking pink bikini that Charlie most certainly enjoyed looking at. It pushed her boobs up, and gave her a great cleavage, and she wasn't about to say no to that! They enjoyed wonderful meals out. Talking. Laughing about situations that had happened in their lives, whether that was in younger days, or more recently. Charlie offered to cook one night, and as he stood over the stove, Michelle came up behind him, and hugged him tightly. She softly began to sing "Two become one," not something she really liked, she actually couldn't stand all that "girl power" bullshit, but the lyrics suited how she was feeling perfectly. Charlie swayed gently as she sang. He wanted to turn and hold her, but she was making sure he stayed exactly where he was.

He asked her a rather awkward question. "Would you go back to the site for me?"

Michelle stepped away, horrified. "What the fuck for!" she exclaimed. Her voice was already high pitched, and Charlie knew this wasn't a good sign.

"I want to teach "Enrique" a lesson." He smiled.

And Michelle saw a steely side to the man she was falling in love with, that she had never seen before. "He will have deleted his profile by now," she came back.

"He will, I'm sure," Charlie said calmly, "but I screenshot all of his "friends" and his "meets" and anything I could get about him the moment Valerie gave you all her login details."

Michelle looked amazed. "You crafty bastard," she smiled. How do you know so much about sex sites?"

Charlie went red. "I was a *very* brief swinger, remember?"

The truth was, Michelle had not remembered. But now she did. And now the ex-girlfriend came back. And she felt anger. "Why?" she snapped a little at him. "What are you going to do?"

"If I find him" he grinned, "I will just make sure he never uses a woman again," and his shoulders raised and fell with a chuckle. He kissed Michelle. "Don't worry princess," he smiled. "I will just have a word with him" and he winked. "NOW!" he shouted. "Come on woman, dinner is served!" Over a decidedly good dinner of lightly poached fish and potatoes, they slowly formulated a plan. Michelle would copy almost to the letter Valerie's profile. Have a similar photo, and well, let "Enrique" find her. As they closed the laptop, Michelle was clearly upset.

"What's wrong Princess?"

"I found you," she whispered, "and I thought I would never need to go back to that bloody awful place."

"You won't, princess," this will all be over, and you will *never* need to go anywhere again."

He held her tightly. She enjoyed feeling him hold her. She felt protected, she felt cared for, and she felt loved! The days counted down. They spent a day at the beach; riding the pedalos, eating fresh fish, swimming, Charlie insisted on buying a diving mask and looking around under the water. Michelle liked it too, but only in short bursts. They kissed; they ate, they drank, and they loved. There was a friendship between them that they both realised they actually *needed.* For Michelle, deeper than the cheap sex she had been having with almost anyone, and for Charlie, a realisation he *could* let someone into his life again. She decided she could even put up with his love of bloody country and western music!

The next morning was their last full day together. They would leave the following morning to go back to reality. And Michelle didn't know whether to feel happy for the wonderful time they had both spent, or sad that it was coming to an end. She overheard Charlie on the phone. "Well, if he can do the deal for around eight hundred, maybe eight fifty, then I will definitely take it. I know I will need to sort out all the legal rubbish. But as long as you can tell him my word is good enough, then if he is happy to trust me, let's make it happen. I know it's not France, but Spain is pretty good!"

As he ended the call, Michelle smiled. "What are you up to?"

Charlie had a devilish grin on his face. "I have just bought a house," he laughed.

"You have what?" she squeaked.

"I have been speaking to Valerie. Well, to her friend Anesh actually. Turns out he has a few properties, and was happy with my offer for one."

Michelle was baffled. "What's going on?" she enquired.

"Well, I figured if, no, when you are able to leave Tommy, you certainly won't want to hang around at home. Even if we go back, you will need to have somewhere safe to escape. So, now you have one!"

Michelle was overcome. "You have really done that for us?"

"Yes princess. If we are going to have a future together, then we need to make sure we (or you!) are safe. I am not scared of Tommy, or Giles, or anyone really, but at the same time, if I can have something in place to make it better, why not. And besides, what else am I going to do with my money? Callum will only buy bloody cars with it!" and he gave a hearty laugh.

Michelle kissed him. Long, hard, and deep. "I love you Charlie Summer!" They spent their last day by the pool. Enjoying each other. Michelle even felt comfortable enough to sing again for him. Though she was worried, as every time she did Charlie's eyes filled with tears. He assured her it was just emotion, and she really was fabulous, but that nagging devil of doubt was in her mind.

As the plane landed, Valerie and Michelle made sure they left together, that Barry collected them, and that Charlie was nowhere to be seen. Charlie didn't mind. He kept the old and slightly run down Z4 so he could have his "slightly poor" image for all to see. Very few people knew what he had stashed away, and even less knew about his man cave. He was quite happy to tell people they were all customer cars. As he got home, he felt wonderful. He had found the woman he should have been with all his life. And he knew it was crazy, risky, even dangerous, but he also knew he couldn't stop. He opened a beer, and opened the laptop. He prided himself on being a pretty good judge of character. And as he opened the site, there he was. He could hardly believe it. As he slowly read through the message "Enrique" (though he was now Paulo) had sent. It was almost word for word what he had sent to Valerie. Charlie was tired. But now Paulo could see his message had been read, Charlie replied, "you sound lovely. I have only just got home from a holiday, so I'm a little tired, but very tanned, perhaps if we get on, I could show you my white bits. Xxx" He pressed send, and closed the computer. Paulo's time would come, of that he was certain. Callum and he would make sure he never got the chance to make any woman suffer what Valerie had gone through.

It was a couple of weeks later, after many messages had been exchanged, and indeed photos of Michelle sent, that the meet was arranged. Michelle had hated the thought of going back there, but the photo "session" had proved to be something very erotic for both she and Charlie, so despite the reason for taking them not making Michelle feel good at all, once they started taking them, they had both enjoyed the teasing and provocative pictures! Charlie also needed Michelle to be there at the "meet", and knew it was always going to be a risk. But Callum in particular wasn't afraid to use his muscle if he needed to, and Charlie didn't mind a scrap when he needed either. Valerie was blissfully unaware of anything that was going on, and he had made sure that her account was deleted now. As they got to the hotel, the pattern was the same. Michelle went up to the reception, and gave the room number. She felt physically sick as she took the envelope containing the blindfold. Her hands were shaking. She pushed the button for the lift, and made her way to the 6th floor. Charlie and Callum following. Both carried bags. She hadn't asked what was in them. It was better she didn't know. As she got to the room, she put the blindfold on. She knocked, and there was a pause. She knew "Paulo" was looking through the small spy window to check if it was her. Then she saw the handle go down. As she did so, Charlie grabbed her as Callum grabbed the door handle. "WHAT THE FUCK?!" shouted at least two voices. Callum was inside now, and Charlie just behind. The door slammed shut. And Michelle ran. She felt sick, and needed to be out of the hotel.

Michelle had been in the car for what seemed like an age. She felt empty, nervous, and lonely. But also happy. Pleased. And angry. Angry at herself for ever entering this awful world of cheap hotels and cheap sex, and even more angry at allowing herself to open the door for Valerie. As she felt the emotions boil inside her, both front doors opened. Bags were thrown into the car, and Charlie slipped the nondescript Saab into gear and sped from the car park. As soon as they were clear of the car park, and rounded the corner, Charlie pulled over. Callum jumped out, and peeled off the stick on number plates. Callum screwed them up and placed them in the bin near the car. They drove back in total silence. Michelle was almost in shock, inside she wanted to know all, but she was too frightened, and too confused to ask.

When they arrived back at Charlie's house, and had gone inside, Charlie spoke first. "Michelle," he said meaningfully, "it's finished. You no longer have to live with those memories, and Valerie can be assured that she will never have to relive anything."

He was calm, measured. Not proud and boasting, but assured and caring. He held her tight and kissed her forehead.

Callum smiled. "It's over Michelle," and looked at her with the same deep brown eyes as his father. Whatever had happened, the bond between these two men was both amazing and unbreakable, and she deeply respected the love father and son were not afraid to show.

"What happened?" she said softly.

Charlie went to speak, but Callum interrupted. "We just made sure that "Paulo" who actually is Peter, nothing more than a low life scumbag who generally likes intimidating women, then leaves it a while before trying to blackmail them with the photos, understood that he had picked on the wrong woman this time. And his mobile phone, which I have here, along with his cronies, will be sent to the police anonymously should he step out of line again."

Charlie smiled. "And we thought a dildo shoved up each of their arses after tying their hands together was only fair under the circumstances," and he laughed.

"ITS NOT FUCKING FUNNY!" Michelle screamed. And then cried, hard. The emotion and worry and fear all coming out at once.

Charlie put his arm around her. "It is Michelle," he said gently. "It's time low life's like him were given a taste of their own medicine, and yes, it *is* funny. But it's also over, no more sites, no more sneaking around, no more of any of that shit! Its US now. And I want to find a way to make Spain, and you and me a reality."

Michelle looked at him, then to Callum. "You know it all?" she questioned.

"He knows it all," Charlie replied. "And you are ok with it Callum?" he replied simply.

"I have always wanted my old man happy. And you make him happy Michelle."

Michelle cried softly. She walked to Callum and hugged him. "Thank you," she said, "he makes me so happy too!"

"I'm going to leave you two alone," Callum said. "I have a date with a pub barmaid," and he grinned.

"Enjoy!" Charlie smiled. "And be careful!"

"*Father,*" he answered, "*I'm twenty five!*" and he belly laughed as he shut the front door.

Michelle felt relief. She didn't know what to say next, Charlie saved the day, "drink?" he enquired.

"Please," she replied.

"I'm going to text Valerie,"

Charlie turned. "If you do, just say you need to see her or talk. *Do not* send anything over text/dial chat/WhatsApp." And he went into the kitchen. When he came back, Michelle had just put the phone down. Charlie opened the laptop. Turned it towards Michelle. "Delete it all," he ordered. Michelle did as she was told. The profile vanished, she blocked the site. And closed the computer as the knock on the door sounded. "Let her in," Charlie said, "I will get a wine. She might need it." Michelle did just that. Welcomed Valerie, and they made their way to the living room.

Charlie followed soon after. As he handed the wine to Valerie, he said, "I have dealt with Enrique."

Valerie looked at him. "And the photos?"

Charlie smiled, "unless he is a genius, he said, "which I doubt, then yes, the photos too. But, if you get anything else. Let me know." Valerie nodded. "And, I know Michelle doesn't think it's funny," he smiled again, that crooked bloody smile. "I took this just for you," and he held up his phone. Valerie looked at it. Then smiled too. Michelle could no longer hide it. She needed to see too.

As Charlie turned the screen, she saw "Paulo" or whatever he was called, face down, hands tied behind his back, with a bright pink dildo sticking out of his arse. His three friends all the same. Hands tied. Dildos inserted. Charlie couldn't help laughing. And slowly, the ladies began to laugh with him.

And as they all raised a glass to the end of "Enrique," Nikki was laying back across the office desk. And Giles slipped his cock into her mouth, as Tommy adjusted the tripod for the video camera, then knelt and buried his head between her legs. As his knees hit the floor, he didn't feel the phone hit the carpet, nor did he realise that he had dialled Michelle as he did so.

Michelle had just gone to the bathroom, when Valerie saw the light flashing on the top of the phone. She picked it up, and saw "Tommy" she took her finger to her mouth, and made sure Charlie understood the need for quiet. As she slid her finger across the screen, she hit speaker, and slowly realised that the call should never have been made. She heard the toilet upstairs flush, and ended the call.

But not before both her and Charlie had both heard, "make her gag Giles," and a belly laugh, as a woman's voice said, "yes daddy, fuck naughty Nikki's mouth hard."

They looked at each other. "Not a word," Valerie said quietly. Charlie nodded.

"Hello princess," he smiled as she came into the room. "What an eventful day!" and the three friends settled to enjoy a couple of hours of each other's company, while in Charlie's mind, he needed to fix another problem, and it was his ex-girlfriend. Valerie too was now thinking deeper about her husband, the deals, her life, and her beloved Jamie. Why had she been so stupid to not leave for him? None of them quite knew what they were going to do, but they knew that they needed to do something. And that one way or another, Michelle needed to find the strength to leave the man she was married to, and live a happy life with Charlie, and she knew she was prepared to do it.

As Giles shouted, "I'm going to come," Nikki wanked him hard into her mouth.

Tommy took an expensive camera, and made sure the photos were both good, and good quality. He was beginning to like the naughty little tramp, she was game for anything, and Giles had made a contact that liked porn more than drugs. Nikki would serve a very useful purpose whilst Tommy learnt a little more about this very lucrative industry. He ordered Nikki to turn over and bend forward. As she did so, he sprinkled the cocaine over her arse cheek. Leant down, and took a huge line. He stood up. His limp cock not interested in sex. He slapped her arse, "get dressed," he demanded. "Go and do your bloody job," Nikki slipped her panties on, rubbed her arse cheek, desperate for just a small taste of the coke, and smoothed her skirt down before leaving the office. "I've found your addiction, Giles old boy!" Tommy laughed.

Giles boomed. "You might just have done so dear boy."

24 "MICHELLE GETS ANGRY"

The following day, Valerie informed Giles she needed to take her car to be looked at. Giles waved her on like she was some sort of inconvenience. She said nothing, but left the house. Seething with rage. It was time for him to learn a lesson. And Tommy. But how? She drove to Summer Autos.

As she drove she called Charlie. "Can you see me?" she asked, sounding a little desperate.

"Of course," he answered, trying to sound as calm as he could.

"Good," she said, realising she was too snappy, he was only trying to help. "I will see you shortly." When she got to the stables, she went inside. Callum was nowhere to be seen. She called out "Charlie, are you there?"

"Do you want sugar?" The question came back. "And come up, I have sent Callum out in the truck"

She went up the stairs and into the office. Charlie was behind his desk, and she could see he was distraught. "I know how you feel," she said. I have always known Giles needed young pussy to make him aroused, but this is taking the piss." She spat the last words out with a depth of anger that slightly surprised Charlie.

He answered rather weakly, "I know."

"So, Mr fixer upper, how do we fix this?"

Charlie had no idea. He needed time. He needed to think clearly. Whatever he wanted, and how desperately he may have wanted it, there was Michelle to think about. And, much as he was ok with Valerie, he also got the feeling she knew perfectly well what Giles did, and to be honest, she wasn't his concern.

She sensed what was in his mind. "I want Michelle to be ok too," she said, calmer now. "Tommy is a monster, and he thrives on it. Giles is a weak man, but also one who enjoys exploiting other people's weaknesses. However, I think Tommy is slowly taking over, and if, and perhaps when he does, it can only end in tears."

Charlie looked thoughtful. "Give me time," he said. "I *know* I will take Michelle away from all this, "*but* ..." he paused, "What about you?"

"Don't worry about me," she answered. "I have enough ammunition and strength to be ok. Jamie was the man I should have been with, but life didn't end up that way. Did you sell the car?"

Charlie told her he had a serious buyer coming next week. "What do you want to do with the money?"

"Give it to charity," she said gently. "Your choice which one," and she smiled at him.

"Ok," he replied. "If you are sure."

"I'm sure Charlie," she said. "I am off, and, for now, all is normal ok. I have spoken to Anesh. He is happy with your word. He trusts me, but never trusted Giles. So, when you have the funds available, let me know, and he will make it happen." She stood up. "Thank you," she smiled. "I seem to be saying that a lot to you lately don't I?"

"Don't mention it" he smiled back. "Let me know when Anesh has everything in place, and I will transfer the money."

Valerie passed her coffee cup. "I will," she said. "Look after her," and she turned on her heel and left.

Charlie couldn't help feeling that things were getting a little out of hand. And his ex- girlfriend was almost *certainly* part of the cause. Perhaps that was his best starting point. He had no idea where she was living now, but was eternally glad she wasn't around anymore. He needed to find out where she was living. And there was only one way to do that. Tommy's nightclub.

He opened WhatsApp. "Fancy going clubbing?" he sent a laughing face with the message. The reply was almost immediate.

"Are you joking old man?"

"Nope," he sent back. I need your help, and I'm too bloody old to go on my own!" More laughing faces.

Charlie's phone rang. "What's up old man?"

"Nikki is what's up."

"For fucks sake, can't you leave her alone?"

Charlie smiled. "See you at my place about 8. Let's eat, and go party."

Callum laughed on the other end of the telephone. "OK, old man," and the line went dead.

Charlie leant back in his chair. It was time to put things in place. The two men met just before 8. Though there were 25 years between them, they both enjoyed the chance to dress well, and tonight was no exception. Armani jeans, smart shirt, loafers. And smelling good. They enjoyed a decent curry, and chatted about the situation. Charlie told Callum pretty much all that was going on. Callum listened intently. He was always a little hot headed. Always a little angry and full on. Charlie both loved it and loathed it in equal measure. But he was fiercely proud of his boy. He and his ex-wife had not spoken in years, and Callum rarely saw his mum. But Charlie had never stopped him, Callum just preferred it that way. As they reached the club, Callum saw the Challenger. Tommy had changed the wheels to bright green and all the lights had bright green halos.

"He fucking ruined it!" Callum laughed.

"I don't want Nikki to see me if we can help it," Charlie told his son.

"Don't worry old man, it's bloody dark in here, you have to be careful who you pull, you might see them in daylight and shit yourself!" and he laughed out loud. The music was deafening. Charlie wanted to walk out immediately but Callum reminded him of why they were there. Charlie found a small booth and Callum went to get drinks. He saw Nikki at the end of the bar. Her eyes wide. She saw Callum, and Charlie could see the recognition, but she made no attempt to say hello. As the night wore on, Charlie became more and more bored. Callum had met his barmaid, and, when he came back for his drink, Charlie checked his watch.

At 12.45 he had had enough. He told his son," I'm going home."

Callum was pissed now, Charlie stone cold sober, "be safe old man."

Charlie wasn't sure he could guarantee that, but his son was now useless as back up. He went back to his car. He had at least 2 hours to kill. He tried to get comfortable, and closed his eyes. His phone alarm went off at 2.45am, he jumped at the noise. Then realised it wasn't the alarm. It was the noise of a loud engine. A V8. An Aston Martin. As the Aston pulled out, the Bentley followed. Charlie followed a distance behind. It was at least a thirty minute drive from the club, when he saw the cars slip into a side road. All the occupants got out simultaneously. He watched Nikki take a packet from Tommy, as Giles laughed. All 3 climbed the stairs to Nikki's flat, Giles put the key into the lock and let them all in. Charlie waited, after around 30 mins, he decided to set the alarm off on both cars. He waited, it wasn't too long before the curtains opened. And there in all their naked glory were the three of them. He opened his phone and took the photo, Charlie had seen enough.

He started the Saab, and left, fast! His eyes wet with anger. He wanted Michelle; he wanted her to leave with him, to be with him forever. The emotions overcame him. And he sobbed as the car sped along. He rang Valerie. A sleepy voice answered.

"Tell Anesh he will have the money tomorrow," and he hung up.

He arrived back at his house, frustrated and angry. He opened Dial Chat. "I love you Michelle," he knew she would be sleeping. He went to bed, still dressed. His mind in turmoil. He needed to make things happen.

He finished the call with the bank, and rang Anesh.

A brief conversation later, he opened dial chat. "It's ours princess."

He sent Valerie, "thank you, Anesh says its done."

The respective replies were "I love you" and "my pleasure." Charlie felt a warm glow, slowly it was coming together. He just needed to tell Michelle all that had happened with Tommy. *Surely* that would be enough to make her leave? But how?

Michelle neither cared, nor wanted to know where Tommy had been lately. She and Valerie had enjoyed each other's company, and, when those two had not been together, Michelle had enjoyed the company of Charlie. Away from the village. They just drove. Sometimes Charlie would bring out one of his "toys" as he called them. She admired how proud he was of the work he had done for each of the cars he owned. She had no idea of values, but she knew that he worked hard to keep them all immaculate, and as the summer began to draw to a close and with Tommy once again not around, (apparently there were "issues" at the club) she was going to take advantage. Tommy always looked really smart. However, she had noticed he had made sure his suits were all clean, his shirts crisper, and he was smelling good. She had always noticed that about him. He had left around 5pm. She knew the club didn't open until 10, and figured he needed to fuck the polish cleaner if he was going in that early. Michelle had called Valerie. But no, Giles was at home. Valerie commented that he had been making more effort lately. Cleaner shoes, etc. Michelle could only agree. Neither of them quite knew why, but it certainly didn't seem to be anything to do with wanting to look good for their respective wives!

Valerie, after her experience with the sex site, had decided that she and Michelle needed to become a "joint force" against the two husbands. Make sure they cover each other's back. She had cried hard. She hadn't wanted to talk about "Enrique" until one afternoon, she invited Michelle and Charlie to the spa. Not for any treatments, but because she finally needed to talk about it. She had admitted that she had been a fool, and tried hard to get over Jamie, in order to accept his death. But the truth was, she knew she would probably never be able to forget the man she had loved from afar, and that having sex with another man was *totally* not the way to do it.

Michelle joked, "you can share Charlie, I'm sure he would help a damsel in distress!" and she laughed.

Charlie went red.

Valerie smiled. "Much as I admire your man, and indeed, have to say he is a bit of alright!" and she returned the laughter "I'm fairly sure that right now I just need to let myself get over Jamie."

Charlie had felt a little left out of the conversation, when he blurted out "I have sold the car."

Valerie looked at him. "Excellent," she smiled. "What did you get for it?"

"68," he grinned.

"Well done," she replied. "So, what do we do with the money?"

Charlie smiled softly. "I gave it to leukaemia,'' he said.

Valerie drifted off back to happier times. She knew Jamie would approve of Charlie's actions. "Thank you," she said.

Charlie replied, "pleasure," Valerie could see that the bond between Michelle and Charlie was more real than ever. Though Michelle knew Charlie had done the deal with the property in Spain, no one had said anything about the future.

As the night wore on, and the booze got them all more and more intoxicated, Michelle needed to pee. "Don't you two be doing anything now!" she slurred. They all laughed. As she went to relieve herself, she suddenly was overcome with a realisation that she *trusted* Charlie. A sensation she had not really encountered in the last five or six years. She had always known that, as Tommy got more powerful, whether he put more weight on or not, he was always going to be able to have women falling for him, for nothing else other than the Aston Martin and money meant they always would.

She had, like Valerie said, just accepted that it was now part of her life. He was losing himself in the empire that Giles funded, but Tommy operated, and with all that responsibility came ultimate power. Something Tommy loved. To control. To manipulate, to order and to boss around. She found herself sobbing gently as she peed. Knowing that somehow she needed to be brave enough to get herself out of this life. Knowing that she wanted the house in Spain, with Charlie. And a chance she believed to spend the rest of her life with a man who loved her. Cared for her. And wanted her. As she sat, Valerie and Charlie discussed what the next move was. Charlie showed Valerie the photo of her husband, along with Tommy, and his ex-girlfriend Nikki, all naked and certainly not because it was hot.

Valerie smiled. "Wow!" she exclaimed. "He does have a cock after all!" and she laughed as she dismissed her husband as the pathetic, weak individual he actually was.

Charlie asked, "how do I tell Michelle? What do I need to put in place to make things safe?"

Valerie was just about to speak when Michelle came back from the bathroom. "What have you two been up to?" she asked. Valerie looked at Charlie, Michelle saw the glance.

"*What?*" she said a little more angrily now. Charlie returned the glance. "WHAT THE FUCK IS GOING ON!" she screamed.

"Calm down princess," Charlie said. "Sit down, I need to talk to you."

Michelle looked worried. "What is it?" she questioned.

"I think Tommy is having an affair," Valerie spat out.

Michelle laughed. "You mean he is shagging the polish cleaner?" she said, still laughing.

"NO!" Valerie answered angrily.

Michelle stopped laughing. "What do you mean?" she said.

Charlie opened his phone again.

Valerie shook her head and carried on. "Has he changed?" she enquired. Her immaculate eyebrows raised.

"I suppose," Michelle replied. "He definitely seems to be smart all the time, but he also seems to be doing more coke than ever too." And her head fell. "I thought it was just because he was getting more, so he was taking more," she said.

Valerie nodded to Charlie. He opened the phone again. And lifted the screen. To see Tommy, Giles, and a woman all naked.

"Who the fuck is that?" she spat out the words.

" *That,*" said Charlie, his head lowering, "is my ex, Nikki." Michelle stopped. She sat open mouthed. Charlie felt guilty as he said softly "I'm sorry." Michelle wanted to slap him.

The anger building in her. Yet why should she care? Tommy had already been screwing others. Why did she care? Because this wasn't a fuck it seemed. This was him *wanting* another woman. Not just sex. But, if both Valerie and Charlie were right, it changed the whole thing. She was having an affair for sure. But Tommy, that meant sooner or later, she might be no longer needed. And if that was sooner, or she stepped out of line, there was no telling what he was capable of.

"Why should I care?" she answered. "I am having an affair, and I am sure he can too."

Valerie took over the conversation. "My dearest Michelle," she said, almost sarcastically, "If I am right, and Tommy might want to be with this other woman, then you may have more than the affair to worry about. All I am saying is, it makes things that much more dangerous. He now has a woman who shares his love of drugs, who clearly likes his power, and, if you are not careful, you will be surplus to his requirements in a *very* short space of time. The affair is irrelevant. What it represents, is dangerous. It's one thing fucking the cleaner over the toilet. This woman is living in Tommy's flat." And she stopped and took a deep breath.

Charlie had been quiet and listening gently. "I have done the deal for the place in Spain princess," he said. "The house is ours."

Suddenly Michelle felt vulnerable. Almost like the club. She felt she was not in control anymore. She knew she could have a future with Charlie. But she needed time, to understand the man.

To make sure, and to be safe. She had been with Tommy for almost 20 years, had a great life. And one that, though she knew Charlie would love her enough, and she knew he had some money, she was terrified that he would not be the man he seemed right now. And once again she would be let down; be alone, be vulnerable.

"How do you know all this?" she babbled. "How do you know that it is Tommy's flat?" she could feel herself preventing believing. She had no idea why. She knew she no longer loved, or indeed even *liked* Tommy anymore. But the sudden reality he might no longer want or need her had never crossed her mind. The rejection. She needed some time to process things. "So what do you suggest?" she said.

Valerie said. "Do as you were, and put things in place. Make sure you and Charlie can get on that plane. That you can sit on the terrace in Spain without looking over your shoulder and shitting yourself wondering who might be there. But ..." and she paused for effect. "Do it quicker."

"Michelle," Charlie said. "I love you. I have a depth of feeling inside me that I never had for anyone else. And I know I want to take the risk to be with you. But I can't make you. It's got to come from you. I didn't know anything about Nikki and the club, much less Tommy and her. But Valerie is right. If he feels anything for her, and doesn't for you, then he is a potential ticking time bomb. And I do not want you in that danger."

Suddenly, Valerie's phone rang. She put her finger to her mouth and answered

"Giles darling," An agitated voice at the other end of the phone. Valerie nodded. And an occasional "yes I see," or "oh that's not good." When she had ended the call, she looked at the pair of them.

Giles is concerned. She said "Apparently Tommy is not doing what Giles needs him to for the business, and he is frustrated that he has taken his eye off the ball. He wouldn't tell me why. But, if my suspicions are right. It's to do with his new found mistress. And while Giles may be a soft and weak walrus, he has others in positions that Tommy might find less pleasant to deal with."

Michelle found it all a little difficult to take in. She had known she wanted someone to care for her, she loved the way Charlie loved her. But she also knew her husband would not accept her leaving him for another man. Yet, in her mind, she now had a reason. And maybe this was fate. Charlie and his ex-girlfriend, Tommy and the club. Her head began to spin. She felt faint. As she did so. Her phone lit up. She glanced at the clock, 7pm.

Valerie saw her face grow into a grin. "What is it?" she asked.

"Oh, Tommy may be late. He needs to sort out a couple of things at the club apparently." and she laughed. Maybe I should go there," she said angrily.

Valerie looked at her. "Leave it a while," she grinned, with that evil face that Michelle had seen before. "Best to make sure you get what you need."

Michelle got changed, she was going to make sure she looked a million dollars. Short skirt, low cut top and heels. Almost tarty. She knew that she would be able to go in the back way to the club. Charlie parked around the corner. The silver Saab came back into use again. It made you invisible. No one would take any notice of a boring silver car. They got to the club around 11.30, she asked Charlie to wait. There was a small public car park. He slid into a space at the back, and lowered the seat. He had no idea what Michelle planned to do, but he knew he needed to be there to make sure she was ok. Michelle entered the club by the back door. She noticed the doorman, Harvey, was standing in her way. She had known him for years. And, despite his injury to his left arm, no one wanted to get a punch from his right. But she knew there was something wrong. She pushed past him, he tried to protest, but he had a soft spot for Michelle. He had always loved her singing, and he missed the club as a live music venue with well to do crowds. Michelle walked to the office her husband used, the door was not locked. She swung inside. Nothing. He wasn't there and the office looked like it was perfect. Nothing out of place. Nothing out of the ordinary. Just as she was about to leave, she heard a crash. Looked over and saw "managers office". She crept slowly towards the door. She could hear voices. And slowly, she touched the door handle. She took out her phone, opened the camera. And pushed the handle down. The door opened slowly. Nikki was bent over the desk, with her knickers round her ankles. She was attempting to snort cocaine as Tommy fucked her. Calling out, "I love my little slut," as he did so. Michelle had no idea what he was taking, but whatever it was, he clearly didn't hear or see anything except that bitches arse. As he slapped her hard and shouted "oh, Nikki I'm going to come," Michelle closed the door. She knew now, she was closing the door on her marriage and her life with Tommy too. She walked past Harvey, and as she did so, she looked into his eyes. He said nothing, but his expression told her all she needed to know. She smiled at him, and marched out of the club.

She found the Saab. Smacked the window. Charlie woke up with a start. He opened the door. "Hello Princess" he said with a smile. "All ok?"

Michelle had an evil grin on her face. "All is just fine," she said. "Now, take me somewhere and fuck me."

Charlie smiled. Put the car in drive, and slid out of the car park. As they left, Michelle undid her seatbelt. She sat forward, plugged it back in behind her. And she rested her head in Charlie's lap. He looked down. She looked back and smiled. "Can I play?" she teased. And began to unzip him.

He grinned. "I love you, you naughty girl," Charlie said.

And she took him into her mouth. His cock began to grow, and, despite having to concentrate and drive, he enjoyed the sensation. The evening was pitch dark. Clear. Warm. Stars filling the sky. He reached over, and, as Michelle lay across her seat, she spread her legs to allow Charlie access to her pussy. He slipped his fingers inside her knickers as he drove. He found her clitoris, and her legs opened wider. His cock now rock hard and hitting her throat, Charlie slipped 2 fingers inside her as he tried to concentrate on driving. He fingered her hard, and she both sucked and wanked him hard. The country lanes meant it was almost impossible to concentrate fully, and, as he slipped another finger inside her, she moaned loudly and said, " I need you to fuck me." Charlie smiled, and saw the small car park ahead. Praying it was empty, he turned off the lights, and drove in. Empty. He stopped the car. Michelle took his cock out of her mouth.

"Come here princess," he smiled. And stepped out of the car. Michelle now neither cared who saw, or what she looked like. Her skirt round her waist. Her pussy exposed with her knickers to one side. She got out, and took them off. She walked to the front of the car. Charlie was standing, his cock shining from her saliva.

She lay back against the bonnet. And spread her legs. He grabbed them, Lifted them, and pushed his cock inside her.

Michelle screamed. And dug her nails into him. Charlie was surprised at her reaction. Michelle knew this was all of her frustration, energy and love pouring out. She was going to orgasm. It would be hard. And urgent. But she was on the edge. "I LOVE YOU CHARLIE!'' she shouted all at once. As she came he held her. Stopping his rhythm, and just embracing her. "Fuck me!" she cried.

And he did as he was told. Faster. His head was spinning. The lust and love mixed into a heady combination that made him feel nothing but desire for the woman laying beneath him. He looked into her eyes. And stopped. Then very slowly. Pushed once more. As he did so, he held her tight. Whispered softly, " I love you Michelle," and she felt him shudder as he released his semen inside her. His emotions were now overtaking him. Tears came, and he held her as tight as he could. Kissing her neck and releasing himself into her. They lay. Peaceful, spent. Charlie whispered again. "I love you Michelle."

Moments later, they were sitting back in the car. Michelle dressing herself. The emotion now turning to anger. "You *must* make Spain safe," she almost begged.

"I will princess," he said softly. They drove back in silence. Charlie stopped outside the house. Michelle kissed him, and the Saab left. Michelle put the key in the door. It was just after 1.30am.

She sent a message to Valerie. "You are right about Tommy." She went to bed that night full of anger and hatred. But the one thing she knew was that she was no longer scared. It was time to fight back.

25 "TOMMY GETS A VISIT"

Anesh ended the call with Valerie. He had always loved her. Despite the bitterness he felt towards Giles, Valerie was indeed a wonderful person who had never questioned his sexuality or friendship. And he did an awful lot for her based only on her word. The money from Charlie had indeed landed in the bank. And Charlie had sent an extra 20,000 euro to make sure Anesh had no problems in any registration or paperwork issues he might run into. Anesh smiled, 20 grand for doing nothing he liked very much indeed. He had around 50 properties at any one time and he had most of the officials that he needed to keep on side in his pocket. So one property deal for a guy like Charlie Summer was a breeze, when he was used to doing them for far more high profile clients. He wanted to keep Valerie happy, so he had done it, "as a favour", and he felt anything that allowed him to get one over on that arrogant arsehole Giles meant a one up for him.

Charlie didn't care about the money. He had worked bloody hard, and also had been very shrewd, it had allowed him to build a fortune that only really his son knew the depth of. Charlie knew that there was a chance of losing everything, but he was pretty confident his son was smart enough, if a little hot headed, to make sure things would be fine.

Valerie smiled as she put the phone down. Anesh was such a sweetie. And, if things went the way she thought they might, she would need all of Anesh's help and know how to make sure that Charlie and Michelle had a chance of making their life what they wanted it to be. She was no longer mourning Jamie, but was determined that she would no longer let herself lose focus. She had lost the one thing she loved dearly. She would not let Michelle do the same. Nor would she let Giles or Tommy stand in her way anymore. She was definitely strong enough to take them on.

Tommy slept late. Michelle was pleased. The last thing she wanted in her mood was him trying to be nice. She had made sure that she could get into the loft, and that suitcases were easily accessible. When the time came, she wanted nothing holding her back. She went into the bedroom where Tommy was sleeping heavily. She smiled, it would be so easy right now. Yet she knew she needed to be practical, nothing stupid. She opened her phone and looked at the photo she had taken of him with that slut. She leant over Tommy; every fibre of her body wanted to lash out, to take revenge. She picked up the scissors. No! she was not about to. She had to take her time and make sure.

Charlie rang Callum. "I need a chat mate, what are you up to?"

A female voice in the background said, "come back to bed."

Charlie smiled. "Tell her your dad said no, he needs a chat."

Callum laughed. "OK old man," he replied. See you in an hour or so."

Charlie smiled, it was 20 mins to his house! Callum clearly was going to make the most of Sam the barmaid before answering his dad's request! Charlie muttered. "Little shit," and went to his man cave. Whenever he felt pressure, Charlie closed the door to the huge garage, and turned up the music. He looked around, it was a strange sort of barn. It had a jukebox: lots of old pictures and signs, some wonderful speakers, and four cars that Charlie would never sell. He just came and looked some days, the fruits of his labour. If everything else went wrong, he had his special cars, that he would never want to sell. But if he had to, he had enough to start again.

Almost bang on the hour, he heard a voice. "Beer or cider old man?"

And he smiled, his son was just as bad as him with the booze at times. And it warmed him that he could trust the business and most of his treasures to his son.

As Callum approached, Charlie wasn't sure how best to speak to his son. He decided just to come out with it. "I'm moving to Spain son,"

Callum looked at his father. "With Michelle?" he questioned.

"With Michelle," he returned.

Callum looked at his dad. "You in love old man?" he smiled.

"I am you little shit!" Charlie replied.

"As long as you are, you know I will have your back, but ... are you sure? You know nothing about her, do you?"

Charlie smiled. "I know enough." He reassured his son. "I will be back. But I need to get away and let the dust settle. We know what her old man can be like," and he held his arms up to show off his muscles. A belly he may have, but the arms still packed a punch.

"Then I'm happy for you dad," his son replied. "Can I have the Aston?"

Charlie threw a bottle top at him. "Not until I'm dead!" he laughed. "Besides, you have enough bloody cars!"

Callum laughed. "But I don't have a DB5!"

"And you still don't!" Charlie smiled. He stood and gave his son a hug. "Thanks mate," he said with affection.

Callum smiled. "That's alright old man. Now, you gonna buy my dinner?" The two men talked late into the night.

Valerie sat in silence with her husband, and Michelle waited for Tommy to leave for the club. And began to sort suitcases, she emptied her jewellery, and smiled. She finally had a reason to smile.

It was around a week later that Giles summoned Tommy to his office. "Ever since you got involved with that cheap tart you have taken your eye off the ball!" Giles bellowed.

Tommy thought for a moment. Giles was a pussy, but Tommy needed him for the time being. He could feel the anger well up.

Giles continued. "She is nothing but a coke sniffing whore. Why on *earth* do you insist on thinking more of her than that?"

Tommy saw red and the punch landed perfectly. Giles reeled backwards, he fell to the ground, holding his jaw. The blood dripped from his nose. Tommy smiled. Giles looked up. "You just made the biggest mistake of your life you prick," he snarled. "Get the fuck out, and you best decide who you want as a business partner, because you are running out of options, and let's get one thing straight, I can break you in a heartbeat you pathetic coke sniffing cheap lowlife."

Tommy raised his fist again, but this time he thought. Said, "don't you dare rubbish Nikki again," and left.

The door slammed with a force that shook both Giles, and his secretary. Giles smiled, he said to himself, "I have him right where I want him," and rose to his feet. As he poured the scotch, and dabbed at his bloodied nose, he heard the Aston leave. "Time to make sure young Tommy knows his place," he smiled.

Dialling reception, he gave a simple request. "Veronica, get hold of Geoff would you?"

"Yes Mr Williams."

Giles took a large swig of scotch. "I will teach that little prick," he said to himself.

Geoff and Eugene followed the Aston for around 20 minutes. As it turned into the small estate and Tommy opened the door, the two men donned balaclavas. Geoff handed the taller slimmer man a baseball bat. "Don't fucking kill him OK," he barked.

And before Tommy had taken more than 5 steps towards Nikki's flat, the first blow hit him on the back of the head. He fell immediately. And then came the blows; to his body and arms, he had no chance to defend himself. It was over in a matter of minutes, and the two men left - silently. The Mercedes disappeared into the blackness.

Tommy lay there, his breathing heavy. Giles. Fucking Giles. He didn't think the old bastard had it in him. But OK, if he thought this taught him a lesson, then Giles was much mistaken. Tommy would bide his time. He knew that he still needed the arrogant fat prick for now. And at least it proved the old bastard could cut it if he needed to. He knocked on the door of Nikki's flat. At least she would give him the sort of relief he needed.

He took out his phone. "Don't wait up."

Michelle grinned. She sent a dial chat message to Charlie. "Tommy is with her. What are you doing?"

Charlie smiled. I'm coming to pick you up," he returned.

Michelle grinned. She was past caring about Tommy now, he seemed oblivious to her. And, whilst she had felt stronger, she still couldn't confront him whenever he became abusive again. "I'm waiting," she smiled.

Her phoned pinged a WhatsApp message - Valerie. "Anesh says you need to get out to Spain and sign everything." Realising she had sent it to the wrong person, she quickly apologised.

Michelle smiled, she dialled Valerie. "Is it really going to happen?" she squeaked.

"Yes my dear Michelle," she replied. "It's really going to happen!"

Michelle said "thank you!" as gratefully as she could. "Without you I couldn't do this."

Valerie replied. "Just make sure you make it work. I have every faith in you and that man. Be safe and make sure you watch your back."

"I will," Michelle replied, and ended the call.

As she did so, she heard deep growl. For a moment she thought it was the Aston, but this was a different sound. She almost ran to the door. Outside, she saw the most stunning car, but she had no idea what it was. She could see the roof down, and she could see it was old. Charlie didn't pull into the drive, even he wasn't that stupid! But he sat at the end of the drive. As Michelle skipped down the drive and opened the passenger door. "This is amazing!" she squealed with delight. "You must have a very trusting customer!"

Charlie smiled as he pulled away. "It's mine," he smiled.

Michelle smiled. "You are a dark horse," she said. This must be expensive!"

Charlie smiled again. "Are you only with me for my money?" he laughed.

She looked at him, not sure how to take it. "NO!" she exclaimed. "I'm with you because I want to be. I love you Charlie," she whispered.

Charlie looked at her, smiled, and as he faced the road again, he laughed and said, "just coz I have a £500,000 car!"

Michelle was shocked, but she slapped him at the same time. "Is that all?" she smirked "and I thought it was valuable!" and she laughed too.

They drove, nowhere special. Just drove. The stars out, and the evening warm. The love between them no longer in doubt. Charlie said "I have to go to Spain."

Michelle was disappointed. "Why?"

"Anesh needs things signed face to face."

"I want to come with you."

Charlie wanted that too, so badly. But he thought it was too risky. "You need to play happy families. Just until everything is done out there. Then, we will just pack, and leave I *promise* princess."

Michelle was disappointed. She wanted to escape now, though if she was honest, Tommy wasn't around much. And she was not afraid of him when he was. He clearly had had enough of her now. She had served her purpose, and a coke snorting, cock hungry 30-year-old was what he needed. She knew Charlie was right. But no matter what, she wanted to be out of the UK as soon as she could. The rage she had felt as Tommy slept had almost been overpowering. And if Michelle hadn't had Charlie, she could have seen herself finding a way to end that *bastards* life. Charlie drove a little faster. The Aston growled and leapt forward. Michelle sat back, looked at the stars, and smiled. It wouldn't be too long. She could wait for Charlie to finish the deal with the house. No matter what happened, she would love this man who loved her, and she was certain, it was forever.

A week later, she was watching Charlie leave for Spain. It would be a long and painful few days for Michelle. She missed him more than she cared to think about, but she knew that this was the only way it would work out. Charlie was both clever, and smart. He was clearly a good businessman, and also a bloody good liar if he had at least one half million pound car, and goodness knows what else!

As he went through the gate, Michelle turned, the tears being held back.

She walked out of the airport lounge, and saw Barry, he smiled. That warming smile she had seen so many times. "Hello Miss Michelle," he said brightly. "Miss Valerie said you might need a lift," and he opened the door to the Mercedes.

Michelle looked inside. Valerie smiled. "Get in woman," she laughed, and Michelle saw the glass in her hand. She stooped to get into the car, and Barry gently shut the door behind her.

"I didn't expect to see you," Michelle smiled.

"I wassshnt supposed to be here" Valerie slurred.

Michelle laughed. "Are you pissed?" she asked.

"On the way!" Valerie laughed.

"What's the occasion?" Michelle enquired.

"My Daaahling Michelle," Valerie began, "I finally told my no good arrogant husband what I think of him screwing that cheap slut!"

Michelle no longer smiled. "You did what!" she said loudly.

Valerie laughed again. "I told the wanker I knew he was shagging the woman at Tommy's club," and she burped loudly. "And do you know what he said?" she smiled.

"He said, it's not me you want to worry about you stupid woman. Perhaps you should look closer to your friends - or their husbands! *Can you fucking believe it?*"

It was Michelle's turn to laugh. "So he has chucked his best mate, golf buddy, and business partner under the bus? *Why?*"

Valerie handed her a drink. "I think they have fallen out," she smirked. Suddenly an air of sobriety over taking her. "So, you best make sure you get things fixed soon. Because if this carries on, I sense things becoming really ugly, really quickly."

Michelle sunk her drink. She was right. Hurry Charlie. Hurry.

Callum finished his pint. Sam was smiling as she pointed to the glass. She mouthed "Another?" Callum shook his head. "Come back to mine when you finish," he said, and slowly walked to the bar. He kissed her hand, and walked outside. As he did so his phone rang, he looked at it, it was almost 11pm. And the simple name - "Tommy – Challenger."

Callum answered. And was greeted with, "you stupid little cunt, what the fuck is that piece of shit you sold me?"

Callum answered swiftly, and precisely. "Fuck off you arrogant prick," and he ended the call. No matter who Tommy thought he was, Callum was young, big built, and definitely had a temper that at times he found difficult to control. As his phone rang again, he took a deep breath. He answered again. "What the fuck do you want now?" angry and harsh. He spat the words out.

The reply was menacing. "The car doesn't work, you best see it does."

Callum laughed. "Fuck off!" and ended the call. As he got home, he text Sam. "I will leave the keys under the mat. Let yourself in, I have something I need to attend to."

"OK," came the reply. "Don't be too long x !"

Callum smiled. He wouldn't be too long. But he was not going to be spoken to like that by anyone, let alone a jumped up shit nightclub owner who dealt drugs. He just needed to let Tommy know he would look at the car, when *he* wanted to, and not when Tommy thought he had to dance to his tune. He slipped the Saab into gear, and drove to the club – fast! The anger and testosterone pumping through his veins. He parked the car in the same car park as his father had a few weeks ago. He made his way into the club. He looked around, checking the bouncers. He knew where the office was, he had been there a couple of times when he was doing the deal over the car. He somehow managed to dodge the security. And it wasn't too long before he was at the door of Tommy's office. He took a deep breath and opened the door. As he did so, he saw Nikki, knickers off, with her legs spread on the winged chair, and Tommy between her legs sniffing cocaine off her thighs.

"Well isn't this cosy," he laughed.

Tommy turned around. "You fucking little prick!" he shouted. And lunged at Callum.

Callum neatly side stepped him and he fell to the floor. Callum laughed again, as Nikki tried to cover her modesty. "Don't cover up on my account you cheap slut," Callum smiled.

She reached for her knickers. Callum stood on them, she looked at him with hatred. "You are just like your fucking dad," and she spat in his face.

Callum heard Tommy get up. He swung the back of his hand towards Nikki, it connected just by her temple and she fell to the floor.

Tommy grabbed him. As he did so, Callum leant forward. Tommy's drugged body both pumped up, and useless in equal measure. He fell again, and as he did so, Callum knelt on his neck. Tommy swung a fist that Callum easily held, he looked into Tommy's eyes. "Don't you fucking dare speak to me like that again, you cunt. I don't care who you are, or who you think you are, you will not speak to me like that."

Tommy's breath came in short spells now. The drugs were making him lose himself all too quickly. "Oooooh oooh OK," he gasped.

Nikki lay spread-eagled on the floor. She held her head and sobbed.

"Shut up you silly cow!" Callum barked.

"Now," he looked back at Tommy. "I will come and look at the car tomorrow, OK?" Tommy nodded. "I'm going to leave now," he said softly. "I never saw a thing, and I certainly won't be running to the cops. But I'm warning you. You fucking speak to me like that again, and you will wish you had never been born."

As he left, Tommy crawled towards Nikki. "You OK?" he said breathlessly. She nodded.

Tommy looked at the door. "Little prick," he muttered. And he pushed Nikki down, opened his fly, and put his soft cock in her mouth. "Suck it!" he demanded. Nikki did as she was told.

Callum got home to find Sam asleep on the sofa.

His mobile lit up. "You OK?" came the question from his father.

"I'm all good old man," he smiled.

"You have been upsetting people I hear."

"News travels fast," he laughed.

Charlie replied. "Just be careful."

"I will old man." Callum sent back.

He felt cheerful. And, as he went to the fridge, and opened the beer, Sam woke up.

Callum smiled. "Hello sleepy head," he said. She rubbed her eyes. "Coming to bed?" he winked, and started up the stairs.

Sam smiled. "YES!" she squealed. Callum turned his phone to silent.

26 "KNOW YOUR FUCKING PLACE"

Anesh poured another wine. He and Charlie sat on the terrace of Charlie's new house. A beautiful, typically Spanish looking 4 bedroom villa, hidden in the hills. Not far from the one he had stayed in with Michelle. Charlie smiled as he surveyed the orange trees, and thought of making a life here with Michelle. "It's beautiful," he commented.

"It most certainly is," Anesh agreed. "Much better in the hills than near the beach. You can absorb the peace when you need to escape, and the beach is a 20 minute drive."

Charlie nodded. "I am grateful," he said.

Anesh smiled. "Valerie is a dear friend. I can't stand her husband, but she and I go back a long way. She doesn't often ask me for favours, and I was happy to help."

Charlie poured more wine. He knew Anesh was gay, so had no need to question if there was a romantic reason, but he was curious. "What happened, if it's ok to ask?"

Anesh looked wistfully into the distance. "Her husband, Giles and I used to do a few property deals. Not always as straight as perhaps either government would want. Giles is a powerful man, but he is also a bigot. He never knew I was gay. Anyway, I got on well with Valerie from the start. She had time for me. We chatted, and were genuine friends. Giles thought I was hitting on his wife. So one night, when I left a club, two guys let me know in no uncertain terms to stay away from her. I spent a couple of days in the hospital. Didn't answer calls, and Valerie was worried. She and Giles went back to the UK. And when I got back home, I told her what had happened. She confronted Giles. She is a *hell* of a strong lady! She told Giles I was gay."

"Giles called me and I didn't answer."

"So he sent me a message," "sorry about the misunderstanding."

"I replied," "Go to hell,"

"And that was the last time I ever saw or dealt with him. But Valerie and I always kept in contact, we are great friends. It's sad that she never managed to make a life with Jamie, she loved him deeply."

Charlie slowly put the pieces together. "I'm sorry for what you went through," Charlie said sympathetically.

"I'm not!" laughed Anesh, it made me clean up my act too, and most of my deals are pretty straight now, and he winked and smiled, "unless it's a rush job for an old friend."

Charlie chinked glasses. "Thank you again," he smiled. And surveyed his house once again.

Callum kissed Sam and went downstairs and into the kitchen. He opened his mobile. "Hope all is good old man, need a pint when you get back," and sent it. He checked the time, 8.30. Shit, he never slept in! He heard Sam moan. And decided he would make her moan some more before starting his day. He smiled to himself, and went back to bed.

Michelle had been up for ages, and she had left Tommy in bed. She was puzzled, she had certainly not expected him home. He spent less and less time there now. She went to the kitchen, made a coffee and sent Valerie a message. Just as she was about to push send, there was a soft knock at the door. She opened it, and Valerie was there.

Valerie stepped inside. "Black, no sugar please," she smiled. "And let's have it in the garden shall we?" and she swept through the house in an almost regal manner.

Michelle smiled. She had absolutely no idea how the woman did it, but she always commanded an audience, whoever that audience might be! She brought the coffee out.

Valerie kicked off her shoes and sat on the sun lounger. It was hardly glorious sunshine, but she clearly had things to say that she didn't want to be overheard. "Anesh called me," she said, "he likes Charlie." Michelle went red. "Don't be embarrassed girl, believe me from that man, that's a massive compliment!" and she laughed, softly. "But ..." her voice hardened. "I am worried for you and Charlie, something is rumbling between Giles and Tommy, and it doesn't feel good."

Michelle looked concerned. "Are you ok?"

Valerie smiled. "I'm ok my dear Michelle, but I have this gut feeling that things are getting ugly. Giles is back to his arrogant self-assured self again. And back to getting a blow job off his secretary it seems, which seems to satisfy him. But there is no mention of Tommy. No golf, no cosy nights out. I don't know why I feel uneasy, but I do."

"What do you want to do?" Michelle said.

Valerie broke, her eyes filled with tears. "I want Jamie back," she sobbed. And made sure her sunglasses hid the emotion.

Michelle stood her coffee down. She put her arms around Valerie. As she did so, Valerie whispered in her ear, "make this work for you," and she held Michelle tight. "He is a good man, and you deserve to be happy."

Michelle sat back. "So do you Valerie."

"Right now Michelle," she sat back and looked at her friend, "if I can help you find your happiness, then that will make me happy. My happiness died the day I lost Jamie, and, one day I might look for more, but right now, I have a focus and a drive to help you get out of this." She waved her arms to demonstrate the house and money, "and have something that fills your heart, not just your bank balance." She took a big swig of coffee. "Sorry for the tears," she smiled. "Now, Charlie is back today, and Anesh tells me everything is sorted. So it's time to decide when you are going, and how you are going to do it. Barry is outside, and I thought we could take a drive."

Michelle smiled. "You are a crafty cow," she said, "here at 11am, and all planned to get me out of the house!"

Valerie laughed. "Of course," she said. "So go get dressed, and let's get out of here!"

Michelle returned less than 15 minutes later. She shut the door and got into the Mercedes.

"Hello miss Michelle." Barry always had a cheery greeting for Michelle. She returned the hello and smiled.

"Where are we going?" Michelle asked. "Sit back and relax," Valerie told her. It took well over an hour to get to the airport.

Charlie was waiting outside. "Morning Mr Charlie." Barry shook his hand.

Charlie smiled. He didn't mind old school. "Morning Mr Barry," and he placed the case in the boot. As he got in, he was greeted by two faces smiling. "I didn't expect a welcoming committee," he beamed. "What do I owe this pleasure to?"

Valerie smiled. "You two need to get your arse into gear," she said softly. "And I intend to make sure you do," and she laughed. So I thought I would take you both out and make it happen. I have spoken to Anesh. He has a couple more small palms to grease, and it's all good to go. So, I guess within a couple of weeks, your Spanish adventure could begin."
Another hour passed, before they drove into a small quaint village. Barry found a small car park, and parked away from everything, over in the corner, out of sight. As the three of them left the car, Barry lowered his seat, and pulled his cap down. Valerie smiled. "Get 40 winks Barry," she laughed.
"Oh er, right, yes, Miss Valerie," he sat up.

They walked to the small pub. A traditional, quaint, thatched roof, low beams, open fire type of English pub, beautifully decorated with hanging baskets, and a wonderful charm.
As they stepped inside, a voice called out "VALERIE!" and a small black guy leapt from the kitchen beaming as he did so.

Valerie greeted him warmly. She introduced her two friends and said proudly, "this is Simon."
"Come in," he enthused, "I have prepared something special for you all." He led them into a small dining room.

"You are just full of surprises!" Michelle commented.

"I try darling," Valerie laughed.

They sat, and Simon brought wine. Michelle exclaimed, "it's not 12 yet!"

Charlie replied swiftly, "It's five o'clock somewhere!" and laughed. Simon poured gently, and asked Charlie to taste. "Superb!" he observed.

Simon looked pleased. And left the bottle. "*Excellent!*" he said as he shuffled off.

"So," Valerie began. "What do you propose to do?"

Michelle and Charlie looked at each other. "No bloody idea!" they said in unison.

"I thought as much," Valerie said sternly. "So, I have taken the liberty of arranging a few things myself."

Charlie spoke first. "Thanks," he said, "but I don't think we need your help. It's down to us."
Valerie shot him a look that would have frozen hell. "You think you can just walk out? You think Tommy wont at least want revenge? *You think you will be able to take him on and that it will be a fist fight and all be done?*"

Charlie thought about going into a long explanation about what he would do, but stopped himself. "I don't know," he said and hung his head slightly.

"Sorry," she said slightly apologetically. "I know he is screwing Nikki, and Michelle and I both think he will want more.

274

But who knows when? Who knows if the cheap little tart suddenly becomes boring and he has no need for her again?"

Michelle shuddered. "So you are saying, jump now, because if we wait for *him* to decide he no longer wants me around, it may be too late?"

Valerie turned to her. *"Yes* Michelle," she said. *"If* you two are sure you can make it work, and that this is what you want, then I'm saying, get ready, and *go for it!"*

Charlie listened. "Ok," he said, "so if he has Nikki, why would he care about Michelle leaving?"

Valerie laughed. "For a bright man, you are very dim," she mocked. "Because he thinks he *owns* her, she belongs to him. Whatever he is doing is irrelevant. Michelle *belongs* to Tommy, and *only* he can decide if he wants to get rid of her. No one can "take" her."

Charlie nodded. "I see," he said. "Ok Valerie," I'm listening."

As Simon appeared with the first course, beautiful salt and pepper squid, Giles was making a phone call. "Tommy dear boy!" he boomed. "Why don't you come over for a chat and let's shake on it and put all this nonsense behind us."

Tommy listened. "Fine," he replied. Puzzled, he listened further.

"Good Man," Giles said, "see you about 2pm for 18?" and he hung up.

Tommy looked at the clock, it was just after 12.30, plenty of time.

He sent a message to Michelle. "Where are you?" the short reply.

"Out with Valerie, don't know what time I will be back."

He smiled, and sent another message, this time to Nikki, "I'm alone for a couple of hours."

As they finished their main course, Tommy was taking Nikki from behind. Bent over the bed that he and Michelle had shared.

Michelle emptied her glass, as Valerie told her that there was a safe flat, owned by Anesh, not too far from the airport. She had used it sometimes to see Jamie.

Michelle laughed. "You are such a dark horse," she smiled.

"I have to be darling," Valerie replied. "When you are married to Giles, you have no choice. You pretend to be the meek and mild kept woman, it suits me."

Simon brought dessert. As he did so, back at Michelle's home, Tommy told Nikki to get dressed, he had a meeting to attend. She teased him, laying on the bed, spreading her legs and her pussy. Doesn't daddy want to fuck me again?"

He glared at her. "Get dressed," he snapped. Nikki saw the anger. She did as she was told.

Giles was already at the golf club when Tommy swung in. He was greeted by Geoff.

There was no love lost between them. "Giles is in his office," Geoff told Tommy sharply.

"Whatever!" Tommy replied, as he locked the Aston.

"Watch your mouth," Geoff returned as he walked off.

"Come in dear boy," Giles boomed in his brash over the top manor. "Sit down, Scotch, or do you still have that hankering for rum?" and he laughed loudly.

Tommy didn't trust him. "Rum is fine," he returned.

Giles handed him a small tumbler. "Now look dear boy," he began.

"Who the fuck gave you the right to call me dear boy?" Tommy exploded.

Geoff entered the room. Along with Eugene.

"I will call you whatever I want dear boy!" Giles spoke loudly, and without fear. "You have taken your eye off the ball dear boy," he smiled. "And that cheap tart is the reason."
Tommy clenched his fists. As Geoff opened his jacket to reveal a gun, Eugene followed. And the silencer on the end of each one meant they didn't care who heard. "Now I don't care who you screw, or what you snort," he snarled, "but when it starts to impact on my business, I have to ask myself, is he the right man for the job?"

Tommy stood to his full height. "You *know* I'm the right man for the job."

As he did so, Geoff took out the pistol. "My dear Tommy," Giles said patronisingly. "I am sure you *were*, whether you still are remains to be seen. However, we have a delivery coming in a couple of weeks. By sea. Discreet. Untraceable. And I need you to oversee it. It will involve a trip to Amsterdam. And then controlling the operation as it progresses. Just a couple of days, but I will be out of the country."

Tommy seethed inside. "Where are you going to be?" he questioned.

"With my darling wife, on a cruise playing the doting husband," and he laughed. "You should try it sometime," he chuckled. "Now get out, and don't forget who runs this show!"

Tommy left quietly. He had not thought much about Michelle since Nikki had appeared. She was always too busy swanning about with Valerie anyway. What did he care? He drove back home slowly. The Aston wanted its exercise, but Tommy needed time; time to think, time to process.

As he drove, Valerie, Charlie, and Michelle were finishing another bottle and congratulating Simon on a simply stunning meal. Valerie told them she had met Simon on a cruise a few years ago. And had been so impressed, she briefly had him as her personal chef for parties and gatherings, even the odd Christmas meal. Giles had enjoyed it, he loved Simon's food, but always had a prejudice against him being black. So slowly, Valerie had encouraged him to do his own thing. Giles had no idea, he just thought that Valerie had gotten bored of him. But she had wanted him to succeed, so she syphoned off enough to allow Simon to buy the pub. And the deal was, he still cooked for her, and repaid the loan interest free. He also knew when to be private, and therefore this was perfect. A great meal, some great friends, and a plan to let two people she loved dearly now, succeed in their life.

Tommy got home. Slammed the door, he was angry! He knew Giles was right. But he liked Nikki; he liked the coke, he liked the sex, he wanted her. Michelle would have to go, somehow. He already knew she was up to something, and was bloody sure it was someone up her! He showered, and waited.

He decided to call Michelle. She picked up immediately. "Hello Darling," she said.

Was that sarcasm? "Where are you?" he snapped. "And who are you with?"

"I'm out," she answered just as angrily, "and with Valerie, would you like to speak to her?"

"Fucking right I would," Tommy smiled.
His smile soon fell, as Valerie said simply "Hello."

Tommy ended the call, and punched the wall. He felt he was no longer in control. And Giles was right, Nikki *had* made him take his eye off the ball. But he couldn't stop; much like the drug he had become addicted to. He *wanted* her, he loved her debauchery and slut like nature. He enjoyed the power over her too. Fucking her like the cheap whore she was made him feel big and powerful and important. And the cocaine she took with him only served to make the experience ten times more intense. Little did he know he had a slut at home who had not needed drugs to make her go places she never thought she would have. Things had to change for sure, especially if he was being trusted to run the whole show while Giles wasn't around. But one thing was for certain, sex and drugs with Nikki were not about to change anytime soon.

As Michelle walked through the door he was waiting. He sat, having moved the armchair to face the door. Like a firing squad with just one member, or perhaps a courtroom with just the judge. He smiled at her as she came through the door. "Where the fuck have you been?" he said.

"None of your fucking business," she snapped back.

He could feel the anger run through his veins. She had never answered back, not like that. He didn't like it, and yet, oddly, he was proud too. Finally she had some balls. He stood and walked to her. "Be very careful," he warned. "I gave you all of this, and I can just as easily take it all away."

Michelle laughed. "You pretentious prick," she started.

As the last syllable came out of her mouth Tommy struck her. One swift yet accurate and deadly blow. Michelle fell to the floor. She lay quiet for a moment. The shock reeling inside her. But this time there would be no tears. "*KNOW YOUR FUCKING PLACE!*" he boomed.

Michelle got to her feet, he was taken aback. She walked towards him. "Be very careful," she whispered, and she walked towards the stairs.

Tommy stood in silence. Michelle padded up the stairs softly. And made her way to the guest room. It was done. She and Charlie would go as soon as possible. It was time to leave. She shut the door, locked it, and fell onto the bed.

Tears filled her eyes, both through the pain of Tommy's fist, and the pain of having to wait just a little longer.

It seemed as though Charlie had a sixth sense. "You ok princess?" the message on Dial Chat read.

Michelle sent back. "I'm ok." She closed her eyes, and sleep came easily. The food, the wine, the journey back, the wonderful company, the laughter, and the crashing blow Tommy had given her, meant sleep was now her escape. She fell deep.

Tommy paced around in the living room. Who was this woman? She had never behaved that way. Who the fuck was she to threaten him! He would make sure she knew she couldn't speak to him like that. Yet, deep inside, he also had a fear. She really had *never* behaved like that before. He couldn't quite put his finger on it. But there was a steely determination oozing from his wife, and he had no idea what was going on in her head, but whatever it was, worried him just a little. He opened the rum bottle.

His phone lit up. "Does daddy want to relax?" came the text.

He threw the phone across the room, turned the TV on, found the porn channel, and took out his cock. He needed nothing and no one. And in a couple of weeks, he would show Giles just how much he no longer needed him. As the film flickered and the sex scenes began to turn him on, he slowly wanked himself to orgasm, before downing the rum and falling asleep. His mind couldn't relax. The troubles in his head may have been slowed by the booze, but they were still battling him, and he woke at 4am sweating and a little confused. He slowly took in his surroundings, and then everything came back to him. Just as he was about to smash upstairs and make sure Michelle understood he was not going to let her get away with what she had last night. He saw the scissors on the table. He could have *sworn* they were not there when he had entered the room, or were they? He took a deep breath and decided that perhaps, just this once, he would let Michelle think she had won the battle of minds.

7am and Michelle woke with a smile. She felt good in herself, and with what she had planned. Tommy had been totally out of it when she slipped into the lounge and placed the scissors on the edge of the table. She grinned to herself as she thought of that moment she could have. The anger, the frustration. The thought that, if she had, she would lose Charlie and a future that she believed would make her happy for the rest of her life. She opened her phone. "Sorry I fell asleep," she sent.

The instant reply. "I figured you had Princess," followed by "breakfast?"

Michelle smiled. "In bed?" She received a photo of Charlie. Naked except for an apron, standing with a frying pan in his hand and his cock hard pressing at the fabric. Michelle laughed loudly. "Give me 30 mins," and she was still laughing as she dressed and left the house. Tommy had finished almost a bottle of rum. God knows when he would wake.

7am and Sam kissed Callum softly, and put her hands on his chest. It has been over 2 years now. When was he going to make an honest woman of her? As she lay looking at him, his hair a mess, his slightly grubby hands wandered down her back, and squeezed her round arse. "Come here," he growled. I want you."

"You are such a caveman Callum Summer," she laughed at him.

"I know," he grinned. And flexed his muscles before kissing her and pulling her towards him. She squealed and kissed him back. Biting his lip as she did so.

7am and Valerie heard Giles singing in the shower, badly! What the hell had made him have such a cheery disposition at this time of the morning?

She looked at her phone. And laughed out loud. Michelle had sent the photo of Charlie. She smiled. Sent back, "enjoy breakfast!" and pondered. She had loved her breakfasts with Jamie, and wondered if she would ever feel like that again. She was certain of one thing. She would never go to a site to look for sex again. If "pinky," her trusty dildo, and her fingers were all she had now, then so be it. But "Enrique," had taught her that sex sites were dangerous. She had no idea how Michelle had done it. And secretly, she admired the crazy woman's bravery. But she also now could see the love for Charlie. Something she needed. Something Michelle had long since lost at home. And as the business and drugs had grown, so had the monster called Tommy. Giles was much easier to work, she had him where she wanted him. Especially as he thought the complete opposite. She smiled to herself. Two weeks, and a cruise. Michelle would be on her own then. But Valerie had planned the cruise, planned to keep Giles out of the way. Made sure Tommy needed to run the drug deal. And it would give Michelle and Charlie the chance to make a clean escape. She couldn't do any more.

Giles came out of the shower. His round body glistening wet, and red from the heat. He waved his cock about and said to Valerie "Would you like me to?"

Valerie raised her eyebrows, "Giles my dear," she said sarcastically, "you have barely raised a smile for me for years, why would now be any different?" and she smiled.

283

He looked defeated, he knew she was right. If they were not young and firm he just couldn't get a hard on. He knew his wife had been having an affair, and that was just fine. His young pretty secretary had kept him more than happy. And when she got too old, he simply employed another. Valerie had always been there though; she knew enough about the business to take him down at any point, but it would take her down too. It worked as a relationship, and he knew he could trust her.

He was about to say "I'm sorry," when Valerie put her finger to his lips. "We both know how it is, Giles. Take me on my cruise, make me smile, and let's enjoy a couple of weeks out of all this shit."

Giles smiled. "Yes dear," he said and the relief that his wife really didn't want his cock was clear. He wandered off to the bedroom, as Valerie shuddered at the thought of ever having sex with him again.

27 "RAYMOND"

Charlie opened the door to the man cave.

It was like a small house; with his prized jukebox, a sofa, a bar, and just about enough to make it liveable at a push. Michelle had enjoyed her breakfast, but not the promise that the photo had made her want. Charlie was a decent enough cook, and the Spanish omelette had tasted good. He purchased good coffee too, and she could forgive rock n roll for decent coffee. It was an acceptable trade off, she said to herself. She took in the end of the room, and saw the beautiful blue Aston Martin that had thrilled her so much. She saw the breath-taking beauty of the other cars. "*Wow!*" she said out loud.

Charlie smiled. "Yes Princess," he beamed, "they are pretty wow!" Michelle had no idea what they were. She saw a Ferrari badge and knew it was old. And the Jaguar she knew was an E Type.

Tommy had always wanted one, but, "too unreliable," he would say. "Like screwing Sharon Stone, looks nice for her age, but soon wears out," and she shuddered as she thought of his crude take on a human being sometimes.

"These are my babies."

Michelle laughed out loud. "So I have to compete with cars for your affection?"

It was Charlie's turn to laugh. "No princess," he said, "nothing compares to you, but, he paused for effect, running his hands over the Ferrari, "she definitely runs close!" and he ducked away, knowing the slap would be coming.

Michelle put her hands on her hips. "And I suppose you thought you were going to get my knickers off did you?" she looked at him. "Well tough baby," she laughed and folded her arms. "Go have fun with your "baby" and she turned away.

Charlie wasn't totally sure if she was joking or not. He came up behind her and put his arms around her. She tried to push them away, but the truth was, she loved being in his arms. Safe, warm, and cared for.

"Don't think you can charm me now!" she squealed. As he bit her neck softly, she gave up the fight. She loved it when he caressed her neck. Her body relaxed, and she allowed Charlie to embrace her. He held her tight. Just gently swaying from side to side as he kissed her neck. She needed his lips on hers, and turned. As they kissed, the warmth of love enveloped them both. It felt good, it felt real. Charlie slowly slipped off her top, her breasts exposed. He touched her nipples softly, tenderly. Michelle moaned softly. As his fingers played and pulled at her breasts. She let her head fall back as he knelt and took first one, then the other nipple in his mouth. His stubble felt good against her breasts, and she held his head as his hands slipped down her sweatpants. She was naked underneath, and kicked off her simple shoes as Charlie paid attention to her pussy with his fingers. Slowly he played with her. Fingering her gently and softly squeezing her ass as he stood up. He led her to the sofa. Slipped down his shorts, and released his cock.

Michelle was about to kneel. "No princess," he said gently. "I want to make love to you," Michelle smiled. She stood and straddled him, gently she lowered herself onto him. Feeling him hard inside her. His arms wrapped around her and slowly she began to move. She looked deep into his eyes, and built a gentle rhythm that made sure her clit was enjoying every motion just as her pussy was. Charlie held her waist. Strong rough hands; working hands, honest hands. She felt wonderful as she rode him, his cock deep in her. She could feel him wanting to go faster.

She knew by now that meant he wanted to come. She looked into his eyes, kissed him deeply, and said, "make me come Charlie."

Charlie's eyes lit up. She saw the love and fire in them, he kissed her again. And slipped a finger into her arse. "Come for me Michelle," he said.

She rode him harder, her orgasm is close now. She wanted them to climax together, her breath was shorter. "Charlie!" she cried, "I'm going to come!"

He fucked her now, his body pressing up in rhythm with hers coming down. The sensations on his cock making him lose his mind as Michelle cried "I'm coming!" and her body tensed.

He felt his own orgasm explode from nowhere, his cock shooting hot semen inside her as she slumped forward and kissed him. His finger deep in her ass. His cock releasing the last drops. He took his fingers out. And as he held her and cried "I love you!" the tears flowed from them both.

Michelle managed to whisper "I love you too" as she collapsed into Charlie.

Tommy woke in a foul mood. The headache he knew he would have was very definitely there. He crashed around the house, but it was very obvious Michelle was not there. He wasn't sure what she was up to, and to be honest he didn't especially care, but she knew about his little empire, and, if she was screwing someone else and opened her mouth, it could all go horribly wrong. He needed to find out, but with that bitch, Valerie covering her every move, what chance did he stand? They were as thick as thieves. He shook his head.

As he sat up, his phone lit up. "Fancy a round dear boy?" *GILES*. Fucking Giles! The last thing he needed. But he knew he needed to keep him sweet until the Amsterdam deal was done.

"Give me an hour," he replied. He needed food, and a shower. One hour later, he swung the Aston into the golf club. Giles's Bentley was already there, and he knew Geoff's Range Rover too. He has the boys with him.

He thought, and smiled. Perhaps he thinks I'm here for trouble. And that feeling of power began to rise in him once more. He swept into the club as if nothing had happened. "GILES OLD MAN!" he boomed.

"Tommy *MY DEAR BOY!*" they greeted each other like old friends.

Geoff stood at the bar with his hand resting inside his jacket, just so Tommy knew he still had his piece with him.

Tommy winked at him. "Won't be needing that old son!" he laughed.

Giles looked at the young man and shook his head.

Geoff turned as the two men left for the course. "I don't fucking trust him one bit," he commented to Jo behind the bar.

She never said much, but she saw it all. "Neither do I," she said as she poured a scotch which Geoff downed. "Keep an eye on him" and she carried on as if they had been talking about the weather.

As the two men played the course, Giles gave instructions to Tommy. What he needed to understand. Where he would be staying. How the shipment would be disguised. What he needed to do to ensure nothing came back to them if it went wrong. Tommy felt like a child being told what to do. But he played it cool, and knew if he pulled this off, he no longer needed Giles. He just needed to work out how to get rid of him.

Nikki woke, feeling even more shit than Tommy. She was pissed at him for not replying, but as long as she had the flat and the coke she didn't really give a shit. The sex was OK, but she knew Tommy would never swing, and she missed the feeling of more than one cock at a time. Somehow she needed to get back to the site, but she knew it was a risk. Tommy has told her she belonged to him now. She laughed, and thought "oh that's sweet, he really likes me." Now she saw all too clearly, she really did belong to him. And the thought terrified her. But her dependency on cocaine meant she couldn't get out, not now. Just let her get straight again. She would get clean then, and get back to a normal life. *Fucking* Charlie Summer. If she hadn't needed him none of this would have happened.

Valerie cried. Long deep sobs. She stared at the photos hidden on her phone. "THE VAULT," had become something she had discovered when she and Jamie had wanted to swap naughty photos at the start. Giles never looked at her phone, but she also knew she had never locked it, so she couldn't start now. She slowly built up a collection of images of both her and Jamie, and sometimes the pair of them, that she had looked at and loved ever since he had passed away. She was slowly letting go. But now, with a little time on her hands, and silence in the house, she allowed herself to go back to a happier time. Gazing at photos of the two of them on a small boat, she had loved that weekend. Neither of them knew anything about boats. So they had gone about half a mile, stopped, and just drunk wine and had sex for 3 days! She laughed through her tears. Life could be cruel sometimes, and the only comfort she had was that for the time Jamie had been in her life, she had at least felt alive and wanted and loved and desired. It had been a beautiful time. And she would cherish the memories she had made.

She sent a message. "Make sure you make this work," she smiled. Nothing would bring Jamie back. But if Michelle could make her life what she had wished hers could have been, she could at least smile inside and know she had helped.

"I will. I know it will work, and I can't thank you enough for what you are doing and have done for me."

Valerie sent a smiling face emoji. It was time to start getting things ready. Her husband was taking her away. He had no idea she had planned it all so Tommy would be away doing the deal to allow Michelle and Charlie the time to escape without either Tommy or Giles being around to cause problems. She smiled to herself. She could be a crafty bitch when she needed to be. She closed the vault. Kissing Jamie's photo as she did so.

Michelle left Charlie and sobbed. The day they could leave together couldn't come soon enough. Valerie had told her of all the plans for the deal. How long Tommy would be away and where. She even had flight numbers and his hotel in Amsterdam. The woman was amazing.

Michelle knew she could never repay the kindness, and sometimes still had to pinch herself to believe it was real. That Valerie had done all this and for no apparent reason. However she also knew that, in just over a week, she would be on her own.

Valerie would be away, and so she had to get everything right. Charlie had assured her he would take care of the flights, the car, and everything they would need to escape. He trusted his son to look after the business, and now he had Sam and she was OK in the garage answering calls and stuff, even if she still worked the pub too, he could see it working out. Callum had spoken of a young black kid, what was he called? Alan? No Aaron! That was it. Who Callum wanted to take on. His dad Harvey worked at Tommy's club. Charlie had sworn it was a bad idea, but Callum was big enough and ugly enough to know what he was doing. Charlie smiled. Just over a week, and he would be with the woman he loved so dearly. And put all of the crap behind him. Once they were settled he would ship his babies, the E-Type: the Ferrari, the baby blue Aston Martin and the Mini Cooper, out to the villa. He would sell his house in England, and, with the help of Anesh, it was time for a new life for both him and Michelle in Spain.

Callum welcomed Aaron. "Tea or Coffee," he said.

The young man looked straight at him. "Coffee please, one sugar."

Callum went off to make it. He was pleased. The kid had shown up on time and seemed clean, enthusiastic, and keen to work. He told Callum how his dad had loved cars and he used to work on them all the time until his arm had been injured. Callum didn't press him, however, he knew on the grapevine it had been a gunshot that ensured Harvey would no longer be doing his own mechanics. He also figured Tommy had something to do with the fact Aaron had answered the advert for the apprentice. Tommy clearly hadn't taken kindly to Callum and his little adventure at the club. Callum was cautious, not wanting to give anything away. He showed the young man around, and got him under the bonnet as soon as he could. As he made sure the young man was ok, his phone rang.

"Hello son," came the cheerful voice.

"Hello father," he replied.

"How are things?" Charlie pondered.

"They are ok I guess, one week to go!"

Aaron's ears pricked up when Callum replied, "you lucky sod, I only wish I could start a new life." Laughter. And a little more banter followed. Aaron listened intently. He could only hear snippets, but it was clear Charlie Summer was leaving the country. Where Aaron had no idea. But he intended to find out. And didn't quite imagine it would be so easy. Callum went up to the office. He wasn't yet sure exactly why the young man was here, as all he seemed to want to do was look around. He certainly wasn't going to let him out of his sight, nor did he entirely trust him. But the help would be good if he could make it work, and now that he and Tommy had an "understanding" then he was sure that, no matter how much Aaron would report back, if there was nothing to tell, then it was all good.

In a few days, he could start to help the old man plan for the rest of his life. And that also meant that Callum would be set for the rest of his life too. He decided he needed to call his dad back.

The phone rang. "Hello son," Callum smiled. His father had always tried to help him. But he knew that there was another person in his dad's life. Who, despite not being at the forefront, he knew the old man would be thinking about.

"Have you spoken to Raymond?" Callum questioned. Raymond was his half-brother.

Charlie had enjoyed a brief fling with a married woman. He had been very young indeed, and she had loved having her "toyboy" right up till he got her pregnant. She had kept the child. But made sure Charlie had nothing to do with the child. As Raymond grew up, she had not told either him or her husband the truth. Until she had been diagnosed with terminal cancer. It was then she told both her husband, and also Raymond, the truth. It hit Raymond massively hard. He had become an angry young man. And had lost all sense of reason with both his "dad" and his mother. He saw her dying, and wanted to hate her for what she had kept from him, but the love a son has for his mother had won out, and he held her on her dying day, stroking her head gently as she slipped out of life. The man he had always known as dad had not been able to cope with the confession. He had loved Raymond and been filled with pride when his wife had told him she was pregnant. His dreams had been shattered when he found out about her unfaithfulness. But he had loved the boy for the last 20 years or so. And tried to continue to do so. His "son" had very quickly become someone unrecognisable to him, as the young man watched his mother die, and slowly lost his mind. He had understood, but had been powerless to change anything. Raymond had disappeared one afternoon. Just left, with no explanation. His "dad" began to lose touch with reality, and found solace in booze. Becoming dependent on the bottle just to get him through every day. Eventually he stopped looking for Raymond, and slowly drank himself to death. Raymond meanwhile, had slipped into the dark world of drugs. It had started as a bit of weed to help him relax. But, as he battled more and more with the demons in his mind and his mother's death, he had found other, more dangerous drugs. As he spiralled out of control, he had begun to look for his biological father.

Eventually he had discovered him via Facebook. He had used messenger to make contact with Charlie. Wanted to tell him

what a piece of shit he was, but found a man who had little idea
that he even had a son. He had been told that Ellen had had an
abortion. The two men slowly "sparred" with their emotions,
neither really knowing how to react. Charlie had been saddened
when they eventually met, at his son's dependence on drugs, and
had battled hard to get him help. Raymond had welcomed the help.
And absorbed the programme of rehab that he was introduced to.
He had been clean for 4 years now, and had gained back his
respect for himself, and also for his father who had stuck by him.
Part of his rehab had been enrolling in some sort of course to give
him a focus and a drive to get up in the morning. Though he had
never given the career a second thought, he took a course to
become a chef. Had even had a famous chef involved, and been to
his academy. Though Raymond had never cooked anything except
beans on toast before, he had really shone. Charlie had helped.
Purchasing knives and a car to get him to work. It would never be
perfect, nothing could make up for 20 years, but the two men
enjoyed a father-son relationship. And Charlie was indeed proud of
his son, who now worked in New York. Had opened a restaurant
that Charlie had funded, and was the talk of the town, with the
restaurant full almost every day and night. Raymond was enjoying
life, and grateful to his father, even if he could never love the way
he wished sometimes he wanted to. Charlie put the phone down. He
knew he had to speak to his other son. He checked the clock, it
was early out there. But he guessed Raymond would be awake.

He dialled the number. A weary voice said "hello?"

Charlie smiled. "Is my son there?"

The sleepy female voice on the other end of the line said
in that long southern USA drawl, "Raaaaaaayyyyyyy, it's your pa."

"Hello father," the brightness in his voice made Charlie
feel good.

They didn't speak much, but when they did, it was always positive, and Charlie genuinely enjoyed the conversations. He wasn't quite so sure he would enjoy this one. "Hello son," he said softly. Raymond wasn't stupid.

"What's up old man?" Charlie smiled. "Why is anything up?" he laughed.

"Coz you only ever use that tone when you have something to tell me!" He paused. "So, who is she?"

Charlie suddenly realised it had been months since he spoke to his son. He had told him briefly that he was seeing someone, and Raymond had been pleased for him, but Charlie hadn't really gone into any details. Raymond was still settling himself into his new life, and Charlie hadn't seen any reason to let his son have anything more to think about than himself. "Are you sitting down?" Charlie questioned.

"Shit father, you are scaring me now!" Raymond laughed.

"Nothing to be scared of son," Charlie said softly, "but I am leaving the UK for a while at least."

The silence was deafening. "Is everything OK?" Raymond replied.

"Everything is fine," Charlie replied, "I just need to disappear for a while. And so does Michelle."

Raymond sighed. "She is the one then?" he asked. Sounding a little disappointed.

"She is son," Charlie replied. "I love her, enough to want to take her away from her marriage, and to make a new life."

"Well father," the young man began, "if she makes you as happy as Hannah makes me, then I can only wish you well. I know I''m not there, but, if things get shitty, you are welcome here you know."

Charlie held back the emotions. He knew that, despite the distance, or perhaps even because of the distance, he felt a pride that right now threatened to show itself in tears. "Thanks son," he said in his soft voice.

"No problem father," came the bright response." As soon as I am settled I will make sure you and Hannah come out and visit," Charlie beamed.

"Cool," was the simple reply. "I have to go get the restaurant ready, we serve breakfast now!" Raymond laughed.

Charlie swelled with pride again. "OK son," he said "go make sure your public are ready for you!" he laughed.

"See ya father," came the reply. And the line went dead.

Charlie texted Callum. "Spoke to your brother, all is cool."

He felt the phone vibrate. "Well done old man."

Charlie smiled. He opened Dial Chat. "Tommy leaves tomorrow," was the message staring back at him.

He smiled even more broadly. "Then I guess it's time to make things happen princess," he replied. A smiling face emoji.

He called Anesh. "Don't worry Charlie," said the soft voice. "Everything is in place. Sunday, you and Michelle will collect the keys, and it's all yours.''

Charlie felt yet another rush of emotions. Pride, pleasure, admiration, but above all, love! Tomorrow was Friday and Tommy was leaving the country. And he and Michelle would have more than enough time to disappear before he got back. Charlie needed to sit down with Callum and put a few things in place for the business, but everything else was taken care of. The plane tickets are done, luggage had already been shipped out. Anesh had taken care of everything. Charlie was pretty sure deep down the extra 20k had not been needed, but he didn't care. It gave him the peace of mind that there would be nothing in the way.

He opened his phone. Was about to text Valerie when it lit up. "Good luck to you both," the message read. And a photo of both Valerie and Giles standing next to what could only be described as the most enormous boat. He had forgotten about the cruise!

He returned, "thank you for all you have done." He saw Michelle typing too, her reply was much the same. He smiled as he took a slow walk to the man cave. He didn't really need a house. Not alone anyway. But, in just a couple of days, he would have a house, have a home. And have a person in his life that he loved deeply enough to want to share it all with.

Tommy was in yet another foul mood. He had just got the text from Giles. The photo of the cruise liner and Valerie looking pleased with herself had done nothing to improve his mind set. And the words attached to the photo, "chin, chin, dear boy!" had almost made him explode with rage.

Michelle smiled. She was enjoying watching him get more and more irate. Suddenly realising that this was probably the first deal he had been asked to handle alone. He was running around the house. Searching out the designer labels. Gucci shoes. 3 pairs.

She muttered, "how long are you going for, for Christ's sake?" but thought better of stirring up trouble. The last thing she needed was Tommy on the warpath. She sarcastically asked, "have you lost something?"

Tommy swung around. "*DOES IT FUCKING LOOK LIKE IT?*" he boomed.

"Er yes," she said, her hands on her hips.

He glared at her. "I will fix you when I get home," he said, low and menacing.

Michelle stepped towards him, "Is that a threat?" she smiled.

"No," he looked back at her, *"it's a fucking promise."* And he went back upstairs.

Every fibre of Michelle's body wanted to attack him. The rage and anger inside her boiled as she fought to keep calm, she needed to be calm. In a couple of days she could be free. Tommy would probably try to find her of course, and you didn't need to be a rocket scientist to know, if he looked hard enough, then he could. But for now, she would bite her tongue. She could hear doors being slammed, and swearing. She sat in the kitchen and laughed. Charlie was so chilled. She couldn't wait to be with him!

28 "AMSTERDAM"

As the ship left port, Giles handed his wife a large gin and tonic. "I say old girl," he beamed, his red face rounder than ever, "haven't done this sort of thing in a while!" and he chuckled to himself.

"Splendid idea," Valerie smiled softly. "It's perfect Giles," she said and chinked glasses. Her mind wasn't remotely on her husband, but her two friends who, with any luck, would be almost ready to change their lives forever.

As the boat left the harbour and the sun began to set, Nikki was getting the last of her clothes together. Tommy had told her it was a business trip and she needed to look professional, but she had packed a couple of slut outfits too. The clubs in Amsterdam were supposed to be amazing, never mind the drugs. If she was having a free weekend out there, she was damn sure she was going to take every opportunity to enjoy herself! She laid out her hold ups. The skirt was a little shorter than "business" perhaps, but hey it was only the 1st day. And she knew Tommy liked her thick thighs. Her breasts were large, and, with the push up bra she had selected, she knew her tits would look good for whoever Tommy was trying to impress. She smiled, and turned on the bath. One more night alone, and then she could have some real fun with him. She wondered just how far he was prepared to go? After all, even Charlie had swung for a while, but he lost interest as the drugs took her over. She laughed to herself, Charlie was such a lightweight. As she stepped into the bath, she took a photo and sent it to Tommy. She sank beneath the water, and slowly began to shave her legs, before venturing higher.

As she did so, the reply "more!" came back.

She smiled to herself, spread her legs and opened herself. She took the photo, pressed send, and waited. It wasn't long before Tommy sent a photo. He was in his office, his cock bulging in his trousers. She slipped a finger inside her, and began playing with herself. She clicked the phone to video, and began to film herself playing. Sending the short clip to Tommy she laughed out loud. He could be so easy to tease. She spread the shaving foam over her pussy and began to shave. She opened a new video, and carefully positioned herself so that she was sure Tommy would have maximum pleasure. Sending the new clip, she was surprised to see him send another. His cock in his hand. A video. Wanking slowly. She cleaned herself. Her smooth pussy, now on display. She rubbed her clit hard, as her phone rang. She opened the video call. And they wanked themselves to orgasm as they watched. She ended the call with, "till tomorrow baby," and as she took herself to bed, she felt the warmth of being naughty and the adventure that was about to begin.

Michelle closed her eyes. Tommy had gone to the club. She didn't care. She had been using Dial Chat most of the night, and had sent some naughty photos, the ones Charlie had demanded. She smiled. She always felt a little conscious of her body, but he made her feel really wonderful. And she knew that, with the connection they had both shared, the fact she had been able to confess pretty much all, and the fact he hadn't run a mile but, had told her he had "swung!" had all made her feel nothing but reassured Charlie was the man she was meant to be with. In a couple of days, she would be able to sit next to him, hold him, love him and look forward to a life that she had always wanted. A man who cared, and who she could care for. Who definitely liked to be a little crazy, but who both loved and respected her in a way that Tommy never had, not even at the beginning. She knew it was a massive risk, but both her head and her heart were telling her this was right. It was more right than she had *ever* felt. And despite the risks, she *wanted* it. She wanted Charlie. And she so *desperately needed* to be away from the man who she had loved once, but who she now realised had no interest in her anymore. She felt the tear fall from her eye. And couldn't decide whether it was a happy tear for her future, or a sad tear for the thought she had wasted the last 20 years. Either way, it was enough to let her drift off to sleep with a warm feeling inside her.

Charlie opened his eyes. Shit! It was not much after 4.30 am. He had always been an early riser, but the pressures of what he was about to do and whether he had covered everything he thought he might need to, were weighing heavily on his mind. He knew this was right. He knew the woman who had so spectacularly entered his life was both the one he was meant to be with, and also the one he was meant to stay with! He hadn't been looking, but when Michelle had hit the back of his car, his world had changed forever. He made coffee and sat in the dark. He checked his phone and was relieved to find nothing. No news was definitely good news.

As he sipped his coffee, Michelle woke gently. Her eyes couldn't focus, but she had a warm feeling inside. This time tomorrow, she will be on her way to the airport. And with any luck, to a life that she couldn't wait to begin.

Tommy's alarm went off. Michelle was in the guest room. She closed her eyes, and listened. Tommy woke, she heard the grunt, and heard him using the bathroom. Making sure she didn't make a sound, she listened intently in the dark. He showered. She opened her phone, nothing. Charlie had his phone in his hand and had been staring at it for the last hour or so. He was nervous, a childish like nervousness that he both loved and loathed in equal measure. Michelle willed the message to come. She felt anxious, was he having second thoughts? Had all this been for nothing? It had been a whirlwind after all. Charlie stared at the screen. All he wanted now was to know Tommy had left. He had already told Callum to go and check out Nikkis' flat. He figured Tommy wouldn't be going alone.

Callum yawned, he didn't like early mornings. But he had done as his father had wanted. And sat watching Nikki rush around the flat. She had not bothered to close the curtains, and Callum could see what his dad had seen in her. She certainly wasn't shy in displaying everything! It was beginning to get light, and as Callum yawned again, the silver Mercedes drew up outside. Callum recognised Harvey from the club. He knocked softly and went back to the car. The lights went off in the flat, and Nikki emerged. She locked the door, and teetered along on heels that clearly she wasn't totally happy with. Harvey put her small pink case into the boot, and closed the door as she got in. Her skirt was definitely too short to hide her charms, and Callum reflected on Michelle, the woman his father had so clearly fallen deeply in love with. She was, it seemed, a troubled soul who had much in common with his father. Whether she was the one, remained to be seen. But he would be there for his dad, and would always be grateful for the opportunities his dad had given him.

He picked up his phone, sent a simple text, "silver Merc,'' and started the car. He would now go back home and get at least a couple more hours of sleep.

Charlie smiled, he sent a Dial Chat message. "Hello Princess, keep an eye out for a silver Mercedes. It isn't empty." And he added "One more day" with a winking emoji and a kiss.

Michelle grinned. Tommy had been as quiet as he could, but she had already heard him whistle and then the muffled sound of his voice. Low and protective of what he was saying. She smiled to herself. As he made his way down the stairs, she heard him mutter, "bollocks!" as he tripped slightly. Michelle laughed to herself. She crept slowly out of the room, and made her way to the window. As the front door closed, she saw Tommy walk down the drive and open the door of the silver Mercedes. She stood far enough away from the window that she couldn't be seen. But if she needed any more evidence that her new life with Charlie was the right thing, she had it now. Tommy had always been too busy to have proper holidays. Michelle knew this wasn't a holiday in that sense, it was nothing more than a deal. But he was taking her. She smiled. An ironic smile. Fuck them both, tomorrow she would be getting on her own plane, and disappearing to find her happiness.

She padded softly back to bed. "He has gone," she sent.

Charlie smiled, "want some company princess?" He sent back.

Michelle grinned, but despite wanting *so* much to, she wouldn't let Charlie come to her house. She didn't need Tommy to know anything. "I will come to you," she responded. "Give me 30 mins or so." She felt warm inside. Yes, this was definitely right. She slipped into nothing more than a tracksuit and slipped out of the house.

As she got to Charlie's cottage, the silver Mercedes pulled up at the terminal building. Tommy and Nikki exited the car, and Tommy took the two small cases. Nikki bent to retrieve hers, and he couldn't resist pinching her arse as she did so. She didn't stop him but squealed with delight. "You are so naughty" she laughed as she looked at him. Tommy smiled. She was so much more fun than Michelle. Who knows, maybe when he got back, he would see about doing something about his marriage and his frigid wife, who barely wanted sex, let alone needed it.

He laughed. "Come on you naughty girl," he squeezed her backside again, and held his arm out, Nikki placed hers in his. And they went into the terminal. Approaching the first class desk, Nikki flashed her best smile and squeezed his cock through his trousers. Tommy went a little red, but returned the smile. The woman behind the desk coughed and beckoned them forward. They both laughed, and presented their passports. Just a minute later, they were walking through to the gate. And to what would prove to be one hell of a weekend.

Tommy of course knew nothing of his wife and her sordid secret past, and inside her she was both repulsed now, but also grateful that she had seen just how unhappy she had become. She had known though, for a long time Tommy wouldn't be her life partner. Never mind a man who she could enjoy sex with. His attitude to her sexually had always been just for his gratifications.

But now, It was *all* he cared about, Charlie loved her. *Showed* her love. Gave it unconditionally. And she absorbed it. Drinking it in and sometimes getting high on the feeling. She *adored* the feelings that Charlie gave her. And it made her see even more clearly the man Tommy had become. Drink, drugs and power and money had taken away the cheeky chappie she had once loved so dearly. To be replaced by a selfish monster who only valued himself.

As she knocked on the door and was greeted by a naked, except for his boxer shorts, Charlie.

She grinned. She stepped inside. Embraced the man she loved so dearly, and said, "take me to bed you sexy beast!"

Charlie picked her up, slung her over his shoulder and marched up the stairs. Michelle screamed and laughed as he spanked her arse. Charlie slipped his hand inside her sweatpants. And found her smooth buttocks beneath his hands. "You sexy little sod," he laughed as he entered the bedroom and threw Michelle onto the bed.

As she lay there laughing, he pulled off her trainers, and grabbed her sweatpants. Pulling them roughly he removed them. She lay naked from the waist down. Covering her pussy shyly, he laughed and pulled her up. Kissing her deeply, he unzipped the top, and removed it quickly. Her nipples brushed his chest and she felt him slip his hand down low and touch her clitoris. Michelle felt her whole body shudder at the touch, both gentle yet urgent. He fingered her gently, playing with her clit softly as their tongues fought in their mouths. She wanted him. Her body aching for Charlie to make her come roughly. Kissing her deeply as his fingers went deeper inside, Michelle gasped and held onto his arm. He fingered her angrily now. Two fingers angled upwards, pulling roughly at her pussy. Michelle could feel her legs getting weak. She felt the juices run from her swollen pussy. And as she climaxed, she squirted hard on his fingers. Her arms held onto Charlie to stop her falling and her mind went blank. Her eyes rolled with ecstasy, and she slumped against his chest. "Fuck!" she exclaimed. "That's never happened to me!"

Charlie kissed her gently. "It was all about you this time princess," he smiled. "Now, are you all packed?"

Michelle was still reeling from the intensity of the orgasm. She wanted to take Charlie's cock out and suck him to orgasm, but she felt spent, exhausted, and also dreamy and filled with ecstasy. "I want to make you come," she said weakly."

"Well," Charlie smiled. "I suggest you sit down first before you do anything," he grinned as he helped her into the chair.

Her face level with his still erect shaft, she pulled at his boxer shorts. "Let me have him in my mouth?" she asked.

His cock sprang free. Slowly Michelle went down on him. Teasing and licking the head. Slowly running her hand up and down him, teasingly flicking the tip with her tongue. It was too much for Charlie. "I'm going to come," he groaned, and as he did so, Michelle pulled the foreskin back harder. Spitting on his stiff cock, she waited for the hot sticky semen to spurt from him and over her breasts. Wanking his shaft, she enjoyed the feeling of power as it was Charlie's turn to have weak knees. The orgasm made him shudder. Michelle kissed the head of his shaft.

"That's better," she smiled.

"It certainly is, you naughty girl!" he grinned.

Michelle stood and kissed him. "Take me away from all of this," she laughed. "Or at least get me a bloody tissue, your spunk is running between my boobs!" After she had cleaned up, she kissed him, and got herself dressed. "I will see you in a few hours, my sexy man," she beamed.

"You will, my princess," he grinned. "I will drive to the airport, Callum is going to pick up my car as he is out with a Bentley this morning, and doesn't know if he will be back.

Michelle looked at him sternly. "You just make sure you are there!" she said.

"I *WILL BE THERE PRINCESS*! he shouted. And pinched her arse.

"*GOOD!*" Michelle shouted back as she ran down the stairs. "OK, it's 9 now. Our flight isn't until 5pm. Make sure you get everything sorted, and I will meet you at the airport."

Charlie smiled. "Ok princess, be safe, and I will see you in a few hours."

Michelle shut the door and felt warm and content inside. She was happier than anyone deserves to be. And in a few hours, she would be with the man she loved.

Callum got to the garage to find Aaron waiting for him. "Been here long?" he enquired.

"Not long," he replied. "I thought your dad might be here to let me in.''

"Dad is away for a few days," Callum said. So I guess for now, you best get used to getting here at about nine," and he laughed. "The old man is always up early, but I definitely am not!"

Aaron laughed, "right!" he said, "is your dad off anywhere nice?"

"Off to Spain tonight," Callum beamed.

"Alright for some isn't it!" Aaron smiled.

"It sure is!"

He said, "what time does he fly out?"

Callum was a little puzzled. "Around 5 I think, why?" he asked.

"Oh, just wondering," he said.

Callum gave no more thought to it but set the boy some simple tasks which he would be able to judge him on. Aaron took out his phone, sent a simple text. "5pm." He returned to work.

Charlie had been packed for ages, just his small bag. He had paid extra already as he knew he would need more baggage, and was dreading what Michelle would bring.

Barry had already been put on stand-by to collect her at around 2pm. First class meant you didn't have to wait around and queue for so long. Or that was what Charlie had insisted. She ran around the house. Checking and double checking. Her phone pinged.

WhatsApp. Valerie. A photo of her and Giles, on one of the decks. Smiling. G & T in hand. They looked like butter wouldn't melt.

The message read. "This is what the outside world sees my friend. You have a chance to make this picture a true reflection of what your life could be. Grab it with both hands, girl. And I don't just mean his cock!" finished with several laughing emojis.

Michelle laughed and burst into tears. Tommy had text. "We are here."

She had been angry. "Fucking we!" she said to herself. Now, she was overcome with emotion. Valerie was right. It *was* time to make it happen for her.

Tommy snorted a couple of lines. Went into the bathroom, took a long pee, and shouted "get dressed!" to Nikki. She had taken way too much. And was wired beyond belief. "And fucking behave yourself!"

Nikki laughed. "Of course," she giggled as she pulled on her knickers. She had managed to persuade Tommy to let her fuck his arse with the dildo this time. It was only a matter of time before she could have a threesome and watch him suck another guy's cock, she loved seeing that! Wanted to just watch, and finger herself, it made her orgasm easily. As she dressed, making sure she put the longer skirt on. She may have been pretty much out of it, but she also had an element of fear of Tommy, which both scared her and turned her on in equal measure. As she walked out of the bedroom and said, "tah dah!" posing like a supermodel, Tommy's phone pinged.

A simple message. "5pm."

He smiled. Sent back. "You know what to do."

Then turned to Nikki. "Don't you look good?" he smiled. And smacked her arse. "Do my cufflinks up would you?" and he held his arms out. Nikki did as she was told. She could see the beads of sweat on his brow, and realised it wasn't just from the cocaine, Tommy was nervous.

"Are you ok?" she questioned.

"I'm good," he replied. A slight shake to his voice. "Just want to get there," and he swung his jacket on. "Let's do this hot stuff," he said, and opened the door.

Michelle climbed into the Mercedes.

Barry greeted her as he always did. "Hello Miss Michelle," she smiled.

"Hello Barry."

As he took her two large suitcases, he smiled. Big day today Miss Michelle."

"Yes Barry," she nodded. He may have been old, but he was wise.

"Good luck Miss Michelle," he said as he shut the door.

Michelle felt relieved. She could almost touch it now. In a few hours, she would be in Spain. She had a chance of happiness. And she was determined to hold onto it with both hands. The car pulled away, and she took a deep breath. Barry chatted, nothing but small talk. It was a good hour to the airport and Michelle was glad of the company. Though she couldn't stop using her phone. A little frantic, she sent Charlie a message.

"Is everything ok?"

Charlie was chilled, he had spoken to Callum. He had the business in hand. He had spoken to Anesh. The car would be at the airport and the villa was ready. It was time. He replied to Michelle. "Hello princess, all is good here, don't tell me you are having second thoughts?"

Michelle smiled. "Not a chance," she replied, "you are mine!"

Charlie laughed to himself. He had already shipped out the clothes he needed. Anesh had made sure all was taken care of. And for 20 grand so he bloody should do! It meant he just needed a bag, a few things to get him through the next day or two. He still had to pinch himself to believe that he had met this woman in such bizarre circumstances, yet he had no doubt in his mind she was the one. He looked around his house, Callum would be happy here. And there was more than enough space to come and stay, and ultimately, if he wanted to come back, Callum was only going to rent out his flat, so he could come back with a bit of notice if it didn't work out. Charlie smiled. He felt good, *this* was good. It was nearly 14.45, and at least 30-40 mins drive to the airport. Callum had offered to take him, but Charlie had wanted to appear as normal as possible. Enough tongues wagged at times about him and who and what he might be doing. So today was discretion. Besides, with Harvey's son working at the garage, he definitely wanted Callum to keep an eye on both him and things. He would use the Saab. It was so nondescript, even he didn't give it a second glance, and he was a car guy! It would be perfect. And he had paid for a months' parking, just in case he needed to come back, so everything was set. He closed the front door, locked it and gave it a push to make sure. He chucked the small case into the huge boot, smiled, and said to himself. This is a bloody good car. He knew a couple of back roads that would get him out of town quickly. As he left the house, he didn't notice the black Mercedes minivan sitting opposite. The driver took out his mobile phone. "On his way," he sent. As Charlie sped along the quiet back lanes, he felt relaxed. Sounds up.

Michelle called his mobile. "Come on man!" she laughed at him. "You are always late!"

He could hear the stress in her voice. "Chill woman," he said softly, "we have first class. No queues or any of that rubbish. I will be there in less than 30 mins."

Michelle shouted back *"ITS ALMOST 3 NOW!"*

Charlie pressed the accelerator a little harder. He actually hadn't figured that it was going to take at least another 30 mins to park, get the paperwork done, leave the keys, and get to the terminal. "*Shit!*" he said to himself, conscious Michelle would panic, he laughed. "Listen you, I will be there, *we* will be there, and in less than 2 hours we will be on that plane and away! so let me get my foot down and concentrate and I will be there to take my princess away!"

He laughed but Michelle got cross. "For Christ's sake Charlie," he heard the wobble in her voice, "just get here please."

"I'm sorry," Charlie replied. "I am only kidding, I am going to be there." He could hear the gentle sobs. Suddenly he felt crap. "Michelle, I'm sorry, I ... "

Michelle heard nothing more; except the sound of metal being torn, of glass shattering, of Charlie screaming in pain, of crackling. Then nothing, just silence. She sat, shell shocked. Unable to move, to speak. The phone fell from her hand and she slumped to the floor. Passengers rushed to her.

The phone still lit up. She heard someone shouting. "Get a doctor."

Her head didn't belong to her right now. She had no idea where she was. Charlie. Charlie. *Fuck!* Her body began to shake, convulse rapidly.

A voice said, "keep her warm."

She felt herself slipping into unconsciousness. She closed her eyes, and lay quietly now. She felt hands on her, and warmth. She didn't want to wake up again. When she finally did wake, she knew immediately she was in hospital. Her head hurt terribly. And she was naked except for the hospital gown. Her mind immediately went back to the phone. She looked left and right. And threw up into the small cardboard bowl.

As she did so, the nurse came in. "Are you OK?" she asked.

"Where is my phone?" Michelle felt the tears as she said the words.

"The police have taken it," the nurse replied. "Try to get some rest," she said comfortingly. "Do you need anything?"

Michelle felt faint again. "I want to have my phone," she said.

"I understand," the nurse replied. "The police would like to talk to you. I haven't told them you are awake."

Michelle exploded. *"I WANT MY FUCKING PHONE!"*

As she did so, a tall gentleman came in. "Detective Sergeant Nicholson," he said as he flashed his warrant card. "Do you feel up to talking?"

29 "THE FUNERAL"

A few weeks later, Michelle stood at the back of the church: black dress, a lace veil, and a small hat. Valerie held her arm. The church was packed, Michelle couldn't see Callum. But she could see Sam. And the woman next to her, she assumed was Marina, Charlie's ex-wife. As she looked around, she saw how liked this man must have been. All these people whose lives he had touched. She could feel the wetness roll down her cheeks. Valerie squeezed her tightly. Michelle fought the tears as the coffin came in. Callum carried the coffin, strong and sturdy. His brother had made the trip from New York and, despite the differences they had had over the years, she was pleased he had made the effort to come. Brian held one other corner of the coffin, and Michael. Older, but Charlie had spoken about him as a very old friend. Michelle stood up straight. The service began. She could feel her tears. Valerie held a tissue. Outside, Barry sat in the Mercedes. He saw the Minivan opposite. Lowered his hat, and pretended to be asleep. This was not a day to cause trouble.

When the congregation came out, and gathered in the courtyard, Michelle stood back. She leant against the wall with Valerie, and wept, hard, desperate tears. Valerie held her friend tightly. Callum came over. He said nothing. Just held his arm out. Michelle went to him. "I'm sorry" she whispered.

Callum wept. "I'm sorry too Michelle."

Michelle needed to leave. Overcome with the emotions of the day she needed to escape. She had booked the plane ticket, Tommy had no idea. He had done the deal, stayed a couple more days in Amsterdam, and then not really been at home much.

Michelle didn't care. When Valerie had arrived back from the cruise, she had called Anesh and explained all. But both she and Michelle would be out to the villa shortly. They both left the funeral. Barry drove them straight to the airport. Giles would have no idea either. As far as he knew, Valerie was comforting a friend who had had some tragic news.

As the two women went through customs, and found the first-class lounge, Michelle stopped crying. She ordered a large Gin and Tonic. As she looked into her friend's eyes. She said simply. "It's my turn."

Valerie looked at her with steely eyes. "It's your turn," she replied. "It's your *fucking turn.'*

ABOUT THE AUTHOR

Hi I'm Will.
Welcome to Bittersweet Summer.
A chance chat with a friend, and a heartfelt story about her late father sparked an idea that led to my (currently) one and only novel.
Bittersweet Summer has been a massive journey of learning, and one that has brought me many highs, (and a few lows!)
I have a day job, (plumbing!) So forgive me as I learn but hopefully with a little help and encouragement, who knows, one day I may be a "real" author!

Printed in Great Britain
by Amazon

35773312R00185